About the

Rachael Johns is an English teacher by trade, a mum 24/7, a chronic arachnophobe, and a writer the rest of the time. She rarely sleeps and never irons. A lover of contemporary romance and women's fiction. She lives in Western Australia with her hyperactive husband, three mostly-gorgeous heroes-in-training, two fat cats, a cantankerous bird, and a very badly behaved dog. Rachael loves to hear from readers and can be contacted via her website – rachaeljohns.com, Facebook or X (formerly Twitter).

Andrea Bolter has always been fascinated by matters of the heart. In fact, she's the one her girlfriends turn to for advice with their love lives. A city mouse, she lives in Los Angeles with her husband and daughter. She loves travel, rock n' roll, sitting at cafés, and watching romantic comedies she's already seen a hundred times. Say hi at andreabolter.com

Susan Meier spent most of her twenties thinking she was a job-hopper – until she began to write and realised everything that had come before was only research! One of eleven children, with twenty-four nieces and nephews and three kids of her own, Susan lives in Western Pennsylvania with her wonderful husband, Mike, her children, and two over-fed, well-cuddled cats, Sophie and Fluffy. You can visit Susan's website at susanmeier.com

Sugar & Spice

Sugar & Spice:
The Chef's Touch

RACHAEL JOHNS

ANDREA BOLTER

SUSAN MEIER

MILLS & BOON

First Published in Great Britain 2024
by Mills & Boon, an imprint of HarperCollins*Publishers* Ltd,
1 London Bridge Street, London, SE1 9GF

www.harpercollins.co.uk

HarperCollins*Publishers*
Macken House, 39/40 Mayor Street Upper,
Dublin 1, D01 C9W8, Ireland

Sugar & Spice: The Chef's Touch © 2024 Harlequin Enterprises ULC.

The Single Dad's Family Recipe © 2018 Rachael Johns
Her Las Vegas Wedding © 2018 Andrea Bolter
A Bride for the Italian Boss © 2015 Harlequin Enterprises ULC

Special thanks and acknowledgement are given to Susan Meier for her contribution to *The Vineyards of Calanetti* series

ISBN: 978-0-263-31981-1

THE SINGLE DAD'S FAMILY RECIPE

RACHAEL JOHNS

To Ann Leslie Tuttle – for making writing
The McKinnels of Jewell Rock a joy!

Chapter One

As Eliza Coleman stared at the door of the new restaurant at McKinnel's Distillery, she forced a smile to her lips. The action ached a little because her facial muscles were rusty from neglect. But today she needed to put the last couple of years in a box and at least feign a little positivity. No way Lachlan McKinnel would want to employ a sad sack as head hostess for his "exciting new venture," the phrase he'd used to describe his new restaurant in the online advertisement she'd read.

She hadn't actually been looking for employment in Oregon but she hadn't *not* been looking either. Living on her grandmother's couch in her tiny apartment in New York wasn't terrible—she adored Grammy Louise—but lately Grammy had been trying to coax her up off the couch and out of the house. She'd even suggested coming along to her salsa class or signing up for online dating.

Eliza shuddered at the thought of both. The last time she'd been on a date was almost six years ago and she'd married that guy. Did people even go on dates anymore? From what her girlfriends told her, hookups were the name of the game now. And she wasn't interested in *them* either.

At first, getting a job had appealed only marginally more than Grammy's other suggestions—at work, Eliza would have to interact with people—but the more she'd thought about it, the more it seemed like a not-too-bad idea. Work would at least help pass the long hours during the day and she couldn't live on her savings forever. On a whim, she'd decided to look far and wide because the idea of getting away from everything—going someplace where no one knew her—held a certain appeal.

And that search had brought her to a little mountain town called Jewell Rock. Her plane had touched down only hours ago in nearby Bend and she'd rented a car and driven straight here, not even pausing to find breakfast, despite the loud complaints of her stomach.

She stood in front of the door, her hand trembling as she lifted it to the handle. Her last actual job interview had been almost as long ago as her last date and the whole concept of selling herself terrified her, but then again, what did she have to lose? After everything she'd already lost, a job in a place she'd never heard of a week ago wasn't the be-all and end-all.

Trying to ignore the debate going on inside her head, she checked her smile was still in place and then pushed open the door. As she stepped inside, her jaw almost touched the polished wooden floorboards. She wasn't sure what she'd been expecting but it wasn't mahogany paneling, flocked wallpaper and Gothic-type mirrors that made her feel as if she'd just stepped back in time.

It felt strangely warm and welcoming, like nowhere had felt for a very long time.

Behind the brass-railed bar were floor-to-ceiling whiskey bottles as if someone had traveled the world and returned with a bottle from each city. If Eliza didn't know for a fact this building was a recent addition to the boutique distillery, she'd have been fooled into believing it was circa 1950s—like the rest of the establishment.

As the door thumped shut behind her, she stepped further into the restaurant and inhaled deeply. The scent of bourbon filled the air but there was also a hint of something sweet that made her empty stomach rumble. Placing a hand against it, she silently willed it to settle, as the last thing she needed was loud gurgling noises emanating from her stomach while Lachlan McKinnel interviewed her.

"Hello!"

It took a second for her to realize the deep-voiced greeting was coming from off to her right. She turned to see a man with thick golden-blond hair, wearing black trousers and a chef's white shirt, standing in the doorway to what was clearly the kitchen part of the restaurant. A very good-looking man. The thought took her by surprise and she blinked as he smiled warmly and walked forward to close the gap between them.

"Eliza?" he asked as he paused in front of her and offered his hand.

She realized she'd been standing there frozen and mute, just staring at him. There was a reason for this— he was much taller and better-looking in person than he'd appeared from the images she'd found online—but it wasn't a *good* reason. She wasn't here to gawk and drool over her potential boss, she was here to impress him. Here to nab herself a job and a new life about as far from New York City and her past life as she could get without leaving the country.

"Um, yes, hi." She shook his hand and silently cursed herself for sounding so staccato. "You must be Lachlan."

"I am." His handshake was firm and she felt a surprising little jolt inside her. Eliza put it down to the fact she hadn't so much as touched a man in almost a year. "It's a pleasure to meet you."

She nodded as he let go of her hand. *Smile. Act happy. Pretend to be someone else if you have to.* "You, too," she answered chirpily, hoping her tone didn't sound as awkward to his ears as it did to hers. "And this place is gorgeous. I can already imagine it full of people. Did you design it?"

His lips quirked a little at one side and she realized he was the one supposed to be asking the questions, but hey, she tended to talk when she was nervous. "The concept was mine but I had a lot of help from my brothers and my sisters. Mac, specifically, handled the construction side and Sophie and Annabel had a lot of input on the interior."

"Obviously a talented family," she said and then immediately regretted the words. He probably thought she was sucking up or, worse, flirting with him. A cold sweat washed over her at the thought.

But he chuckled. "Don't tell them that, or they'll get big heads. Now, shall we get started?"

"Yes, good idea." The sooner they got down to business, the less likely she was to say something stupid.

He led her over to one of the tables—she noticed her résumé waiting there—and held out a chair for her to sit down. As she lowered herself onto the seat, her breath caught a waft of his sweet-and-spicy scent. She couldn't tell if it was an actual aftershave or if he'd been cooking and the delicious aromas of his creations lingered on him.

"Can I get you a drink? Coffee? Whiskey?" He winked as he said this last word, yet at the same time she didn't think he was entirely kidding. It might not be afternoon yet, but this *was* a whiskey distillery.

She played it safe. "Surprise me."

He nodded once and then retreated behind the bar. The urge to turn her head and watch him was almost unbearable but she resisted, choosing instead to take in more of her surroundings. Her eyes were drawn to an old grandfather clock that stood between the doors leading to the bathrooms. It was beautiful and fit right in with the rest of the decor. She could just imagine glancing at it to check the time when she was working.

"It's a beauty, isn't it?"

Eliza snapped her head to the bar at the sound of Lachlan's voice and saw him, too, admiring the old clock.

"My grandfather bought it out from Scotland. It was his father's, and it's over a hundred years old. Never misses a beat."

"It's gorgeous," she agreed as he turned back to what he was doing.

A few moments later, he returned to the table and set a glass mug in front of her with what looked (and smelled) like coffee in the bottom and cream on the top. "You told me to surprise you, so I thought I might as well try you out on what I hope will be our signature drink."

She drew the mug toward her, picked it up and inhaled deeply, the strong concoction rushing to her head and making her mouth water. "This isn't just coffee, is it?"

Lachlan grinned, shook his head and placed a second mug down on the table. Then he discarded the tray on the table beside them, pulled out the chair opposite her and sat. "I don't plan to offer our patrons *just* anything here. Go on, taste it!"

She felt his intense gaze boring into her as she took a sip and relished the quick burn of whiskey as she swallowed. It likely wasn't a good idea to drink on an empty stomach, but she welcomed the little bit of Dutch courage right now. Something about him set her on edge—she told herself it was simply that she needed this job, so she wanted to impress him, but that wasn't the full story.

She'd been around so many chefs in her life she thought herself immune to the uniform, but the way her pulse sped up around Lachlan McKinnel said otherwise. And he wasn't even wearing the whole kit and caboodle. *Not good.* Her hormones needed to calm their farm because whatever ideas they might suddenly have, she wasn't planning on acting on *any* attraction, but especially not with someone she worked for.

"It's good," she said as she set the mug down on the table again.

"Just good?" The smile he'd been wearing since she arrived drooped a little, making her feel as if she'd kicked a puppy.

"No. Of course not." She rushed to reassure him. "It's fantastic. The best coffee I've ever tasted. I could get addicted to this stuff."

As if to prove her point, she lifted the mug again and took another sip.

He threw back his head and laughed long and loud.

"It's okay, I was just kidding. I'm not that pathetic that I need constant reassurance, but I'm glad you like it."

Eliza hadn't laughed in what felt like forever and appeared to have lost the ability to recognize a joke or playful banter. She summoned that smile back as she lowered the coffee to the table again, not wanting him to think her some straitlaced grump who wouldn't be able to sweet-talk the customers.

"Anyway." Lachlan folded his hands together on the table between them, his expression suddenly serious. "You've got quite an impressive résumé. The list of restaurants you've worked for reads like the Michelin Guide."

"Thank you." Her cheeks flushed a little but her stomach tightened as she anticipated his next question: *Why did you leave your last job?* She'd already decided only to tell him the bare basics and hope he didn't scrounge around too much online, but miraculously he went much further back than that.

"Can you tell me how you got into the restaurant business?"

She nodded, knowing he'd eventually ask the inevitable but happy to put it off a little longer. "My father was a restaurant critic and my parents were divorced. On the weekends I spent with my dad, he often took me along when he dined for a review. I guess his passion for good food rubbed off on me. I've wanted to work in restaurants for as long as I can remember."

He quirked an eyebrow. "If you loved food so much, why not become a chef?"

Although she willed them not to, she felt her cheeks turn an even brighter shade of red. She dreaded this question almost as much as the other one. A tiny voice inside her head told her to lie, but she knew from experience that doing so could get her into very hot water. Besides, with Lachlan's big brown eyes trained so intently on her, she didn't think she'd be able to tell even the smallest fib.

"Because I can't cook," she confessed.

When his expression remained blank, she went on. "I've tried. Lord knows, Dad paid for every cooking school he could get me into when I was a teenager, but after the fire department had to be called when I burned down the kitchen, word got around."

A small smile broke on his face. "Seriously? You burned down a kitchen?"

She hung her head in shame and mentally kicked herself. *Probably not the best way to sell yourself, Eliza.* "It was not my finest moment, and after that my grandmother tried to convince me to go into medicine or journalism or law, anything that kept me away from food, but I just couldn't give up, so I got a job as a waitress instead. Finally, I found something I was good at. Talking about food, serving food and customer service. I haven't looked back."

"Well, usually at this point, I'd ask what your favorite dish to cook is, but I'm predicting microwave popcorn or something, and that's not really what I had in mind."

She grimaced. "Good. Because I burn that, as well."

"At least you're honest. Lucky I'm not interviewing for the kitchen. So tell me your favorite dish to *eat* instead."

Millions of foods whirled through her head—it was like asking someone to pick their favorite child, not that she would ever know how that felt. "That really depends on the situation," she said, mentally shaking her head at the dark thoughts that threatened. "If I'm dining out somewhere classy, you can't go wrong with duck confit or a good pan-seared salmon fillet, but if I want comfort food, it's mac'n'cheese every time."

Her heart squeezed a little at the thought of Grammy Louise's mac'n'cheese—the food she'd practically lived on the last couple of months.

"Then you'll be pleased to know I actually plan on having a mac'n'cheese on our menu—not just any old mac'n'cheese, of course. You haven't lived until you've tasted my whiskey-and-bacon take on the old favorite."

Her mouth watered. "That sounds amazing. What else are you planning for the menu?"

Obviously pleased by this question, Lachlan began to speak animatedly about the dishes he'd been experimenting with. "I want hearty food with a unique flair, showcasing McKinnel's whiskey as much as possible. Every table will get a complimentary basket of whiskey soda bread, and for starters, we'll offer things like smoked turkey Reuben sliders, scotch deviled eggs and a whiskey-cheese fondue to share. The mains will be even more whiskey focused, featuring slow-cooked bourbon-glazed ribs, a blue cheese burger in which I mix whiskey into the ground beef…"

He went on and on—listing more delicious dishes, including a steak sandwich with bourbon-sauteed mushrooms and a vegetarian option of butternut squash gnocchi with whiskey cream sauce. Eliza made a conscious effort not to drool.

"I love the sound of all of that," she said, genuine excitement pumping through her body. "You're making me very hungry."

"Really?" He grinned, clearly pleased by her response. "And I haven't even started on dessert yet."

"I can hardly wait," she replied. Food was something she could talk about till the cows came home and talking about it with Lachlan made her realize how much she'd missed it.

"How does caramel-and-whiskey sauce with steamed sponge pudding sound?"

"Oh. My. God." She couldn't help moaning at the thought.

"Or are pumpkin pancakes with bourbon-vanilla maple syrup more your style? Perhaps you like the sound of blueberry-bourbon-cream-cheese pie or maple-bourbon ice cream."

The way he spoke about the food sounded almost seductive and she felt goose bumps sprout on her arms.

"Please stop!" She begged, an alien bubble of laughter escaping her throat. "I didn't eat breakfast and I can't take this anymore."

His lips twisted with amusement. "Why didn't you say so? I just happened to have been playing with my recipe for an Irish apple crisp. How about you taste test for me while we finish the interview?"

Lachlan pushed back his chair to stand before she could reply, and as he did so, the door to the restaurant flung open and they both turned to look. A tall, skinny woman with immaculate makeup and peroxide-blond hair stood there, a girl with a sullen expression at her side.

"Linda! Hallie! What are you guys doing here?" He rushed toward them, stooping to give the girl a hug. "Why aren't you at school? Is something wrong?"

"I need you to look after Hallie for a while," said the woman Eliza presumed must be Linda. "I'm going to LA to look after my sick aunt. She's got cancer."

Eliza's heart went out to the woman and her aunt, but when she looked to Lachlan, the smile he'd been wearing seconds earlier had vanished from his face.

"You don't have an aunt!" he exclaimed.

Linda narrowed her eyes at him. "You don't know everything about me, Lachlan. Maybe if you'd paid more attention, our marriage wouldn't have ended in tatters."

"What the...?" Lachlan's eyes bulged, but he took one look at Hallie and didn't finish his question. When he spoke again, it was clear he was trying to control his annoyance. "Aunt or no aunt, you can't just take Hallie to LA. And if you think you can..."

"Re-lax." Linda's tone was condescending. "Of course, I can't take Hallie with me. That's why she's staying with you for a while."

"What?"

Ignoring Lachlan's one-word question, Linda bent and drew the little girl into her arms, kissing her on her golden pigtailed head. "Be good for Daddy. I'll call you from LA."

She straightened again and took a step toward the door as if that was that, but Lachlan's words halted her in her tracks. "Oh, no, you don't, Linda. We need to talk. Kitchen. Now."

Linda glanced at her watch, let out a dramatic sigh and then flicked her long hair over her shoulder. "Fine, but I don't have long. My plane leaves in two hours."

Lachlan looked to his daughter and smiled warmly. "Hallie, you wait here. Mom and I will be out in a moment." Then, dragging the woman by the arm, he led her into the kitchen and slammed the door shut, leaving Eliza alone with the little girl.

She stared at the child. Lately, she couldn't even handle being around her best friend's children, never mind strangers' offspring.

"Hello," she said after a few moments of silence. Despite her own discomfort at finding herself in the middle of a family drama, Eliza felt for the girl. Although she didn't know the ins and outs of the situation, it was clear this child was Lachlan's daughter, that her mother was dumping her here unexpectedly and her father didn't seem pleased with the news.

However dire her own life was, this was a stark reminder that she wasn't the only one with problems. And a kid as cute as this one should not have to deal with such rejection. It made her blood boil.

"Who are *you*?" the little girl replied.

"I'm Eliza," she said with what she hoped was a friendly smile. "Your dad is interviewing me to work in his new restaurant. Did I hear your name was Hallie?"

"Yep." The girl shuffled forward and flopped into the chair Lachlan had just vacated. The sigh that slipped from her lips sounded far too heavy for someone who could only be about eight years old, nine max.

Before either of them could say another word, raised voices sounded from the kitchen.

"Do you not *want* her?" Linda shouted.

"Do you want to play a game?" Eliza asked loudly. She'd borne witness to a number of screaming matches between her own parents before they divorced and she didn't believe any child should have to hear such things. Especially not their mom questioning their dad's love for them.

Hallie rolled her eyes. "It's okay. I'm used to my parents fighting and I've been waiting for this day for as long as I can remember."

"What do you mean?" Eliza found herself asking. "Has your mom's aunt been sick for a while?"

Hallie laughed. "I've never even met my mom's aunt. I meant I've been waiting for her to get rid of me like she did my brother." Before Eliza could ask what she meant,

Hallie added, "My twin brother has got a condition called cerebral palsy that made Mommy not want him."

The little girl's words shocked Eliza and she found herself unsure of what to say, but Hallie continued on in a matter-of-fact way, "Oh, that's not the story she or Daddy will tell you. They say they grew apart like grown-ups sometimes do and took a child each, but I'm not stupid. I go to Daddy's house every second weekend but Mommy never takes Hamish. That's my brother by the way."

"I see." Eliza's heart hurt—in her research for the interview, she'd read an article on the internet saying that Lachlan had sole custody of a son with special needs, but she'd never imagined the reason why.

"And if Mommy can give up Hamish, then I always knew that one day she might also give up me."

"But she's not giving you up," Eliza rushed to reassure the child. "She's going to look after your sick relative."

Hallie shrugged. "I'm actually glad. Daddy and Hamish live with Grandma Nora, and now I will, too. She's the best. And I already have my own bedroom there."

Despite the child's attempt at bravado, Eliza saw her lower lip wobble and knew the girl was close to tears. Poor precious little thing. Eliza didn't blame her. But she *did* blame her parents. Fighting within earshot of her and both carrying on as if looking after her was a hassle. Some people didn't know how lucky they were.

The voices in the kitchen grew louder, more irate, and no matter Hallie's declaration that she was used to this kind of thing, Eliza couldn't just stand by and do nothing. She got to her feet and held her hand out to the little girl. "Will you show me round the distillery gardens?" *While we wait for your parents to finish*, she added silently. "I loved what I saw when I drove in."

Hallie raised an eyebrow and took a moment to reply as if she knew this was a ploy to get her away from the firing line, but then she pushed her own seat back and stood. "Okay," she said. "If you insist. Come on."

As Eliza followed Lachlan's daughter to the door, she glanced in the direction of the kitchen… This interview was not at *all* going how she'd hoped.

Chapter Two

"Tell me this is some kind of sick joke, Linda!"

Holding her chin high, she folded her skinny arms over her surgery-enhanced chest and glared at him. "Joke? Looking after my ailing aunt is not a joke."

He raised an eyebrow. "Cut the crap. There is no aunt." Her father had never been on the scene, and as far as he knew, Linda's mother was an only child.

Linda let out a long, deep, clearly irritated sigh. "She's my mom's estranged sister if you must know."

"So why isn't Carol trekking across the country to look after her, then?"

"What part of the word *estranged* don't you understand?" she said, speaking slowly as if he were five years old. "Besides Carol has just started a new job in Bend, she can't just take time off when she feels like it."

"But you can, because you have never worked a day in your life." He was about to ask her if she had any idea what it was like to look after someone with a terminal illness—Linda had never been the nurturing type—but he figured she'd work that out pretty quickly.

"There's no need to be such an ass about this." She blew air between her lips, flicking her platinum blonde bangs upward as she did so. "You'd think I'd asked you to sail around the world naked, not look after your *own* daughter."

"Keep your voice down," he growled, glancing toward the shut door. He'd been in such a good mood five minutes ago—thinking that he might have finally found the perfect person to lead his waitstaff—but now he could almost feel the steam hissing from his ears. "You've got some nerve. You know I want her. I've always wanted her *and* our son, but your timing couldn't be worse. I'm trying to open a new restaurant here, and you interrupted me in the middle of an interview."

Linda smirked. "Oh, that makes sense—for a moment there, I thought you were on a date."

He hated himself for it but he took the bait. "And why would that be so amusing? You don't think I date?" She'd be right. He couldn't remember the last time he'd been on a date—between having permanent custody of their son, every second weekend with both kids and work, he didn't have the time—but he wasn't about to admit that. Not to her.

"Keep your pants on," she said, obviously highly amused. "I just meant that woman isn't your type. She's a little too... How should I put it? Rounded?"

His hackles rose even further. He didn't have a type—not anymore—but he didn't like the way Linda spoke about Eliza. She might not look anorexic like his ex-wife, but she had womanly curves in all the right places and he thought that was a hell of a lot more sexy than someone who was afraid to eat carbs.

"So how long do you think you'll be?" he asked, his voice louder than he'd meant. Already he was mentally calculating the extra things he'd have to do now that he had Hallie full-time. He loved his daughter—and his son—more than life itself, but he also understood that kids required time as well as love. Hallie had dance and singing classes and she went to school in Bend, not Jewell Rock, which would mean an hour round-trip twice a day. All this on top of Hamish's therapy appointments and his extracurricular activities. Had Linda thought any of this through?

Again, his ex-wife rolled her eyes as if she were talking with a plank of wood. "She has cancer, Lachlan, I can't give you an exact time and date when she's going to breathe her last breath."

"Isn't there anyone else who can look after her? I'm opening the restaurant in a month!"

"You want me to dump our daughter on strangers?"

"Shh," he hissed again. Then he firmly added, "I *meant* your aunt."

She shook her head. "Can't you show a little compassion? Besides, your mom and your family will help you look after Hallie. It's not like one extra person in your massive family is going to make much of a difference."

They stood there for a few moments, glaring at each other like two opponents in a boxing ring. How dare she assume his mom could help? Although he knew she would do her best, he didn't like asking her to do any more than she already did. And with two family weddings imminent and his two future sisters-in-law pregnant, Lachlan's mom had enough on her hands already. He wasn't a violent man and he would never hit a woman, but the frustration coursing through his body right now made him want to pick something up and throw it against the wall.

Only the thought of his daughter and Eliza in the next room held him back.

Eliza. What must she be making of all this? Would she still be there when he went back out? It was definitely not the first impression he wanted to make on a potential new employee.

Feeling resigned and realizing they'd left their daughter with a stranger, Lachlan let out a long breath. "I take it you've packed Hallie's school uniform?" Linda might have seen fit to take her out of class to bring her to him, but he didn't want her missing any more because of this.

"Of course."

"And can you give me a list of all her extracurricular activities?"

Linda smiled like a child who'd just been told they could stay up past their bedtime and eat junk food. "I'll text everything to you while I'm waiting to board my plane. You're a good man, Lachlan McKinnel."

She moved forward as if to throw her arms around him but he held up a hand, warning her off. If she thought him so good, why had she looked elsewhere for excitement when they were married? Maybe he wasn't good, maybe he was just a pushover. A pushover who had been blinded by Linda's looks and the fun they'd had together when they'd first met but had been paying the price ever since.

"Go say goodbye to Hallie," he said instead and then turned and opened the door for her to go through.

"She's not here!" Linda exclaimed, then turned to him in horror. "Who *was* that woman? What has she done with our daughter?"

"Will you stop being so dramatic?" Lachlan snapped. "They're probably just outside." Although inside, his heart clenched as if someone had wrapped string around it and was tightening quickly. Where *were* Hallie and Eliza?

He strode quickly to the door and breathed a sigh of relief when he opened it and spotted Hallie and Eliza a few yards away, seemingly deep in conversation in the garden. Eliza glanced up as if sensing his presence and the look she gave him told him exactly why they'd moved outside.

Shame washed over him and he felt heat creeping into his cheeks that a stranger had thought it best to intervene so his daughter didn't hear the raised and bickering voices of her parents. At the same time, he was thankful that she had. However many times he told himself not to let Linda rile him up, he always failed miserably in this resolve.

"She's out here," he told his ex-wife.

The possible-kidnapping drama forgotten, Linda rushed over to Hallie and made an elaborate show of bidding her farewell. "I'll miss you, my darling. Be good for Daddy and Grandma Nora. I'll call you every night." She clung to her a few more moments, then kissed her on both cheeks and stepped back.

"Au revoir, folks," she said with an irritating wave of her fingers, before turning and tottering away in her ridiculously high heels to her car. She seemed more like someone off on a beachside vacation than someone off to play nurse.

As Linda sped off down the long drive, Lachlan turned to Eliza. *This is awkward*, he thought, wondering what she must make of arriving in the middle of his family drama. "I'm sorry about that," he said. "That was my ex-wife."

"I guessed." She nodded and her shoulder-length, chocolate-brown hair bobbed a little.

"I had no idea she was going to come over like that or I wouldn't have scheduled the interview."

"I guessed that, too," Eliza replied, but her lips didn't even offer a hint of a smile.

"Daddy." He felt Hallie tugging at the side of his shirt. "Dad-dy. I'm hungry."

"Wait a moment. Can't you see I'm talking?" The moment his words were out, he realized how snappy they sounded.

"Sorry, Daddy," she said, a quiver in her voice and her eyes glistening.

He swallowed the frustration at his daughter—none of this was her fault—and took her small hand in hers. He squeezed it gently three times, which was their secret, silent way of saying *I love you*. "It's okay, glitter-pie. Everything's going to be okay. Can you just give me a moment and then we'll go get some lunch?"

She nodded solemnly and squeezed his hand three times in reply. His heart flooded with warmth. No matter how angry he was at her mother and however untimely this new arrangement was, he never wanted to make Hallie feel like she were a burden.

He looked back to Eliza and offered her a conciliatory smile. He could tell she wasn't impressed with his and Linda's behavior. Although it really wasn't any of her business, he wanted to stick up for himself, wanted to give her a little history of the last tumultuous decade with his ex-wife. But he would never speak badly of Linda in front of Hallie. And besides, there were still so many questions he wanted to ask Eliza about herself and her own professional experience.

Sadly, conducting an interview with his eight-year-old daughter in tow was also not ideal. He was about to ask her if she'd mind if they rescheduled the interview for later in the day or even tomorrow but decided he didn't really have the time. Opening night was four weeks away and so far he'd interviewed ten people for the job and none of them had been suitable.

Yet from the moment Eliza had walked in the door, he'd thought she was the one. There was just something about her that made her look like she belonged in the restaurant—he could already imagine her weaving between the tables on a busy night, chatting to the customers, directing the waitstaff, helping make McKinnel's the place where people wanted to be.

His older brother, Callum, would probably berate him for hiring someone without calling their references or finishing a proper interview but this was *Lachlan's* restaurant and sometimes you had to go with your gut. He ignored the voice in his head that told him how wrong his gut had been about Linda—there'd been adolescent hormones involved there, so it didn't count.

As far as he could see, the only thing against Eliza was that she couldn't cook—but considering he wasn't hiring her for the kitchen, that didn't actually matter. It was her personal skills that counted and the way she'd taken Hallie away from the drama impressed him. Not that Hallie was difficult but he believed Eliza would be able to handle difficult customers, leaving him to focus on the restaurant, which was his area of expertise.

"When can you start?" he asked her.

"What?" She blinked. "You're offering me the job?

Don't you want to ask me more questions? Check my references?"

"I'll call your references later but they won't change my mind, will they?"

"They better not," she said. "Wow. Okay."

"Is that a yes?"

She deliberated so long, he thought she was about to reject his offer, but finally she said, "Will Monday be okay? I have a few things I need to organize first."

As today was Friday, that seemed reasonable. "That would be fine, but if you need a little longer, that's okay, too. And let me know if there's anything I can do to help. Now, my daughter here is hungry and I think I recall you saying you were, as well. Would you like to have an early lunch with us?"

Again she deliberated, but not quite so long this time. "If it's not an imposition?"

"Not at all. It will give us a chance to talk a little more and you can start to try some of the dishes I'll be putting on the menu. Come on, let's head back inside."

"Can we have mac'n'cheese, Dad?" Hallie asked as they started toward the restaurant.

"Of course," he replied.

"That's my favorite food, too," Eliza said, smiling down at his little girl and Lachlan felt the tension that had built inside him with Linda's arrival start to dissolve again.

They went inside and Hallie and Eliza sat at one of the tables while Lachlan went back into the kitchen to make lunch.

He made two separate dishes—one for his daughter sans the whiskey and one for his newest employee with *all* the trimmings. As he worked, he kept one ear to the door, smiling as he heard Hallie chattering away to Eliza, telling her about school, the distillery and the fact her two new aunties were both having babies very soon. It didn't sound like she was too affected by her mother's sudden departure and for that he was grateful. Although Eliza didn't say much, her replies were soft and encouraging and the belief he'd made the right decision in hiring her solidified inside him.

"This smells delicious," she said a few minutes later when he emerged from the kitchen, carrying three bowls of steaming pasta.

"Thanks, Daddy," Hallie said before picking up her fork and diving in as if this were the first meal she'd had in months. He had to wonder if Linda had given her breakfast but again he bit his tongue.

"Let's hope it tastes as good as it looks." Lachlan sat down beside the girls and waited in anticipation as Eliza tasted her first mouthful. He was a good chef but he knew from her résumé that she'd worked in restaurants with some of the best chefs in America and he found he really wanted to impress her.

"Wow," came her one-word reply after a few moments. It wasn't the word but the way she said it and her almost-black eyes that lit up as she did so that made his heart soar.

"It's okay?"

She smiled. "*Okay* is an understatement."

He let out a breath he hadn't even known he'd been holding and picked up his own fork. But before he'd even loaded it with macaroni, the door of the restaurant burst open again and in came half his siblings.

"What's for lunch?" Mac said, before he, Blair and Sophie—his youngest sister by two and a half minutes—halted in their tracks.

"Sorry," Blair said.

"We didn't know you had company," Sophie added.

Lachlan stood and gestured to Eliza. "This is Eliza. I've just offered her the position of head hostess. Eliza, these are three of my siblings, Sophie, Mac and Blair." He pointed to each of them as he spoke.

"Wow. Cool. Hi. Nice to meet you." Sophie rushed forward, offered her hand to shake Eliza's and then pulled out a seat at the table.

Mac and Blair also followed with handshakes and Lachlan couldn't help noticing the way his younger brothers looked appreciatively over his new employee. Mac's appreciation wasn't surprising—he might not date much since splitting with his longtime girlfriend a year ago, but he wasn't dead. And Lachlan had to concede you'd *have* to be dead not to notice how easy on the eye Eliza was.

But Blair's interest surprised him—granted, he was divorced but most of the time he and his ex-wife, Claire, acted like newlyweds. It was very confusing for everyone.

Whatever, he made a mental note to warn them both off Eliza later—he didn't want any flings with his brothers getting in the way of her doing her job.

"Hi, Auntie Sophie, Uncle Mac and Uncle Blair," Hallie said through a mouthful of macaroni.

"Hey, short stuff." Sophie ruffled Hallie's hair. "What are you doing here? Shouldn't you be in school?"

Sophie half looked at Lachlan as she said this and he mouthed back, *Linda.*

Sophie nodded—he'd fill her in later—then she leaned in and sniffed Hallie's lunch. "Mmm, that smell's to die for."

"Okay, okay." Lachlan shook his head as his brothers

also pulled up seats. "I'll go get you all a serving." He knew he wouldn't get rid of them until he did so.

"So where are you from?" Sophie asked when they all had steaming bowls of the best mac'n'cheese in Oregon in front of them.

"New York," Eliza replied.

"Long way from home," Blair commented.

Eliza shrugged. "I'm looking for a change of scenery and a new adventure."

Mac nodded. "I can relate. So where are you living?"

"Um…I actually came straight here from the airport," she admitted, glancing over and meeting Lachlan's gaze. "That's one of those few things I need to organize."

"Hey, why don't you check out the apartment next door to us?" Sophie suggested. "The old tenants moved out last month, and the landlord is still looking for a new one. It's nothing flashy, but it's cozy and not far from here."

"Us?" Eliza asked.

Sophie grinned. "Me and my twin sister, Annabel. She's a firefighter, but I'm sure you'll meet her soon enough. If you're interested, I could call the landlord and see if she can show you round this afternoon."

"That would be wonderful. Thank you. And then I'll need to deliver my rental car back to the airport and work out more permanent transport."

"We can probably help you with that, as well," Blair said.

"I can draw some pictures to go on your new walls," Hallie—never one to be left out—offered.

Everyone laughed.

"Thank you," Eliza said, "that will be wonderful."

Then she looked to Mac. "So are you the genius behind this building?"

"Sure am." As Mac's face glowed with pride, Lachlan felt a pinch of something like jealousy inside him. It might have been Mac's handiwork but much of the concept was Lachlan's and he'd got his hands dirty a few times during the construction. But he bit down on the impulse to state these facts as he knew how uncharitable it would sound—besides, even when they egged him on, he'd never been the type to compete with his brothers, so the feeling was weird. Perhaps he was still unsettled after Linda's dramatic arrival and departure.

Lachlan refilled his brother's bowls and poured Hallie a glass of milk while conversation continued around him. Eliza got along well with his siblings, she showed lots of interest and asked lots of questions about the history of the distillery and the café that had been open until recently.

"We closed it a month ago—in April—so we could finish the construction and decorate the restaurant," Lachlan explained. "It's ideal to have somewhere to eat on the premises as customers tend to buy more whiskey when they can linger for a snack, hence why I want to open up as soon as possible."

"Fantastic," Eliza said, wiping a tiny smudge of cheese-and-whiskey sauce off her bottom lip. "I'm excited to be here at the ground level."

Mac chuckled. "I hope you're prepared to work hard because I can attest to the fact that Lachlan here is a slave driver. I've barely slept in a month."

Lachlan glared at him but Eliza didn't seem perturbed.

"Bring it on," she said as she met his gaze. "*Workaholic* is my middle name."

And something inside him fizzed at this declaration. Someone who wasn't afraid of a little hard work was exactly who he needed in this position. Eliza's good looks had absolutely no bearing on his decision whatsoever.

Chapter Three

Everything was happening so fast, Eliza thought as she flopped back onto her bed in a cute little boutique hotel in Jewell Rock. Unlike the neighboring town of Bend, whose popularity was rising by the second, Jewell Rock was still a national secret and therefore there wasn't an abundance of places to choose from to stay. The few options were all high-quality, rustic, mountain-lodge-type places. Lachlan's sister Sophie was so very friendly that she'd offered Eliza the couch in her and Annabel's apartment for the night, but Eliza had politely declined the generous invitation.

Once upon a time, she'd have accepted such an offer from near strangers—thought of it as an adventure—but things had changed and now she preferred to keep to herself and take new friendships slowly.

Her cell phone beeped and despite the fact that her limbs felt heavy from exhaustion, she rolled over and reached to grab it from the bedside table. Speaking of friends…a message from Lilly, her best one, popped up on the screen.

Just checking in. How was your day? Any news on the job yet? xx

While part of her felt too tired for a conversation, calling was easier than typing out what would inevitably be a long message. She pressed Dial and less than two seconds later, Lilly picked up.

"Tell me the interview was a disaster and you're not moving halfway across the world."

Eliza almost smiled as she snuggled back into the pillows. That was classic Lilly—no time for greetings and a tendency for theatrics. "Oregon is *not* halfway across the world."

Lilly groaned. "Oh, no. You got the job, didn't you?"

"Yes. I start on Monday."

"Monday?" Lilly exclaimed. "How on earth are you going to come home and pack all your things and get back there in that time? Where are you going to live?"

"I'm not coming back to New York." She couldn't bring herself to call it home—without Jack and Tyler, nothing felt like home anymore. "Not yet anyway. The restaurant is opening in a month, so there isn't really time. I don't need much. I'll have a uniform for work and I'll buy whatever else I need locally. And I've already found a place to live. It's an apartment, only a five-minute drive from the restaurant—I might not even need a car. I'm thinking of buying a bicycle and getting fit."

Lord knew after all the comfort eating she'd done

over the last eighteen months, it wouldn't be a bad thing if she lost a few pounds.

"Getting fit?" Lilly sounded horrified. She was married to a chef, wrote food reviews for a popular mommy blog and believed life was too short to waste time exercising.

"It's an idea," Eliza said.

"A crazy one if you ask me," Lilly replied, "but moving on. Where are you living? What was Lachlan McKinnel like? Will you get free whiskey as part of the package because…in your situation, I'm not sure if that's a good thing."

Lilly always asked more than one question at once.

"Don't worry—I'm not going to become an alcoholic," Eliza promised. "This fresh start will be good for me, I can feel it in my bones. In answer to your other questions, I'm moving into an apartment next door to Lachlan's twin sisters. I met one of them this afternoon and she just happened to mention the place next door was vacant. She set me up with the landlord and I checked it out this afternoon. It's perfect, so tomorrow I'm going to buy a bed, a fridge and maybe a couch, a microwave and a TV. That should do me for starters. And as for Lachlan, I'm not sure what to think of him."

"Whoa. There's a lot to unpack here. What do you mean, you're not sure about him? Didn't you like him?"

Eliza pondered her response a few moments before she told her friend about Lachlan's ex. "They're a close-knit family," she added. "Anyway, my opinion of him personally doesn't matter—he's definitely a good chef and he's serious about making the restaurant a success. Since he's going to be my boss and not my friend, I guess that's the main thing."

"Yes, I suppose that true. But are his sisters at least

nice?" Lilly asked. "Perhaps you'll become friends with them. I don't like to think of you all alone across the other side of the *country*."

"They seem nice. A bit younger than us, though—different zone. Sophie asked me if I wanted to join Tinder. Apparently they've both signed up."

Lilly snorted. "Tinder! Jeez, I'm so glad I met Matthew before the dating scene changed so dramatically."

"Mom-my!"

Before Eliza could say anything to that, Lilly's two-year-old daughter, Britt, hollered in the background.

"Mom-my, I did poos in the potty."

Eliza felt torn between laughing and crying at the excited little voice. Jack and Britt had been born only three months apart and every milestone Britt crossed felt like a knife twisting in Eliza's gut. She wanted to be happy for her friend but all she could think about was the fact Jack would never do any of the things Britt was doing.

"I'll let you go," she said, choking up. "Tell Britt I said well done, and I'll send you some photos of my new place tomorrow night when I've furnished it a little."

"All right, my love," Lilly replied. "Chat soon."

Eliza had barely disconnected from her friend when the phone started ringing again.

"Grammy," she said as she answered.

"Hello, my darling," came her grandmother's sing-songy voice down the line. "I've just got in from salsa and I'm dead on my feet, but I couldn't go to bed without checking in on my favorite granddaughter."

"I'm your only granddaughter."

"Even if I had a hundred grandchildren, you'd be my favorite," Grammy said. "Now, tell me, did you get the job?"

"Yes." Eliza filled her grandmother in on her day.

"Wow—that's quite a jam-packed day. But tell me, is Lachlan McKinnel as good-looking in person as he is in his photos?"

Eliza frowned. "How do you know what he looks like?" Although he'd appeared on a local TV show cooking segment, until she'd seen the advertisement for the job and searched online, she'd never heard of him and she was pretty sure her grandmother hadn't either.

"You don't think I'd let my favorite granddaughter fly all the way to Tombouctou without doing a little research." As far as Grammy was concerned, anywhere outside of Manhattan was the end of the earth. "Well, *is* he good-looking?"

Something quivered low in Eliza's belly—indicating that she wasn't as numb as she'd thought. It was quickly followed by guilt that she could be feeling anything so frivolous. "It doesn't matter what he looks like. What matters is that he's passionate about food and has offered me the fresh start I need."

"So he *is* good-looking." Grammy sounded victorious. "I might have to jump on a plane and come and check him out myself if there's potential for a romance."

"I think he's about forty years too young for you."

Grammy laughed. "I meant for you, my dear."

That's what Eliza had been afraid of.

"I'm not looking for love," she said, trying to put her grandmother straight. Her heart had been so full of love once and she'd lost it all in the most tragic of circumstances. Even thinking about loving another left her feeling chilled.

"Did I say anything about love?" Grammy tsked. "Not all relationships have to be serious you know? Fun and mutual pleasure are just as important. I should know."

Eliza blushed. She should be used to her grandma's frankness about sex by now, but it still made her want to cover her ears.

"Even if that's true," she said, "getting involved with my boss would be asking for all sorts of trouble. Been there, done that before, and you know how it ended."

"What happened with Jack was not because Tyler was your boss," Grammy said almost tersely.

But as much as she loved her grandmother, Eliza really didn't want to get into all that—again—right now. "It's a moot point anyway," she said, equally as terse. "I'm not ready for another man in my life yet."

Deep down, she didn't think she'd ever be ready but if Grammy thought there was a slight chance, maybe she'd stop pushing.

"Okay," Grammy relented. "Tell me about Jewell Rock instead, then."

And despite the tiredness she felt from getting up at the crack of dawn, flying across America, getting a job and house hunting all in one day, this was something she could give her grandmother.

"It's beautiful. The complete opposite of New York, but I think you'd love it. There's a big gorgeous lake near where I'm going to live and I'll wake up every day to a view of the mountains. I'm going shopping tomorrow to buy stuff for my apartment, but over the weekend, I hope to have some time to play tourist. I'll email you some photos."

"I'd rather you send me a bottle of McKinnel's whiskey!"

Eliza puffed out a breath of amusement. "I think that can probably be arranged. Now, as much as I love talking to you, I'm exhausted and I've got a big few days ahead so I need to try to get some sleep."

Try being the operative word—sleep hadn't been something she'd easily achieved for a long while.

"It's not even midnight here," Grammy proclaimed. "You young things these days have no stamina. But you're probably right. I need my beauty sleep." Then her tone turned serious. "I love you, cherub. Look after yourself and remember I'm always here—any time of the day or night—to talk if you need it. I might not have suffered a loss like yours, but I'm an old woman and I've experienced enough in my long life to know that when you're hurting you shouldn't bottle it all up inside. Promise me you'll call when you're feeling low."

Eliza tried to swallow the lump that rose in her throat and blink away the tears that came at her grandmother's loving concern. "I promise," she whispered and then quickly disconnected the call before she lost it.

No matter how far she ran from the scene of her heartbreak, she knew she'd never escape the pain but, somehow, she had to learn to live with it. And maybe McKinnels' Restaurant was exactly what she needed to help her do so!

Chapter Four

Lachlan hated to be late on Eliza's first day but getting two kids ready and off to school in the morning took *three* times longer than one kid. And Hallie's hair was responsible for almost half an hour of that time. Thankfully, his mom had offered to take Hamish, so he could drive Hallie into Bend and talk to her teacher to make sure everyone knew that he was the first point of contact for the foreseeable future. Hallie seemed to be taking the change in stride but he'd wanted to spend a little one-on-one time with her just to be sure.

When he finally arrived back at the distillery, his new head hostess was sitting on the restaurant's front step, her elbows resting on her knees, waiting for him. A bicycle was off to one side, leaning against the building. Even though he'd told her she could wear casual clothes until they'd sorted out the uniforms—one of the many jobs on his to-do list for the next few days—Eliza looked professional in smart black trousers, a short-sleeved pink blouse and her hair held back off her face with some kind of pink clip. Pink looked good on her, he thought as he approached—a color he'd never seen the benefits of before now.

"Good morning," he said as she stood to greet him. "Sorry I'm late."

"Isn't that usually the employee's line?"

He grinned, feeling some of the tension dispersing that had built up inside him since Hamish woke at 6:00 a.m. "Perhaps, but I don't like being tardy and I am genuinely sorry you had to wait. Can I get you a coffee to make up for it?"

"Sounds good. Thank you." She hitched her purse against her shoulder as they headed toward the door.

He slipped the key into the lock, pushed the door open and then held it as Eliza went through. The scent of caramel wafted by as she passed him and he wondered if it was perfume or if she'd had something sweet for breakfast. He'd never smelled such a scent on a woman before—his mom, sisters and ex-wife all preferred floral aromas—and he liked it. A lot.

"How was your weekend?" he asked, pushing the thought of caramel to the back of his mind as he flicked the switch so light flooded the restaurant. "Sophie told me you took the apartment. Are you all settled in?"

"Yes," she said, putting her purse down on one of the tables. "Everything seems to have fallen into place. Your sisters are wonderful."

"They have their moments," he said, secretly in complete agreement. His younger sisters were pretty fantastic and the best aunts he could want for his kids, always helping out whenever they could. They'd both make great moms one day, but so far, neither of them had been lucky in the love department.

"What about you?" she asked. "How was your weekend?"

"Busy," he replied as he went behind the bar and turned on the coffee machine. "I played cabdriver to Hallie and my son, Hamish—they have better social lives than me—and then in the evenings I came in here and experimented with a few more dishes."

He yawned at the thought, his body in dire need of a caffeine injection. He'd already had one cup of coffee this morning but it wasn't enough, not at the moment when he was burning the candle at both ends.

"Anyway, how do you like your coffee? Cream? Half-and-half? Sugar?"

Eliza came across to join him, pulling out a stool on the other side of the bar. "Half-and-half and no sugar, please."

"Sweet enough already, hey?" It was supposed to be a joke, but she looked horrified and he mentally kicked himself in the shins. He didn't want her to think he was flirting with her, because he hadn't meant it that way and he got the impression she already didn't have the highest opinion of him. He blamed Linda for that. Eliza had seen him at his worst before she had the chance to find out that he was really a pretty nice, fair and level-headed guy.

"I'm sorry, I didn't mean to make you uncomfortable," he said. "It was just a stupid joke."

"It's okay."

Awkward silence lingered while he finished making the coffee and by the time he placed the mug on the bar in front of her, he decided he needed to clear the air before they got down to business.

"Look, I wanted to apologize properly for the way your interview unfolded the other day. I'm not proud of what you witnessed between me and my ex-wife," he said. "And I want to thank you for taking Hallie outside so she didn't hear our discussion."

Eliza's lip quirked upward at one edge. "Is that what you'd call it?"

"Okay. A *heated* discussion. What you heard may not have given you the best impression of me and that's probably because Linda tends to bring out the worst in me. To be honest, I can barely stand to look at her and if it wasn't for Hallie, I wouldn't have anything to do with her."

"Your personal business isn't any concern of mine." She wrapped her fingers round her mug and drew it up to her lips.

"Still, I'd like to explain. Linda and I got married fairly young—we thought attraction was enough to build a marriage on, and I won't lie, things were good for a while. But then we had twins and everything changed. Our son was born with cerebral palsy and she couldn't handle it. She gave all her attention to Hallie and refused to even hold Hamish. It broke my heart but I hoped in time, she would learn to love him."

He paused a moment, emotion swamping him.

"Hamish is the most lovable kid on the planet, but Linda never came to feel this way. Instead she drew away from me, too—she came to resent the love and attention I gave Hamish—and so she had an affair. I wanted custody of both the kids but she fought in court to keep Hallie and has never so much as acknowledged Hamish again since. So when she came barging in here the other day and said she was off to take care of some sick relative I've never even heard of, the anger I usually manage to contain exploded. How can she give herself to look after a near stranger when she's never given any of herself to her son?"

"I don't know." Eliza twirled a few strands of her hair between her fingers. "But that's really sad. How do you explain that to Hamish?"

Lachlan let out a heavy breath. "So far I've just skirted around the issue. He gets lots of love and attention from me and my family and I hope that we give him everything he lacks not having a mother. I guess because it's always been this way, he's never questioned it. Hamish isn't a dumb kid but his condition has left him with a moderate intellectual disability—he amazes me. He can play things like chess almost as well as an adult, but he takes longer to catch on with things like schoolwork than most kids, and perhaps this has been an advantage when it comes to the absence of his mother."

Eliza smiled sadly. "He sounds like a great kid. I can't imagine how any mother could just abandon their child."

"He is." Lachlan nodded. "And I'll never understand Linda either. Hallie's always been great with Hamish, though, and it may not have sounded like it the other day, but I'm glad to have her with me, too. I'd have appreciated Linda giving me a little more notice, though, so I could organize everything better."

"That's understandable." Eliza took another sip of her coffee and he found himself wondering and wanting to ask about her background. He knew from her résumé when she'd graduated college, which put her in her early thirties, about the same as him—she couldn't have got to that age without some kind of serious relationship. Did she have a crazy ex in her past, as well? Was that why she'd chosen to leave a perfectly good job in a fancy restaurant in New York to come here? She'd told his siblings she was looking for a change of scenery and a new adventure, but people didn't usually look for such things unless something or other had gone wrong.

These were questions he might have been able to ask at the interview, but he felt like the chance had passed him by and that if he asked them now, it might sound like he was prying. Lachlan told himself that Eliza's personal life wasn't any of his business anyway, that as long as she worked hard and did the job he needed her to do, then he didn't care, but he couldn't help being curious.

Pushing that thought aside, he also took a sip of his coffee. Man, that tasted good. Just what he needed, and hopefully with caffeine in his system, he would focus on what mattered—getting the restaurant ready for the grand opening.

He put down his mug. "I thought I could give you the grand tour of the distillery first and introduce you to everyone who works here and then we can come back and go through the list of everything we need to achieve over the next few weeks."

"Sounds good." She downed her last bit of coffee and stood.

Although he still had almost a full mug to drink, Lachlan decided it would be better to get the tour started. Things felt weird between them and he wanted to get back to the easy conversation they'd been having before Linda rudely interrupted the interview.

"I grew up here," he said as they started out of the restaurant, "and, like my brothers and sisters, I'm very passionate about the whiskey and the distillery, even though until now I haven't worked here. What I'm trying to say is all of us can tend to go on a bit about the history of the place, and so if we start boring you to tears, let us know."

Eliza let out a sound that was almost a laugh, but not quite. "I'm sure I'll be fascinated."

Was she nervous? What would it take to get this woman to relax? He hoped to God he hadn't made a bad decision in hiring her. He wanted a head hostess who was chatty and friendly, happy to flirt a little if necessary and laugh with the clientele. For a moment, he wondered if he—like Mac and Blair—had been bamboozled by her looks.

"The gardens are beautiful," she said, jolting his thoughts.

And he grabbed hold of the topic, happy that she'd initiated something. "Thanks. My mother is the family green thumb and she does a lot of the work herself, although she does have help these days. We've got a full-time gardener on staff."

"I read that your mom lives here at the distillery, and that your father died recently. I'm sorry," she offered.

"Thank you." It was good to see she'd done her research. "Yes, we lost Dad to a heart attack just over a year ago and a lot has changed around here since then. My older brother has taken over as head of the distillery and where Dad was all about tradition, Callum wants to take the distillery to the next level. In addition to opening the restaurant, he's branching out in the types of whiskey we make. We're now selling McKinnel's touristy merchandise as well, and he's hoping to buy some land next door and actually start growing our own grains."

"Sounds like a lot going on."

"There is, but you don't need to worry about any of that. Our prime concern is the restaurant." He gestured to the building they were approaching. "We'll start in here. You met Blair the other day—he's our head distiller. If you've got any questions about the making of whiskey, he's the one to ask."

Both Blair and Lachlan's other brother Quinn were in the distillery and they stopped talking to welcome Eliza to the distillery family.

"Quinn's in charge of our warehouse," Lachlan explained. "And he recently got engaged."

"Congratulations," Eliza said.

"Thanks heaps." Quinn smiled broadly and the goofy expression that crossed his face whenever he spoke about his fiancée, Bailey, appeared. "We're also expecting twins."

"Quinn and Bailey are going to get married at the distillery and we'll do the catering in the restaurant. Bailey's an event coordinator and we're hoping that with her on board, we'll get to host a lot more weddings here. The first one is actually going to be our oldest brother, Callum, and his fiancée, Chelsea, in two months' time."

"I hope you like weddings," Blair said with a chuckle.

"Who doesn't like weddings?" Eliza asked, but again she didn't smile.

Lachlan let Blair show her round the actual distillery, which—whether she liked it or not—included a brief lesson in whiskey making and then Quinn took them into the warehouse for a quick look. From there, Lachlan took Eliza to the shop and office building. Sophie was busy with customers doing a tasting, so although she offered them a quick wave, they headed down the corridor to Callum's office to find him and Chelsea locked in a passionate embrace.

Lachlan cleared his throat and rolled his eyes at Eliza

as he rapped on the open door. "You two should get a room!"

Chelsea sprang out of Callum's arms and her cheeks turned pink as her gaze fell on Lachlan and Eliza. Callum seemed less embarrassed—in fact, his smug, satisfied smile as his gaze met with Lachlan's made Lachlan try to recall the last time he'd kissed a woman.

He pushed that thought aside. "This is Eliza," he said. "And these two are my brother Callum and his fiancée, Chelsea."

"It's so great to meet you," Chelsea gushed as she rushed around Callum's desk and offered her hand.

"And you, too," Eliza replied with a smile.

Callum also shook her hand. "Welcome to Mc-Kinnel's—Lachlan showed me your impressive résumé. Sounds like we're very lucky to have you here."

"Thanks. I'm excited to be here."

"If you ever need anything or have any questions, my door is always open."

"Maybe you should shut it more often," Lachlan quipped.

Callum gave him the finger and Chelsea reprimanded him. "Don't mind these two," she said. "They're very professional most of the time."

The four of them chatted for a few more moments until Chelsea excused herself. "I'm really sorry," she said, placing her hand on her small bump. "I have to get to a prenatal appointment."

"It's fine." Lachlan smiled at his future sister-in-law. "We should be getting back to the restaurant anyway."

"It was lovely to meet you both," Eliza said.

Callum nodded as he wrapped an arm around Chelsea and pulled her close. "You, too, we'll see you around."

Leaving his brother and Chelsea to no doubt partake in a passionate goodbye, Lachlan led Eliza back down the corridor.

"Oh, do you mind if I buy a bottle of whiskey for my grandma?" she asked, glancing across to where Sophie was just wrapping up a sale.

"Of course." He took her over to the polished wood tasting bar, but neither he nor Sophie would hear of Eliza paying for her bottle.

"Call it a welcome-to-the-team gift," Sophie said as she placed the bottle in a special case for mailing.

"You're close to your grandmother, then?" Lachlan asked as he and Eliza finally headed back to the restaurant.

"Yes. I've been living with her the past few months and she was kind of like a surrogate mom for me in my teens."

"Oh?" Lachlan didn't know if he sounded nosy but he couldn't help asking, "Was your own mom not around?" He remembered her saying her parents were divorced.

"She died when I was thirteen, in a helicopter crash."

It was his turn to say, "I'm sorry," but he couldn't help being happy that she'd shared a little of herself.

"Thank you." Her reply was almost a whisper. "Until then she had full-time custody and I stayed with Dad every second weekend, but after her death I went to live with him and Grammy moved in until I was old enough to take care of myself. We became very close."

"Do you have any brothers or sisters?"

"No. And sometimes I'm not sure if that's a blessing or a curse. Did you like growing up in a big family?"

He chuckled. "Sometimes I loved it and sometimes I hated it. My siblings can be my worst enemies or my best friends. Speaking of family..." He slowed his steps.

"I just remembered, I'd better take you to the house to meet Mom before we head back, or my life won't be worth living. Although she's not involved in the day-to-day running of the distillery anymore, she likes to be kept in the loop."

"Hallie told me you lived with your mom," she said.

"Yes, when Linda and I split up, I moved in with my parents, so Mom could help me with Hamish. It was only supposed to be temporary," he admitted, "but nine years later and we're still there. Sounds pretty pathetic, doesn't it? A thirty-three-year-old man still living with his mom."

There was a hint of a smile on her lips as she met his gaze. "Hallie also told me how much she adores your mom. I can't wait to meet her."

"Come on, then. And let me hold that." He took the box with the whiskey from her grasp before she could refuse and gestured for her to follow him toward the main house, pointing out the smaller cottage on the property as they passed it. "Callum and Chelsea live there—it used to be our grandparents' place. It was the original house they built when they moved over from Scotland in the 1950s."

"It's quaint."

"Yeah, I suppose it is," Lachlan said as they continued. "Blair also lives at the main house with Hamish, Mom and I."

"He's not married?" she asked.

Lachlan tried to detect if there was interest in her question or if she was simply making conversation. "He's divorced, too. But more recently. And it's kinda complicated."

"What divorce isn't?"

He chanced a glance at her as they walked but

couldn't read anything from her expression. "You sound like you speak from experience."

Her forehead crinkled and then she nodded. "I'm smack-bang in the middle of one myself."

"I'm sorry." Suddenly her move across the country made complete sense.

"Thanks. Don't really want to talk about it, though."

"Fair enough." His divorce was ancient history now and still not his favorite topic of conversation, but he couldn't help wondering about hers. Who was the party at fault? Had Eliza and her husband simply drifted apart? Had he been abusive? Was that why she was trying to get as far away as possible from him? Or was she still in love with him?

Lachlan pondered these questions as they walked in silence the rest of the way to his mom's place. The list of things he'd like to know about Eliza was growing longer by the second.

Chapter Five

After meeting Nora McKinnel, who was as friendly and welcoming as the rest of her family, Eliza sat down with Lachlan and started going through his to-do list. As he shared his dream and ideas for the restaurant, she listened intently and couldn't help catching some of his enthusiasm. He asked her questions, valued her experience and was eager to listen to her opinions and suggestions for going forward. It felt good to have a project—something to focus on other than her own woes—and once again, she found herself relaxing in his company. The uncomfortable awareness of earlier in the day had made her tongue tie every time she tried to speak.

As he talked her through the menu, business matters and his vision, she decided her initial opinion of Lachlan as a good guy was more accurate than the one she'd started to form when his ex was there.

Besides, really, who *was* at their best when interacting with their ex-partners anyway?

She'd surprised herself by telling Lachlan about Tyler—well, not *exactly* Tyler, she hadn't mentioned any names or details—but, after he'd been so open and honest about his family situation, it hadn't seemed such a big deal to share that tiny bit of herself. She was glad he hadn't pried and for a moment, she'd wondered if she shouldn't tell him the whole sorry story but she'd bitten her tongue, reminding herself why a move across the country had been so appealing.

In Jewell Rock, she wasn't met with sympathetic looks and awkward conversation because people didn't know what the right thing to say to her was. Over the past couple of days, she'd met the whole McKinnel clan, her landlord and a number of other people as she purchased things for and set up her apartment. None of them had treated her like a leper as many of her friends in New York seemed to now.

"Are you all right?" Lachlan's concerned question drew her out of her musing. "Shall we take a break? I feel like I've been overloading you with information."

She blinked and shook her head. "No. I'm fine. Was just thinking how exciting all this is. I might have worked in lots of restaurants, but I've never been part of the grand opening of any of them."

A smile crept onto his lips. "Me either. Sometimes I have to pinch myself that this is actually happening. And other times, I wonder if I'm crazy, trying to do all this while looking after two kids."

"I don't mean to pry, but how exactly do you plan on running a restaurant while being a full-time single dad?"

"I'm not under the illusion it's going to be easy," he said, "but in some ways, being my own boss will mean

I can be more flexible with my working hours. I've hired another very experienced chef to work with me. The dishes will all be mine to start with, but I'll take the lunch roster most days and he'll take the nights. That way, I can be around for my children in the afternoons, put them to bed and then come across here to help close."

"I see." It sounded like a lot to take on but it wasn't her place to question her boss. And plenty of women managed to work full-time while also being single moms. Why shouldn't a guy be able to do the same? "Did you want me to start making phone calls to set up interviews?"

They'd just finished going through the pile of résumés from people applying for waitstaff jobs. Lachlan had explained they had a few people staying on from the café but as that had only been open a few hours during the day for the lunch period and given the restaurant's expanded hours of operation, they needed to employ quite a few new people. He'd already hired a team of kitchen staff who were due to start soon, but as the waitstaff would be under Eliza's supervision and management, he wanted her to be involved in choosing them ASAP.

"Yes, that would be awesome. I've got a few things I need to do in the kitchen, but how about I make you a cup of coffee before I get to that?"

"Thanks. That sounds good." She smiled to show her appreciation. A boss who made coffee as well as he did was definitely a keeper.

Lachlan stood and headed into the bar area. As she heard the coffee machine whir to life, Eliza looked down at the short list of names they'd drafted together and then picked up the restaurant's cordless phone to call the first one.

She'd made two interview appointments by the time he returned with a steaming mug of coffee and a plate of something that looked and smelled sinful.

"You never ended up trying my apple crisp the other day and I'm eager to hear what you think," he said.

Her mouth watered just looking at it and she knew if it tasted half as good as the hamburger he'd made her for lunch, she'd lick her plate clean. Thank God she'd invested in that bicycle over the weekend.

"I'm sure I'll love it," she said as she picked up her fork and dug it into the dessert. He watched in anticipation as she lifted it to her mouth, which was slightly unnerving, but the taste that exploded in her mouth was worth it.

"That," she proclaimed, "is like no other apple crisp I've ever tasted. And trust me, I've had my fair share."

He grinned smugly. "That'll be my secret ingredient."

"What is it?" she asked, mentally going through the flavors she could taste and trying to work it out. Of course, there was the whiskey, but there was also something else she couldn't quite put her finger on.

He wriggled his eyebrows up and down. "That would be telling. And the only people who will know will be my kitchen staff and they'll be sworn to secrecy."

"That's not fair. You know I can't cook."

He shrugged one shoulder. "I could teach you."

The way he said it sent a ripple of heat through her body and she imagined the two of them working together intimately for lessons. Pushing that thought aside, she laughed it off. "What makes you think you'd be better at teaching me to cook than any of those who have tried and failed before you?"

"You can't be *that* bad," he said, leaning back against one of the other tables and crossing his feet at the ankles.

"No. You're right. I'm worse, but thanks for the offer."

He flashed her a smile of encouragement. "I meant it. Anytime you'd like to learn a few new skills, I'd be happy to teach you a few tricks. I'm actually a pretty patient guy."

"Thanks. I'll give it some thought," she lied and then turned her attentions to finishing the apple crisp.

While she ate, Lachlan talked about setting up a Facebook page and an Instagram account for the restaurant. "Sophie reckons we need one," he said, but the expression on his face made it clear he didn't relish the task. "And some catchy hashtags or something."

Eliza cocked her head to one side and winked playfully. "Hashtag—happy to help with that." She'd recently closed down her own social media accounts because watching everyone else's updates about their children had been too depressing, but a business account would be different. And it would also give her something else to occupy her free time.

Lachlan laughed. "Thanks. That would be awesome." And then with another one of his endearing smiles, he collected her plate and disappeared into the kitchen to do whatever it was he needed to do.

Feeling full and totally satisfied, Eliza continued making her phone calls and then typed up an interview schedule on Lachlan's laptop. Sorting through the applicants and hiring staff would take up the best part of a few days but they both agreed that getting the right people for the job was the most important thing. It felt so good to be busy, being productive again. The time flew by, so that when the door of the restaurant opened and Annabel walked in with Hallie and a little boy that had to be Hamish in tow, Eliza couldn't believe it was almost four o'clock.

"Hi, Eliza." Hallie skipped over to her, peeled her little backpack off her back and dumped it on a chair. "I'm glad you're here. I wanted to give you these." She pulled some hand-drawn pictures out of her bag and laid them on the table in front of Eliza. "I hope you like them."

"Wow. They're gorgeous. Thank you," Eliza said as she gazed down at rainbows and cats. "I can't wait to get home and stick them on my fridge."

Hallie beamed proudly, then turned around and beckoned the little boy who was hanging close to Annabel and holding on to two crutches. "Hamish, come meet Eliza."

As Annabel said, "Hi," and lifted her hand in a wave, the boy stepped forward, the crutches supporting his body as he walked toward them unevenly. But it was his smile that squeezed Eliza's heart—it lit up his whole face as he said, "Hel-lo. I'm Ham-ish."

"Hi, Hamish." Eliza pulled out a chair. "It's nice to meet you. Would you like to sit down?"

He nodded and expertly put the crutches to one side as he lowered himself onto the seat. "Do you...play ch-ess?" he asked, his words slightly slurred.

She wished she could say yes because, although part of her didn't want to get close to anyone else's children, knowing that this poor boy's mom had rejected him made her see red. It made her want to say yes to anything he asked her. "Sadly, I don't," she admitted.

"I could te-ach y-you," Hamish said, his voice buzzing with excitement and reminding her of his dad's offer to teach her to cook. Even before she could reply, he added, "There's a set over there at the bar."

"That sounds like fun," she replied, "but I'd have to check with your dad. I'm supposed to be working, you know?"

"I hope my brother hasn't been working you too hard." Annabel, dressed in her firefighting uniform, pulled out a seat and sat at the table.

"Mostly he's been feeding me," Eliza confessed, patting her stomach.

Annabel bowed her head. "He's a good cook. I'll give him that."

"I thought I heard voices." Lachlan emerged from the kitchen with a tray full of milk shakes and some massive chocolate chip cookies. "How are my two favorite people this afternoon?"

"Don't you mean 'three favorite'?" Annabel asked with a chuckle as she reached forward and picked up one of the milk shakes.

Lachlan rolled his eyes as he stooped down and placed a kiss on each child's head.

Eliza's heart twinged at his obvious affection for his children, whom he'd mentioned frequently throughout the day. His love and desire to put Hallie and Hamish above all else confirmed her decision that he was a good guy.

"We're good, Dad," Hallie and Hamish said together. Then Hamish added, "Can I te-ach 'liza to play ch-ess? She s-said I had to ask you 'cause she's wo-working."

Lachlan reached out and ruffled Hamish's hair. "Not now, she's not. It's knock-off time. But Eliza might want to get home to do other things."

Strangely, Eliza found herself in no hurry to escape. Today had been the best day she'd had in a long while.

Work had done what she'd hoped it would, and the prospect of a night home alone in her new apartment left an emptiness in the pit of her stomach. It was when she was alone that her thoughts turned dark and a loneliness that was impossible to ignore engulfed her.

"It's fine. If you guys have the time, I'd love to learn to play."

"We have all the time in the world, don't we, Dad?" Hallie said, then took a slurp of her milk shake.

Lachlan laughed and pulled up a seat. "Today we do, glitter-pie, as it's the one day you don't have any after-school activities." He looked up at Annabel. "Thanks so much for picking these guys up from school. I owe you one."

"It's always a pleasure hanging out with them. I'm on the same shift tomorrow if you need me to get Hallie from school again."

"Thanks. I'll let you know," Lachlan said as Annabel pushed to a stand.

She looked at Eliza. "Sophie and I are ordering in pizza tonight if you want to come have dinner with us. No pressure, but I thought you might not be in the mood to cook after your first day at work."

"I'm not sure I could eat another bite after today," she said, "but thanks for the offer, I'll think about it." The lie came easily. As much as she liked the twins, she didn't plan to accept. Making friends meant getting close to people, and getting close to people meant sharing things, which she didn't want to do here in her new town.

"Okay. We might see you later, then." With those words, Annabel hugged Hallie and Hamish goodbye and then left.

Lachlan retrieved the chess set from behind the bar

and mouthed *thank you* to her. Hamish took out the pieces and laid them on the board, his tongue sticking out in concentration as he did so.

"Go easy on her." Lachlan winked at Eliza as he said this.

Eliza felt heat rush to her cheeks as he did so. She didn't think he was flirting with her, but her stupid body reacted as if he were and that made her feel uncomfortable.

She dropped her gaze from him and focused on his son as Hamish began to explain what the pieces were called and what moves they could and couldn't make. Hamish's skill and passion toward the game impressed her. And although she tried hard to concentrate, the most she could hope to remember was the name of the pieces. First game, he beat her in three moves, and the second one, with Lachlan leaning close and trying to give her tips, she did only fractionally better.

"I think I'm going to need a few more lessons," she said, "but I'm afraid that's all I'm up for today. I'm suddenly feeling rather tired."

Hamish's lips collapsed into a frown but she had to get out of here. While Annabel was sitting chatting with them, it hadn't felt so awkward. Now that she was left alone with Lachlan and his two kids, it felt too much like they were playing happy families. That thought brought tears rushing to the surface of her eyes.

She shouldn't have stayed so long.

Eliza stood fast, needing to escape before the tears broke free and her new boss thought her a sore loser, crying because a small boy had beaten her at chess.

"Thanks for everything," he said as he also stood. "Get a good night's sleep and don't rush in tomorrow morning as I have to do the school run again before work."

"Okay," she managed. Then she collected her purse from where it still sat on one of the tables by the door and hurried outside. She was just throwing her leg over her bicycle, the first tear sneaking down her cheek, when a little voice called out to her.

"Eliza. You forgot these."

Wincing, she wiped the tear quickly from her cheek and turned her head to see Hallie rushing toward her, waving the rainbows and cat drawings in the air.

"Thank you," she whispered, before opening her bag and depositing the pictures inside.

"Have a good night." Hallie waved, seemingly oblivious to Eliza's torment.

"You, too," Eliza called as she started peddling down the long driveway as hard and fast as her legs would allow. Her lungs struggled to keep up and her thighs began to burn. Maybe if she peddled fast enough, her legs would ache so badly that they would distract her from the pain in her heart.

But it didn't work. When she arrived at the apartment, she simply had sore limbs to go along with her sore heart and was pleased to see no sign of Sophie and Annabel or anyone else, thank God. She was in no mood to pause and make small talk with strangers.

Inside, she dumped her handbag on the counter and pulled out Hallie's drawings. She'd promised to hang them in pride of place on her fridge but as beautiful as they were, she couldn't bring herself to do so. Hanging up another child's art would feel like a betrayal to Jack.

So instead, she opened a bottom drawer and stashed the pages there as tears cascaded down her cheeks.

Chapter Six

"Daddy, do you think Eliza liked my drawings?" Hallie asked as Lachlan stooped to tuck her into bed.

Since getting home hours ago, she and Hamish had waxed lyrical about the virtues of Eliza Coleman. He himself still wasn't 100 percent convinced. While she'd relaxed a bit as the day went by—they'd even enjoyed a little fun banter about the secret ingredient—and had been friendly and engaged with his kids, her sudden departure had him unsure all over again.

One minute, she'd been happily trying to hold her own in a game of chess, the next minute, she'd been rushing out the door as if her chair had caught fire.

What had happened that had made her so skittish?

He wasn't questioning her expertise to do the job he'd hired her for—her résumé was more than impressive, her references had all gushed about her and it was clear to see she knew the restaurant business as well as, if not better, than he did. But he needed her to charm customers and to manage staff without being so awkward. Since the interrupted interview, she'd rarely smiled and he wanted a head hostess who never *stopped* smiling.

"Dad?" Hallie reached up and palmed her hand against his cheek. "I *said*, do you think Eliza liked my drawings?"

"Of course, she did. How could anyone not love your drawings?" he asked, stifling a yawn as he leaned over to kiss her good-night. "Now, you need to get some sleep. School tomorrow and dance after school."

"Okay. I'll try," Hallie promised, although her eyes sparkled as if she wasn't tired in the slightest. Hamish had been the same when he'd put him to bed five minutes earlier. Where did kids get their energy from? If only there was some way he could transfer their energy over to himself, because right now he felt like he could sleep for a month and he knew things were only going to get worse as the opening day loomed.

He needed more hours in the day.

With a final, "Good night, sleep tight, don't let the bed bugs bite," he switched Hallie's light off and then headed down the hallway with a wistful glance into his own bedroom. His bed looked very welcoming but he knew, despite his exhaustion, he wouldn't be able to sleep until he'd ticked a few more things off his to-do list.

Although he'd pretty much finalized the menu—they were off to the printers next week—he still wasn't satisfied with all of the dishes. He wanted each item on the menu to be a unique take on the traditional, which required a little more experimentation before he felt ready to introduce them to the rest of his kitchen team. The team that was due to start a few hours a day next week.

"Would you like to join Blair and me for a nightcap?" His mom held up a bottle of McKinnel's finest as he entered the living room to ask if she could keep an ear out for Hamish and Hallie.

"No, thanks. I was hoping to head back to the restaurant to do a few things. Do you mind listening out for the twins?"

As Blair aimed the remote at the TV and flicked through the channels, his mom frowned. "Of course, I don't, but you're working too hard, honey. Why don't you take a night off?"

While he appreciated her concern, it also frustrated him. He could slow down once the restaurant was open and running smoothly but you only got one opening night. And he wanted to wow the town and do his family proud. He might not be a success when it came to relationships but this he *could* control.

"I'm fine, Mom," he said, stifling another yawn. "Please, don't fuss. The twins should be asleep soon, but buzz me if there are any problems."

"Okay, sweetheart." She relented with a sigh. "Don't stay out too late."

"I won't," he said, having no intention of coming home before he was good and ready. That was the problem with still living at home in your thirties—your mom sometimes forgot you were an adult. Maybe it was time to get a place nearby for him and the kids and hire a nanny to help him out, rather than always rely on his family. Then again, he wasn't sure he could trust anyone else to look after Hamish the way he deserved.

Blair lifted the remote to wave goodbye. "Catch you later, bro."

And Lachlan decided opening the restaurant was enough for now, that the other stuff could wait a little longer. Without another word, he headed out of the house and across the property to the restaurant.

Over the next few days, some of his anxiety about Eliza started to abate again. Every day, she arrived punctually (often before him), dressed to impress and proceeded to work hard for all the hours they were in the restaurant together. She still didn't give much insight into herself but then again, with back-to-back interviews, there wasn't really much time for deep and meaningful conversation.

She shone in the interviews, asking all the right questions, posing scenarios of difficult customers that the applicants had to role-play their way out of. He had to admit her businesslike manner was rather attractive and a number of times he found himself staring at her when he should have been concentrating on the task at hand. Thankfully, he didn't think she'd caught him out.

In the rare moments between interviews, she showed him the progress she'd made on the social media accounts and he fed her to show her his appreciation. Watching anyone enjoy food that he'd thrown his heart and soul into gave him a buzz, but watching Eliza eat, he sometimes found himself harboring rather *un*professional thoughts. The way her lush red lips closed around her fork and her long eyelashes fluttered as she closed her eyes in satisfaction made him wonder if that was the expression she'd have during hot sex.

"Oh, my God, this is amazing." Eliza almost moaned as she finished her first mouthful of butternut squash gnocchi with whiskey cream sauce, and he felt his trousers get a little tight. He loved a woman with a healthy appetite. Thank God there was a table between them hiding the evidence.

"Thanks," he said—secretly pleased at her words—as he picked up his own fork to start on his lunch.

"Is there anything you can't cook?"

"I'm not that good at scrambling eggs," he admitted. Silently adding that he wasn't *bad* either.

She laughed. She actually laughed—and he felt as if he'd won a gold medal in the freaking Olympics. Although their interactions had grown easier the more time they spent together, a smile from Eliza was as rare as a red banana. And it made him want to tell her all his best jokes, simply for the reward of another upward flicker of her lips.

"But when on earth are you finding the time to make all this delicious food?" she asked. "There's been no time to cook between interviews."

As if her question reminded his body of its fatigue, he had to stifle another yawn. "I usually come over here and play in the kitchen for a few hours after the twins have gone to bed."

"No wonder you drink so much coffee," she said, nodding toward the mug in front of him.

He shrugged. "It's a necessary evil right now but I know it won't be forever. I just want to make sure the recipes are right before the kitchen staff starts."

She rubbed her lips together. "Well, this one tastes pretty much perfect."

"Thanks." He couldn't help beaming at the compliment—late nights and eyes that felt like they needed to be kept open with matches would all be worth it if it got McKinnel's on the map.

"Where did you learn to cook?" she asked. "And more to the point, why?"

"I always liked cooking. It used to drive Dad wild that I'd rather cook with Mom than watch soccer with him and my brothers—he was very traditional like that. Don't get me wrong, I don't mind soccer—you kinda have to when you have a brother like Mac, who is so good he makes the state team and then goes on to play with the bigwigs."

"Mac, who built this restaurant?" she asked, wide-eyed. "He plays professionally?"

"Uh-huh." Lachlan nodded, forgetting that not everyone knew Mac's history. "Well, he did until recently but he retired a year ago." There was a lot more to that story—more he suspected than Mac had admitted even to them—but it wasn't his story to tell.

"I'm sorry," she said. "I'm not really very sporty."

He laughed. "It's fine. Anyway, as I was saying, I used to cook a lot with Mom and my grandma when she was alive, but I never really considered doing it for a career until I went to Scotland. I always just assumed I'd follow in my father's and grandfather's footsteps and become a distiller. There's kind of this rite of passage in our family where we all go back to the county in Scotland where my dad is from and spend some time working at a distillery there.

"Only the year I went, the distillery had a fire and their operations had to close while they rebuilt. I still had six months left on my ticket and didn't want to come home early, so I got a job in a hotel in Inverness, working in the kitchen. I loved it so much more than I had working at the distillery and I knew then that this is what I wanted to do more than anything. Dad wasn't very impressed, but luckily Callum was already working at the distillery and Blair had his sights set on a career as a distiller as well, so he got over it."

"I guess that's one of the benefits of having so many siblings," she said. "It takes the parental pressure off you."

He wanted to ask her then what her childhood had been like—aside from the divorce and the tragic helicopter crash—and whether her mom and dad had certain expectations for her, but she got in with another question first.

"Did you have any formal training?" she asked.

"Yes. When I came back from Scotland, I went to the Oregon Culinary Institute." He went on to give her a brief rundown of his career to date and then asked her about the places she'd worked and the ones she liked the best while they finished their lunch.

She'd worked with some quite-famous chefs and he laughed as she told him some not-so-favorable stories about some of them.

When she'd scraped her plate clean, she stood and went to pick up both their plates. "I guess we should be getting back to work," she said.

But strangely, he was in no hurry to do so. He'd enjoyed sitting, eating and chatting with her far too much—he felt as if they were finally getting to know each other a little better—and he didn't want it to end just yet.

"Leave that," he said, standing and gesturing to the empty plates. "I'll deal with them. And can I get you some steamed sponge pudding with caramel-and-whiskey sauce to finish? It won't be quite as good heated up as it is fresh out of the oven but…"

When he'd been working on perfecting the sauce last night, the caramel component kept reminding him of Eliza and that alluring scent she wore. It had almost driven him to distraction and for the first time in his life, he'd nearly burned the sauce.

"Are you kidding?" She placed her free hand on her tummy. "That sounds amazing and I already know not to expect anything less from you, but if you keep feeding me like this, I'm going to end up the size of a house. Not even a week of working with you and already my clothes are getting tight."

It wasn't an invitation to rake his gaze over her body but he couldn't help himself. And what he saw—delicious curves in all the right places—had all the blood in his head shooting south.

"I think you're perfect just the way you are," he admitted, his voice low.

Her cheeks grew pink but their eyes met and held for a few long moments. He held his breath, wondering if he'd overstepped the mark by voicing such thoughts. It was hardly professional to be making eyes at the staff and the last thing he wanted to do was make her feel uncomfortable, but the words had just slipped out.

Lachlan was about to apologize when she said, "Thank you," and smiled. "Maybe I will have a taste of that pudding after all. I mean, I can't tell our customers how wonderful it is if I haven't tasted it myself, now, can I?"

"Definitely not." Silently, he let out a breath of relief as he headed into the kitchen to plate it up.

Following dessert, they discussed all the applicants they'd interviewed and made a short list of who they wanted to offer jobs to. While Eliza spent the next hour making phone calls to the lucky candidates, Lachlan sat at his computer and did some book work, which included finalizing an advert for the local paper. They passed the next few hours in companionable silence until Annabel arrived with his kids and any hope of silence flew out the open door as they rushed in.

Hamish and Hallie exploded with news about what they'd been up to that day, both talking over the top of each other. He laughed at their enthusiasm as he tried to direct the chatter and although he was glad to see them, he also couldn't help feeling disappointed that his time with Eliza had ended for another day.

Chapter Seven

Late Thursday night, a week after Eliza had arrived in Jewell Rock, she lay in bed staring at her ceiling, wondering if she would ever sleep again. Working alongside Lachlan made the days almost bearable but they went far too fast and the nights dragged on like decades. She'd started taking an extralong detour on her way home from work, not only to take photos of Jewell Rock to send to Grammy, Lilly and Dad and to kill some of the calories she'd consumed at work, but also because it helped shorten the hours between getting home and going to bed.

Every time she closed her eyes, an image of Jack's sweet little face popped into her head, quickly followed by his lifeless one—the latter of which she'd never be able to eradicate from her head.

Almost eighteen months after the day she'd lost her son, that afternoon still haunted her.

If only she'd decided to do something else that day. If only Jack had slept longer, then they wouldn't have had time to visit her friend Kiana and her new baby. If only Kiana didn't have a fishpond. If only...

Eliza tried to read books and watch a series that Lilly raved about on Netflix to distract herself from the "if only" game, but her concentration for such normal things—things she used to love doing to relax—was shot. For about five minutes, she'd considered getting a pet—imagined that it might be nice to have a cat to come home to and snuggle with or a dog she could take on walks—but then a little voice reminded her that if she couldn't keep a child alive, what made her possibly think she was responsible enough to look after an animal?

She understood why Tyler couldn't forgive her, because she could never forgive herself either.

And thoughts like that brought on the tears that she worked hard each and every day to keep away.

At ten o'clock, feeling as if she'd go insane if she lay there any longer, Eliza flung the covers off and jumped out of bed. She pulled on her comfiest jeans, a T-shirt, a light sweater, her sneakers and then tucked her cell in her pocket and headed outside. As she climbed onto her bike, a little voice in her head warned her that it was late and dark out and possibly not the smartest move for a woman (or anyone) to be out alone. But aside from the streetlights, the whole of Jewell Rock seemed to be asleep, and she figured if she stayed on the roads where there were plenty of houses, she'd be safe from wildlife.

An even darker voice wondered if it would truly be the end of the world if something bad did happen to her, but she pushed that aside. She peddled hard but kind of aimlessly, listening out for traffic and any other dangers as she circled around town hoping to finally exhaust herself enough for slumber.

After about twenty minutes, she found herself slowing in front of the entrance to McKinnel's Distillery and guessed her legs had come here on autopilot. She paused, pushing herself high up on the pedals and balancing as she looked over the bridge and into the distance. The lake glistened beautifully in the moonlight and most of the buildings were in near darkness but light shone from the restaurant. She thought about Lachlan's confession earlier that day that he was working late most nights.

Not really sure what she was doing—but knowing that when she was at the restaurant she felt better than when she was anywhere else—she dropped back to the seat and started over the bridge. Thankfully, she didn't need to go near the residential buildings to get to the restaurant as the last thing she wanted to do was wake Lachlan's family. She dismounted the bike and leaned it up against a post, then slowly made her way up the couple of steps onto the restaurant's porch.

As wood creaked beneath her feet, she froze. What the hell was she doing here this late at night? What if Lachlan got the wrong idea? She didn't know exactly what that would be but she knew she didn't want him to get it. Working in the restaurant was the only thing she had to live for at the moment and she didn't want to do anything to mess that up.

She'd all but made the decision to retreat when the door opened and Lachlan's silhouette appeared. "Eliza? Is that you?"

He wore faded jeans and a long-sleeved black T-shirt pushed up to the elbows, giving her a lovely view of his nicely sculpted forearms.

"Hi," she said, feeling like someone who'd been caught trespassing.

He frowned and stepped into the porch light. "Did you forget something today?"

She deliberated a second, racking her mind for a logical excuse for her late-night appearance, then opted for the truth. "I'm not really sleeping well at the moment, so I decided to go for a bike ride. I didn't really think about where I was going and my bike brought me here."

"I'm glad," he said, stepping back and holding the door as he gestured for her to go through. "I wouldn't mind some company and a second opinion on a syrup I've been experimenting with. Want to come in?"

"Okay. If I'm not gonna get in the way?"

"Not at all." He smiled warmly as she stepped past him and then shut the door behind them.

As they headed into the kitchen, he asked, "Why can't you sleep?"

"Probably all the coffee we've been drinking during the day," she said. Not wanting to tell him the truth, she quickly changed the subject. "So what exactly are you making?"

He crossed to the commercial-sized stove and turned the heat on under a pan. She guessed he'd turned it off when he'd trekked outside to investigate the noise. "Bourbon-vanilla maple syrup. It's going to go with pumpkin pancakes, but I'm still trying to get the quantities right. Here, try it for me and see what you think."

Then he took a teaspoon, dipped it into the saucepan and held it out for her. She took the spoon, brought it up to her lips and almost orgasmed on the spot as the flavors melted on her tongue. "I don't think it needs any more experimentation," she said. "The balance between bourbon, vanilla and maple is exquisite. It will go perfectly with pancakes."

"Then let's make some and see."

She raised an eyebrow at him. "I hope by *let's*, you mean you."

He chuckled. "Pancakes are easy."

She snorted. "Easy for you maybe."

He grabbed an apron off a hook on the wall and held it out toward her. "Put this on. I'll show you. We'll keep it simple and just make the plain variety."

"You're going to regret this," Eliza said, but she found herself reaching out and taking the apron from him. Their hands brushed against each other in the process and she tried to distract herself from the little jolt inside her as they did so. The late hour and lack of sleep was obviously messing with her head.

"How come *you* don't have to wear one of these?" she asked as she lowered it over her head and began to knot the ties behind her back.

"Because I don't care about my clothes, whereas yours look nice."

She felt his gaze on her as he spoke and awareness spread across her skin, but once again, she tried to ignore it. Probably she was imagining the heat in his eyes anyway. His ex-wife looked like a supermodel, so he'd hardly find someone like her attractive.

"What? These old things?" She injected a lightness she didn't feel into her voice. But they *were* old—if she'd known her legs were going to lead her to her boss, she might have made more of an effort choosing a nicer outfit.

He shrugged one shoulder and gestured to his clothes, which she saw were covered in splashes of various ingredients. "Either way, I think for me the horse has bolted. Now, shall we get started?"

"Yes." She averted her gaze from his fitted T-shirt. "But only if you promise not to fire me if I burn down your kitchen."

He laughed and shook his head. "I think you're going to surprise yourself."

Together they collected the ingredients from the pantry and got out a frying pan. She was hoping his lessons would be more watch and learn, but he talked her through every step of the process—making her sift the flour three times, add pinches of salt and baking powder, a spoonful of sugar, and then mix milk, egg and a "dash of vanilla" together before whisking the combo into the flour.

"My arm is killing me. Are you sure this isn't whisked enough yet?" After two minutes, her muscles throbbed with the unexpected exertion.

"The secret to fluffy pancakes is in the whisking— no one ever does it as long as they should."

"You're a slave driver." She pouted as she continued, secretly enjoying the task.

He grinned as if pleased by this description. "Okay, that's probably enough," he said a few moments later. "Now taste the batter to ensure it doesn't require any more sugar or salt."

He passed her a teaspoon, which she dipped into the mixture and then brought to her mouth.

"Well?"

She licked her lips. "I think it tastes good, but I'm no expert."

"Yet." He winked as he took the spoon from her. "Now it's time to cook them."

She swallowed. Making batter was one thing, but

her hands shook as he instructed her through placing a dab of butter in the pan and then pouring a measure of batter on top. It sizzled as the batter spread out to the edges of the pan.

"You're doing really well," Lachlan said, his voice low as he stood right next to her and encouraged her like he might a child learning to ride a bike. Only she didn't *feel* like a child when she was around him. Anything but.

"Thanks," she whispered as they both gazed down at their efforts.

"There, see those bubbles? That's how we tell it's time to flip."

Thankfully, he didn't expect her to do some snazzy trick with the pan but handed her a flipper instead.

She barely breathed as she slid the flipper under the pancake and lifted it, but as she tried to turn it, the whole thing fell into a heap in the pan. She let out a shriek of annoyance. "See, I'm hopeless."

"You're not going to give up that easily, are you? Come on, we'll do this next one together."

He expertly cleaned the pan of her mess, then tossed another drop of butter in. "Try again."

And despite feeling as if this was a lost cause and she was wasting his ingredients, Eliza poured another measure into the sizzling pan.

Neither of them spoke, watching until it began to bubble, then Lachlan said, "Grab the flipper again."

But this time when she picked it up, he placed his hand over hers, then gently guided the utensil under the half-cooked pancake and helped her turn it over properly.

"There, that wasn't too hard, was it?" As he spoke, his warm breath tickled her ear and undeniable attraction rippled through her. It had been so long since she'd been this close to a man and it left her feeling a little unsteady on her feet.

Somehow she managed to reply, "But you did that, not me."

"Seriously, Eliza," he said, turning his head to look at her. "It's not that hard. You just need to have a little faith in yourself."

And somehow—under Lachlan's kind and patient instruction—she lifted this first pancake out of the pan and onto a plate and then continued on to make a more than passable batch.

She grinned as she stared at the pile sitting there, begging to be eaten, unable to recall such a sense of achievement in quite some time. Maybe she really had just never had the right teacher before.

They didn't bother going out into the restaurant to eat them but piled two plates high, poured his special syrup over the top and then ate them right there, leaning back against the countertop.

"This is the best midnight snack I've ever had," she said after swallowing the first bite.

"And you didn't burn the kitchen down. Next time, we'll try something a little trickier, like mac'n'cheese. If a girl can cook pancakes and mac'n'cheese, I reckon she's set for life."

She laughed and realized that in the last week working with Lachlan, she'd started to laugh a lot more. She'd started to *feel* a lot more again—emotions other than sadness and grief. Part of her felt guilty about this fact but another part of her wanted to enjoy it.

"I was thinking," she said, "about opening night…"

But he shook his finger at her. "No talking about

work tonight. You're not on the clock now. I want to know about you."

She swallowed, nerves suddenly rushing up her throat. "What do you want to know?" There was only one thing that came to her mind and she didn't want to talk about that with him. Or anyone.

A pensive expression lingered on his face a few moments. "Let's start with the basics. What's your favorite color?"

"Pink," she said with an apologetic shrug. "I guess I never grew out of it."

"No wonder you and Hallie get on so well. Mine's brown."

"Brown?" Eliza couldn't help but scoff. "Whose favorite color is brown?"

"Mine," he said defensively. "It's the color of all my favorite things—chocolate, coffee and…caramel."

"Fair enough." She stifled a smile. "I'm not going to judge you on that. What's your favorite movie?"

He took a moment, rubbing his chin between his thumb and forefinger as if this was a difficult question.

"Let me guess. *The Sound of Music?*"

He laughed. "No, but close. *Mary Poppins.*"

"Seriously?" She raised an eyebrow. "Now you're pulling my leg."

He shook his head. "Uh-uh. I swear. The bank scene where all the grumpy old men are floating up near the ceiling, laughing their heads off—sometimes I watch that if I'm in a bad mood or sad about something, and it never fails to brighten my day."

She frowned, trying to remember the plot—it had been a long time. "But didn't someone die in that scene?"

"Yes, but he died laughing. What better way to go?"

A lump formed in her throat at the notion of there being any good kind of death—she felt tears welling—but thankfully, Lachlan didn't seem to notice. "My turn."

"What?"

"It's my turn to ask a question," he clarified. "Could your ex-husband cook?"

She blinked, startled that he'd gone from impersonal, almost-silly questions to something immensely personal.

"If you can't cook—or couldn't," he added, "because I'm pretty certain I could teach you—I just wondered if he could. Or did you guys mostly eat out?"

Eliza tried to ignore the tightening in her chest that the conversation was heading to a place she didn't want it to go. "He was a chef, so yes, he cooked—or we ate out at work. As we were both in the restaurant industry, that's generally what we did."

"Did you work at the same restaurant?" he asked.

"Yes." She hoped her one-word answer told him that she didn't want to talk about her ex. She'd come out to try to escape dwelling on the past and up until now it had done the trick. "Most embarrassing thing that's ever happened to you?"

He took the bait and within moments, she was laughing. "The night I lost my virginity, I walked my girl-friend back to her parents' place. We were supposed to have been at the movies but instead we made out in the distillery warehouse. Her mom and dad asked me in for cocoa when we got back and then afterward, as I stood up to leave, the used condom fell from my pocket onto their kitchen floor."

"Oh, my Lord, no!" Her hand rushed up to slap her

mouth. "Why hadn't you got rid of it? You weren't keeping it as some kind of trophy, were you?"

He screwed up his face. "What kind of sick freak do you think I am?" But he was laughing, too. "No, I didn't want to dispose of it in the distillery in case my parents found it, so I stuffed it in my pocket, wrapped in tissues, to get rid of later."

"What did her parents say?" Eliza almost couldn't ask the question, she was laughing so hard.

"I thought her dad was going to shoot me, so I feigned shock as if it was the first time I'd ever seen a condom in my life. I said it must have been on the bus and stuck to my butt when I sat on the seat or something."

She snorted. "And they bought that?"

"No. Her dad turned and left the room and I thought he might be off to get his gun, so I hightailed it out of there."

"Was the girl Linda?" she asked, knowing they'd got together young.

"Nope. Her name was Rose. Sweet girl, gorgeous inside and out. But after that episode, her parents sent her away to boarding school. Pity… Perhaps if we'd stuck together, I wouldn't have met Linda."

"But then you wouldn't have Hamish and Hallie."

His expression turned serious. "Yeah, that's true. And I wouldn't swap them for the world. What's your most embarrassing moment, then?"

"I don't think I want to tell you."

He chuckled. "Come on… It can't be worse than mine."

"Oh, it's not." She found herself smiling again at the thought of his. "I don't know if much could top that, but mine involves a restaurant faux pas and I'm worried you might regret hiring me if I tell you."

He leaned back in his seat and rubbed his hands together. "Fair's fair. I told you mine, now you have to tell me yours. Besides, I like nothing better than a restaurant faux pas—as long as it's not mine."

She sighed. "Okay, then. I threw up on a customer."

His lovely green eyes widened. "You mean, like… vomited?"

She nodded slowly.

"Hey, that's not so bad. You can't help being sick. What was it? Gastro or food poisoning? If it was food poisoning, it's more an embarrassment for the chef."

Pregnancy, she almost said, but couldn't quite bring herself to do so. They were having such a lovely time and if she told him she'd been pregnant, he would ask her what happened to the baby and that answer would end all easy conversation between them from here on in. She liked that he could talk and even joke a bit with her without worrying that he might put his foot in it.

It's amazing how many common, everyday phrases related to dying. She'd found that out soon after Jack died. Friends and family would be chatting away and suddenly say something like "I'd kill for a coffee right now" or "it scared me half to death" and then they'd get all flustered and apologize to her for putting their feet in it, when she wouldn't actually have noticed if they hadn't pointed it out.

"Some kind of twenty-four-hour bug," she said, hoping Lachlan hadn't noticed her hesitation.

"Hardly your fault, but yes, embarrassing." And then, he started to yawn. He tried to cover it but the action made her realize how late it was.

"I should be getting home," she said, pushing back

her seat and starting to collect their plates. "We've got a busy day tomorrow."

For a moment, he looked as if he might try to convince her to stay a little longer, but then he, too, stood. "Leave the plates. We can do them in the morning. I'll drive you home."

"No." The word came out harsher than she meant it to. "I've got my bike and I don't want to put you out."

"Your bike will fit in my truck, or you can leave it here and I can come get you in the morning after school drop-off, but there is no way I'm letting you ride home alone at this time at night."

"No bogeymen got me on the way over," she said.

But he wasn't taking no for an answer. "You were lucky. But my mom would never forgive me if I didn't drive you, and more important, I wouldn't forgive myself. And I'd expect any respectable guy to do the same for my sisters or for Hallie when she's old enough to sneak out late at night. Now, are we going to stand here arguing about it, or are you going to let me give you a lift, so we can all go home and try to get some rest?"

"Okay." She relented. If he was putting her in the same realm as his sister and his daughter, it wasn't like he'd expect her to ask him in for "coffee." Part of her actually felt a little disappointed by this fact, but she told herself it was a good thing. She needed a friend and a job more than she needed to complicate her life any more than it already was. Besides, her surprising physical feelings for him were probably simply because he was the first guy (aside from her dad) she'd spent any time with since Tyler.

"Great. Let me just switch off the lights."

Eliza waited by the door as Lachlan turned everything except the security lights off and then they went outside. It was only as he was locking up that she realized his truck was a few hundred yards away at the house.

"I don't want to wake your family," she said as he gestured for her to follow him that way.

"The kids and Blair sleep like the dead and Mom's probably still up watching the late-night movie. No more excuses."

And although it was dark and he couldn't see, she smiled. If she'd told him about Jack, he'd now be berating himself and apologizing to her for that sentence. Instead, they walked easily across the gravel to the main house, like two people who had just enjoyed a pleasant evening in each other's company. And *that* felt good. Her heart pinched a little with guilt at this, but she told herself to ignore it—this was why she'd moved to Jewell Rock, to learn to live again.

"Thanks for keeping me company tonight," Lachlan said ten minutes later as he lifted her bike out of the bed of his truck and set it down on the ground in front of her apartment block.

"Thank *you*," she replied. "It sure beat counting sheep."

He laughed. "I'm making chocolate, whiskey and bacon chili tomorrow night if you have trouble sleeping again."

"What *is* that?" she asked, unsure whether to grimace or rub her lips together in anticipation.

He cocked his head to one side and winked. "I guess if you really want to know, I'll see you tomorrow night."

And with that, he turned, swaggered around to the driver's side and climbed back into the truck. Smiling, she lifted her hand and waved good-night as she started to wheel her bike toward the building. She secured it out front and then turned back to see him still sitting there, watching her. Only when she went inside and closed the door behind her did she hear him finally drive off down the road.

Chapter Eight

"You guys all set in here?"

Lachlan looked up to see Eliza peering her head around the door to the kitchen. Alongside him worked his assistant chef and three of their new kitchen hands ready for the first ever dinner service. They weren't open yet—the big day was still two weeks away—but Eliza had had the brilliant idea to have a couple of rehearsals. So tonight and next Friday, he'd invited members of his family and the family of his staff to have dinner at the restaurant on him.

"Yep. We sure are." He smiled, loving the sight of her in their new uniforms, the McKinnel's logo in pride of place on her breast pocket.

"Good. Because our first customers have just walked in the door." She winked at him and then turned and hurried into the restaurant to welcome them.

Lachlan gave his kitchen team a quick pep talk and

then took a moment to peek out and watch Eliza and the waitstaff welcoming people and leading them over to tables. Behind the bar, their mixologist was ready and waiting to make magic with the drinks. Everyone and everything was exactly as it should be and Lachlan felt a buzz of pride fill his lungs as he looked on. Granted, they still had a few hours and many dishes of food to get through before they could celebrate their night as a success, but with himself in the kitchen and Eliza making sure everything went smoothly in the dining area, he felt as if he could conquer the world, so a simple restaurant should be a piece of cake.

Eliza looked up from where she'd just seated his mom, her best friend, Marcia, and the twins. As their eyes met, she gave him a slow smile that he felt right down to his toes.

"Daddy!" Hallie spotted him, rushed out of her seat and threw her arms around his waist. "Can I have some french fries, please? Hamish wants french fries, too. Don't you?" she said, glancing back to her brother as if daring him to disagree.

Lachlan smiled as he carried his daughter back to the table. "I was hoping you'd be a little more adventurous than that," he said, lowering her down into her seat, "but if you choose something from the menu, we might be able to do some fries on the side."

"Yay." The twins punched the air in unison.

He chuckled and glanced to his mom and Marcia, who would soon be Quinn's mother-in-law. "Welcome, ladies, so glad you could join us tonight."

"Thanks for inviting me," Marcia said, gazing around. "This place looks fantastic and I feel so privileged to get to try it out before the rest of the town."

"We wouldn't miss this for the world," Nora said,

standing to give him a hug. "I'm so proud of everything you and Eliza have achieved so far."

Lachlan liked the way his mom spoke as if he and Eliza were a partnership and wondered if somehow she could tell that his feelings for the head hostess were growing into something a little more than professional. He'd pretty much finished experimenting with the dishes now—the menu had already gone to print—but their nightly rendezvous hadn't stopped.

And he found himself looking forward to them more and more.

During the day, his conversations with Eliza were strictly professional—revolving almost entirely around what needed to be achieved in the lead up to opening the restaurant—but at night, he forbade them to talk about work. At night, while he taught her to cook, they made easy conversation, which got a little bit more personal with every passing day. He hadn't enjoyed a woman's company this much in as long as he could remember.

"I can't take any of the credit." Eliza scoffed but her cheeks flushed.

"That's not the way my son tells it," Nora said. "He told me these preopening dinners were all your idea. But I do worry the two of you are working far too hard. I hope Lachlan is leaving you some time to relax and settle into your new apartment. How are you finding life in Jewell Rock?"

"Oh, I love it." Eliza smiled. "Everyone is so friendly. I've never lived in a small town before—so it's a little weird that the people at the supermarket already know me by name—but aside from that, I like the slower pace of life. In New York, everyone is always in a rush, but here, no one seems to be in such a hurry they can't stop and say hello."

"Splendid. Now, what are you doing on Sunday?"

Eliza's brow furrowed slightly. "Um, nothing. I'll probably end up cleaning my apartment."

"Nonsense. Sundays are supposed to be days of rest. Housework is strictly forbidden." His mom clapped her hands together. "You'll come to lunch at my place instead."

Eliza looked a little flustered.

"Mom," Lachlan said. "It's customary to *ask* people, not *tell* them when you invite them over for a bite to eat. Eliza might have had enough of us McKinnels during the week and prefer to spend her weekends by herself."

Although secretly he loved the idea of hanging out with her on Sunday, as well.

His mom rolled her eyes. "I'm sorry, Eliza. If you don't have a *better* offer, would you *like* to come have Sunday lunch with me and my ever-growing tribe?"

Eliza laughed. "That would be lovely, thank you. Now, can I get you some drinks to start with?"

That was his cue to head back into the kitchen, and with one last lingering look at Eliza, he did so. He needed to ignore his errant thoughts and focus on cooking.

The next few hours flew by. The kitchen was a hive of activity with Lachlan and his team working seamlessly together, creating dishes he was proud of. There were only two mishaps—a batch of bourbon-glazed brussels sprouts slightly overcooked and one broken plate—but nothing that could be classified a calamity.

Once the desserts had been served, he took a few moments to go out into the dining room and chat to his friends and siblings, who all raved about their dinners.

"We did it," he said to Eliza, meeting her as she was halfway back to the kitchen with an armful of dirty plates. He took them from her, their hands brushing against each other in the process. Her skin was silky smooth and he wanted to reach out and touch it again.

"Did you ever have any doubt?" she asked, her eyes radiant as she grinned at him. "We make a good team."

But she turned and went back to keep clearing tables before he could agree.

Although the cooking and serving part of the evening went fast, the next couple of hours dragged. No one seemed in a hurry to leave and conversation lingered over mugs of Spanish coffee. When the kitchen was sparkling clean, he and Eliza dismissed the rest of the staff, saying that they could handle any last drinks and the locking up of the restaurant. He sent each of his new employees home with leftovers, and when his friends and family finally called it a night, he was overjoyed to be left alone with Eliza.

"You hungry?"

"Famished," she said with a sigh, reaching up to pull her hair free from its ponytail. "But what a night. That went even better than we hoped."

"I agree." He tried not to stare at her gorgeous brown locks, but all he could think about was how silky smooth they would feel if he reached out and ran his fingers through them. "How about we raid the leftovers for our own dinner and I crack open a bottle of wine to celebrate?"

She raised an eyebrow. "While that sounds just about perfect, how am I going to ride home or you drive me home if we drink a bottle of wine between us?"

"Hmm." He rubbed his jaw as he pondered this problem. *Dammit*. "How about a glass, then?"

She chuckled. "A glass sounds like a good idea. Any

more and I might fall asleep anyway. Why don't I grab the wine while you get the food?"

"Good idea. What do you want?"

She shrugged one shoulder. "What's left?" Before he could answer, she added, "Actually, surprise me."

While Eliza poured the wine, Lachlan went into the kitchen and retrieved two bowls of chili. When he returned, they sat down at a table together and talked over the evening. Although everything had gone even better than they'd hoped for, they agreed on a couple of things to finesse in this week's training before the second rehearsal next Friday. When Eliza yawned, Lachlan realized that they'd both been working pretty much nonstop since early that morning.

"Come on," he said, pushing to a stand. "I'll drive you home."

He didn't want to—although physically exhausted, he could happily spend all night talking to her—but she didn't object and together they loaded their plates into the dishwasher, then locked up and headed out into the night.

"What should I bring to your mom's place on Sunday?" she asked as they climbed out of his truck at her apartment block and headed around to the truck's bed to retrieve her bike. This had become a nightly ritual but he suddenly realized that once the restaurant was properly opened, their late-night cooking lessons would likely come to an end and he didn't want them to.

"Just yourself," he said as he held the bike toward her. "There's always enough food to feed a small country."

She chuckled as she reached out to take the bike and once again their hands touched in the interaction. Their gazes collided—her dark eyes glittered in the moonlight, her lips parted slightly and he felt the connection like a physical jolt.

"Thank you," she said, her voice low. "For bringing me and my bike home again."

"Any time," he replied and then, before he could think the ramifications through, he leaned forward and touched his lips to hers. What started as a tentative brush across her mouth, what could have almost been a platonic kiss good-night between friends, turned serious very quickly when she kissed him back. As her tongue slipped into his mouth, muscles all over his body tightened and his heart went into overdrive.

He took his hands off the bike and lifted them to her face, cradling her cheeks in his palms as he deepened the kiss. Eliza let out a little moan of pleasure and it was the most beautiful sound in the world.

A little voice in his head told him that they should take this inside, that at any moment either of his sisters might glance out the window and become an unwitting spectator. It seemed that Eliza was thinking the same thing, for she pulled back and looked up into his eyes.

His heart halted as he waited for her to speak. Had he misread the signs? Perhaps she hadn't enjoyed that kiss as much as he did?

But then she opened those beautiful lips again and whispered, "Do you want to come inside?" Her tone and the expression on her face made it crystal clear what she was offering.

It was all he could do not to shriek for joy. That pesky little voice from earlier tried telling him that maybe he should decline—that sleeping with an employee was quite possibly the worst thing he could do—but his desire for Eliza was stronger than anything else. For two weeks, he'd barely been able to think about anything but kissing her and now that he had, there was nothing he wanted more than to do so again.

"I'd love to," he said, reluctantly dropping his hands from her face so he could take the bike from her grasp and lean it up against the wall.

After that, no more words were necessary. Eliza offered him her hand and he took it happily, his pulse racing as she led him into the building. They grinned conspiratorially at each other as they tiptoed past his sisters' apartment and he felt like a kid about to do something very, very naughty.

But he couldn't wait and thanked the Lord for the just-in-case condom in his wallet.

Chapter Nine

Eliza knew she'd been playing with fire all these late nights she'd been spending with Lachlan but until he'd kissed her, she'd deluded herself into believing that the attraction she felt was one-sided. She'd ignored the way he sometimes looked at her and the way such a look spread heat from her core right down to her toes, telling herself it was all in her imagination. She'd even deluded herself that if such attraction *were* mutual and *if* he ever made a move, she'd be able to resist him on the grounds that they worked together and it wasn't a good idea.

But the moment she'd felt his lips on hers, she'd known she was a lost cause. She couldn't push him away if her life depended on it and neither did she want to.

Adrenaline raced through her body now as she fumbled to find her key in her purse. She shoved it in the lock and pushed open the door. The moment they were inside, Lachlan kicked it shut behind them. Eliza managed to switch on the hall light before her purse and key dropped from her grasp.

They reached for each other again, his hands drawing her face to his, and hers finding their way around his back and sliding up under his shirt. His bare skin was hot and smooth beneath her touch and her mouth watered at the thought of licking it.

She honestly didn't know what had come over her but standing here in her tiny hallway kissing him wasn't nearly enough. As if Lachlan could feel her desperation in her kiss, his hands started to wander. As one thumb teased the skin at her décolletage, the other went lower, gently and teasingly skimming over her breasts.

Fire lit within her—she felt as if she might combust if she didn't feel his hands on her skin. More daring than she'd ever been before, she ripped her hands from beneath his shirt and started undoing the buttons of her own.

She wanted everything and anything he could give her.

As if encouraged by her wantonness, Lachlan's lips followed in the path of his hands, dropping tiny kisses along her neckline that caused her skin to gooseflesh. Heat pooled between her legs and her heart rate went crazy as he expertly unclasped her bra and replaced it with his hands instead.

"You're incredible, so beautiful," he whispered, teasing her nipples with his thumbs. His words made her feel alive, and when he took one nipple into his mouth, she cried out. The pleasure shot through her, right to her core and her knees buckled.

Lachlan was right there to catch her, one arm sliding around her back and holding her close to his lovely, hard chest.

"Which way to the bedroom?" he asked, his voice low and gravelly, exactly as she imagined sex would sound if it spoke.

Unable to speak, she thrust her head in the right direction and squealed as he scooped her up into his arms and carried her into her bedroom like she weighed nothing more than a silk scarf. Her curtains still open from that morning, the moonlight sneaked in and fell across the bed, giving them enough light to make their way to it without switching one on.

They tumbled onto the bed together, legs tangling as their lips sought each other once again. Her hands scrambled for his shirt, but chef's whites weren't the easiest to remove in the near dark while on the brink of sexual satisfaction.

"Help me," she moaned. "I want to feel your skin."

Lachlan sat up, his knees on either side of her hips, his body hovering just above her as he whipped off his upper layers.

Had she ever seen anything so intoxicating as this gorgeous man doing as she'd begged?

She reached out her hand to touch him. More slowly, enjoying the anticipation now that what she wanted was within reach. She felt his quick intake of breath as her fingers glided down his chest, following the arrow of hair to the top of his trousers. Her hand covered the bulge beneath and her insides tingled as she touched him through the material. He felt so good and she could only imagine how much better he would feel inside her.

"Take them off," she demanded.

Slightly groaning as if trying to control himself, Lachlan lifted her hand from his groin and shook his head. "You first," he said. Then, he sat up, ripped off

her shoes and yanked her trousers and panties down
her legs in one swift move.

Self-consciousness about being fully naked in front
of him lasted only seconds, because then he was back,
his body stretched out over the top of hers like a warm
blanket she wanted to enfold herself in. She could feel
his erection against the apex of her thighs and she
pressed herself upward, instinct taking over as she
rocked herself against him.

He pushed himself up on his arms and swore as he
gazed down at her. "Eliza, you do any more of that
and this will be over in seconds. Let me take care of
you first."

And take care of her he did.

With those words, he claimed her mouth again with
his, but this time, his fingers trekked far lower than they
had before, sliding between her legs and touching her
where it mattered most. He stroked her gently at first,
but then the intensity increased as he pushed his finger
deeper and circled her bud.

She felt her core tightening, her whole body going
still as the pleasure built within her. As if that wasn't
maddening enough, he tore his lips from hers and
dipped his head, once again twirling his tongue around
her nipple and then sucking it right into his mouth. It
was almost embarrassing how quickly her first orgasm
rolled through her, her body shaking and her inner muscles shuddering against his touch.

It had been so long since she'd felt such intense physical relief. The man had magic fingers but she needed,
she *wanted* more. Barely able to move due to the sensations flooding her body, somehow she voiced her desire.

"Lachlan. You're killing me. Please, take off your
trousers. I need you."

He looked up from where he'd been pleasuring her breasts and grinned around her nipple. It was the most erotic thing she'd ever seen.

"Just a sec."

And then he pushed up from her again and treated her to a one-man revue as he unbuckled his belt, then shucked his shoes, socks, trousers and underwear in what had to be world-record time. He was a good-looking man fully clothed, but standing at the edge of her bed, moonlight dappling over his bare skin, he was simply glorious.

Lachlan seemed far too busy to go to the gym, so she wondered what he did to get such lovely muscles. She couldn't help gaping at his impressive erection, but she didn't have time to stare or wonder for long.

He stooped and picked his trousers up off the floor. For one horrifying moment, she thought he'd changed his mind and was going to put them back on, but relief flooded her when he pulled out his wallet and conjured a little square foil packet instead. As he ripped it open with his teeth and sheathed himself quickly, she silently thanked the Lord that Lachlan had the forethought to think about it, when she'd almost lost her head.

And then he was back on the bed beside her, taking her in his arms, kissing her like their lives depended on it and making her hot all over again. This time, it was Eliza who slipped her hand between them, moved it lower and wrapped it around his long, hard shaft. She squeezed a little, tentatively at first, but when it grew even more beneath her touch, her own desire took over.

She lifted her hips a little, nudged her entrance with his erection and then hooked her legs up around his back. He plunged inside, not needing any more encouragement, driving deep into her, his hands pressed against the mattress, their eyes glued on each other as he brought them both quickly to release.

It might only have been missionary sex—boring sex, as Tyler used to say—but nothing felt ordinary about this connection. Banishing Tyler from her head, she cried out as her second orgasm in what felt like a matter of minutes rocked through her, the pleasure so strong she thought she might combust.

Lachlan grinned down at her, then covered her mouth with his, silencing her as he kissed her hard once again. Afterward, they lay there, so still, so quiet, she could feel his heart pumping against her own chest.

What the hell have I just done?

But with him still deliciously inside her, she found she couldn't summon one iota of remorse. A little guilt perhaps that she could feel so wonderful, so alive, but with the aftershocks of pleasure still doing their stuff, definitely no remorse. Sex that good could never have been regretted, no matter what came next.

After what felt like ages but was probably only a minute or so, he pushed up again and looked down at her. "I'm going to go deal with the condom," he said and then slid out of bed. "Back in a sec."

She admired his cute butt as he walked naked to the en suite and then stretched out in bed wondering if that was his only condom. She'd stopped taking the Pill months ago when it became obvious that sex with her husband wasn't on the agenda anymore, but she wouldn't mind if more sex was on tonight's agenda. Now that she'd broken her pact with herself not to get involved with anyone, it seemed silly not to indulge herself with such a willing partner.

As she rolled over, her heart halted in her chest as she came face-to-face with the photo frame with her little boy's smiling face sitting next to her on the bedside table. She sat up so quickly, her head spun as she snatched up the frame, then yanked open the bedside drawer and shoved it inside.

The lightness that had filled her body vanished as she realized how close she'd come to Lachlan seeing it. What on earth had she been thinking, sleeping with her boss of all people? The last thing she wanted was for him to start asking questions she didn't want to answer and now that they'd slept together, he might think he had the right to pry further into her personal life.

What else would he expect? Would he hope tonight was a prelude to something more? Fear turned her heart to ice at the thought. If she'd needed sex, she could have gone to a bar and picked up some stranger or joined that silly app that Sophie and Annabel were obsessed with.

But her boss? *Oh, Eliza, you stupid, stupid girl.*

She heard the toilet flush and then the door clicked open and Lachlan stood there, still in all his naked glory. She froze like a deer in headlights.

He took a step back into the bedroom and then paused, frowning as he met her gaze. "Are you okay?" He sounded uncertain. That would make two of them. "You look like you've seen a ghost."

She rubbed her lips together. "What did we just do?"

His brows furrowed a little more. "We just had incredible sex. At least I thought we did."

Incredible didn't even come close to describing what they'd just done. Her cheeks flushed at his directness and she quickly pulled the blankets over her, feeling suddenly self-conscious. "But you're my boss."

His lips flicked up at the edges and he took a step closer to the bed. "I could be your boss with benefits."

As he peeled the covers back and lay down next to

her again, heat ripped through Eliza's body at his suggestive tone.

Yes, please, shouted her hormones. Boss with benefits? How freaking fantastic did that sound? Forever was a long time to go without sex simply because she didn't want the intimacy and commitment she'd always thought went hand in hand with making love. She thought of Grammy Louise's advice that sex didn't always have to be serious and hope flared in her heart.

She smiled up at him. "Are you serious? You'd be happy with that kind of arrangement?"

Lachlan blinked, his hands pausing on their way to her body. When he'd suggested "benefits," he'd been joking. For one, he didn't think Eliza was that kind of girl; two, he respected her too much to use her for her body; and three, he also liked her, which meant for the first time in a long while, he wanted more than just sex from a woman. But the smile on her face and the tone of her voice gave him pause.

It sounded almost as if she liked his indecent proposition.

"Um...I... What do *you* want?" he asked, looking directly up into her dark eyes.

"Well." She rubbed her lips together and her chest rose and fell with a heavy breath. "I really like you, Lachlan. You're the first guy I've slept with since my marriage ended and it was amazing. I've really loved spending time with you these last few weeks—during the day and especially at night. Your passion for food is contagious and thanks to you, I've smiled more in the last few weeks than I have in the last year. But I'm still incredibly hurt and raw from my separation, my divorce isn't even final yet and my head isn't in the right place to start another relationship."

"I see. Of course." He nodded fast and summoned a smile, trying to cover over his shock and disappointment. Wasn't it usually the guy quoting such lines? And since when had he wanted a relationship anyway? His kids came first and considering Linda's rejection of Hamish, he'd never allowed himself to dream about finding a woman who might want him *and* his children.

Still, he couldn't help being curious about Eliza's reticence. "Do you think there's a chance you and your ex might get back together?"

His heart squeezed at the prospect and he couldn't help the rush of relief as she shook her head. "No. I loved him with all my heart but he hurt me too badly to ever recover from that."

"He abused you?" His own feelings forgotten, Lachlan clenched his fists as he harbored violent thoughts about a man he'd never met.

"Oh, no, nothing like that. He didn't hurt me physically. Tyler…" She sighed deeply and paused as if considering how much to tell him.

Was she holding back because she didn't want him to think badly of her ex? Obviously she still had feelings for the guy, no matter how much she professed otherwise, and Lachlan couldn't help feeling a tad jealous.

"It's all right," he said encouragingly, trying to ignore his own discomfort. "You can tell me anything, but if you don't want to…I understand."

"Tyler had a drug problem," she said after another few long moments. "When he was young, he dabbled in recreational stuff, but he swore he'd stopped by the time we started going out. I believed him but eighteen months ago, he started up again. Instead of turning to me when…when things got tough, he turned to drugs and his usage quickly started affecting his work. Eventually, with the assistance of his family, I convinced him to get some help. He sought counseling and it appeared to be doing him good. So good it turns out that he decided he liked his counselor more than he liked me."

Eliza sniffed and a tear slid down her cheek. She brushed it away as if embarrassed by it and went on. "Three months ago, he told me he'd been sleeping with her and asked me to move out of our apartment. That's when I moved in with my grandmother again."

His heart went out to this gorgeous woman lying beside him and he stupidly blurted, "Isn't sleeping with a patient breaking some kind of professional rule?"

Something between a scoff and a laugh escaped her lips as she met his eyes. "I think adultery goes against the rules of marriage, too, but you know as well as I do that rules don't always hinder people."

"That's true." He put his hand over hers and squeezed it in a show of support. "But it still sucks. And for what it's worth, I think your ex-husband must be a damn fool, choosing someone else over you."

In fact, Tyler had to be stupid *and* blind because right now, Lachlan couldn't imagine another woman that could give Eliza a run for her money on any level. She was pretty close to perfect.

"Thank you," she whispered, linking her fingers through his and staring down at their joined hands. "That means a lot."

Part of him wanted to hunt this Tyler dude down but another part of him wanted to thank the asshole because while Eliza might not be ready for another relationship right now, at least she was a free agent. Their chemistry was impossible to deny, so perhaps in time, if he was patient, if he played his cards right, he might stand a chance for more than just sex with her.

There hadn't been a woman he *wanted* to stand a chance with in a very long time.

"I mean it," he said, "and if you ever want to talk about any of it, then I'm all ears. It might have been a while ago, but when Linda cheated on me, she taught me a few important life lessons and I've come out the other side relatively unscathed. I believe you will, too."

"Let's hope so," she said with a slow smile. "I feel like moving here, getting away from my past and helping you open the restaurant is a very good step in the right direction. I should probably have mentioned this in my interview, but my last job was working in Tyler's family restaurant. I changed my name back to my maiden name so the connection wouldn't be obvious on my résumé, but when our relationship exploded, I basically lost my job, as well."

Lachlan couldn't believe what he was hearing. "They fired you for *his* indiscretions?" He thought back to the call he'd made to her last employer for a reference—they'd been over-the-top gushy but now he wondered if that wasn't simply because she was good at her job, but also because they didn't want her to cause a fuss about being let go.

"Oh, no, not exactly. His parents were very upset by his behavior and they didn't actually fire me, but I couldn't be comfortable continuing to work there after everything that had gone down. I've had firsthand experience with how dangerous mixing business with pleasure can be and that's why *this*—" she bit her lip and pointed her finger back and forth between them "—scares me. I like being in Jewell Rock. I like my new apartment, living next to your sisters. I like working with you. I didn't want to mess all that up for..."

Her voice trailed off and he finished the sentence for her. "For a bit of fun between the sheets?"

Her lips twisted and her cheeks flushed that beautiful pink color again. Her long dark lashes fluttered as she looked down, not meeting his eyes when she said, "Exactly. But perhaps that's too late. If things are going to be awkward now that we've slept together and you'd rather I quit, then...I understand."

"Quit?" His heart shuddered. The thought of Eliza handing in her notice made his insides turn almost as much as the thought of never *being* inside her again. "Don't talk such blasphemy," he said, turning and finally pulling her into his arms again. "I do *not* want you to quit. I do not want to talk about your ex-husband. But I do want to kiss you again."

And then, before she could say another word, he did exactly that, taking her beautiful face once again between his hands and claiming her mouth with his. Man, she tasted good, no food could ever possibly compare. And if sex was all she was offering, then he'd be an idiot to turn her down. It wasn't like he had a lot of time for anything more right now either.

A moan slipped from her mouth into his, their bodies smashing together as her silky smooth legs entwined with his. They kissed like a couple of crazed teens, their hands wandering, exploring and driving each other to distraction.

Eventually, Eliza tore her lips from his and rolled over so that she was straddling him. Her hair swished from side to side as she smiled seductively down at him with her hips rocking torturously against his growing erection.

"Do you have another condom?" she panted as her hand once again closed around his penis.

Every muscle in his body tensed at her touch. "No. Hot damn. That was my only one. I don't suppose you have any?"

She shook her head.

He groaned. "I'll take a trip to the drugstore tomorrow and stock up."

"Yes. You do that," she said, "but in the meantime…"

And then she smiled suggestively, wriggled down his body and dropped her head to his groin. Seconds later, she had him in her mouth. And a minute later, he'd lost the ability to think straight.

A boss with benefits? Yeah, maybe he could get used to that title.

Chapter Ten

Eliza's phone rang as she was getting herself ready for Sunday lunch and her heart kicked up a notch. Could it be Lachlan? Her body buzzed in anticipation at the thought of seeing him again. But more likely, the caller would be one of three people—Grammy Louise, Lilly or Dad. Sometimes she wondered if they'd set up some kind of roster among them because hardly a day went by when at least one of them didn't call her.

As much as she loved all three, she didn't always feel like talking to them. It was draining to have to re-assure them that she wasn't about to jump off a cliff or drown herself in a lake.

But today, still on a high from Friday night, she wouldn't have to put on too much of an act. She scooped up the phone and swiped to answer. "Hi, Grammy."

"Hel-lo, my gorgeous girl. Happy Sunday."

"You sound out of breath," Eliza said. She carried

the phone back into the bathroom, put her phone on the vanity and her grandmother on speaker so she could continue her hair and makeup as she listened to her grandmother talk about her new beau.

"I'm actually going out to lunch in a moment," Eliza said. She knew for a fact this would make Grammy very happy. "Nora McKinnel, my boss's mom, asked me over for Sunday lunch with their family."

"Ooh, that's lovely. It's so kind of his mom to try to make you feel welcome."

"It's not just Nora," Eliza admitted. "All of the McKinnels have been very friendly and welcoming. I think you'd like them."

"If they are looking after my girl, I already adore them," Grammy said.

"Oh, they are." Eliza blushed, thinking of exactly how well Lachlan had looked after her on Friday night. "In fact, Lachlan's sisters, Sophie and Annabel, will be arriving any minute to give me a lift to the distillery because my bike was stolen."

"What?" Grammy sounded horrified. "Are you okay? What happened to your old one? You'd barely had it five minutes."

"I didn't lock it up properly on Friday night and someone stole it."

"That would never happen in New York, but it's not like you to be so careless either. What happened?"

While smirking at the New York comment, Eliza wondered if she should tell her that she'd been in such a haste to go inside after Lachlan kissed her so they could rip each other's clothes off that she hadn't been thinking straight. Grammy would probably rejoice at such news but something stopped her from being forthright.

She worried if she told her grandmother, Louise might make more of it than it actually was.

"Eliza? Are you still there?"

"Sorry, Grammy. Yes, I was just tired the other night, I think, and I forgot about securing the bike."

"Lachlan's not working you too hard, is he?" There was a hint of if-he-is-I'll-give-him-what-for to her tone.

Eliza bit her lip. Being with Lachlan never felt like work at all. "No, Grammy. I'm loving getting ready for the opening of the restaurant and I'm actually learning to cook a little, as well."

This news was met by silence on the other end of the line. Eliza could not recall another moment in her life where Grammy had been stunned silent.

"I think my hearing's failing me, sweetheart," she said after a few long moments. "I thought you just said you were learning to cook?"

"I am," Eliza replied, pride zapping through her. "Not anything too complicated, but Lachlan has taught me to make pancakes, mac'n'cheese and how to grill a steak."

"My Lord, wonders never cease. This new boss of yours must be some kind of miracle worker."

Eliza thought of the way he listened when she told him her woes, of the way his fingers played her body like she was a violin and him a member of the symphony orchestra. "I think he might be," she said.

"Have you told your father?" Grammy asked.

"What? About me learning to cook?"

Before her grandmother could reply, the intercom buzzed. "Sorry," Eliza said, "but my ride's here. I'm gonna have to go."

"That's okay. Jonathon and I are heading out for an

early dinner and then a Broadway show. You have a lovely lunch."

"I will. You, too, Grammy, but don't do anything I wouldn't do," she teased.

The older woman chuckled. "That, my dear, would make for a very boring date." And then she disconnected.

"You ready?" Sophie's voice sounded through the front door—or was it Annabel's? Eliza couldn't tell the difference unless she saw them in the flesh. And even then it wasn't easy.

"Yes," she shouted so her voice would carry out of her bedroom and down the hallway as she grabbed her purse and the box of chocolates she'd bought for Nora.

A few moments later, she opened the door to find both Sophie *and* Annabel standing there.

"Hi," she said chirpily.

"Wow, you look lovely," the twins said in unison by way of a greeting.

They were both in jeans and casual T-shirts, whereas Eliza had gone for a floral jumpsuit and strappy, heeled sandals. She'd also spent a ridiculously long time blow-drying and straightening her hair.

"Thanks," she said, feeling her cheeks flush. She suddenly felt vastly overdressed and hoped the twins couldn't guess that she'd gone to all this effort for their brother. Although this was a family lunch at his mom's and there wouldn't be any opportunity for shenanigans, her body buzzed in anticipation of seeing him again and she couldn't help wanting to look good for him. She wanted him to be *thinking* about having sex with her, even if he wasn't able to. Her cheeks heated even more at the thought and she wondered what kind of person she'd become. That familiar tug of guilt pulled at her heart.

"And thanks so much for the ride," she added, silently telling her guilt to take a hike—this had *nothing* to do with Jack.

"It's not a problem." Sophie waved a hand in front of her face. "I still can't believe someone stole your bike! I thought this was a safe neighborhood."

Eliza pulled her door shut behind her, then tested the handle to make sure it had locked. "It was my own fault for being careless."

"Have you reported it to the police?" Annabel asked and for a moment, Eliza thought she was talking about the sex.

"What?" A flutter ran through her and her lips tingled traitorously as if Lachlan's had been there only moments ago. Then, once again, her brain caught up. "*Oh*, the bike." She shook her head as they walked together down the corridor to the building's exit. "Not yet. Do you think I should? I figured whoever took it will be long gone by now."

"Maybe, but you should definitely report it," Sophie said, "because if the culprit is caught later for another crime, and they find your bike in his or her possession, then they'll be able to charge them for that, as well."

"I'll think about it."

Seemingly satisfied with this, Lachlan's sisters led her to Sophie's new model orange Mini Cooper and Annabel folded herself into the back seat.

"I don't mind sitting in the back," Eliza offered, but the twins wouldn't hear of it.

"You're our guest today," Sophie said as she settled into the driver's seat.

On the short drive to McKinnel's Distillery, the twins

kept the conversation rolling, talking about a trip Sophie was planning to Scotland the following summer and Eliza did her best to listen—hopefully making the right noises in the right places—when all she could think about was the fact that within minutes she'd be seeing their brother again. The closer they got to the distillery, the more the butterflies in her stomach kicked up.

She was really excited about seeing him but also a little nervous, fearful that despite the arrangement they'd decided on, things would get weird or awkward between them. Today would be a test and she desperately wanted them to pass it.

"I hope you're hungry," Sophie said as she slowed the car to a stop in front of Nora McKinnel's impressive stone-built house.

"Starving," Eliza said, although the truth was there was only one thing she felt very hungry for right now. How the heck was she going to sit through a civilized lunch with Lachlan and his family when all she could think about was sleeping with him again?

"Good, because Mom's cooking is not to be missed," Annabel added.

After that, Eliza got out of the car and held the door as Annabel climbed out behind her. Together the three of them headed for the house but even before they'd gone a few feet, the front door opened and Hallie burst out, waving and screaming, "Hello, hello, hello," as she ran toward them. Eliza assumed she was excited to see her aunts, so she couldn't hide her surprise when Hallie threw her little arms around Eliza's waist.

"I was so happy when Granny Nora said you were coming for lunch. Can you sit next to me?"

She laughed and patted the child on the back as she extracted herself. It was lovely to feel wanted but she also couldn't bring herself to get too close. "Hi, Hallie. Let's see where your grandmother wants to put me."

And then she looked up again to the house and saw Lachlan appear in the doorway. He looked absolutely edible in faded jeans and a tight black T-shirt that highlighted all the muscles she'd become intimately acquainted with the other night. Her mouth went dry.

"Hey there." He lifted a hand to wave and any worries she'd been harboring evaporated as he hit her with a smile that made her pulse tingle. It wasn't the only part of her that tingled and she decided that perhaps sitting next to Hallie would be safer than sitting next to him. The way she felt right now, she wasn't sure she'd be able to keep her hands off him if they got so close.

"Hi." She smiled back at him, desire curling low in her tummy.

"You okay?" Annabel asked, turning back and looking quizzically from a few steps ahead.

Eliza felt Hallie tugging on her hand and realized she'd stopped dead in her tracks and was gawking at Lachlan as if he were the first good-looking man she'd ever laid eyes on.

"Oh, yes, sorry…" She tore her eyes from his, summoned a smile for his sister and squeezed the little hand in hers. "Coming."

As she took the few steps onto the porch, Lachlan stepped out of the way and held the door open, gesturing for the four of them to go through.

"It's good to see you again, Eliza," he said as his sisters followed the din into the kitchen. "I hope you had a good Saturday and got to relax a little after Friday night."

Heat flared within her at his words. As far as anyone who could hear their conversation would assume, Lachlan was referring to their busy rehearsal at the restaurant, but that's not what his words conjured in her head.

"Yes," she replied. "I did, thank you. I chilled out on the couch, watching Netflix."

"Sounds blissful," he said.

"And what about you?" she asked.

"I spent most of the day at a dance concert for Hallie." He looked down and grinned at his little girl, who was still clutching tightly onto Eliza's hand. "And then the three of us had a movie night, so yes, it was relaxing enough."

"Ooh, what movie?" She attempted small talk for the sake of Hallie still attached to her hand, when all she wanted to do was press her lips against Lachlan's and take what she needed. *Down, girl.*

"Beauty and the Beast," the little girl replied, seemingly (and thankfully) oblivious to the sparks flying above her head.

"The recent one? Weren't you scared?" Eliza asked. "I've heard it's quite terrifying in places."

Hallie held her chin high. "I'm really brave."

"You most certainly are," Lachlan said. "But why don't you run ahead and see if Granny Nora needs any help? I just need to talk restaurant business with Eliza for a few moments."

Hallie sighed deeply and pouted her outrage but did as she was told nonetheless, leaving Eliza and Lachlan as alone as they could be in a house full of people.

He stepped a little closer and spoke quietly. "It's *really* good to see you." And although he didn't touch her, the way his gaze skimmed down her body sent a familiar current through her.

"You already said that," she whispered, breathing

in his unique male smell, which sent a potent rush to her head.

"It was worth saying again. Although I'd much prefer it if we were alone," he added with a suggestive wriggle of his eyebrows.

"Me, too."

"What are you up to ton—"

But before he could continue, Nora appeared down the hallway and Lachlan cleared his throat. "I'd like you to come in early tomorrow to help me sort through the uniforms before we hand them out to the staff," he said, as if they'd been talking business all along.

"Not a problem. Of course." Eliza hoped his mom didn't click that the staff had already been wearing their uniforms on Friday night at the rehearsal.

"Lachlan, the poor girl has come to lunch. She's not on your clock now. Leave her alone." Shaking her head at her son, Nora reached out and pulled Eliza into a hug. "Welcome. I'm so glad you made it."

"Thanks," Eliza managed.

"Sophie told me your bike was stolen," Nora said as she released Eliza from her embrace. That's shocking—if I ever find out who took it, I'll skin them alive."

"Someone took your bike?" Lachlan asked, concern creasing his brow.

She nodded. They'd exchanged a couple of brief messages yesterday, but she hadn't mentioned the bike as she didn't want him to feel responsible. "I must have forgotten to lock it up Friday night."

His eyes widened as realization dawned.

"I've just remembered," Nora continued, "I have an old bike in storage if you'd like to borrow it. It's nothing flashy but I think it still does the trick."

"Thank you. If you're sure. That would be wonderful," Eliza replied.

"Of course, I'm sure. I can't remember the last time I used it—I think the twins might still have been in high school." She laughed. "I'll get one of the boys to dig it out for you after lunch."

"Thank you. Oh, and by the way, these are for you." Eliza handed the older woman the box of chocolates.

Nora grinned. "Ooh, these are my favorites, although you didn't need to give me anything. It's a pleasure to have you here. Now, come on through and say hi to everyone."

She turned and started back where she'd come from, gesturing for Eliza to follow behind.

Eliza looked to Lachlan. "After you," he said, and then he reached out his hand and placed it on the small of her back to guide her. It was like he'd flicked a match against the cotton of her jumpsuit, but somehow she managed to put one foot in front of the other and head into the country-style kitchen.

It had felt enormous when Lachlan had brought her to meet his mom a couple of weeks ago, but now, with so many people crowded around the table, it didn't feel so big. There was a buzz of noise as all Lachlan's family chatted amicably.

"Everyone!" Nora exclaimed loudly. The chatter immediately died out as all eyes turned to them. "Eliza's here."

"Hi, Eliza," everyone around the table chorused.

Nora turned back to look at Eliza. "Is there anyone you haven't met yet?"

Before Eliza could answer, a tall, slender woman with long red hair down to her butt lifted a hand and waved.

"Hey there. I'm Claire, Blair's ex-wife—everyone's been telling me so much about you, so it's nice to finally meet."

Claire was sitting next to Blair and Eliza vaguely remembered Lachlan mentioning something about Blair's divorce being complicated. She tried not to show her surprise as she said, "Hi. Lovely to meet you, too."

"Take a seat," Nora said, nudging Eliza toward the table.

"Is there anything I can do to help you?" she asked Nora instead.

The older woman tsk-tsked. "Don't be silly. I didn't invite you here to work—you've been doing enough of that lately. There are plenty of others here to help. Now, make yourself comfortable and I'll get you a drink. What do you fancy? Tea, coffee, orange juice or something stronger?"

"Can I have some water, please?" Eliza asked as she sat down at one of the few empty seats. She needed something to cool her down.

"I hear you're from New York," Claire said from across the table. "I love New York so much. Do you miss it?"

Eliza smiled and made small talk about her hometown for a few moments, but all the while she spoke she was conscious of Lachlan's gaze. Before long, the casserole dishes were delivered to the table and once everyone was served, they all seemed to talk again at once. Eliza found it hard to keep track of any one conversation—she wasn't used to such big family gatherings but Lachlan playing footsie with her under the table didn't help either.

At first, it was just his shoe, gently nudging hers, but then he slipped it off and as his foot trekked slowly up her calf, it was all she could do to stop moaning and squirming in her seat.

"Are either of you off to another one of your Tinder dates tonight?" Mac asked his sisters, a smirk on his face telling them exactly what he thought of the hookup app.

Sophie stuck out her tongue at him. "Don't mock it until you've tried it, bro. You should sign up—might get you out of that permanent funk. You used to be fun, you know."

Trying to ignore Lachlan's wandering foot, Eliza looked between the siblings, enjoying their banter. There was only herself, her dad and her grandma in her family and although Tyler had two siblings, none of them spoke to each other so she'd never experienced anything like the fun and warmth that filled this room. Even when the McKinnels teased each other, it was done in love and Eliza could see why Claire would be so loathe to lose her place here.

"Oh, darlings." Nora frowned at the Tinder chat. "I've heard all about that app. All the men on there are only looking for one thing."

Quinn snorted. "Most men are only looking for one thing." His fiancée, Bailey, elbowed him. "Ouch!"

"Wh-at one thing?" Hamish asked. Everyone pretended not to hear him.

Annabel chuckled. "Mom, I thought you wanted Sophie and me to find Mr. Right and give you more grandbabies."

Nora's expression remained serious as she reached beside her and squeezed Annabel's hand. "I just want you to be happy again, sweetheart."

Annabel took a few seconds before she smiled and Eliza recognized a sadness there—similar to the one she saw in the mirror everyday. During their late-night sessions in the restaurant, Lachlan had shared stories about his siblings and Annabel's was the saddest of all.

Her high-school sweetheart was in the military and a few years ago went missing in action, presumed dead after an explosion.

"I know, Mommy," Annabel said, "and this is the first step. I've actually met some really nice guys. Not everyone on Tinder is only looking for hookups. In fact, I'm seeing a really nice man—he lives in Bend—and I think it could get serious."

Nora's eyes sparkled and she clapped her hands together. "Oh, that's simply marvelous."

"Chill, Mom," Mac said, "she said it *could* get serious. There aren't any wedding bells yet."

Everyone laughed, then Callum said, "Probably a good thing. I think two weddings and three babies in a year are enough, even for our family."

Nora then looked to Eliza. "What about you, dear? Are you single?"

Lachlan's wandering foot pressed into the junction at Eliza's thigh. They exchanged a look of two people who shared an illicit secret and it was all she could do not to squeak. Instead, she squeezed her knees together and managed to say, "Yes. I am."

"You should join Tinder, too," Sophie suggested and then laughed. "I've been exchanging horror stories with Annabel but it sounds like she might not need the app much longer, so I'll need another partner in crime."

Eliza saw Annabel blush and bite her lower lip as if to stifle a smile. Yep, she looked like a girl who was falling in love, something that Eliza herself didn't think she'd ever have the capacity to do again. Love could be amazing but then there was the flip side. "I'm not really looking for a relationship right now," she said.

With her words, Lachlan pushed back his seat and

the chair legs scraped loudly against the tiled floor. Everyone looked at him.

"Eliza, come with me. I'll get that bike for you now."

"There's no rush to do that now, sweetheart," Nora said to Lachlan. "Plenty of time to—" She stopped midsentence as she and Annabel exchanged a pointed look. "*Oh*. Take your time, dears."

"Can I come, Da-ad?" Hamish asked, starting to get up from his seat.

"Dad won't be long," Annabel said to her nephew. "And I need you and Hallie to help me clear the table."

Eliza felt heat rushing from her core, painting her neck and body red. What was Lachlan playing at? It was obvious Annabel at least suspected he was summoning her to scratch an itch and she could already imagine the gossip that might ignite once they left. Yet, despite this and the fact they'd agreed to keep their liaison a secret, she couldn't stand up fast enough.

He didn't say one word to her as they hurried out of the house, her following behind like some lovesick puppy dog at his heels, but the moment they were out of sight, he took hold of her hand. With the jolt that shot through her at the connection, the last of her scruples or embarrassment evaporated. Her panties were already wet with desire and the knowledge that he was equally desperate for her only compounded that desire.

"This way," he said as he led her round the back to the garage and let them in through a side door. He shut it behind them and then slid the lock across to hinder interruption. The sound of the lock clicking into place sent a shiver of lust down her spine and when Lachlan turned back around to look at her, she saw the heat she felt reflected in his eyes.

"You were very naughty back there," she whispered, feeling very naughty herself.

He shrugged one shoulder lazily but didn't sound very apologetic when he said, "It's your fault. You drive me to distraction."

And then the conversation ceased as he dragged her toward him. As their lips met, Eliza's hands went straight for his belt buckle. After their interactions under the table, they were way past foreplay and she wanted him inside her without delay.

"You got a condom?" she panted.

In reply, he slipped a tiny foil packet from his pocket and held it up in front of her face. "I stocked up."

Those three words were perhaps the sexiest ones anyone had ever spoken.

"Good," she said as she conquered the buckle and pushed his jeans and underwear down his legs. She took the condom from him, ripped it open and he groaned as she slid it down his deliciously hard length.

But when Lachlan tried to rid her of her clothing, he struggled.

"What in the world is this thing?" he asked as he pulled his head back to gaze at her outfit.

Eliza silently cursed her choice of attire, but when she'd chosen it that morning, the last thing she'd thought was that she'd end up in a garage having sex. This was so out of character for her, but also so invigorating. The illicitness of their situation only spurred her on more.

She undid the jumpsuit and let it—along with her panties—slither to the floor, feeling sexier and more alive than she had in a long while as she stepped out of it and stood before him in nothing but heels and her bra.

Lachlan sucked in a breath as his gaze raked down her body. His eyes widened at exactly the moment she realized her mistake. When they'd slept together at her house, she'd made sure not to turn on the lights and figured that somehow when they slept together again, she'd manage a similar trick.

But it was light in here and, in the heat of the moment, she'd felt as if she were a different person and had completely forgotten about her scar.

"What's this?" he asked, his voice soft as he reached out and touched it.

Although her stomach fluttered as his finger ran a line along her skin, her body went ice-cold. How could she have been so careless?

"Um." She swallowed. Her mouth parched, she was all of a sudden aware of her nakedness. A voice in her head told her to ignore his question, to simply kiss him till he forgot it, but she couldn't.

She scrambled for her jumpsuit—this was no conversation to have sans clothes—and tried to collect her thoughts as she hurried to put it on again. She could lie. What other reasons were there for such a scar across her abdomen? But although there must be a zillion, her brain came up with not one.

"Have you got a child?" he asked, his voice a little rough but his gaze trained on hers so she couldn't look anywhere else.

She shook her head and felt tears spring to her eyeballs. "Not anymore."

Chapter Eleven

Not anymore. What on earth did that mean? For a moment, Lachlan wondered if, like Linda, Eliza had abandoned a kid to her ex, but he found himself unable to believe such a thing of her. His heart rate slowed as a number of other possible scenarios ran through his head.

"What happened?"

"I lost him," she whispered as a tear snaked down her cheek.

Lost? "You had a stillbirth?" he prodded gently.

Again she shook her head and another tear followed the first. "His name was Jack. He was fourteen months old and he was beautiful."

Every bone in Lachlan's body turned to ice. Fourteen months wasn't a stillbirth. That would have been bad enough, but this…this was so much worse than he'd imagined. He had no words, but in his head, he swore.

"One day I took Jack to visit a friend and her new baby. I was cuddling the newborn, talking to my friend…" She sniffed again, but it didn't stop the flood of tears down her cheeks.

He grabbed his jeans off the floor and dug in his pocket for the handkerchief his mom had made him carry from an early age. He held it out to her and when she took it, their fingers touched, but the current that usually flowed beneath them was different now.

"Thanks." As she wiped her eyes, Lachlan quickly pulled on his jeans, not wanting his nakedness to make her uncomfortable.

"Jack was playing quietly with some toy cars on the floor behind us and we didn't hear him wander off. As it was my friend's first child, their house wasn't fitted with all the usual child-safety devices yet, and somehow Jack let himself out the back door and into their yard." She took a long breath. "They had a fishpond."

Shit. He could see where this was heading and almost could not bear to listen. He wanted to put his hands over his ears but if *he* couldn't bear listening, how much worse must it be for her to be relating this nightmare to him? Instinctively, he reached out again and took her into his arms.

As he pulled her close, her tears already soaking into his shirt, he whispered, "It's okay. You don't have to tell me any more."

But she did.

She pulled her head back and looked up at him, her dark eyes wide with anguish. "I should have been watching him. If I'd been paying attention, I would have seen him leave the room and I would have followed him outside. He loved water… He was just being curious." Again, her face crumpled. "I don't know how long he was there, his little face under the ripples. Did he know what was happening? Did he wonder where I was? Why I wasn't helping him?"

Although she kept talking, her words blended together in her distress, becoming almost impossible to decipher. But he knew the gist. She blamed herself for the death of her child and he honestly couldn't comprehend how anyone could ever get over that.

He felt compelled to say, "It was a terrible accident. It's not your fault. You can't think like that."

But she countered quickly, "Tyler thinks it was. He can never forgive me, but what he doesn't see is that I understand that, because I can never forgive myself either. I don't blame him for finding solace in someone else."

Again, Lachlan wanted to tell her that Tyler was a fool, but deep down he understood where they were both coming from. He already didn't like the man, but he understood that grief caused people to do terrible things, to make unwarranted statements. There were no winners in this game of blame and he didn't think many marriages could recover from something like this.

But what would be the point in saying that? His words couldn't change the past.

Feeling utterly helpless, he held her tighter, wishing he could do something to take away her pain. Yet he knew that was impossible.

How could you ever get over the death of a child?

His mind went to Hamish and Hallie, and his chest tightened at the thought of anything ever happening to either of them. Due to Hamish's condition, he was more susceptible than most kids to illness. There'd been times when he'd been so sick Lachlan had feared the worst might come, but his son was a fighter and had always bounced back. As Hamish's cerebral palsy was mild, the doctors believed he had a good chance of living a reasonably long life.

But Lachlan had to wonder how he'd cope if the prognosis was different, if Hamish were taken from them. He wasn't honestly sure he'd be able to.

Perhaps having Hallie to live for would help, but Eliza didn't have that.

And the person who should have stood by her through all of it had turned against her. Somehow, despite everything, she'd managed to get out of bed day after day, to come into work, to paste a smile on her face when smiling was probably the last thing she felt like doing. Somehow, despite experiencing two of life's most traumatic things—the death of a child and the breakup of a marriage—she'd attempted to continue living. And that only made him admire and respect her more.

"I'm sorry." She suddenly pulled back. "You don't need me falling apart on you like this. I just…"

"Don't apologize," he said, perhaps more forcefully than needed, but the last thing he wanted was for Eliza to feel like opening up to him had been a burden. They may have known each other less than a month, but he already cared deeply for her. All those sleepless nights suddenly made a lot of sense and he wished she'd told him earlier, so he could have supported her. "Let me be here for you. If you ever want to talk about Jack, I'm happy to listen. I can't even imagine what such loss would feel like, but…"

Anger flashed across her face. She fisted the handkerchief into a tight ball in her hand. "I don't *want* to talk about it! Talking doesn't help, it only makes the ache worse. That's why I moved here—to start afresh—and the only hope I have of achieving that is if people don't see me as the woman with the dead baby. That's why I didn't tell you before, because I didn't want you to look at me the way you are now."

He opened his mouth to object, to tell her that he would never think of her in such terms, but then he felt the pity etched in his face and he knew she was right.

Eliza cast her gaze around the garage and thrust her finger at the old bicycle leaning against the wall off to one side. "Is that the bike your mother said I could have?"

"Yes."

"Tell her I'm sorry but I'm not feeling well and I had to go home," she said as she crossed the garage to retrieve it.

"Eliza, please. Don't go. I'm sorry, I…" he called after her, but she waved a hand at him.

As she unlocked the door, she turned back and Lachlan's heart squeezed with hope. "Can you promise me one thing?" she asked.

He nodded. "Of course. Anything." After the conversation they'd just had, she could tell him to run a marathon on hot coals and he'd give it his best darn shot.

"Can you not mention this conversation or…my… Jack to anyone? It's not that I want to forget him," she said, as if he would ever think anything of the sort, "but it's easier this way."

He took some comfort from her request as it made it sound as if she didn't plan on quitting and leaving Jewell Rock or anything like that. Perhaps he hadn't just lost the best employee he had. But no matter how much he loved and wanted the restaurant to succeed, it wasn't the restaurant worrying him now.

"I won't," he promised.

"Thank you," she said, before opening the door and disappearing with the bike.

Lachlan wanted to go after her, to make sure she was okay, but he didn't want to risk making things even worse than they already were. And if he didn't head back to the house soon, they'd probably send out a search party. The last thing he felt like doing was going inside and playing happy families.

Leaning back against a workbench, he dropped his head into his hands and sighed. Talk about complicated. When Eliza had leaped at the chance to enjoy some no-strings-attached sex, he should have wondered what the catch was.

After a few moments, he straightened his clothes and forced himself to go back to the house. His mom was just serving her famous marionberry pie for dessert when he returned, and all his family looked past him quizzically.

"What have you done with Eliza?" Blair asked, amusement in his voice.

"She wasn't feeling well," Lachlan said, crossing over to his seat and ruffling Hamish's hair as he sat back down beside him. He had a sudden urge to hug both his kids. "She had a really bad migraine."

When Sophie raised her eyebrows, he elaborated, not meeting his sister's or anyone else's eye. "It came on really quick and she just needed to get home and lie down."

Lachlan knew he'd never been a good liar and this falsehood was probably written all over his face, but he was hardly going to tell his family the truth—whether there were kids present or not.

"But she left her stuff behind." Hallie stooped down

and picked up Eliza's purse from where it had been sitting on the floor by her feet.

Lachlan cursed silently. He guessed her cell and house key were in the bag and the fact she hadn't even thought about this proved just how upset she was. Although he didn't think she wanted him to go after her, part of him was glad for an excuse to do so. He pushed to a stand. "I'll take them to her," he said, reaching across the table to take the purse from Hallie.

Before anyone could say anything else, he was out of there. He grabbed his keys from the hallway table as he rushed out of the house and headed for his truck. Eliza hadn't made it far and he saw her on the road just past the entrance to the distillery. He slowed the vehicle and jumped out. "Eliza!"

She looked up and her eyes widened as she held up her hand to halt him. "Please, Lachlan, I can't. I just… don't want to. Not now."

Her cheeks were red and blotchy, her eyes bloodshot and her mascara was running down her cheeks, mingling with her tears. To him, she still looked gorgeous and it took all his willpower not to rush at her and hold her close. He longed to help, to offer her comfort.

Instead he took a tentative step toward her and held out her purse as if he were holding out a treat to a wild animal. "It's okay. We don't need to talk, but you left these behind."

Horror flashed across her face. "Oh, Lord, what must your family think of me?"

"Don't worry about them. I told them you had a migraine and I'm a pretty convincing liar."

"Thank you. I didn't even realize."

He nodded. "You're welcome." And then as much as

it pained him to do so, he turned and went back to the truck because that's what she wanted him to do.

His cell started ringing in his pocket as he parked back in front of his house. Could it be her? Hope lit in his heart as he yanked the phone out. If she needed him, he would turn right back around. But the hope was short-lived when he glanced down at the screen and saw Linda's name staring back at him.

Damn. He wanted to speak to his ex-wife even less than he wanted to go inside, but he knew that if he didn't answer, she'd keep calling until he did. Better to get it over with. With a resentful sigh, he slid his finger across the screen to answer and lifted the phone to his ear. "Linda."

"And a good afternoon to you, too, Lachlan."

"What can I do for you?" he asked, ignoring her obvious dig. He was in no mood to deal with her antics.

"I've got some good news!"

"Your aunt has had a miraculous recovery?" Although he hoped that was the case for the sake of this woman he'd never met, his stomach clenched at the thought that he would have to give Hallie back. It might have been crazy and exhausting trying to juggle her activities with Hamish's and the restaurant preparation, but they'd managed and he'd loved having both his kids with him, where he'd always wanted them to be.

"What?" She sounded as if she didn't know what he was talking about. "*Oh*, um…yes actually, she seems to be doing much better, but the really good news is I've scored an acting role in a new sitcom. I'm going to be famous!"

"Excuse me?" He shook his head, wondering if he'd heard right. Linda had always proclaimed she'd one day make it big as an actress but, as far as he knew, she'd never taken any steps toward this so-called dream.

She repeated herself. "Isn't it exciting?" When he didn't say anything, she added, "Oh, Lachlan, can't you just be happy for me for once?"

"I knew there was never an aunt!"

Her irritating giggle sounded through the phone line. "Actually there was. The role I'm playing is a woman looking after her dying aunt. Apparently I nailed the audition and they might actually make this woman's character bigger than it was originally going to be."

His body filled with loathing. He didn't give a damn about any of that. "What about our daughter? Where does she fit in this new life of yours?"

"Well, that's why I'm calling. To let you know I'm going to be busy for a while focusing on work, but once I've set myself up in an apartment, I guess she can come live with me in LA."

"You *guess*?" Lachlan's grip tightened on the phone. This day was going from bad to worse. He thought of Eliza, of the tragic conversation they'd just had and how she would do anything to get her child back. And here was his ex, so blasé about their children. "What about the fact her family and friends are here?"

"She'll make new friends and there are such things as airplanes, you know."

"Over my dead body will she be moving to LA," he growled. "If you go through with this, that's it. I'll file for full custody again and this time, I'll make sure I get it."

"Don't take that tone with me, Lachlan. I'm not your wife now. But," she added, "perhaps you have a point. I don't really think I'm cut out for motherhood. I need some time to find who I really am, so maybe it would be better for Hallie if she lives with you permanently and comes to visit me for holidays."

Not cut out for motherhood? His ex-wife was damn lucky they were having this conversation over the phone because he'd never been more angry in his life. Linda didn't give two hoots about what was best for Hallie, she was only thinking of herself. His heart ached for his daughter, who deserved more than a mother so willing to pass her on to someone else to look after. He wanted his daughter's mom to fight for her, to want her.

Hallie, *and* Hamish, warranted so much more than a mother who was more invested in her own life than she was in her children's. He couldn't remember what he'd ever seen in Linda. The less she had to do with his kids the better. Heaven forbid Hallie would grow up to be anything like her narcissistic mother.

"Good. It's settled, then," he said. "I'll have my lawyer draw up the papers and send them to you." Then before she could say another word, he disconnected the call.

He stared at the phone in his hand, feeling totally conflicted. A big part of him wanted to celebrate the fact that he'd soon have full custody of both his kids—although he wouldn't put it past Linda to make things difficult just for the sake of it—but there was another part at a loss.

What would he say to Hallie? She'd seemed nonplussed about Linda going off for a while, but how could he tell her that her mother wasn't coming back? Abandoning Hallie to look after a sick relative was one thing, but choosing to star in some stupid sitcom over her daughter was quite another.

And celebrating anything after the conversation he'd just had with Eliza didn't sit right.

Lachlan felt like he'd been put through the emotional wringer—in less than an hour, he'd gone from highly aroused to the depths of sadness, then raging anger and now desolation again. But as much as he cared for Eliza, his focus needed to be on Hallie and making sure she was protected in all this. He'd need to think carefully about what to tell her and how to tread from here on in.

With that thought, he let out a heavy sigh, shoved his cell back into his pocket and went inside to face the music.

Chapter Twelve

Eliza couldn't get back to her apartment fast enough. Her legs and lungs burned with the exertion and her eyes stung almost as bad. Not wanting to have another bike stolen, she took the bike into the building and then hurried into her apartment where she went straight into the bedroom and pulled out the photo of Jack. She flopped onto the bed, looked down at his perfect little face and then clutched it desperately to her chest.

Her whole body ached at the knowledge this was as close as she would ever get to holding him again.

After all the tears she'd sobbed, she didn't think there would be any left, but she knew that tears didn't have a limit. Only right now, she wasn't sure whether she was crying about her loss or the fact she'd done what she'd promised not to do and told Lachlan about her son.

Probably a combination of both.

Jewell Rock had felt like a safe haven when no one

knew her dark secret—even her apartment had begun to feel like a home—but now as she looked around, she felt like a stranger in her own place again and was terrified she'd blown everything.

It was one thing, Lachlan knowing about Tyler's betrayal. Lots of people could relate to a cheating ex; Lachlan himself even had experience in that department. But it was quite something else when they knew you'd lost a child.

She would never forget Jack—that would be impossible—but in New York, she'd almost come to wish that other people would. There, where everyone knew what had happened, her grief had become like a prison. It was the elephant in every conversation, the first thing people thought of when they thought of her. Her loss had consumed her, the sadness becoming who she was, suffocating.

In Jewell Rock she'd started to breathe again. She'd started to notice the beauty in her surroundings when, for eighteen months, she hadn't been able to see anything but sorrow. In Jewell Rock, she got to be someone else, even if only for a few hours a day, and allowing herself to be that other person was the only way she could cope.

But the one person whom she spent the most time with now knew about Jack.

She swallowed as her hand subconsciously went to her pocket, closing around the handkerchief Lachlan had given her when she'd become teary, and recalled the horror on his face when she'd told him. Horror that quickly turned to sympathy.

She drew the small square of cotton from her pocket and stared down at it. Crisp and white when he'd given it to her, it was now streaked with black lines from her mascara. She shuddered to think about what her face looked like now. Would Lachlan ever find her attractive again after seeing her snot-cry like that?

He'd been so kind, so gentle in his endeavors to comfort her, but it wasn't comfort she wanted from his hands. She wanted the release, distraction and oblivion that came when his lips touched hers.

Eliza drew the handkerchief up to her nose, hoping to smell him on it, but all she could smell was her own heartache and anger. Shame and mortification washed over her when she thought of how she'd treated him. Rejecting his offer to talk, pushing him away, running as fast as she could and leaving him to explain her sudden departure to his family. Hopefully they'd bought his excuse that she had a migraine, but she'd put him in a terrible position and the thought of facing him tomorrow made her nauseous.

But she also couldn't keep running from her problems forever.

Besides, how could she run out on Lachlan so close to the opening of the restaurant?

As scary as the prospect was, she needed to face him again and to apologize for today's behavior. It was probably a pipe dream but she hoped they could at least try to go back to the easy way things were between them. She didn't want to give up sleeping with him but even more important, she didn't want to lose her new job. Work had given her purpose again, a reason to get out of bed every morning.

With a deep sigh, she put Jack's photo back on the bedside table and twisted the handkerchief between her fingers. She should wash it and give it back to him.

She also recognized that if she wanted to recover from today, she needed to reach out. To apologize for her meltdown this afternoon and for rushing out like that. Her Grammy always said you shouldn't let the sun go down on an argument and although this wasn't an argument as such, she wouldn't be able to attempt sleep if she didn't at least try to make amends.

With that thought, she reached for her purse, which she'd dumped on the bed, and retrieved her cell. Then, her fingers shaking a little, she typed out a quick message to Lachlan.

I'm sorry I freaked out today. Thanks for covering for me. I'll pop in to see your mother tomorrow and say thank you. xx

Just before she pressed Send, she deleted the two kisses, horrified that she'd almost sent them to her boss. Granted, they'd become a little more than chef and hostess but kisses in messages were definitely *not* part of their arrangement. And she didn't want to muddy the waters.

Perhaps she should send Nora some flowers, she thought, as she waited for a reply. She felt as if she should do something to make up for her behavior today, but maybe flowers were a little over-the-top. They might make more of a big deal about this than she wanted it to be. *And* she'd already given Nora chocolates. Feeling at a loss, she glanced again at the framed photo of Jack.

What do you think I should do, little man?

And then the most ridiculous idea entered her head—so ridiculous she almost believed it had come from her little boy. Children believed anything was possible.

I should make Nora cookies!

She let out a little laugh of disbelief. *Her*, cook for someone with the expertise of Nora McKinnel? A few cooking lessons did not make her an expert and the idea that she could cook anything on her own was farcical. All the same, the idea refused to be silenced and Eliza found herself pushing off the bed and heading into the kitchen, wondering what would be the worst that could happen. She'd be very careful, but if she *did* set the kitchen on fire…well, Annabel would probably be home soon and had the skills to save them all.

And if the cookies were a disaster, no one would ever have to know that she'd attempted them, but how many people did she know who found comfort in baking? Perhaps she could find some, too.

Decision made, she flung open her food cupboard and immediately came across a problem. Like Mother Hubbard, her cupboard was bare, but this only deterred her for a few moments.

You're not going to give up that easily, are you?

There was a supermarket down the road and, thanks to Nora, she had a new bike to take her there. The prospect of heading out now—when her head hurt and her whole body ached from sobbing—had her heart filling once again with despair, but a little voice told her she needed to be brave. She needed to step out of her comfort zone and try new things, or she would be the opposite of brave and flounder.

The next morning Eliza arrived at the restaurant before anyone else and, carrying her purse under one arm and a plastic container in the other, let herself inside with the key Lachlan had entrusted her with. Although they were still only training staff and preparing for their grand opening, she felt as if she'd been here a lot longer than a few weeks. She'd spent as much—if not more—time in this beautifully designed space than she had in her apartment and many of the happy memories she was starting to collect had taken place here.

She only hoped they would continue.

With that thought, she went around, pulling back blinds and turning on lights, rousing the coffee machine to life and trying to ignore the nerves that fluttered in her stomach at the knowledge Lachlan would be here any moment.

In the middle of her baking efforts yesterday afternoon, he'd sent her a short response to her message: It's all good. See you tomorrow.

But until they were face-to-face and acting normal again, she wouldn't be able to completely relax.

Trying to distract herself, she peeled back the lid on the container of cookies and took a sniff before popping them in a safe spot behind the bar. Even though she'd had breakfast not long ago, her mouth watered at the sugary aroma that teased her nostrils. Triple chocolate chip cookies. If her kitchen hadn't looked like a disaster zone after her efforts, she might not be able to believe that she'd actually succeeded in making them. Without any assistance.

She'd followed the recipe she found on the internet to a T and had set up a chair in front of the oven and watched as the cookies had been baking, terrified she'd leave them too long and burn the lot.

The sound of the front door opening jolted her thoughts and she looked up to see Lachlan coming in.

"Coffee. I need it now." He grunted as he stalked toward her and came around the bar to stand alongside her.

She blinked, unsure what to make of his brusque tone, and then registered how terrible he looked. Well, as terrible as it was possible for one of the best-looking guys she'd ever laid eyes on to look. His hair was way more disheveled than usual, dark circles hung beneath his eyes and there was a shadow along his jaw as if he hadn't had the time or inclination to shave that morning. Usually she didn't mind a little sexy stubble on a man but his whole demeanor erased such an effect.

His ashen appearance couldn't possibly be because of what had happened between them yesterday. Could it?

"I'll make you some," she said and immediately set to work to do exactly that. He was much better at making coffee than she was but in the state he was in, she guessed he wouldn't be fussy.

"Thanks." He lifted a hand to his mouth to try to cover over a yawn. Then he said, "Are you okay? After yesterday?"

She pursed her lips and nodded, still not wanting to talk about Jack but comforted by the fact he didn't seem to be angry at her.

He smiled sadly, then leaned back against the bar. Almost immediately, he frowned and stepped forward. Eliza realized the container of cookies on the shelf beneath the bar hadn't quite been pushed in far enough and he'd felt it.

"What are these?" he asked as he peered beneath the counter and picked up the box.

Her heart did a ridiculous flip as she watched him peel back the lid. It felt as if he were doing so in slow motion. *Oh, Lord.* What had she been thinking, bringing them in here? They might have tasted okay to her but maybe that had been wishful thinking. Her fingers trembled around the metal jug as she said, "I had a bizarre urge to bake yesterday afternoon."

"*You* cooked these?"

She nodded. And then before she could snatch them

away from him, he plucked one out and took a bite. Every part of her froze as she waited for his verdict. But instead of saying anything, he took another bite and then another, devouring the cookie entirely.

"Man, these are excellent," he said finally, grabbing another. "And I really needed that sugar boost."

"You really like them?" she asked, entirely distracted from her task of making coffee.

"I do," he said, his gorgeous lips twisting up at the edges. "I knew you could cook if only you believed in yourself. But if these are for anything special, then you'd better take them off me before I ingest the lot of them."

She shook her head. "They're all yours." It seemed silly now to say she'd made them for his mom to apologize for her weird behavior yesterday—she didn't want to bring all that up again—but she was glad he appeared to be enjoying them. She doubted he'd eat them all, but if he did, she'd think of something else to give his mother.

"In that case." He took another. "I'm comfort eating."

She almost laughed, having never heard the phrase "comfort eating" come from a man before, but he didn't appear to be in a laughing mood.

"Why?" she asked instead. "What's the problem?" Again, her heart hitched a little as she silently prayed it wasn't her. He'd been nice about the cookies but after yesterday, did her presence here now make him uncomfortable? She didn't want to leave but perhaps he'd prefer her to.

"Kid trouble." He let out a deep sigh. "Between Hallie and Hamish, I think I got maybe two hours of sleep max."

"Oh, no. Are they sick?" Both of them had seemed

happy and in good health yesterday—well, as in good health as Hamish ever was with his condition—but she remembered clearly how a child could go from rosy cheeked to feverish in a matter of hours.

Lachlan deliberated a moment as if contemplating how much to share, but when she handed him his coffee, he wrapped his fingers around it and said, "Thanks. Hallie was upset because I gave her some bad news last night. Linda called and told me she's not coming back and that she thinks it would be better if Hallie lives full-time with me now."

"Linda's staying with the sick aunt indefinitely?"

"There was no sick aunt," he said and then went on to inform her that Linda's real purpose for heading to LA was to audition for acting roles.

Eliza felt her eyes boggle as he told her the whole story. She could not imagine a woman so easily deserting her children, but then again, Linda had done it once before with Hamish. Anger burned within her at the thought.

"Hallie had such a fabulous day yesterday, and I thought it was better to tell her the truth and get it over with. I tried to make it sound like her mother loved and wanted her to move to LA but believed that Hallie would be happier staying here with me and Hamish, but…" He sighed and ran a hand through his hair, obviously distressed. "She's a smart kid and she saw right through my attempt to soften the blow. For all she acts tough, she was heartbroken. She bawled her little eyes out into my chest until she finally fell asleep, still shuddering."

"Oh, the poor sweet girl." Eliza tried to swallow the lump in her throat. The last thing Lachlan needed was another crying female on his hands, but her heart broke for Hallie.

He nodded and took a sip of his coffee. "Then I'd just climbed into bed myself when Hamish woke up with really bad muscle spasms."

Eliza thought of the little boy who had physical disabilities but always seemed so chirpy and optimistic. She was relieved to hear that she was not responsible for Lachlan's lack of sleep but deeply saddened by his explanation. "Does he get them a lot?"

"We're really lucky in that he doesn't have as many debilitating symptoms as some CP kids do, but he goes through patches where the pain is pretty bad and sleep is always the first thing to be affected."

"What can you do for him?"

"I do a little bit of massage, offer him pain relief, sit with him and make stupid dad jokes to try to distract him…" His voice trailed off as if she wasn't the only one trying not to cry.

"It must be heart wrenching watching him go through that."

"It kills me," Lachlan said simply. No wonder he looked like he'd been hit by a bus.

She didn't know what to say. What could she say? He spoke again before she had to.

"And it makes me question all of this." He made a sweeping gesture with his arm, indicating the restaurant.

She frowned. "What do you mean?"

He laughed, but it wasn't an amused kind of chuckle. "How the hell do I think I can cope opening a restaurant, *running* a restaurant and being the father I need to be at the same time? I must have been delusional!"

"No. You're not." Without thinking, she reached out

to touch his arm. His skin was warm beneath her fingers and it was on the tip of her tongue to offer to help with the kids, but she reminded herself he had family for that. "And you are not on your own doing any of those things. Don't worry about the restaurant—we've got it covered, it's going to be awesome—and Hallie and Hamish are going to be so proud of their dad."

He glanced down at her hand on his arm and then looked back up into her gaze. It was wrong to feel such attraction during such a conversation, but she couldn't ignore the way her insides bubbled. And the way his pupils dilated told her he felt it, too.

Her tongue darted out to try to moisten her suddenly parched lips, but it wasn't her own mouth she craved. Almost of its own accord, her hand traveled up his arm, across his broad shoulder to rest at the back of his neck.

She might not be able to fix his kid and ex-wife problems, but she could attempt to take his mind off them for a few moments, to give him some of the relief his touch had given her. And with this goal in mind, she stepped up close, pulled his head toward her and stretched up to kiss him.

Within seconds, Lachlan's hands landed on her back, sliding upward and into her hair as he deepened their kiss. Her body melted as her breasts pressed against his hard chest and his knee slid between her legs. Her heart rate went berserk and all thoughts of propriety left her head as she reached between them for her prize.

Lachlan groaned as her hand slid into his trousers and closed around his hot, getting-harder-by-the-second penis. Then he tore his mouth from hers and muttered, "Are you sure you want this?"

"Uh-huh." She nodded, knowing he was referring to yesterday. "Do you?"

"Stupid question. Come on, we don't have long." Grabbing her hand, he led her over to the door, which he quickly locked, before all but dragging her into the kitchen and kicking that door closed behind them.

As it shut, they came together like magnets, kissing and touching as if it were an Olympic race and they were going for gold. The knowledge that their staff would be arriving any minute meant they didn't have long for fondling and caressing. But that didn't matter. The moment Eliza had touched his arm, the moment he'd looked hungrily into her eyes, she'd been ready for this.

Her body mourned the loss of his touch as he retrieved a condom from his wallet, undid his belt buckle, freed and sheathed himself in a matter of seconds. Then he lifted her up against one of the counters, pushing her skirt up around her hips as he did so. No time to take off her panties, he pushed that scrap of lace aside as well, and two seconds later, he was inside her.

She cried out in bliss as he thrust hard and she wrapped her legs around his waist, urging him deeper. The pleasure that ripped through her was so intense she had to hold on tight to his shoulders to anchor herself. His orgasm followed quickly on the heels of hers and they held each other, their foreheads pressed together as they waited for their heart rates to return to something like normal.

He was still inside her when they heard knocking on the front door. She snapped her head back and looked into his eyes, horrified that her fellow colleagues might guess what they'd been up to. But when she saw his smile and the color once again in his cheeks, she thought such a discovery was worth it.

"You are amazing," he said, then claimed her lips in

another quick kiss before drawing out of her. "I need to go to the bathroom. Do you think you could unlock the door and let in the troops?"

"Sure." She smiled as he turned away and then she slid off the counter and straightened her skirt and panties. As she walked out of the kitchen, she pulled her hair out of its now-messy ponytail and redid it with her fingers.

"Sorry," she said to the group gathered, faking a frown. "The lock must be playing up. But come on in. Ready for a big day?"

A couple of the female staff looked at her quizzically as if they didn't quite believe her faulty-lock excuse, but she turned away and set off to begin the working day. They still had much to prepare for the grand opening next week.

Chapter Thirteen

"Good morning," Nora said as Lachlan wandered into the kitchen. "Can I pour you some coffee?"

"Yes, please." He summoned a smile for her as he sat at the table and then ran a hand through his still-wet hair. He'd been up at the crack of dawn to have a shower in peace before the kids woke up. "Have you heard anything from Hallie or Hamish yet?"

She shook her head. "Not a murmur, but I've just popped some blueberry muffins in the oven for their breakfast."

"Thanks," he managed, still too tired for too many words but grateful for all his mom's help where his children were concerned. She'd been especially good with Hallie, making sure they did girlie things together to try to distract her from Linda's absence.

"So, one week until the big day!" Nora said brightly as she placed a mug of steaming caffeine in front of him. "Excited much?"

He made some sort of grunt in response and then took a big gulp of coffee. This was his *dream*. Since he'd first decided to become a chef, he'd harbored the secret (and then not-so-secret) fantasy of opening his own restaurant. The fact that he was also helping expand the family business should have made it even more exciting, but with everything else going on in his head right now, he just couldn't drum up the enthusiasm he'd once felt.

Or maybe he was just nervous, anxious that everything would go right on the opening night. Eliza and Sophie had been working hard together to drum up some media attention and the pressure was on to impress those who'd promised to turn up next Friday night.

"Did you hear Annabel's bringing her new beau?" Nora asked, seemingly oblivious to his disenchantment or putting his almost-monosyllabic responses down to him still being half-asleep. She continued without waiting for him to reply, "I can't wait to meet him. Has she told you anything about him? She's been very cagey with me. I'm sure Sophie knows more than she's letting on as well, but you know how vault-like those two are with each other's secrets."

She finally paused and looked at him expectantly. "Well?"

He shrugged. "Well, what?"

"I was asking you about Annabel and her new man."

"Sorry. If anyone has said anything—and I don't think they have—it's gone in one ear and out the other. Between the kids and the restaurant—" *and my sneaky sessions with Eliza*, he added silently "—I don't have room in my head to focus on anything else right now."

"Hmm." Nora frowned and then leaned back against the counter. She stared at him long and hard, making him squirm a little. "I'm very proud of all you've done so far with the restaurant but I am worried that you're overworking yourself what with the restaurant and the kids, and I don't want you to burn out. That wouldn't be good for anyone, especially those gorgeous grandchildren of mine."

"I'm fine, Mom. Things will calm down in a few months when we've been open for a bit. Don't stress."

"It's not my stress I'm worried about. Look," she said, with a tone that said she meant business, "I was thinking, why don't I look after the twins tonight and maybe you and Eliza could go out and get dinner together, have someone else cook for you for a change? And as it's Saturday, there's no reason to rush up in the morning, so you can stay out as late as you like! You both deserve a last hurrah before the restaurant opens."

His mom grinned from ear to ear as if immensely pleased with herself for presenting this offer, but getting a babysitter wasn't the issue. He had plenty of family always ready and willing to help with the kids if asked, but he and Eliza simply didn't have the kind of arrangement where dinner was involved.

In theory, things had been good since that awful afternoon in the garage. The next morning, they'd had mind-blowing sex in the restaurant kitchen and had been at it almost every day since, finding moments before the staff arrived or after they'd left for the day.

But he missed hanging out with her like they used to do when he'd been giving her cooking lessons late at night. Most nights, he ended up with Hallie in bed with him and as much as he adored his daughter, she was like an octopus, her arms and legs flying all over the place while he was trying to dodge them. On the rare occasions he found himself alone, he fantasized about what it would be like to have a woman in bed with him instead.

But not just any woman.

Still with Hallie's nighttime neediness, he couldn't risk sneaking out of the house and having her wake up to find him gone. He didn't begrudge his daughter his time and attention, but he missed talking and laughing with Eliza.

During the day while they worked, moments for conversation were few and far between and there was always another person within earshot. At night, instead of being with Eliza where he longed to be, he lay in bed, thinking about her and flicking through the books on grief he'd borrowed from the local library. He knew he was a fool to get involved with a woman who had shut off her heart to anything more than sex but he couldn't help himself.

"Don't you think asking my employees out for dinner is overstepping the line?" Lachlan said.

His mom blinked, looking genuinely confused. "Well, I…I thought Eliza had become a little more than an employee to you. She came to lunch with us and—"

"*You* invited her to lunch," he interrupted, not wanting to be reminded about that afternoon. Since then, things had changed between them. And he didn't think it was because of him like Eliza had predicted. Although his heart hurt every time he thought about what she'd lost, he'd done his best not to treat Eliza any differently, but she'd retreated again into herself. Only when they were in the throes of passion did he really feel as if he had any chance of getting close to her.

"Yes, but we all saw the way you two were with each other when you were here. It was clear to all of us you were attracted to each other. And then you went out to get the bike together and—"

Again Lachlan interrupted but didn't meet his mom's gaze as he said, "There's nothing between Eliza and I."

"Really?" Nora raised an eyebrow. She'd always had the annoying knack of being able to read him and his siblings like picture books.

And he'd never been able to lie to her face.

He sighed. "Okay, you're right. I do like her. How could I not? And, I admit, there have been a few moments, but…" He paused, considering how much to tell her. "She's not ready for a romantic relationship right now. She and her husband have only recently separated and she's still hurting from his betrayal."

"Ah…" His mom nodded. "So that's it."

Now it was his turn to look confused. "What's what?"

"The first time I saw her, I thought there was something troubling her. She has a lost look in her eyes and I thought maybe she was grieving the death of somebody close."

A chill prickled his skin as once again he considered telling her about Jack. He longed to ask her opinion about whether she thought Eliza could ever recover from losing her son. Although Nora had never lost a child herself, she was a mother and could probably put herself in such a position to give him advice. She'd also lost her husband only recently so she understood grief. The question was on the tip of his tongue, but he swallowed it, not wanting to break Eliza's confidence.

He'd have to make do with the books.

"Don't think so," he said, staring into his coffee so again he didn't have to look her in the eye. "Her mom's dead but she died a long time ago."

"But she's grieving the loss of her husband. Someone doesn't actually have to die for you to go through the stages of grief." She smiled encouragingly at him. "Give her time, honey. And be patient. I've got a good feeling about this one."

He had to laugh, because she said "this one," like Eliza was one in a long line of women he'd been interested in, when the truth was she was the first. He hadn't been a complete monk and had enjoyed a few flings over the years, but no one had ever occupied his headspace the way Eliza did.

She was special. And she was broken.

"Anyway," he said, pushed back his chair indicating this conversation was over and tried to shake her from his thoughts, "I don't have time for a relationship right now. The kids need me."

And as if to prove his point, Hallie wandered into the kitchen at that moment. Her hair was fuzzy from sleep and she had her favorite teddy bear in a headlock. Since his conversation with her about Linda, she'd started carrying the bear everywhere, where previously she only snuggled it at nighttime.

"Hey, glitter-pie," he said, forcing chirpiness into his voice as he went across and scooped her up into his arms. "How's my favorite girl this morning?"

She buried her head into his chest and he heard a muffled, "Hungry."

"That's good because Grandma's made you some delicious blueberry muffins."

"I want cereal," she demanded.

Usually Lachlan would insist she ate something healthy for breakfast, but today he didn't have the energy to object to the sugary cereal she requested and besides, he'd do practically anything to see his little girl smile again. "Okay, just this once I don't think Uncle Blair will mind if we raid his secret cereal stash."

She looked up into his eyes and almost smiled. "Thanks, Daddy."

His heart leaping at these two words, he lowered her onto a chair and set about getting her what she wanted.

His mom again raised her eyebrows from where she stood against the counter. "Don't start," he said, under his breath. "She's allowed to eat sugar occasionally."

"I agree. I wasn't thinking about Hallie's breakfast and I promise this is the last thing I'll say on this, but whether Eliza will go out to dinner with you or not, maybe you should call some friends and take a night off. Lord knows I've had to tell Callum this before, but all work and no play…"

"D-a-ad!" Hamish's voice carried down the corridor from his bedroom, saving Lachlan from hearing the rest of his mom's lecture. He looked at the door.

"I'll get Hallie's cereal," Nora said, her tone resigned. "You go get our boy."

"D-a-ad!" Hamish called again just as Lachlan got to his bedroom door. Once again, he summoned a smile for the benefit of his son and silently told himself to stop being so pathetic.

"Hey, champ. How are you feeling this morning?"

Hamish screwed up his face and stretched his arms over my head. "A little sore, but it's not too bad. Can I smell Grandma's blueberry muffins?"

"You sure can. Let's get you out of bed so you can have some." He reached for Hamish's crutches. "Do you need to go to the bathroom before breakfast?"

"Not yet," Hamish said. "My tummy is more loud than my bladder right now."

Lachlan laughed as he helped his son to stand.

Hamish never failed to help him put things in perspective. If anyone had any reason to grumble about the lot they were given in life, it was his son, but Hamish rarely complained or dwelled on his disabilities.

"Are you going to work today?" Hamish asked as they slowly made their way toward the kitchen.

"No," Lachlan said, making the decision at that moment. "I'm going to spend every minute with you and Hallie."

After weeks and weeks of experimentation, he was as happy with the menu as he was ever going to be—even his kitchen staff could cook it almost as well as he could—so there wasn't any need to go into work today.

"Really?"

"Really," Lachlan said, feeling guilty that Hamish sounded surprised by this. He thought he'd been doing a good job of spending time with his kids and working, but perhaps not. "What say we take a picnic to the river and maybe even go for a swim?"

"Yippee." Hamish punched the air in excitement. "Can we take our bikes?"

"Hallie! Slow down," Lachlan called as the three of them peddled along the path by the Deschutes River. It was a beautiful day and the riverbanks were busy with locals riding bikes and walking dogs and tourists taking photo after photo of the gorgeous scenery, which Lachlan had to admit he took for granted, having grown up on the river.

"Why can't *you* hurry up?" Hallie shot back and Lachlan chanced a glance sideways at Hamish, who was doing his best, peddling hard on his adaptive bike. Usually Hallie was very caring and considerate of her brother, but occasionally she got frustrated at him not being able to do everything as quickly or efficiently as she could. Since Lachlan had told her about Linda, these episodes of frustration seemed to be coming more frequently.

"Sorry." Hamish's shoulders slumped and he stopped peddling altogether.

"You're doing great," Lachlan said, "but I'm ready for a break. Hallie," he called ahead again, "let's stop for lunch."

"O-kay." She reluctantly turned around and came back to join them.

"How about under that big tree over there?" Lachlan pointed to a spot not far from the playground.

The three of them peddled over and once their bikes were secure, Lachlan pulled the picnic blanket out of his backpack and started to unload the feast.

"Hallie, can you pour everyone a drink of juice?" he asked, handing her the carton and pointing to the plastic cups he'd just unloaded.

She made a noise of annoyance with her tongue but did as she was told.

"Thank you, Hallie," Lachlan said when the drinks were poured and he'd laid the containers of food down on the rug between them. "Now, eat up."

When the kids filled their plates and started to eat, Lachlan became aware of the silence between them. Usually when the three of them were together, Hallie chattered endlessly, and he and Hamish were hard pressed to get a word in, but today she barely said anything.

"How're things at school?" he asked, trying to draw her out of her shell.

She shrugged one shoulder. "Okay."

He tried a different tack. "Are you looking forward to

the summer break?" Hallie was booked into a dance and drama camp and Hamish would also attend a summer camp to enable Lachlan to continue to work. He pushed aside the smidgen of guilt that sneaked into his heart at this, but he knew the kids would have a ball, much more fun than if they were stuck at home or the restaurant with him.

"Maybe."

Feeling defeated, Lachlan looked to his son. "What about you? Ready for vacation?"

But rather than answering the question, Hamish pointed his finger toward the river and shrieked, "Hey. Isn't that 'liza?"

Hallie spun around and her face lit up for the first time that day. Before Lachlan could stop her, she'd scrambled to her feet and was racing off toward the riverbank in the direction of a woman who was, if not Eliza, then her doppelgänger. A tingle pulsed beneath his rib cage as he registered her sitting on the grass, her knees against her chest and her arms wrapped around them as she looked longingly into the distance.

He hadn't expected to see her today and his body reacted predictably at the sight of Eliza in denim cutoff shorts that highlighted her tanned, shapely legs, a pink fitted T-shirt and a cap that held her gorgeous brown hair captive, but the jolt of attraction waned as he followed her gaze to the playground. The playground full of toddlers with their smiley parents helping them navigate equipment they weren't quite ready for.

Did any of those children look like Jack?

He didn't know, because Eliza hadn't told him anything else about her son. He'd tried to bring him up a couple of times when they were alone, but they were alone so infrequently and when they were, she usually brushed him off, using sex to distract him.

The sex was off the charts—better than any sex he'd ever had, which is why he was so easily distracted—but you didn't need a psychology degree to know she was using it to try to ease her pain. He was happy to help her in any way he could, but all the books he'd read about grief indicated that this was an avoidance tactic and that what people who suffered such a tragic loss really needed was to talk about it. To talk about the person who had passed.

He wondered if she'd ever had counseling or if she talked about Jack back in New York. He hoped so. The books encouraged friends of the bereaved to speak about their dead loved one, but he didn't even know if Eliza classified him as a friend.

And that hurt, because he wanted to be her friend.

"Are you coming to see 'liza?" Hamish asked, and Lachlan realized that while he'd been pontificating on grief, his son had pulled himself up with his crutches. Hamish started off after Hallie before Lachlan had a chance to reply.

He stood, thinking that he'd better rescue Eliza from his excitable offspring. They didn't know about Jack so they were liable to say something to upset her. As he thought this, he suddenly realized that he was doing exactly what she said people did—second-guessing her feelings. But he'd seen the sad expression on her face as she'd watched the kids playing and he couldn't help wanting to protect her.

As he got closer, Eliza looked up and waved. Her lips curved into one of her punch-him-in-the-chest smiles. Relief mixed with joy that she seemed happy to see him and his kids.

He tried for a casual smile as he slowed in front of her. "Fancy meeting you here," he said.

She laughed. "It's such a beautiful day, I thought I should get outside and make the most of it. I still feel like I'm walking through a postcard when I come down here. Jewell Rock really is pretty, as pretty as any place I've ever been."

Not as pretty as you. But he managed not to voice this thought. "It really is," he said instead, "but I have to admit, growing up here kinda makes you take it for granted."

"I can understand that. Did you and your brothers and sisters spend a lot of time down here?"

He nodded. "Mom and Dad used to send us off in the morning with a packed lunch and we'd spend the day climbing the trees and swimming here. It wasn't as touristy back then and the playground was much more basic."

"Sounds blissful," she said.

"D-dad." Hamish tugged his hand. "Can we get an ice cream?"

"Yes. *Please!*" Hallie jumped up and down, her moodiness from earlier seemingly forgotten now that she had her hand in Eliza's. Eliza chuckled and smiled down at her.

The sight of them together made his heart squeeze—a little girl who desperately wanted a mother who cared, a woman who had lost her child and her way.

"Would you like to get an ice cream with us?" he asked Eliza.

"Ooh, yes, please do," Hallie said, another little jiggle accompanying her words.

Lachlan predicted Eliza would say no, offer some excuse because hanging out with his family was definitely outside of their arrangement, so he almost couldn't believe his ears when she said yes. Maybe she simply didn't want to disappoint his kids, but whatever the reason, he was happy for the chance to spend some time with her outside the restaurant and with their clothes *on*.

"Right this way, then," he said.

The ice-cream truck was parked in the lot and close enough that he could see the picnic blanket and their bikes, so they walked over without packing up.

Hamish went for his usual choice of triple chocolate and peanut butter, but Hallie deliberated for what felt like hours, until Eliza asked for a caramel ice cream and Hallie decided she'd have the same. Lachlan didn't get anything, explaining that he usually had to finish one if not both of the kids' cones, and then the four of them walked back to the picnic blanket and sat down to eat.

It was surprising Hallie managed to eat hers at all because she spoke incessantly, which at least meant there were no awkward pauses in conversation.

Eliza listened earnestly as she licked her ice cream and Lachlan had to admit he liked watching her do so. Occasionally she'd ask Hamish a question, but before long, Hallie always took control of the discussion again. Lachlan tried to contribute as well, but he kept trying to work out if Eliza was really enjoying hanging out with them or biding time until she could retreat.

"Can you braid?" Hallie asked Eliza as she handed Lachlan her half-eaten cone.

Eliza blinked. "You mean braid hair?"

Hallie nodded excitedly. "Yes. Stacey at school always has pretty braids and Daddy only ever does bunches for me. Can you braid my hair now?"

Holding his daughter's ice cream, Lachlan was about

to tell Hallie to leave Eliza alone, but Eliza popped the last bit of her cone in her mouth and nodded.

"Sure I can," she said, repositioning herself onto her knees and patting the space in front of her. "Come, sit here."

Hallie didn't need to be asked twice and as Eliza did his daughter's hair, Lachlan and Hamish ate the rest of the ice creams and watched.

"You make that look easy," he said with a chuckle when she'd finished.

She shrugged. "I find doing hair quite therapeutic. Happy to do it whenever you want me to, Hallie."

"Thank you." Hallie gave Eliza a big hug, then looked to Lachlan. "Can I go play now, Daddy?"

"Sure, but wait for your brother," he said, reaching across for Hamish's crutches. Not only did Hallie wait, but she gave her brother her hand to help him up and then kept close to him as they headed off to conquer the playground together. It warmed his heart to see her happy and caring again.

"She sure can talk, can't she?" Eliza said with a chuckle.

"That's an understatement," he replied. "But actually she's been uncharacteristically quiet since I told her about Linda. I'd hoped bringing her out today would help her out of her shell again."

"And it looks like it has."

He nodded, choosing not to tell Eliza that this hadn't been the case until she'd shown up. He didn't want to put that kind of pressure on her but he couldn't help noticing how his little girl adored his employee. And he couldn't blame her—Eliza was easy to like and actually listened when Hallie talked, unlike her own mother.

Perhaps Eliza was simply a good actress but she genuinely seemed to be enjoying hanging out with them.

He couldn't help imagining how different their lives could be if Hallie and Hamish had a mother like Eliza instead.

But the moment that thought entered his head, he berated himself for it. Was that why he liked her so much? Because secretly he was looking for a substitute mother for his children? He didn't *think* that was the case, but even so, fantasies like that were asking for trouble because, even before she'd told him about Jack, Eliza had made her position crystal clear.

"She's really good with Hamish, too, isn't she?"

Eliza's observation broke Lachlan's thoughts and he followed her gaze to see Hallie staying close to her brother as he climbed one of the structures. "Most of the time, yeah."

"He's pretty amazing, though," she continued. "He doesn't seem to let his condition keep him back. You should be really proud of your kids."

"I am."

They spent a few more minutes talking easily about Hallie and Hamish and as they chatted, Eliza planted her hands on the blanket and leaned back as if she was settling in for the long haul. Not wanting to monopolize the conversation with his kids, he asked after her grandmother and her father, whom she'd spoken a little about during their stolen moments together.

Her eyes lit up when talking about her grandmother in a way he'd only ever seen them do on rare occasions. "Grammy's such a character," she said and he laughed as she told him about her dating escapades.

And then a little boy toddled toward them, chasing a bright blue plastic ball that had got away from him and

Eliza's relaxed expression vanished as the ball rolled onto the blanket. As the toddler got closer, she picked up the ball and held it out to him.

His chubby little fingers closed around it just as his dad arrived beside them. "Sorry," he said, slightly breathless. "This little guy has suddenly got fast. Thanks."

Eliza seemed lost for words, so Lachlan smiled back and said, "You're welcome. Have a great day."

"Thanks." As the man scooped up the kid and jogged away again, Lachlan looked back to Eliza. She'd gone pale, as if she'd seen a ghost.

"Did Jack liking playing with balls?" he asked. His heart pounded in his chest as he did so but he believed here in the park with his kids only a short distance away, she couldn't change the subject in the manner she usually did.

Seconds ticked by. Eliza's mouth opened as if she were about to open up to him, but then she glanced at her watch and sprang to her feet. "I've just remembered something I have to do. Thanks for the ice cream. Say goodbye to Hallie and Hamish for me."

And then she turned and fled in the opposite direction of the playground. As Lachlan watched her run, he cursed under his breath and punched his fist into the ground. He'd pushed her too far. Hadn't she told him she didn't want to talk about her son? Why couldn't he just respect those boundaries and be patient like his mom had advised him?

Chapter Fourteen

"**O**h, my goodness! What are you guys doing here?" Eliza shrieked in a most unprofessional manner as she looked up and saw her dad and Grammy Louise coming through the restaurant entrance. She almost tripped over her feet in her rush to get to them and she didn't know who to embrace first. So she threw her arms around both of them and pulled them into a group hug.

"Careful, dear, you'll ruin my hair," Grammy said.

She laughed and let them go to take a good, hard look at them. It was only a month since she'd last seen them but it felt like years. "Your hair looks fabulous, Grammy. And you look great, too, Dad. Nice shirt." She reached a finger out to touch it and found herself grinning uncontrollably. "I've missed you guys."

"We've missed you, too, sugar," her dad replied.

Grammy grabbed hold of Eliza's hands. "You're looking gorgeous, darling. This mountain air obviously agrees with you."

"Thanks," she said, thinking that it wasn't the mountains that had put the glow in her cheeks. "I still can't believe you're both here." Tears sprang to her eyes as the emotion of seeing them again got to her.

Her father reached out and brushed his thumb over her cheek. "You didn't think we'd miss this, did you?" he asked, glancing around at the rapidly filling restaurant.

There was a local band playing in the corner and the drinks were already flowing as her waitstaff seated and welcomed the patrons. She wanted this night to be perfect for Lachlan. At that thought, her heart squeezed and she asked her father, "Are you here in a professional or personal capacity?"

"Can't I be both?" he joked.

As more people came in the door behind them, Eliza decided she didn't have time to worry about the prospect of him writing a bad review. Besides, she had a more pressing issue. Like where to seat her family? Her mind scrambled as she searched for a solution. The restaurant was fully booked for opening night but she couldn't possibly turn them away when they'd come all this way.

As if reading her mind, her grandmother leaned closer and whispered, "We're booked under a false name. Your lovely boss called me last weekend and asked if we would like to come and we cooked up the aliases Mr. and Mrs. Brown so you wouldn't find out."

Lachlan had arranged for her dad and grandmother to come? Her heart bumped against her ribs at this news. How did he even get Grammy's number? Immediately she remembered that she'd listed her grandmother as next of kin on her employment forms because her father was always so hard to pin down. Grammy wasn't much better but at least she stayed in New York and had a landline to contact her on.

Although she'd changed her name back to her maiden one, long before that her mother had changed both of theirs back to *her* maiden name, so she and her father didn't share the same surname and Eliza realized she'd never actually told Lachlan exactly *who* her father was. A restaurant reviewer, yes, but not *the* restaurant reviewer with his own column in the *New York Times*. Which meant Lachlan had no idea that he'd invited one of America's most famous restaurant reviewers into his world.

"Splendid," she said, telling her nerves to take a hike. Unless something went terribly wrong in the kitchen, it was much more likely her father would write a glowing review as Lachlan's food was unlike anything she'd ever tasted before. And *that* would put McKinnel's on the map. "Come right this way, then."

Eliza led them to a table by the window, which looked out onto a gorgeous view of the lake at dusk. And just happened to be next door to the long table crowded with McKinnels. Nora was there with her children, their partners and her grandchildren, including Annabel's hunky new man, whom she'd introduced on the way in. Apparently he was a colleague at the fire station who'd swiped right on Annabel when he came across her on the infamous dating app.

"Grammy, Dad, I'd like you to meet the McKinnels," she said and then quickly introduced them individually. They all shook hands and Eliza couldn't help but notice her dad held Nora's hand a fraction longer than necessary. He had a bit of a reputation as a Casanova and she hoped he'd behave but she didn't have time to worry about that either as more patrons arrived.

"Stella, your waitress for the night, will be with you in moment," she said before kissing Grammy on the cheek, then turning and heading back to do her job.

The rest of the evening passed in a blur. Eliza didn't get the chance to talk to her family, but at one stage, she glanced across to see that the McKinnels had made room for Grammy and Dad at their table. Grammy was in her element, sipping whiskey and holding court, everyone looked to be hanging on to her every word, all except her father and Nora McKinnel, who appeared lost in a conversation of their own.

She was happy her family was being looked after and couldn't wait to spend some time with them herself. Couldn't wait to sit down and slip off her heels once most of the patrons had gone home. Her feet were aching from overuse but the only time she got five seconds' reprieve was when Lachlan came out of the kitchen when all the entrées had been served.

The musicians quieted as he borrowed the singer's microphone and Eliza leaned back against the bar to listen. Even before Lachlan spoke, the crowd erupted in applause, which wasn't surprising, considering the compliments to the chef she and the waiters had been receiving all night.

"Welcome, everyone," he said, grinning out at the patrons. "I want to thank you all for joining us tonight for the grand opening of McKinnel's. It's good to see some new faces and also some familiar ones, people who have been friends and supporters of the distillery since my father and his brother first opened. I wish Dad was here today to see us working hard to expand his legacy and I want to thank my brother Callum for believing in me to open a restaurant to complement the amazing things he, Blair, Quinn and Sophie are already doing with the distillery."

He smiled in the direction of his family table and then lifted an arm and gestured around him. "And thanks to Mac and his craftsmanship for taking my and Callum's ideas and creating this amazing building. To Mom, for keeping us all from killing each other as we continue to grow the distillery and to Annabel, who is always on hand in case of an emergency."

Everyone laughed and Lachlan continued, his voice getting a little choked, "McKinnel's truly is a family affair and there are two other people who also deserve a special mention. Thank you, Hallie and Hamish, for putting up with me working ridiculous hours. One day, you'll know that everything I do is for you guys."

Eliza sniffed as a tear slid down her cheek. If Lachlan went on much longer like this, she didn't think there'd be a dry eye in the house. As she listened to him thank his assistant chef, their talented kitchen hands and the enthusiastic front-of-house team, she felt so proud and happy for his success. Not only was he a very good-looking man and a generous lover, but he was a hard-working, kind man and a dedicated father. He'd told her he thought Tyler a fool for leaving her. Well, she thought exactly the same about his ex-wife.

Lost in these thoughts, it took a second for her to realize people were turning to look at her and that Lachlan was no longer smiling at his family but at her. She'd thought he included her when thanking his front-of-house team but…apparently not.

"Without Eliza, this last month would have been harder and nowhere near as much fun."

Her tummy flipped as their gazes met and as he spoke, she felt as if they were the only two people in the room. She knew the fun he was referring to and felt her cheeks heating but couldn't do anything to stop them. Later she would tell him off for singling her out like that and then she would show him her gratitude.

As he continued singing her praise, she felt her cheeks getting redder by the second. Just when it was getting really embarrassing, he finally wrapped up, "You've been my right-hand gal in every decision and I count my blessings for the day you walked into this building."

Thank you, she mouthed back.

"I think that just about wraps up my thanks. Those who know me know I don't like public speaking, so now that I've said what needed to be said, I will leave you all to order and enjoy dessert. Thanks again for coming and, if you've enjoyed your meal tonight, please tell your friends and share on social media. And don't forget to tag McKinnel's."

As everyone applauded at his final words, Lachlan stepped away from the microphone and began circling the tables, chatting to the patrons individually. Eliza wanted to go and congratulate him and also introduce him to her family but, too busy with diners herself, she didn't get the chance to do so. She did see Lachlan shake hands with her dad, kiss Grammy and embark on what looked to be a deep and meaningful conversation before he headed back into the kitchen.

If possible, dessert service was even more of a success than the entrées. It wasn't until everyone was on to coffees or whiskeys that Eliza finally slipped into the kitchen to take a breath.

Lachlan immediately came across to her and touched a hand to her arm. "Why didn't you tell me your dad was Raymond Starr?"

She shrugged a shoulder and answered with a question of her own. "Why didn't you tell me you invited my family?"

He gave her a coy smile. "Are you mad at me?"

"Are you kidding?" she whispered, leaning perhaps a little close when they had the eyes of the kitchen staff on them. "Later, when we're alone, I'll show you exactly how grateful I am."

"As amazing and tempting as that sounds, I wouldn't want to monopolize your time tonight when your grandmother and father are here. Rain check?"

Her heart sank. As delighted as she was to see her family, she'd been looking forward to a private celebration with Lachlan when all the patrons and staff had gone home. "Do you know how long they're staying? Or where?" It suddenly crossed her mind that she'd been so startled by their arrival, she'd failed to ask either of these questions. Perhaps they'd want to stay with her?

"I think they booked into the hotel for the weekend, but you'll have to check with them. And right now, we both need to get back to work." He kissed her with his eyes and then turned to help his staff begin the cleanup.

As Lachlan had predicted, Eliza's family was among the last people to leave the restaurant. Not knowing that her boss with benefits often gave her a lift home, her father insisted she let him drive her to her apartment in his rental car. All the way, he raved about the evening—how outstanding the food had been and how enjoyable the company.

"Does that mean you're going to write a good review?" Eliza asked from the back seat.

"You'll have to wait and see," he replied with a chuckle.

"Tease."

"I must admit I was dubious about your move here," he said as he caressed the steering wheel. "I worried about you being in such a small town, not knowing anyone, but you looked in your element tonight. It's good to see you smiling again."

"Thank you, Dad," she said, a lump forming in her throat. Part of her still felt a little guilty when she felt happy but that part was getting smaller and smaller. "I'm getting there."

"I'm glad."

"Me, too," added Grammy, glancing out the front window. "And I have to admit you were right about this little place being picturesque. New York will always be my first love, but I guess small towns can have their charm, too."

"They sure can," Eliza said. "And I don't start till two tomorrow afternoon, so how about I give you both the grand tour? The river walk is a must and there are some delightful old Craftsman homes to admire."

"That sounds lovely," Grammy said as Eliza's father slowed in front of her apartment block.

Although physically exhausted, Eliza knew she wouldn't be able to attempt sleep with the success of the evening still buzzing through her veins. "Do you want to come in for a nightcap?" she asked.

Her father turned her down, citing the desire to write his review while the food was still fresh in his head, but Grammy jumped at the idea, choosing to stay with Eliza instead of going back to the hotel.

The apartment didn't have a spare room and the couch was too small to slumber comfortably on, but this didn't matter because she and her grandmother had shared a bed numerous times in the past.

While Eliza attempted to make two cups of cocoa without burning down the kitchen, Grammy evaluated the apartment. "It's a little poky," she said, "but it has potential if you add a little more color and maybe a few photos or pieces of art."

"Maybe you can help me shop for something tomorrow morning before you leave?" Eliza suggested.

Grammy's eyes glistened. Along with drinking and flirting with men, shopping was one of her favorite pastimes. "Now you're talking."

They carried the mugs into the small living room, kicked off their shoes and cozied up on the couch together. "It's so good to have you here." Careful not to spill her drink, Eliza leaned her shoulder against her grandmother's. Although they talked on the phone almost every day, nothing was as good as having her here in person.

"It's good to be here," she replied, patting Eliza's knee. "And Lachlan is even better-looking in person than you gave him credit for. Why didn't you tell me you were sleeping with him?"

Cocoa spluttered from Eliza's mouth and this time she did spill some. Grammy had never been one for beating around the bush, but she hadn't been expecting *this*. As she put the mug down on the coffee table, she opened her mouth to deny her grandmother's accusation, but she felt the older woman's gaze boring into her and knew it was futile. "How did you know?" she asked instead, as she reached for a tissue to address the stain on her work shirt.

Grammy smiled victoriously. "A blind person could see the sparks flying between the two of you. I wouldn't have been surprised when he was speaking about you tonight if he got down on one knee and proposed."

"Propose?" Eliza cackled at the absurdity of such an idea. "I've only known the guy a month."

"When you know, you know," Grammy countered. "I'd known Raymond's father two hours before I knew he was the one for me."

Eliza shook her head. Her situation was very different from that of her grandmother and the grandfather she'd never known because he'd died when her father was a child. "That may be true, but my stance on relationships hasn't changed. I'm not looking for love or marriage. We're…" How should she put it? "We're having *fun* together."

When Grammy just raised her eyebrows, Eliza added defensively, "You were the one who said not all relationships had to be serious, that fun and mutual pleasure are valid reasons for being with someone."

"Maybe I did." She sighed. "And maybe for an old woman like me, that's true, but you're still young, you deserve love and companionship as well as physical intimacy."

Before Eliza could say that she didn't want love ever again, Grammy continued, "And so does Lachlan. He might be happy with sex for a little while, but it's clear to see he's a family man and eventually he'll want more. Nora confided in me about his ex-wife—she sounds like a ghastly woman, abandoning those two beautiful children, but not all women are so stupid. Lachlan is not only a handsome man, but he's smart, successful, caring, a good dad…"

As Grammy listed all the things that had gone through Eliza's head only a few hours ago, the cocoa she'd barely drunk grew heavy in her stomach.

"He's a very eligible bachelor and I'm sure there are

plenty of single women in Jewell Rock who'd be happy to take on the role of his wife and his children's mother."

Eliza's shook her head, her heart thrashing about in her chest at the thought of Lachlan being with another woman. "But he's happy with our...arrangement." The last word tripped on her tongue as it suddenly sounded tawdry.

"Are you sure about that?" Grammy turned her head to look seriously at Eliza and took hold of her hands. "Because I'm an old woman. I've seen a lot in my eighty-two years and I think Lachlan already sees you as way more than just a colleague or a quick tumble between the sheets."

The thrashing in her heart slowed almost to a stop as her grandmother's words sank in. She thought of the way Lachlan treated her—how his face lit up when she walked in the door and the tender way he caressed her body when they slept together. But mostly, she thought of the way he tried to get her to talk about Jack and the hurt in his eyes she tried to ignore when she shut those conversations down.

He wasn't a man who was just using her for his body. All the signs were there that he wanted to get to know her more. And then she thought back to that very first postsex conversation. Had he been joking when he suggested he be her boss with benefits? He'd been quick to assure her he was happy with a fling but what if he'd only said so because of what she'd said?

Her mind whirled with confused thoughts. Maybe Grammy was reading more into the situation than was actually there. Maybe she was seeing what she wanted to see because she didn't like to think of Eliza all alone. But alone was safe. Not getting emotionally entangled meant her heart couldn't break, so why did it hurt so much at the thought of Lachlan finding someone else to make a family with?

Because you're already falling in love with him.

But no, she shook her head vigorously. She didn't want to love him. Tears sprang to her eyes at the thought. She certainly didn't want to love Hallie and Hamish.

Grammy squeezed her hand. "I think you're fooling yourself if you think you can keep your body and heart separate where Lachlan is concerned. I know *you*, and I know you want more out of life. Don't let fear and grief stop you from living because doing so won't bring Jack back but it could leave you leading a very lonely life."

"But isn't that what I deserve?" Eliza sobbed, an image of her little boy's lifeless face once again appearing in her head. "If I was a better mother, he'd still be alive."

"Oh, precious girl." Grammy drew her into her arms. "Stop punishing yourself. You were a wonderful mother—you *are* a wonderful mother—and you need to learn to forgive yourself. You moved here to this beautiful town to start again, but you're not allowing yourself to truly do so."

Eliza couldn't stop the tears that fell and she sat there with her grandmother's arms wrapped around her, the old woman gently stroking her hair, until they finally started to subside. "I'm so glad you're here," she said, pulling back a little so she could look into Grammy's wise eyes.

"Me, too. But now this old girl is getting tired. Shall we head to bed?"

Eliza nodded, thankful that her grandmother wasn't going to push the issue anymore. Then she stood, collected their mugs—one empty and the other half-full of now-cold cocoa—and dumped them in the kitchen sink to deal with tomorrow. She lent Grammy a set of cotton pajamas and gave her a new toothbrush, and they both readied themselves for bed.

Within seconds of climbing beneath the covers, Grammy was sound asleep—probably from all the whiskey she'd drunk that night—but Eliza, not wanting to disturb her, lay there quietly, staring into the darkness as she fought the urge to toss and turn. A war of thoughts raged inside her head as she went over and over the conversation they'd had on the couch.

Was her grandmother right? Did Lachlan want more from her?

And if he did, could she risk her heart on love again?

Or should she put an end to their affair and try to protect them both before it was too late?

Chapter Fifteen

Lost in thought and wondering if he would ever conquer sleep, Lachlan took a few seconds before he registered the strange noise coming from outside his bedroom window. He frowned and listened earnestly as another tap sounded on the glass. Flicking on his bedside light, he glanced at Hallie, who looked like a sleeping angel, and tried not to disturb her as he climbed out of bed and crossed to pull back the curtain.

The silhouette of a woman looked back at him and it took a moment for his eyes to adjust in the moonlight and register who it was. *Eliza.* What was she doing here? Was this a booty call? Or perhaps he'd fallen asleep after all and this was some kind of weird dream. Nevertheless, he pushed open the window and whispered, "Eliza?"

"Can you come out?" she asked. Her voice sounded weird and his heart kicked over in concern.

"I'll be right out. Wait there." If it weren't for the damn screen, he would have climbed out the window. Letting the curtain fall back, he yanked on a pair of jeans and a T-shirt and then hurried out to join her as fast as he could.

She met him on the front porch and he finally got a proper look at her. Dressed only in a thin summer dress, she clutched some kind of book to her chest.

"You haven't got any shoes on?" he asked. He didn't either but he'd just climbed out of bed, whereas Eliza had presumably come from her apartment.

"Oh." She looked down at her feet as if surprised by this fact as well and shook her head slightly. "There wasn't time."

He frowned. "Are you okay?"

She nodded, although the expression on her face told him she wasn't completely sure. "I wanted to show you something."

At three o'clock in the morning? He managed not to voice this thought because he didn't want to make her feel bad and if there was a problem, he was glad she felt comfortable enough to come to him with it.

"Okay," he said instead. "Shall we go across to the restaurant? I'd invite you inside but I don't want to wake everyone up."

Again she simply nodded.

"I'll just go get my keys," he said and then retreated inside the house.

"Come on, then," he said when he emerged less than a minute later. He wanted to take her hand but she was still cradling the book like it was a precious treasure so he would have had to ask to do so. They walked the short distance to the restaurant in silence. It wasn't uncomfortable but it wasn't comfortable either. Lachlan had no idea what was going on, whether her late-night visit was a good one or a bad one and he didn't want to put a foot wrong.

When they arrived, he unlocked the door and switched on the lights. "Can I get you a drink?" he asked.

"Coffee?" she said.

Usually he didn't drink caffeine after dinner but it wasn't like either of them were going to get any sleep now. He smiled at her. "Two coffees coming right up. Do you want to sit down?"

"Thank you." She sounded so damn polite—like a stranger almost—as she lowered herself into one of the two leather couches by the door where patrons could sit with a drink while they waited for a table.

Nerves twisting his belly, he set about making two cups of coffee and then carried them over to her. He put them down on the coffee table and hesitated, unsure whether to sit opposite or beside her. When Eliza put down her book on the table, picked up a mug and took a sip, he lowered himself down next to her.

She put her mug back on the table, picked up the book, edged a little closer to him. When she opened up the book, he realized it was a photo album. His heart pinched as he looked down to see the most angelic little child staring back up at him. With masses of thick curls the same delicious color as Eliza's hair and a cheeky smile that filled his whole face, there was no doubt in Lachlan's mind that this was Jack.

"He did like playing with balls," Eliza said, her voice not much more than a whisper.

Tears prickled at the corner of Lachlan's eyes as she answered the question he'd asked her almost a week ago.

"In fact, we had quite a collection of them. He also

loved the color yellow. I could only buy him yellow clothes because he threw a tantrum if we tried to make him wear any other color." She turned the page to the next photo of a little boy curled up with a Big Bird toy that was almost bigger than him.

Lachlan felt like he should say something but no words would come.

"Dad bought him Big Bird and he rarely let it out of his sight. Grammy bought him a packet of the most beautiful crayons. He was just starting to scribble with them but only the yellow one ever came out of the box."

Again she flicked the page and this time Jack sat in a high chair, a bowl on his head and what looked to be custard dripping down from his hair. His smile said he thought the situation hilarious.

"The obsession started to worry me when he refused to eat anything that wasn't yellow, but Tyler told me not to worry too much. That there were plenty of good yellow foods—bananas, cheese, pineapples, eggs, custard—and that he'd grow out of the quirk but…"

She paused, sniffed long and hard, as if trying to hold it together. "He didn't have the chance to grow out of it."

Eliza might be just keeping it together, but there was a lump in Lachlan's throat and he didn't know how much longer he could hold back his tears. He didn't know what to say. Life was so unfair, so terribly unfair, but what was the point in stating the obvious? Should he tell her how adorable her son was? Did she want sympathy and comfort or would she blow up and run again if he tried to give it?

"Why are you telling me all this?" he found himself asking.

She twisted her head to look at him and blinked. "Because I thought you wanted to know."

"I do." He reached out and laid his hand beside hers so their pinky fingers were touching. The warmth from her skin emanated onto his. He wanted to know this and everything else she had to tell, but as much as he wanted to be there for Eliza, he was now all too aware that his heart was on the line.

He was falling hard and fast in love with her. "But I want to know what it means," he said.

"I miss him so much," she confessed. "I feel so empty, like there's a hole inside me that will never go away. The only time I even begin to feel half-human again is when I'm with you and that terrifies me. I'm petrified of getting close to you and to your beautiful children and then losing one of you. I don't think I could ever survive that kind of pain again, but no matter how much I've tried to protect myself, I realized tonight that I'm fooling myself. And not being fair to either of us. I already have very strong feelings…not only for you, but also for Hallie and Hamish."

Hope flared in Lachlan's heart. Her words were music to his ears.

"Of course, maybe I'm being presumptuous." Again her voice shook. "Maybe you're happy with things as they currently stand?"

"I'm not going to deny that I like sleeping with you," Lachlan said, choosing his words carefully, "but from the moment we first slept together, probably before that, it was a lot more than just physical for me. Like you, I'm wary of opening my heart again but you make me want to give love and family a second chance."

She edged her hand even closer and linked her fingers through his. "You do that to me as well, but I've got to admit that taking a risk on both those things— love and family—is a huge deal for me. Not only am

I scared of messing up again, but I'm not really sure I deserve that kind of happiness."

"Everyone deserves that kind of happiness," he said, lifting her hand to his lips and brushing a kiss against her knuckles, happy she didn't pull away.

Eliza was quiet a moment. "Maybe. But this is all a bit overwhelming for me. Do you mind if we take things slow?"

Although in *his* heart he felt ready to propose, he put his arm around her shoulder and drew her into his side. She fit so perfectly there and if it meant being able to hold her like this whenever he wanted, then he could be patient. He would be. "Yes. We can do that."

"Thank you. I don't want the pressure of the staff knowing we're together yet."

He nodded. "But what about my family? I think most of them already suspect there's something going on between us."

Color rushed to her previously pale cheeks. "We weren't very subtle at your mom's lunch, were we?"

He laughed and shook his head.

"You can tell Nora, your brothers and sisters, but do you think we should see how things go before we tell Hallie and Hamish? I adore them but…"

"They already adore you, too," he said, "so maybe that's a good idea." He didn't want to vocalize the possibility that things might not work out between him and Eliza. But Hallie had recently all but lost her mom, so he didn't want her to get too attached to another woman until they were both sure of the future.

"Okay, then." Eliza inhaled and then exhaled deeply. "My grandmother really likes you by the way. And I think my father does, too. He was going back to the hotel to write his review right away."

Lachlan should feel anxious about the prospect of a restaurant reviewer as famed as Raymond Starr commenting on his new venture, but right now with the guy's daughter in his arms, he couldn't even care if he trashed it. "I can't wait to read it," he said.

Then he retrieved the album from Eliza's lap and turned to the next photo. "This is the cutest kid," he said, recalling one of his grief books telling him it was best to refer to the dead loved one still in present tense. "Thank you for showing me these photos of Jack and telling me about him. I hope as time goes by, you'll tell me more, but if you ever need space to grieve quietly, then you tell me that, as well."

"Thank you. I promise I will."

Chapter Sixteen

Eliza stifled a yawn as she smiled at the young couple coming in the entrance of the restaurant. "Good evening, welcome to McKinnel's," she said. "Do you have a booking?"

The guy nodded. "Table for two under Justin."

"Excellent." As she glanced down at the evening's booking register, she breathed a sigh of relief. If they didn't have a booking, she would have had to turn them away and she always felt so terrible when that happened. Whether it was due to the social media efforts she and Sophie had put out to broadcast the new restaurant or her dad's raving review in the *New York Times* a week ago, business had been booming. They'd had a full house every night since opening and the lunch service was always busy, too.

Eliza couldn't be happier with this result, but it was starting to take its toll on her energy levels. Although if she were honest, she couldn't entirely blame the restaurant for her fatigue. Since she and Lachlan had decided to give a relationship a go, they'd been stealing as much time together as they could outside working hours, as well. This was hard due to Hallie and Hamish's needs— not that she begrudged his children his attention at all— so he'd often sneak over to her house in the middle of the night when they were finally asleep.

And they didn't always have sex. Sometimes they just lay together in bed and talked. Other times they'd watch a movie. They made plans for more cooking lessons once things were less crazy at the restaurant and Eliza couldn't wait, but at the moment they were both just struggling to keep their heads above water.

She looked back up from the register and spoke to the couple. "You've got my favorite table right near the window. The view outside is magical at night. Come this way."

As she led them through the restaurant, she had to curb another yawn. If there was time, she'd take a break and get a coffee but the moment she settled this couple, the door opened and another group arrived to be seated. With a sigh, she told the couple their waitress for the evening would be with them in a moment and then made sure her smile was still firmly in place and hurried back to do it all over again.

"Eliza?" Troy—one of the younger waiters—nabbed her the moment she'd settled the group. "Can you come and talk to a woman over here? She wants to know why almost everything on the menu has whiskey in it."

Annoyance flared within her and she felt the beginnings of a headache prickling her scalp. "Did you tell her this is a *whiskey* distillery?"

"I tried, but she still doesn't seem to get it. She says she doesn't like whiskey."

Oh, boy. Telling herself to stay calm—she'd dealt with hundreds of awkward customers in her life—she told Troy to get back to serving his other tables and she'd deal with it.

"Hi there," she said to the lady, pasting a smile onto her face that was so big it hurt. "Would you like me to run through the menu with you?"

"I can read it myself, thank you. I came here because everyone's been talking about the quality of the food but it all reads like boring fare with a dash of whiskey to try to make it original."

Boring? Usually she prided herself on being a fairly patient and tolerant person, but hearing this woman insult Lachlan's talent had her harboring homicidal thoughts. "I can assure you that all the chef's dishes are very original," she said, her tone saccharine, "and flavorsome. If whiskey isn't your thing, however, we do have a lovely salmon dish and a chicken pasta that don't have—"

The woman screwed up her nose as she interrupted, "I don't want salmon or chicken. Let me speak to the chef!"

Not wanting to cause a scene and guessing that once Lachlan opened his mouth to speak, he'd have this difficult customer eating out of the palm of his hand, Eliza said, "I'll go see if he's available for you," and retreated before she said something she regretted.

As she stepped into the kitchen, the aromas of the various dishes hit her like a food truck. Although these smells usually made her mouth water, today she fought a wave of nausea. Trying to ignore it, she called across the kitchen, "Lachlan, do you have a moment?"

He looked up, smiled, said a few words to one of the kitchen hands, who took over his place at the commercial-sized stove and then crossed over to her. "What's up?" Before she could reply, he frowned and touched his hand to her elbow. "Are you okay? You're not looking so great."

"Jeez, thanks." She shook his hand off, still not wanting the staff to suspect anything between them. "I'm just tired, but never mind about me. Can you come and talk to a lady out here?" She explained the problem with the whiskey.

He chuckled. "It'd be my pleasure. Lead the way."

Eliza did as he asked and then happily left to go and chat to more amenable patrons. Lachlan defused the situation, wrote down the table's order himself and then returned to the kitchen. When the meals started to be served, things got hectic and Eliza ran back and forth to the kitchen, trying to help the waitstaff get everything delivered before it got cold.

"Thank you. That smells divine." A gentleman smiled up at her as she put a steaming bowl of whiskey-and-bacon chili in front of him. Usually she'd agree, but as she opened her mouth to reply, another wave of nausea rocked her and she shut it quickly as bile shot up her throat.

Covering her mouth, she turned and fled toward the restrooms, horror washing over her at the realization she'd almost vomited over a customer. *Again.* Locking the cubicle door behind her, she collapsed onto her knees and hurled into the toilet bowl.

No. This cannot be happening.

The door of the restroom opened. She stilled, willing this episode to be over.

"Eliza?" came the voice of one of the waitresses.

"Are you okay? Lachlan saw you rush off and told me to come check on you."

Oh, Lord. Somehow she managed to speak. "I'll be fine. Think I must have eaten something that didn't agree with me."

The waitress chuckled. "Hopefully not from this kitchen."

Eliza could not laugh. There was *nothing* funny about this.

"Okay, then," said the girl after a long pause. "Do you need anything?"

"No. Just go back to work," Eliza managed. "I'll be out in a minute."

She waited until she heard the door click shut again and then she forced herself off her knees. She wiped her mouth with toilet paper, flushed it and then went out to check her reflection in the mirror. It wasn't pretty but she pinched her cheeks to add a little color and told herself to get back out there and worry about *this* later.

Yet, as she opened the door and stepped back into the hallway that led into the restaurant, she almost slammed into Lachlan's chest.

"I'm going to ask you again," he said as he put his arms out to steady her. "Are you not feeling well?"

She wanted to lie, to keep on working, but she didn't want to make another scene. "I've felt better."

"I'm taking you home," he said. "I'll just get my keys."

"No!" She shook her head furiously. "You can't leave now." It was the assistant chef's night off. "I'll be okay," she managed. "I probably just need to sleep it off."

In the end, Lachlan reluctantly agreed to let her go on her own as long as she took his truck and promised to call him the moment she got home.

"I will." Without saying goodbye to anyone else, she grabbed her purse and headed out into the night. As she walked toward his vehicle, her breaths came in rapid jolts and she told herself to chill before she gave herself a heart attack.

This was probably a false alarm anyway. Maybe she really was just sick. She tried to remember the last time she'd had her period but life had been so busy lately she'd lost track. Was it just after she arrived in Jewell Rock? That was well over a month ago now, which would make her late but…

No! She and Lachlan had used condoms every single time they'd made love. Weren't condoms 99 percent effective or something? Probably tomorrow morning, she'd wake up and discover her tiredness and nausea was a new premenstrual symptom.

Clinging to this possibility, she climbed into the truck and started toward her apartment with a quick detour to the drugstore just to be sure. As much as the idea of being pregnant terrified her, she wouldn't be able to sleep if she didn't know for sure.

With shaking hands and hoping nobody there recognized her, she grabbed a pregnancy-testing kit and took it to the counter. Less than ten minutes later, she was in her apartment, staring at the little white stick on her counter.

The word *pregnant* glared up at her.

This felt like déjà vu; the last time she'd been in this situation, she'd been over the moon, but her world had changed since then. She didn't want another baby. She'd only just begun to consider the idea of becoming a stepmom. So much for taking things slow with Lachlan. The fears she'd slowly been starting to conquer these last few weeks reared up inside her once again.

She whirled around and threw up into the toilet. Only this time, she wasn't sure the nausea was down to morning sickness or because she was more terrified than she'd ever been in her life.

Lachlan lost count of the number of times he checked his phone following Eliza's departure. Why hadn't she called yet? Had something happened on her way? An image of her slumped over the steering wheel, the car in a ditch (or worse), haunted him and for the first time since the restaurant had opened—for the first time in as long as he could remember—he burned someone's dinner and had to start again.

If there'd been an accident, you'd have heard about it, he told himself as he tried to focus on cooking. But it was no good. He couldn't get her out of his head. Taking a break he couldn't really afford due to the full restaurant, he slipped outside and tried to call her. When her phone went to voice mail, he cursed and called Annabel.

She answered just as he was about to give up. "Hey, big bro, how can I help you?"

"Are you at home? Eliza left early because she wasn't feeling well and I was wondering if you could go check on her?"

"Sorry. I'm in Bend at Noah's house," she said, naming her new boyfriend.

"Is Soph at home?"

"She's out on a date."

He cursed. Why had his sisters suddenly decided to throw their hearts and souls into dating when he needed them? "Okay, thanks. Bye."

He shoved his phone back into his pocket, then headed back into the restaurant and willed everyone to leave early. Then, when all the desserts had finally been delivered to the tables, he handed the reins over to his barman—who was the most senior employee still there that night—and asked him to close up.

Only outside did he remember he'd insisted Eliza take his truck. He deliberated all of two seconds between taking her bike or jogging to the house and borrowing his mom's car before he jumped on the bike. It might take him slightly longer but he wouldn't have to explain himself to his mom or Blair, which would waste time.

Less than ten minutes later, he saw his truck parked outside her apartment building and pressed his hand to his heart as relief washed over him. But there was no time to catch his breath—he was still worried and knew he wouldn't be able to sleep if he didn't at least check on her before going home. He leaned the bike against a wall, went to the entrance and punched his sisters' code into the security pad to let himself inside.

Less than thirty seconds later, he was pounding on Eliza's front door. "Sweetheart, it's Lachlan."

No reply was forthcoming. He tapped his shoe against the floor, contemplating his next move and was just about to knock again when he heard the click of the lock and the door peeled back.

"You'll wake the neighbors," Eliza hissed.

He put his hand on the door and pushed it enough to let himself inside. "At least two of them are out and all I care about is you anyway." Frowning, he lifted his hand and put it against her forehead. "You don't have a temperature. Is it your stomach? Maybe you should lie down."

She raised an eyebrow as she pulled away from him. "That's what I was doing until someone knocked on my front door."

"I'm sorry," he said, feeling slightly chastised. "But I was worried. You didn't call me to say you'd got home safely."

"I forgot." She hugged her arms to herself.

"Never mind. Let's get you to bed and all snuggled up. I'll look after you." He shut the door behind him and reached for her again, ready to lead her into the bedroom and play nurse, but she all but pushed him away.

Lachlan blinked. He hadn't seen this side of her before but she was kind of cute when she was grumpy. "You're a little feisty when you're sick, aren't you?"

"I'm not sick," she snapped. "I'm pregnant."

And then she promptly burst into tears.

He stood there frozen for a few moments, watching the tears stream down her cheeks but too stunned to do anything about it. *Pregnant?* How could that possibly be? They might have had a lot of sex but they'd also used a lot of condoms.

Finally he found his voice. "Are you sure?"

"I can show you the positive pregnancy test if you don't believe me," she said, her words punctuated by sobs.

"No, of course, that's not necessary," he rushed, feeling like a real asshole. He chuckled nervously and thought of his two pregnant soon-to-be sisters-in-law. "There must be something in the water around here right now."

When Eliza didn't laugh, he took a breath and a tentative step toward her, trying once again to take her into his arms. This time, she didn't resist. And as Eliza's body molded again him, he tried to collect his thoughts.

They'd been so happy the last couple of weeks—the more he got to know Eliza, the more he wanted to know and the more they found out they had in common. He loved their conversations even more than he loved sleeping with her. When she walked into a room, his heart lifted and he always felt a mixture of nerves and excitement. They were in that new, wonderful stage of a relationship where they couldn't get enough of each other and whenever they were apart, he found himself counting down the moments until he could see her again.

It might only be early days and although they'd promised to take things slow, he knew without a doubt that he wanted to spend the rest of his life with her. Getting her pregnant was not ideal but it wasn't the end of the world.

And they couldn't just ignore it.

"Come on, let's go sit down," he said eventually.

She let him lead her over to her couch and as she lowered herself into the chair, he added, "Can I get you anything? Is the nausea still bad? I could go out and get you some ginger soda if you want?"

He remembered that when Linda had terrible morning sickness with the twins, the only thing that helped was anything ginger.

She shook her head, so he sat down beside her and reached for her hand. "It'll be okay," he said.

"I don't know how this happened," she whispered. "We've always been so careful."

And then it hit him. *Oh, God.* "You know that first time we slept together?"

She looked at him warily and nodded.

"That condom had been in my wallet for quite a while." He grimaced. "It could have been out of date."

Her eyes widened and she glared at him. "So this is *your* fault?"

"I don't know." He ran a hand through his hair. "But if you are pregnant, it'll be okay. I love you, Eliza, and although a surprise, the idea of a little baby that's part of you and me is beautiful."

"You...*love* me?"

"Yeah. Yes, I do." He grinned—although he'd suspected as such for a while, this was the first time he'd truly admitted to himself that things had progressed this far for him. He placed a hand against her stomach. "And you know what? I already love this little girl or guy, as well.

"You're probably tired, and today's been massive," he continued, "but tomorrow we should get you in to see the local doctor. Chelsea and Bailey might be able to recommend their obstetricians to you, and of course, you'll need to start on folic acid tablets right away. I'll pick some up tomorrow for you, if you like. And if you're not well enough for work or need to sleep longer then..."

Suddenly registering the expression on her face, he stopped rambling and realized that the best-case scenario to his declaration of love was one of her own, but maybe she was overwhelmed by everything.

"I'm sorry," he said, "we can talk about all this tomorrow but for now—"

She interrupted, once again pushing his hand off her, "You're acting like we're keeping it."

He blinked, confused.

"How could you think I'd be happy about this?" she cried, jumping to her feet.

Lachlan flinched at her harsh words. A baby might not have been in their plans but not for a second would he ever want to get rid of it. Hallie and Hamish were hard work at times but they were also absolute blessings and he'd never once regretted his and Linda's decision to have them.

Is that what she meant? She might not want to go through with the pregnancy. His gut churned at the thought and suddenly Eliza looked more like Linda to him than she ever had before.

"What do you mean?" He couldn't help his icy tone.

She threw up her hands in the air and shouted, "I don't know! I need some time. I need to think about all this."

"Time?" His heart quaked.

"Yes. You promised that you'd give me space if I needed it."

It took a couple of seconds for him to recall the vow he'd made in the early hours of the morning when she'd finally talked properly to him about Jack. But this was different. There was another baby involved now. *His* baby. A child he'd known about less than half an hour but would already do anything to protect.

"This has nothing to do with Jack," he growled.

"It has *everything* to do with Jack," she countered. "And I'm done talking about this with you right now. Your truck keys are on the table by the door. I'd like you to leave."

As hard as it had been to let her go that afternoon in the garage when he'd first found out about Jack's death, it was a hundred times harder to walk away now. He'd never felt more conflicted. He was angry and scared but also worried about her. He didn't want to leave her in this state but it was late, he was losing his cool and maybe they could both do with a little space.

Reluctantly, he pushed to a stand and stared her right in the eye. "Okay. I'll go now. But promise me you won't do anything drastic before talking to me."

She took a long moment to reply. Then she said, "I'll talk to you later."

It wasn't lost on him that she didn't promise him anything and, as he scooped up his keys and headed out to his truck, he fought the urge to turn around and beg her.

Chapter Seventeen

When the plane touched down at JFK airport, Eliza did not feel like she'd come home but she hadn't known where else to go. She hadn't told Grammy, Dad or anyone that she was coming as she didn't want a big welcome at the airport, where she was liable to fall apart. She still wasn't sure whether she was going to tell her family about being pregnant, but she hadn't been able to stay in Jewell Rock a moment longer.

Although Lachlan had let her be last night, she wouldn't be able to think straight seeing him day-to-day and she didn't know how long he'd be able to resist making her talk about their "situation." As everyone around her un-clicked their seat belts and bolted upright to scramble in the overhead compartments for their things, Eliza switched her phone on and held her breath as she waited for the inevitable.

Sure enough, within seconds, a message arrived in reply to the one she'd sent Lachlan just before she'd switched off her cell for takeoff, telling him she wouldn't be coming into work for a few days.

I wish you would talk to me.

She read his reply three times and her heart squeezed with the knowledge she was hurting him. The expression on his face when she'd told him she didn't know if she wanted the baby was still as clear in her mind as if he were standing in front of her now, but he couldn't understand how she felt.

Should she reply or should she just leave it?

"Are you going to get up?" came a grumpy voice from beside her. She turned to see the guy who'd been sitting in the window seat glaring at her.

"Sorry," she said, grabbing her purse from beneath the seat in front of her and shoving her phone inside it. Then she unbuckled her belt and rushed to stand, joining the line of passengers slowly shuffling out of the plane.

As she followed the crowds toward the arrival area and then waited by the luggage carousel for her stuff, she noted how crowded this airport was in comparison to the quiet one she'd left only seven hours ago. She'd never really thought about how busy New York was before, but as people bustled around her now, pushing and shoving in an aim to get their things, she wished they would all just disappear.

She'd hoped for silence when she got into a cab but was cursed with a chatty driver. In the end, she told him that she wasn't feeling well and didn't want to talk and he accepted that, so when they arrived at her destination, she thanked him with a generous tip.

"Not a problem. Hope you're feeling better soon," he replied as he lifted her suitcase out of the trunk.

"Thanks." She forced a smile when the last thing she felt like doing was smiling and then let herself into the apartment building that had been her home less than two months ago. It felt like a lifetime ago.

When she got to her grandmother's door, she knocked loudly to announce herself in case Grammy had a gentleman guest. When there was no reply, she used her key and pushed open the door. The apartment was deserted except for the lingering scent of Grammy's perfume. Usually Eliza liked it but today the aroma went straight to her stomach, so she dumped her things and rushed to the bathroom.

As she emerged five minutes later and went to get herself a drink of water, she wasn't sure whether she was happy for her grandmother's absence. Part of her longed for the comforting embrace that only Grammy could give, but another part of her just wanted to be alone. Perhaps she should have gone to a hotel instead or maybe flown somewhere else entirely but when she'd headed to the airport that morning to catch a flight, she hadn't been thinking straight.

Although mentally, emotionally and physically exhausted, she hadn't slept a wink last night or on the plane. Now, standing in the kitchen, her eyes started to droop and she thought if she didn't go to bed, her grandmother might return later to find her asleep on the kitchen floor. With that thought, she found a piece of paper and scribbled a note to leave in an obvious place on the counter in case she actually did achieve slumber before Grammy got home.

Surprise. Came back for a few days' break and am exhausted after an early flight. See you in the morning. xx
Eliza

Then she took herself off to the spare room, which still had much of her stuff in it from when she'd moved in earlier in the year, pulled back the covers on the bed and buried herself beneath them.

Lachlan stared at the roster for the next week and found he wanted to screw it up and hurl it across the restaurant. Five days since Eliza had gone home sick. Five days since he could think about nothing but what she'd told him. Five days since they'd been understaffed.

With a sigh, he dragged his phone out of his pocket and glanced down at the screen for what had to be the five thousandth time. She hadn't replied to the message. His knocks went unanswered but he hadn't even contemplated the fact she'd left town until one of her neighbors saw him turning away from her door and told him she'd seen Eliza get in a cab a couple of mornings ago and didn't think she'd been back since.

He passed his phone from hand to hand, wondering if he should try to call her or message her again. Surely she knew how unfair she was being to him—not only because he didn't know whether he should be looking for another head hostess for the restaurant but because every waking hour, he tortured himself with one question.

Is she still pregnant?

For someone who hadn't imagined ever having more kids, the thought that she might not be haunted him and left his heart cold. But the fact that she'd refused to talk and had shut him out so completely hurt even more. And he missed her more than he thought it possible to ever miss anybody.

He tortured himself with what-ifs and if-onlys. If only…he'd been more gentle with her the night she'd told him. He'd been in shock but he should have realized how hard this would be for her after losing her son not so long ago. Could he have done something, said something different? Unprepared for this news, he possibly hadn't handled the situation as carefully as he should have.

A shadow appeared in the doorway to the restaurant's office and Lachlan glanced up from behind the desk, thinking it was one of his employees. He was about to bark an order for them to get back to work, but he shut his mouth when he saw his older brother standing there instead.

Without a word, Callum stepped into the room and shut the door behind him. In his hand, he held a bottle of McKinnel's finest and two glass tumblers.

"Oh, boy, this looks serious," Lachlan said as Callum lowered himself onto the seat on the other side of the desk. "Is this an official visit?"

Callum had a look of consternation on his face as he unscrewed the lid on the bottle. "I guess you could call it an intervention and I'm here in two capacities—that of your older, wiser brother and also that of the director of this distillery."

"I see," Lachlan said, watching his brother pour amber fluid into the two glasses. When Callum pushed one toward him, he lifted it to his mouth and took a sip. *Why not?*

Callum echoed the action, but when Lachlan took another, his brother put his glass back down on the desk and made an appreciative noise with their tongue. "Man, we're good," he said, nodding toward the bottle.

"We are," Lachlan agreed, although he got the feeling Callum wasn't here to praise their product, and besides, nothing tasted that great at the moment. "What can I do for you?"

Callum leaned back in his chair and clasped his hands behind his head. Although his posture gave off an air of ease, the expression on his face did not. "You can cut the crap and tell me what's really going on with you and Eliza."

"What are you talking about?" Lachlan asked. He'd told his family and the restaurant staff that there'd been a family emergency in New York, which meant Eliza had to go back there for a while. At least, that's where he guessed she'd gone. "I told you, she's visiting her family."

Callum's eyebrows stretched up to his hairline. "You are quite possibly the worst liar I've ever known. If this wasn't affecting the restaurant, I'd mind my own business and tell Mom to mind hers as well, but as it is, I can't. We all know Eliza hasn't gone back to New York for a family emergency—if that were the case, you wouldn't be charging around like a wounded bear and Sophie wouldn't have been fielding complaints from your staff about you being grouchy and unreasonable."

"What?"

Callum nodded gravely. "She wouldn't tell me names but your crew aren't happy campers at the moment and that's not good for business."

So much of the staff was Eliza's, too. In such a short time, so much of his had become theirs. And right now, he didn't really give a damn about business but he guessed that wasn't the answer Callum was looking for. He sighed and took another sip of whiskey. Maybe he should bring Callum into his confidence—he'd had more experience dealing with the fairer sex than Lachlan had lately.

"Eliza's pregnant," he blurted.

"Holy shit. That was fast." Callum chuckled and then grinned. "Congratulations. There must be something in the water round here."

"That's what I said, too," Lachlan replied, "but hold the congratulations."

Callum's smile faded. "So this is why she went back to New York? I know you might not have been planning a baby so soon but surely it's good news?"

"I don't even know if she is in New York," Lachlan admitted. "All I know is that she isn't here and wherever she is, the last time I saw her, she told me she was pregnant but that she wasn't sure whether she could go through with the pregnancy."

Callum frowned. "Jeez. Wanna talk about it?"

Lachlan hesitated a few moments. Despite everything, he didn't want to break the promise he'd given to Eliza not to tell anyone about Jack. But then again, maybe being older really did make Callum wiser, and thus maybe he'd be able to help. He leaned forward and refilled his glass.

"Eliza recently lost a child," he began and Callum listened intently without saying a word as Lachlan filled him in. "She came to Jewell Rock for a fresh start, so it took ages before she opened up to me about any of this. She's still hurting so badly."

Callum finally spoke. "I haven't even met my kid yet and already I can imagine the pain I'd feel if we lost it. I'm not sure losing a child is something you ever stop hurting from. Being pregnant has probably—"

"I *know*. I get that," Lachlan interrupted, feeling the frustration rise within him again. "Even agreeing to start a relationship was a massive thing for her. We definitely didn't plan this pregnancy but her shutting me out is killing me. I don't seem to be a very good judge of character when it comes to women."

"This isn't about you. And don't be an ass by comparing Eliza to Linda. Even I can see they're totally different people. From what you've told me, she's obviously terrified of being a mother, of feeling such intense love and then losing it all over again."

Lachlan threw his hands up in the air. Eliza might not be Linda and maybe Callum was right, but he was still at a loss as to how to handle her or the situation. "Even if that is the case, what can I do about it?"

"Do you love her?" Callum asked.

"Yes."

"Do you want this baby?"

"Yes."

Callum nodded once slowly. "Then there's your answer. You need to do whatever it takes to make her feel safe—you need to make Eliza feel like she has options."

"And what if she doesn't want any of us? The baby or me? Hallie or Hamish?"

Callum shrugged. "You're already a single dad. And a good one. You might not want to do it alone, but you can, and any child would be lucky to have you."

If only it were as simple as Callum made it sound. "How am I supposed to achieve any of that when she won't talk to me? She won't even answer my messages, never mind her phone. I can't force her to talk to me."

"Not sitting there behind your desk feeling sorry for yourself, you can't. But you can show her how much she and the baby matter by going to her. Don't leave her to go through this all alone, even if that's what she thinks she wants. Sometimes in life, you've got to fight for what's important, little brother."

"Even if what's important is in New York—and I can't be certain about that—I can't just go there."

"Why not?" Callum challenged with another irritating shrug of his shoulders.

"Because I can't just leave Hallie and Hamish. And what about the restaurant?"

Callum shook his head. "Hallie and Hamish will be fine with us and what's your priority? Your love for Eliza or your career?"

The answer came quick and easy. "Eliza, of course." In a matter of weeks, she'd become one of the most important people in his world, along with Hallie and Hamish, and the last five days without her in it had been hell. "But I thought as director of this distillery and therefore my boss, you might be against me rushing off to New York. Especially when the head hostess is missing, as well."

As he said these words, he realized this was what he'd wanted to do since he'd turned up at her apartment and found her gone.

"I'm your big brother first and your boss second. Family trumps work every time, buddy, and I believe that you and Eliza have what it takes to make a beautiful family. Chelsea had some restaurant experience years ago, she can help out in front of house and you've got a very capable assistant chef. We'll be fine."

Something a little like hope kicked over in Lachlan's heart. "Are you sure?" he asked.

Callum grinned again and nodded. "What are you waiting for?"

Chapter Eighteen

I should have cancelled, Eliza thought as she walked through Central Park to meet Lilly for lunch at Tavern on the Green. Perhaps it wasn't too late. She couldn't imagine she'd be very good company. But Grammy had apparently run into Lilly at Macy's yesterday and let slip that Eliza was back.

Her friend had been extremely hurt that she hadn't called her and had been on the phone immediately, reprimanding Eliza for not telling her she was home and demanding they catch up for her to dish the dirt.

She already felt enough guilt over leaving Lachlan in the lurch and she didn't need to add being a bad friend to her list of sins, so she'd agreed to a lunch date. After five days of thinking time, her thoughts were no clearer in her head than they were when she'd left Jewell Rock. She missed Lachlan so much that she found herself watching *Mary Poppins* to feel close to him. But every time a wave of morning sickness came over her, her whole body filled with a crippling terror and the thought of facing him left her shaking in her shoes.

She'd decided maybe a little fresh air would help.

Yet now as she walked along the paths toward her destination, she remembered why she favored being a hermit. When you were upset about something, life had a habit of flaunting it in your face. Today, everywhere she looked, there were couples in love, young moms jogging with strollers or pregnant women tenderly caressing their blossoming bellies.

No. I can't do this.

Yanking her phone out of her pocket, Eliza began typing out an apology message to Lilly and as she did so, she turned and started back in the direction she'd come. She was just about to press Send when her foot caught on a crack in the path. A yelp left her mouth as her phone flew out of her grasp and her whole body shot forward. Instinctively, she put her hands out to try to save her fall, but it didn't quite work out. Two seconds later, she found herself lying flat on the path, a small crowd quickly gathering around her.

Her first thought wasn't the pain on her head or the embarrassment of falling so spectacularly in such a public place. It wasn't even, *Where is my phone?*

"You okay?" asked a man, crouching down next to her and depositing her phone on the ground.

"Let me through, I know first aid," boomed a very familiar voice from somewhere above as Eliza attempted to pick herself back up.

"Oh, my God, I know her," shrieked Lilly, dropping to her knees beside her.

Eliza had never been happier to see her friend in her life. She stopped trying to get up and instead burst into tears—it seemed crying was the only thing she was good at these days.

"Oh, Lize." As the strangers dispersed, Lilly helped her into a sitting position, then dug around in her purse and conjured a small packet of tissues as she spoke. "What have you done to yourself? You've got a horrible gash on your forehead." She thrust a tissue against the spot and held it firmly. "Do you think you can stand, or are you feeling dizzy? If you can get up, we should go into the restroom and clean you up. That way, I'll be able to have a proper look and see if you need stitches."

But Eliza didn't care about the blood trickling down the side of her face. She was almost numb to the pain that accompanied it. Her hands rushed to cradle her stomach as she thought about the new life growing there.

What if this fall makes me lose it?

Then the pain came—in the form of a big whoosh to her heart.

"My baby," she whispered.

"Huh?" Lilly blinked and her hand fell from Eliza's forehead as her gaze dropped to Eliza's stomach. "What did you just say?"

"I'm pregnant." Eliza said the words for the first time since she'd told Lachlan. Grammy knew that something was going on but Eliza hadn't been able to bring herself to mention the baby yet. Part of her had thought if she didn't tell anyone, maybe it would just go away but suddenly she knew with absolute certainty she didn't want that.

As terrifying as the idea of being a mom again was, as scared as she was of messing up and experiencing more pain, she wanted this chance and she wanted to have it with Lachlan. Sitting on this hard ground now, she craved his arms around her. But what if she did lose the baby? Lachlan might think she'd got rid of it on purpose.

As these thoughts whirled through her head, her sobs came harder and faster.

"Oh, honey." Ignoring the blood now, Lilly drew Eliza into her arms. "It'll be okay."

Her friend held her until her tears finally started to subside and then she gently suggested they go clean Eliza up. "Do you want to go back to my apartment—Britt will still be out with my mom—or do you still want to have lunch?"

"I don't think I could eat anything right now," Eliza said.

So Lilly gave her a hand up off the ground, then held her close as they headed to find a cab. In the car, she gave their driver her address and then held Eliza's hand the whole way to her place. Neither of them said anything—a silent agreement not to air her dirty laundry to their cabbie—and when they got into Lilly's house, she took Eliza straight into the bathroom and tended her wound before anything else.

When the blood had stopped, the area was clean and Lilly had applied antiseptic cream to Eliza's forehead, she stood back and said, "If you're unlucky, you'll end up with a Harry Potter scar on your forehead."

Eliza almost laughed. Her life might be a shambles but Lilly always had the ability to make her feel a little better.

"So…I would offer you wine," Lilly said, "but in the light of what you've just told me, maybe juice would be better for this discussion. Want to come sit down?"

Eliza nodded and a few minutes later, they were both sitting on Eliza's couch, nursing a glass of juice. She took a sip and then put her drink down on the coffee table. "I'm not really sure where to start."

"How about who the father is?" Lilly said.

"Very funny. I told you I'd started seeing Lachlan."

Lilly nodded. "But you also told me you were taking things slow. Next thing you tell me, you're knocked up."

"It was a shock to me, as well," she said as she told her friend about her resolve not to ever have another baby. "I even told Lachlan I wasn't sure I wanted to have the baby," she concluded.

Lilly's eyes widened. "You thought you might get rid of it?"

"I don't really know," Eliza admitted. "I hadn't thought as far as logistics. All I knew is that I couldn't face the thought of becoming a mother again and so I came back here to try to get my head together."

Lilly reached for Eliza's hand. "And has it worked? Have you made a decision?"

Eliza let out a long, deep breath. "I've thought about nothing else for five days but until that moment I fell today, I was as confused and terrified as ever. I couldn't help feeling that if I allowed myself to feel anything for this baby, it would be a betrayal to Jack. But when I tripped, my first thought was of the baby's safety and suddenly I knew..." She sniffed as tears threatened once again. "I knew that whether or not I want to, I already love this child. And not only do I also love its father, but I love his two gorgeous children, as well. My heart feels like it could burst with love for them all."

"Oh, Eliza." Lilly squeezed her hand. "Just because you love another baby doesn't mean your love for Jack is any less. I know how scary this must be but you are the bravest person I know and you can do this. You deserve to be happy again."

"But what if Lachlan doesn't want me anymore?" She remembered the look on his face when she'd said she wasn't sure if she wanted to have the baby and a chill filled her heart. How could she ever have thought such a thing?

Maybe she'd already ruined things with him.

"I haven't met Lachlan," Lilly began, "and I can't tell you what he thinks or feels, but from the little bits you've told me about him, he sounds like a caring and reasonable person. Go back and talk to him. Tell him what you just told me."

At the thought of seeing him again, Eliza's cold heart sped up. It was time to stop running and face her fears. Time to stop waiting to wake up from her nightmare and start living again.

She lifted her arm and looked at her watch. "I wonder what time the next flight to Oregon is?"

Lilly's face split into a grin. "Leave that to me. You go pack your bags and I'll book you on it."

"I thought you didn't want me to live in Oregon," Eliza said, braving a smile.

"I didn't. I *don't*. But I do want you to be happy, so I'll learn to live with it."

When Eliza turned her key in the lock of her grandmother's apartment twenty minutes later, she wasn't surprised to hear voices. Barely a day went by without one friend or other of Grammy's dropping in for a drink. But she stopped dead in her tracks when she registered the male voice.

No. It can't be. The voice belonged to someone much younger than Grammy's usual gentleman friends and maybe she was hallucinating but it sounded very familiar.

Light-headed, she almost tripped again in her haste to get into the living room and let out a shriek at the sight of Lachlan sitting on the couch. He offered her a tentative smile, but it was Grammy who spoke first.

"Hello, Eliza," she said calmly. "I was just about to message and say you had a delivery. How was your lunch with Lilly?"

"It was fine," Eliza found herself saying and then realized that was a lie. "Actually we didn't eat lunch. I…" Her words failed her as she met Lachlan's gaze and her heart filled with love. It was *so* unbelievably good to see him.

"Good Lord." Grammy pushed out of her armchair, crossed the room and touched her hand to Eliza's forehead. "What have you done to your head?"

Lachlan swore and rushed to his feet. Both of them stood before her, fussing.

She brushed her grandmother off and kept her gaze on him. "It's nothing. I'm fine."

"In that case, I think I'll take myself for a walk around the block," Grammy said and then, with a quick pat on Eliza's arm, she retreated.

The moment the door clicked shut, Lachlan spoke. "Are you sure your head's okay?"

She nodded.

"Look," he began, "I know I said I'd give you time but there's something I want to say and it can't wait a moment longer."

"Me, too," Eliza said. "In fact, I was just coming back here to pack my bag and fly back to Oregon."

"Really? Does that mean…?" His voice broke on the word and he paused a moment before continuing. "Does that mean you've made a decision?"

She nodded. "I'm sorry I've caused you pain and

stress these last few days, but getting pregnant felt like a nightmare. Having Jack was the best thing that ever happened to me and losing him the absolute worst. I'm terrified that something might happen to this baby, that I might make another fatal mistake."

"You didn't make a mistake," Lachlan said, a flash of anger in his eyes. "What happened to Jack was a terrible accident and there are no guarantees in life. I'd be lying if I promised you we won't have hardships, but I *can* promise you this. I love you, Eliza Coleman, and therefore I'll respect whatever decision you make regarding our child. If that means me taking on the baby because you don't think you can, then I will. And I will love it and look after it with all my heart."

Eliza's heart clenched with even deeper love for this man. Already he had his hands full with two children, yet he was willing to take another one on all by himself.

She opened her mouth to tell him but found she couldn't speak past the lump in her throat.

"But," he continued, "I need you to know that I believe in you. I think you can do this, I think you're stronger and braver than you give yourself credit for, but if you choose motherhood again, then you *won't* be alone. If you choose us, I promise whatever we face from now on, whatever highs and lows life throws at us, we'll face them together. I want to be there for both you and the baby. I want the five of us to be a family. But the question is…what do *you* want?"

And despite the decision she'd made in Central Park and as much as Eliza wanted to accept Lachlan's offer, as much as she wanted to believe in herself and them as much as he did, a tiny voice from the past was still crying out to her.

"Tyler made those same vows to me," she found herself saying, "yet when everything—"

"I'm *not* Tyler," he said forcefully and he stepped forward and took hold of her hands, bringing them up to rest on his chest. "But this is your decision."

And as she looked into his lovely blue eyes, she knew his words to be the absolute truth. Life had already thrown a lot of pain and drama at Lachlan but he hadn't turned to illegal substances like Tyler and he hadn't tried to run away from his problems like she had. He was a good, *good* man. The very best man. And he was offering himself and his beautiful children to her.

She'd be an idiot not to accept him.

"Is it my turn to speak yet?" she asked.

Lachlan's lips twisted slightly upward. "Go ahead."

She took a quick breath and then told him about the last five days in which she'd missed him like she'd miss a limb. "I wanted to come back to you, but I still wasn't sure I could face the idea of parenthood again. Then today…" She slipped her hand out of his and gestured to her head. "I slipped badly in Central Park and as I fell onto the pavement, everything fell into place in my head. I realized that this baby is a blessing and so are you."

"Really?" He blinked and sounded choked.

"Uh-huh. I was rushing back to Oregon to beg your forgiveness and tell you how much I love you and Hallie and Hamish and that I want to be a family with you all."

"Really?"

She nodded and laughed. "Is that all you can say now?"

And in reply, he took her face in his hands and kissed her till she was breathless. It didn't take long. His mouth had that kind of effect.

"I love you, too," he said again, "and I'm so proud of you."

She glowed inside but suddenly had a thought. "Who's looking after the restaurant?"

He grinned. "My family and our wonderful staff. Apparently I'm an ass to work and live with when you're not around, so they told me not to bother coming home without you."

She wasn't sure if she believed him or not, but before she could say this, he said, "You know how I told you my favorite color was brown?"

Eliza half laughed, half grimaced. "How could I forget? It's the only thing not quite perfect about you."

Still smiling, he gently took a chunk of her chocolate-brown locks and twisted it around his finger. "Until I met you, my favorite color was blue."

Epilogue

"Mama!"

Eliza jolted from sleep at the sound of her little boy happily calling to her from the crib in the next room, but Lachlan's arms shot out and he wrapped himself around her, preventing escape.

Her body immediately melted at his touch, but she pretended to put up a struggle. "Let me go," she laughed. "I'll bring Henry back in a second."

But even before he could reply, they heard laughter coming from their baby's bedroom, telling them that Hallie and Hamish had got to their little brother first. She relaxed back into the bed and rested her head against Lachlan's chest as they listened to their three children playing happily together.

Sometimes she still had to pinch herself when she woke up to Lachlan lying beside her and the sounds of Hallie, Hamish and Henry began to fill the house. It wasn't always easy holding down a relationship, running a restaurant and parenting three children with very different needs, but there was nowhere else she'd rather be and no one else she'd rather be sharing these responsibilities with.

"What are you thinking?" Lachlan whispered to her, his hands sliding suggestively down her body.

"I'm thinking I want you to feed us all pancakes for breakfast."

He laughed. Even though she was getting much better at cooking—and loved experimenting in the kitchen—he still made better pancakes than her and it wasn't only the kids that loved them.

"All right. You twisted my arm." With a quick kiss, Lachlan rolled out of bed and headed out of their room, saying, "But you can pay me back in kind later."

"It's a deal," she called out to him as she hugged a pillow to her chest and gazed over at the photo that still had pride of place on her bedside table. Only now, the bedside table was in a bedroom she shared with her husband, in a house they shared with the three kids who had become her world and, together with their father, given Eliza a reason to truly live again.

The day Henry was born, Lachlan had popped the question. He joked he'd been waiting for a moment when she wasn't thinking straight, but Eliza knew the truth—he hadn't wanted to rush her into anything. However, by then, they'd already been renting a house together in town while they waited for Mac and his team to build them a forever home, so it felt as if their fate was already sealed and she didn't want it any other way.

They'd waited only a few months before having a simple wedding at the distillery with only their closest family and friends and then the five of them had gone away on a honeymoon to Disneyworld together. She knew people thought they were crazy, going to such a place and taking their children with them, but Eliza hadn't been able to even contemplate the thought of leaving Hallie, Hamish and Henry with anyone else.

Even now, she sometimes panicked when she had to leave their baby with his grandmother or one of his uncles or aunties to go to work, but she loved working in the restaurant and each time, it was getting easier. With Lachlan's patience and the help of a counselor, she was dealing with her grief, her guilt and her fears. And the last thing she wanted to do was stifle Henry because of her past and her hang-ups.

"Mom! Time to wake up!" Hallie burst into the bedroom with Henry on her hip and Hamish not far behind them.

"I *am* awake!" Eliza proclaimed as she turned away from the photo. She laughed as Hallie plopped Henry into her arms and climbed up beside them. "How could I sleep with the noise you three make?"

"So-rry," Hamish said, looking a little sheepish as he stood with his crutches alongside them.

"Don't be silly," Eliza said, grinning at him. "Come up here and give me a hug."

Hamish didn't have to be asked twice and Eliza's heart swelled with love as Henry settled into her lap and the older children snuggled in on either side of her. As Lachlan clattered about in the kitchen making breakfast, she and the twins took turns making faces and trying to make Henry giggle while they waited for the pancakes to be ready.

Just when she thought Henry might explode if he laughed anymore, Lachlan popped his head around the door. "Sounds like I'm missing out on a lot of fun in here, but breakfast's ready."

"Yay! I'm starving!" As Hallie leaped from the bed and rushed past him, Hamish scrambled after her and Henry looked longingly after them both.

Eliza met her husband's gaze and smiled. "The moment this one can walk, we're in trouble. He'll be chasing after them for sure."

Lachlan nodded as he stepped up to the bed and held out his hands for their baby son. "True," he said, scooping Henry up into his arms. "But I wouldn't have it any other way. Now, are you coming to join us in the kitchen or doth the lady require breakfast in bed?"

She laughed. "I'm coming." As much as that idea appealed to her, sitting down and eating with her family appealed even more and so she tossed back the covers and climbed out of bed.

A few moments later, Eliza was sitting at the table, surrounded by the people she loved most in the world. Family, food and laughter, she thought, as she glanced from face to face—these were the simple things in life and they were the best.

* * * * *

HER LAS VEGAS WEDDING

ANDREA BOLTER

For Barbara and Moe

CHAPTER ONE

"Here comes the bride." Daniel Girard stood to greet his daughter as she entered his office. Audrey Girard plopped her flight bag down on a chair and gave her dad a peck on the cheek. As both the heiress to the Hotel Girard chain of fine boutique hotels and its director of public relations, she had a slew of things to take care of before their grand opening in Las Vegas. Not the least of which was to organize her wedding.

"When does Reg get in? You probably have more information about my fiancé's schedule than I do," she said. After all, her dad and Reg's father, Connor Murphy, had been planning this marriage between their offspring for the past couple of years. Connor owned the Lolly's chain of casual breakfast eateries that operated in several of the Girard hotels, and the families had been in business together for a decade.

"His flight comes in from LA later this afternoon."

Audrey's intended, Reginald Murphy, was the business half of Murphy Brothers Restaurants. His younger brother, Shane, was the long-haired, mercurial chef. Expanding the Murphy family's interests in the restaurant business, the two brothers had started their own venture. Together, they had crafted the upscale Shane's Table restaurants. After creating a destination dinner spot that was a hit from the moment it opened in New York, they duplicated the success with a second location in Los Angeles. Now they were collaborating with the Girards on this Las Vegas property and hoping Lady Luck would shine upon them here.

"Explain to me again why we're rushing the wedding?" Audrey asked her dad.

"We had never set a date."

"So why now?"

"You've seen the financial statements. We need a big opening for this hotel. A high-profile wedding will really showcase our special-events capabilities."

"So I've got one month to plan the whole thing?"

"We'll make the engagement announcement in two weeks to start generating a buzz."

"When I talked to Reg on the phone a couple of days ago, he didn't sound certain that he was on board with doing the wedding now."

"Connor has concerns about their financial position, as well. The Murphys need this hotel launch as much as we do."

"Gee, I'm glad my future has been reduced to profit and loss statements."

"You know that's not the only reason. Come on now, you're twenty-eight. Reg is, what, thirty-six?"

"You're right, Dad, I'm virtually an old maid."

"You can't blame a couple of fathers for pushing to get their kids to settle down. We want to see you two create a life together. You both work too hard. You should enjoy yourselves. Bring us grandchildren. Not to mention the next generation of hoteliers and restaurateurs."

"Dad, we've talked about that. Children are not in the picture." Not after what Audrey had been through. That was nonnegotiable.

"Never say never."

They moved to the spacious office's reception area, where each sat down on one of armchairs that faced the floor-to-ceiling windows. Audrey took in the view of a couple of the huge hotels and casinos on the Las Vegas Strip, and the majestic red mountains behind them in the distance.

The Hotel Girard Las Vegas sat on a small piece of real estate in between two of the giant monoliths on the Strip. It was originally built in the early 1960s as the Royal Neva Hotel, a sort of bargain casino with one-penny slot machines for visitors who weren't high rollers staying at the big palaces. The lone restaurant had offered two-dollar breakfast specials and the four floors of guest rooms were dirt cheap. The hotel never had the Rat Pack panache of Vegas's heyday, but the architecture was in the midcentury style that defined that era. When it went on sale after closing due to lack of upkeep, the Girards decided to make their first foray in Las Vegas.

With two hundred hotel rooms, as opposed to the three and four thousand of its neighbors, the Girards set out to refurbish the property to appeal to the trend toward boutique hotels, which were their specialty. There'd be no noisy casino. Instead, luxurious suites and amenities, a splendid rooftop pool, unique special-event spaces and exclusive cocktail lounges would provide a chic den for hip guests. The crème de la crème would be Shane's Table, a world-class dining establishment to attract travelers and Vegas locals alike.

Unfortunately, they'd encountered one problem after the next with the project. The original structure was in far worse condition than was initially thought. There had been mold and rot within the walls that required a costly teardown in sections of the hotel. Partial renovations during the years before the Girards bought the property hadn't included solar power or technical upgrades, and energy costs were double what they should have been.

There had been other setbacks to the business, as well, beginning three years ago when Audrey's mother was dying and Daniel was distracted from his duties as CEO.

"I think weddings are going to do it for us at this hotel," Daniel said enthusiastically.

Audrey's business mind agreed. "Special-occasion bookings will bring us a lot of revenue. We have so many great event spaces with this hotel. Showing off the property with a lavish wedding should be publicity gold."

"The marriage of hotel and restaurant royalty will brand the hotel with glamour that will stick in people's minds."

"I had some ideas on the flight here. We can shoot the engagement tea in the garden and a guys' night out at the cigar lounge this week. We'll calendar the press releases and photo spreads to hit after the engagement announcement. No one will know we shot the events ahead of time."

"You and Reg will be an imperial couple. It'll be the romance Las Vegas has always been known for."

Except for the actual romance part, Audrey thought. That was not in her plans. Love was a gamble she wasn't going to bet on. Love involved trust. She'd never fall for that hoax again.

Which is why she had become so contented with the agreement that she and Reg would wed. Yes, the arranged matrimony felt a bit like something involving territorial feudal kingdoms and armies. Yet, in a different light, having their future spouses decided by their fathers was a smart outsourcing of labor that neither she nor Reg had the time for.

The two were friendly toward each other. They had dinner if they were in the same city, spoke on the phone and had discussed the challenges that their lifestyles would bring to the marriage. With seven Girard hotels throughout the world and a soon-to-be third Shane's Table, they both traveled to and from their businesses almost all of the time and didn't foresee that changing. Reg was a workaholic just like Audrey.

Any comradery they could share would be healthy for her. Currently, she spent what little free time she had by herself. After a childhood where she'd so often been alone, pairing with someone would be a blessing.

She and Reg had concurred that while romantic love was right for some people, it wasn't for them. That compatibility was crucial. What a relief it would be to answer the social pressures to couple off, to find a significant other. There would be no more questions about her dating life from the well-meaning staff at the hotels. She'd always have a companion for events. There might even be shared hobbies and simple dinner-and-movie dates. The list went on.

Most importantly, it was utterly perfect that Reg had zero sex appeal. What Audrey surely didn't need was a man like Reg's brother, chef Shane. A hot-blooded beast who dripped raw power and primitive demands. Reg would never make her pulse flutter like Shane had since the moment she met him. Never cause her to shiver in anticipation of his every move. Never keep her up at night imagining secret pleasures.

"Is Shane on track with his cookbook?" Audrey asked her dad.

"I hear that's not going as smoothly as it should."

She wrinkled her nose, although the information didn't surprise her. With Shane Murphy's bad-boy chef reputation, not to mention his wife's sudden death two years ago, being behind on a deadline would come as no shock.

A peculiar warmth flushed down her neck when she thought of the photo of Shane she'd seen recently on a magazine cover, his almost-black eyes piercing whoever looked at the image. Her reaction to even a photograph of him was involuntary but a little embarrassing, especially as he was to become her brother-in-law. Anything to do with Shane seemed to affect her on a chemical level that she had no control over.

"I'll check into it. Not having the cookbook on schedule could turn into a major problem." Shane Murphy's first cookbook was another essential component of the publicity schedule for the Vegas opening.

"Shane is cooking dinner for you and Reg tonight at the restaurant. You can talk about it then."

Daniel filled his daughter in on the outcome of a meeting he'd had with the human-resources director earlier that day while she'd been on the flight. And about a resolution with a furniture distributor for their hotel in St. Thomas.

Mention of the island brought a wry half smile to Audrey's face with the memory of that weird moment with Shane a decade ago. To this day, the recollection still replayed often in her mind.

It was at the Hotel Girard St. Thomas in the US Virgin Islands that she'd first met the Murphy brothers. When she'd first encountered the volcanic force of nature known as chef Shane Murphy.

Audrey had been a short eighteen-year-old, hiding in baggy shirts because her body hadn't yet settled into its shape. Shane Murphy was the *enfant terrible* of the culinary world at just twenty-four. Reg, the staid older brother at twenty-six. Connor was opening the Lolly's café at the hotel and Shane was there to do a tasting menu in the hotel's formal dining room. The first Shane's Table had already become the hottest dinner reservation in New York, making Shane an instant star.

The two brothers couldn't be more different. Though both were tall, Reg was thin and tidy, save for a perpetually sweaty upper lip. He kept his hair closely cropped and always donned a tailored suit. In contrast Shane's dark curly hair brushed the shoulders of the rock band T-shirts he wore with his jeans. Reg, the immaculate professional, and Shane, the soulful artist. Black and white. Night and day. Shane had made an impression on her that she still carried to this day.

She hadn't seen Shane in person in many months other than through teleconferences, which he would often leave before they were halfway done. Audrey wondered how much his impatience or inattention had to do with the death of his wife two years ago. She knew firsthand how a loss like that could color everything that came after it.

Helping herself to a glass of icy cucumber water from the clear pitcher on the office bureau, she took a much-needed sip. As always seemed to be the case, mere mention of Shane Murphy made Audrey thirsty.

She paced in front of the windows of Daniel's third-floor office. Prior to the renovation, there had only been a couple of picture windows on that exterior wall. With the new sweeping vista she could look out to the hotels and casinos, or peer down to see street-level activity on the always-crowded Strip.

Audrey's eyes fixed on a couple. The young woman, blonde, short and curvaceous like she was, wore a white minidress and a clip-on bridal veil that looked like it hadn't cost much money. Her groom had on black suit pants and a white shirt with his tie loosened. The two laughed and passed an open bottle of champagne between them to sip from. The bride held her left hand up to the sunlight to admire the ring on her finger. They stopped walking and threw their arms around each other for a passionate kiss.

Las Vegas.

Land of hope. Of gambles. Of chances. Of love.

What would it be like to arrive in Vegas to wed the person you were in love with? Audrey wondered. To embark on a life together, sharing ideas and dreams and romance?

Audrey had no time for thoughts like that. She had her own, practical marriage to plan.

Having made her way from her father's office to the central courtyard of the hotel, Audrey stepped outside into the dry Nevada breeze. The main structure of the building formed a square with a public space in the center with walk-throughs to the Strip and parking so that patrons could enter the restaurants, bars and shops from both inside and outside the building. She was eager to settle into one of the freestanding suites at the back of the property they called the bungalows, where she'd make her home for the time being.

For the past couple of months, she'd been utterly buried by work in her small office at the hotel chain's Philadelphia headquarters. There were splashy incentives to organize and newsworthy stories to cull in order to promote all of the seven hotels for the summer season. Winter had thawed into spring without her really taking note of it.

Along her walk, she said hellos to construction workers and to staff members who were onsite to begin readying the hotel for the opening. This week she'd check in with every department to see what was new and note-worthy that she could use for publicity.

For now, though, she wanted to drop her luggage and check her emails and messages and texts. And see Reg, who had sounded so tentative when she last spoke with him.

As she crossed diagonally through the outdoor public area, she froze on her heels. The Shane's Table restaurant, not yet open for business, appeared to be fully finished, at least on the outside. In front of its door stood a life-sized cardboard cutout photo of chef Shane Murphy.

What the heck?

Audrey was director of public relations and any kind of promotion that went on at Girard hotels came across her desk. It was she who authorized press releases if one of the hotels even so much as bought new towels. If a landscape designer decided on an unusual type of plant for the grounds. When one of the hotels offered a Valentine's Day package that included breakfast in bed.

Yet she'd heard nothing about this horribly tacky six-foot-two-inch shrine to the male ego. What a monstrosity! Not at all befitting the elegance and restraint Girard hotels represented. Nor worthy of the Shane's Table reputation for integrity and excellence.

She didn't know who approved this amateur-hour attempt at marketing for the restaurant. But she was going to find out.

Bustling over, Audrey stopped dead in front of the display. Barely clocking in at five-foot-two herself, she had to crane her neck back to fully study Shane's likeness. The discomfort she always felt in his presence was just as palpable here in this massive photograph.

A wild toss of dark hair seemed to grow from his scalp in every direction as though it belonged on a mythological Medusa. A folded blue bandanna was tied across his forehead and under his hairline. Those black-as-night eyes were framed with long eyelashes and crowned by heavy brows. A straight nose led to full lips, parted slightly, surrounded by beard stubble above his mouth and across his lower cheek and square jaw.

The look on his face was a dare. To say this man was smoldering and dangerous was the understatement of the century. He was almost too much to take in, even in cardboard form. Thank goodness she was marrying safe Reg.

Audrey bit her lip to stay grounded and continue her survey of Shane.

His chef's coat fit well from one broad shoulder to the other. The coat's sleeves were cuffed twice to reveal hefty forearms with a dusting of dark hair. The arms crossed at his chest showcased black leather cording that formed bracelets wrapped around each wrist. One huge hand held a chef's knife.

An embroidered insignia on the chest of the chef's coat depicted his restaurant logo of a four-legged table with the name Shane scripted above it. The coat's hem hit Shane at mid hip, shorter than a typical chef preference. Fitted jeans encased the lower half of his body, with its straight hips and muscular legs. The jeans gave way to black motorcycle boots. One foot crossed over the other in a defiant stance.

Audrey's eyes did a ride up from the boots to the powerfully built chest to the heart-stopping lips. She followed individual locks of jet hair as each made a different wavy descent down around his face.

All she could say to herself was "Whoa!" as that flush swept across her neck again.

Audrey hated cardboard cutout displays that presented a person as some sort of whacked-out Greek statue or national monument. To her, they were a crass and crude form of advertising. But there was no question that Shane Murphy was a drop-dead sexy man. She was painfully aware of it every time she was around him. While it didn't directly have anything to do with his cooking, she wouldn't doubt that his fiery good looks contributed to his restaurants' success.

Nonetheless, Audrey was not about to have that eyesore muddy the sophistication of a Girard hotel. So she lifted cardboard Shane Murphy at his waist, tucked him under her arm and proceeded to her bungalow. As soon as she swiped her key card and let herself in, she propped Shane in a corner of the room facing the bed.

Dropping her bags, she made a three-hundred-sixty degree turn as she took in the finished renovation of the bungalow. The photo and video tours she'd seen didn't do it justice. An interior archway divided the suite into two distinct areas. In the sleeping portion, teal and brown bedding appointed the king bed, a palette that evoked the original sixties style. But a flat-screen smart TV mounted on the wall and tech stations on the two lightwood nightstands brought the room straight into the needs of today's guests. An armchair upholstered in stripes echoed the teal and added in green and cream colors. A reading lamp perched on an end table beside it.

Through the archway, a lightwood desk and chair provided a place to work or eat. Bright abstract paintings adorned the walls. A sitting area with a sleek gray sofa and low coffee table gave way to the sliding-glass door. Each bungalow had a private patio with two forest-green lounge chairs shaded by a partial veranda to give protection against the desert sun.

Audrey delighted at the perfection of the remodel. This was what put the Hotel Girard brand on the map. Everything carefully crafted from fine materials and designs perfectly executed.

Except for that stupid cutout of Shane Murphy, of course.

"There he is." Daniel nudged Audrey as they sat in a finished section of one of the hotel's cocktail lounges.

They both stood as Reg Murphy approached. Audrey's future husband was a slim man who stood ramrod straight. He wore a three-piece pinstriped suit. Audrey couldn't remember the last time she saw a man wear a vested suit.

She hadn't had a chance to unpack but had pulled an outfit from her garment bag for the evening. A conservative gray sheath dress and black sandals.

"Nice to see you, Reg."

"I guess this is finally it," he said as he extended his right hand as if to shake hers. Then he seemed to change his mind midstream and instead lifted her hand and turned it over to kiss the back of it. His supple palm pressed her fingers against his open lips. The whole maneuver was awkward and a bit moist.

"How was your flight?" Daniel asked as Reg vigorously shook his hand up and down.

"Fine, sir."

Audrey remembered Reg as being a bit more poised. Perhaps it was wedding jitters that made him appear so nervous. He stared at Daniel slack-jawed like he wanted to say something, but instead pulled a white handkerchief out of his jacket pocket and dabbed his upper lip.

"Are you in Vegas now until the opening?" Audrey asked.

"I may have to fly back to New York. You?"

"Yeah, I'm here. I've got our wedding to coordinate."

"Right." Reg nodded as if it were just sinking in. He glanced at his phone and read something on the screen that brought a huge smile to his lips. "Please pardon me a moment while I return this message."

He tapped onto the screen, grinning the entire time.

"Well," Daniel said using his right hand to pat Audrey's back and his left to tap Reg's, "I'll leave you two to your evening."

"Thanks, Dad."

After Daniel walked away, Reg and Audrey each perched on a stool beside the table. One of the four bars on the property, this space was located inside the main lobby and had stylish fun in mind. The decor was done with white barstools upholstered in deep purple velvet set around chrome pedestal tables. Behind the chrome cocktail bar was a giant glass tank filled with undulating purple goo similar to the lava lamps of the 1960s.

Once again, Girard's interior designers had worked through an idea to perfection. And then capable crews were able to bring the vision to fruition. Audrey could imagine the lounge with chic music playing in the background and filled with trendy patrons choosing drinks from a cocktail menu that offered libations with names like *Flip-Out Frappe* and *Yin-Yang-Yum*.

"After all of the talk about us marrying, this has come about rather suddenly, hasn't it?" Reg asked.

"Is there a problem with that?"

He seemed to be a million miles away. "Not at all."

"I think the extra push makes sense. Do everything at once. Open the hotel and Shane's Table. Shane's cookbook. Our marriage. It's a cascade of publicity on several levels."

Audrey knew that the Girard hotels had never really recovered from the events of three years ago. When her mother was dying and her father was unable to concentrate on the business. Audrey had tried as best she could to fill in for him. It was a gift to have the work to focus on since her mother hadn't wanted her at her bedside.

All of her life, it had been assumed that she'd grow up into the family business. As a teenager, she developed a knack for coming up with advertising ideas and events. The marketing side of the brand was a perfect fit for her after college.

Hotel Girard Incorporated was Audrey's entire world. Running around the properties as a kid, she had known every secret passageway. Every painting that hung in every guest room. Every item sold in the gift shops. Any happiness she could recollect took place within the borders of the hotels. The staff were loyal to Audrey and she was loyal to them. She'd do anything needed for their good. Even get married.

Besides, she thought Reg was a good match and she had become quite amenable to the marriage idea. He was smart. Nice-looking, too. Maybe a little too much hair product. Those short curls might look better if they weren't so stiff. He was poised and polite and she didn't know what the medical condition was that made a person have a sweaty upper lip but, hey, she thought she could overlook that.

And he was, safely, nothing like his brother. That split second ten years ago on St. Thomas flickered in her mind again. A freeze-frame in time that she still secretly compared everything else to.

"Should we go to dinner?" she asked. Reg seemed so uneasy tonight, perhaps a change of atmosphere would help. Devotion to the hotels was one thing but she wasn't going to go as far as to beg him to wed her if he didn't want to.

"Shane is cooking for us in the restaurant." Reg took Audrey by the bony part of her elbow and lead her out of the bar. "We are essentially the first guests at Shane's Table Las Vegas."

Along the way, Reg stopped to read and respond to another message on his phone. The same amusement that had come across his face earlier returned while he typed.

But he hesitated when they reached the restaurant's entrance. "Where is the display that's supposed to be here?"

"You mean that awful stand-up photo of Shane?"

"Name recognition is what Shane's Table is all about."

"I'm well aware of that. But that cardboard cutout was absurd. Brash advertising like that is not how Girard maintains its reputation for taste and understatement."

Not that a life-size photo of hottie Shane Murphy was hard on the eyes, but it was, nonetheless, inconsistent with the Girard style.

"You personally removed my advertising?"

She'd stood it up in her bungalow for the time being and now didn't seem the right time to confess that. "Reg, I'm head of public relations. I work alongside a marketing team and together we decide when and how best to…"

"I built Shane's Table into what it is today."

Wow, Audrey wasn't expecting this. She assumed Reg would respect her authority on this topic. He should have at least proposed the display prior to just having it planted it in front of the restaurant's doors, which was technically Girard property.

Audrey attempted to smooth ruffled feathers. "You know, Reg, perhaps I'm not a hundred percent clear on what our contracts state about my role concerning the PR specifically for the restaurant."

"I'll have my lawyers call yours in the morning."

She stroked his thin arm once up and once down in a

gesture of calming affection. "That's a great idea. Can we just put the issue aside for now and enjoy our dinner? I can't wait to see the completed dining room."

The pacifying technique worked because Reg pulled from his pocket a deadbolt key and an access fob to open the front door of the newly finished construction. He reached to flick on a temporary lamp that stood just inside the entrance.

Rock 'n' roll blared from the far end of the restaurant. Reg gestured for Audrey to follow him across the dark dining room and through the double doors leading into the kitchen.

The lone man in the cavernous space stood with his back facing them, but Audrey easily recognized that long curly hair and the broad shoulders that filled out his chef's coat. The music was turned up so loud that he hadn't noticed anyone had entered. His head bobbed and his hips ground to the beat as he sautéed something smoking hot on the stove in front of him. Reaching for a spoon, he tasted from the pan.

"Garbage," he decreed and, in frustration, threw the spoon into the nearby sink.

Only then did he turn enough to be startled by Reg and Audrey's presence. He grimaced. His gorgeous full lips twisted. A pulse beat in his neck. His eyes locked on Audrey.

"Audrey," Reg yelled above the music, "you remember my brother, Shane Murphy."

CHAPTER TWO

"HI, SHANE," Audrey said, turning on the polish. In reality, his intense stare made her heart skip every other beat. "Can you believe it was a full year ago when we stood right here after the old restaurant had been gutted?"

Shane slowly, sinfully, with no restraint whatsoever, inventoried her. From the part in her blond hair, across her face, down every curve of her fitted dress and shapely legs, through her sandals to the tips of her orange-painted toes.

Her legs twitched from his gaze.

He mashed his lips together as he shifted something internally and turned his attention to his brother. "I mixed a white sangria and put it on the bar. Why don't you take Audrey into the dining room and pour it, Reg?"

"Join us for a glass, won't you?"

Unspoken communication passed between the two brothers.

"I'll be out with some appetizers in a few minutes."

Reg ushered Audrey out of the kitchen and turned on the overhead lighting.

The restaurant was a showstopper. One entire wall made of glass looked out to a furnished patio. A wood-burning oven, large grill and two fire pits would allow for al fresco cooking. The open-air space was enclosed by a semi-circular wall made of small stones. At three points, waterfalls rained down. The effect was that of a private outdoor world far from the bright lights of Las Vegas.

Inside, shaded lighting fixtures hung from the ceiling to cast a play of light and shadow throughout the room. Tall-backed chairs cushioned in an olive-colored fabric, teakwood tables and booths dotted the dining room, each placed with enough space between them to allow for dinner conversation. Carpeting in a subtle diamond pattern of khaki and red would muffle the din of a full house. Stone tiling on the walls gave the room a lodge feel that was posh but comfortable.

Audrey took her time inspecting it all. "Everything turned out spectacularly."

Reg guided Audrey by the tip of her elbow again, a trend she wasn't enjoying, to the one table in the center of the dining room that had been set for dinner.

"I'll get the wine," he said as he pulled out one of the chairs for her. Then he hopped down the three steps to the bar to retrieve a carafe. "Shane used a 2009 pinot gris from the local Desert Castle vineyard we're working with," Reg announced as he poured each of them a glass. Crisp green apple slices and chunks of fresh peaches floated in the drink.

"Nice," Audrey said after a quick sip, never one to drink much alcohol. Not after what she had witnessed. "You're staying in a condo in Vegas?"

"In the Henderson suburb. I suppose when the two of us…" Reg stopped, seemingly at a total loss of how to complete the sentence. "Shane leases a flat behind the Strip," he added and ran the back of his index finger under his nose.

"Will he base himself mostly in Vegas?"

"For a while. When we first opened in Los Angeles, it took a year until we were functioning smoothly."

"It takes a long time to build a core staff that you feel confident in. People don't work out. You hire new ones."

"Shane is very exacting in what he expects. As you'll recall."

A flush of heat spread down Audrey's neck.

"Ten years was a long time ago." Audrey made reference to the St. Thomas collaboration. "I was just starting college so I wasn't really involved, but I do have a vague memory," she fibbed when, in fact, she remembered every second of that summer.

The twenty-four-year-old wunderkind chef and his demands in the kitchen had been legendary. "Didn't the controversy begin with some herb we couldn't get onto the island?"

"I still don't know how I was supposed to make a yellow mole without hoja santa." Shane's thick vibrato filled the dining room. Audrey didn't know how they had failed to hear him come out from the kitchen.

The surprise sent a blush all the way under the neckline of her dress.

"And your idiot sous chef suggested I use cilantro."

"I was all of eighteen so, believe me, I was just an innocent bystander at the time."

"We were on a tiny island, Shane." Reg lifted his palms. "They weren't able to fly in your herb."

Shane held two small plates. Audrey took notice of the black leather cords he had roped around his wrists like the ones he wore in the cardboard cutout. There was something so rebellious about them. She'd never known a chef to wear jewelry on his hands. Yet she found them as mysterious and exciting as the man who donned them.

His hands were so massive they made the dishes of food he carried look tiny.

"Nevada appears to be the motherlode for the ingredients I need," Shane said as he placed one plate in front of each of them. "Chiles en nogada. Poblano stuffed with pork, pear and mango and topped with a walnut cream sauce."

Audrey's eyes widened at the striking presentation on the plate. She knew that the sprinkle of diced red and green peppers on top of the white sauce was in homage to the colors of the Mexican flag. The foundation of Shane Murphy's menus was in the flavors of the Spanish-speaking world.

While Shane waited intently, she took a bite, careful to get a little morsel of each ingredient onto her fork. The rich cream fragrant with ground walnuts brought a decadent lushness to the pork, yet the dots of fruit kept the dish from being too heavy.

Audrey closed her eyes to savor the combination.

Depriving herself of sight, she could sense even more powerfully how Shane's eyes bored into her face. Making her feel somehow exposed and beautiful at the same time.

She whispered upon opening her eyes and looking at Shane again, "Magnificent." Possibly in reference to the food.

Shane pulled a fork out of the back pocket of his jeans and showed it to Reg. "There was a mistake with the order that came in today. Three tines? Am I serving Neanderthals?"

Without another word, Shane turned and returned to the kitchen.

Audrey noticed the four tines on the fork she was holding. She appreciated how important every small decision was for these consummate professionals. It was the same level of concern the Girards applied to their hotels.

"Audrey, I need to talk to you."

They were only on the appetizer and she was already feeling unfocused and exhausted from being around Shane. Reg had just said something, but she hadn't really heard him. "Has Shane always been so—" she chose her word "—fierce?" Although she guessed the answer.

"Since the day he was born." Reg shook his head. "Our grandmother Lolly, who taught him how to cook her old Irish recipes, used to call him Mr. Firecracker. Of course, since Melina died he's been grappling with his own demons. Forks are the least of his problems."

The loss of his wife had left behind a wounded ogre. Audrey knew the story. The young woman who had been killed instantly in a car accident during a snowstorm in the woods of upstate New York. She hadn't seen the Murphys very often during that time period, but her dad had sent flowers and reached out to Connor to offer his support.

Audrey asked Reg, "Does Shane talk about her?"

Reg dabbed under his nose and sounded exasperated when he questioned, "Why are we spending so much time discussing Shane?"

In his kitchen, Shane took out his frustration on the mint he tore for the salad. With a syncopated rhythm, he ripped leaves from their stems and threw them onto a work board. His preferred soundtrack of hard rock music did little to squelch the thoughts stomping through his head.

When he'd first heard this master scheme of Audrey Girard being matched up with his brother, he heartily approved. Reg spent far too much time agonizing over spreadsheets, finding fault with staff members and riding Shane about the cookbook or the lagging business. Hopefully a wife would take up some of Reg's attention and get him off of everyone else's back.

But now, face-to-face with Audrey again, the whole idea angered him. Wasn't she just a little too pretty, a lot too sexy and even a bit too independent to be with up-tight Reg? He loved his brother and wanted the best for him, but Audrey was too fine a lamb to be offered up for this sacrifice.

During the meetings regarding the new restaurant, he'd observed petite but voluptuous Audrey Girard in action. In her tight business skirts, she moved with the charged-up energy to match the clack of her high-heeled shoes. In fact, memories of her would linger in his mind for days after every encounter.

While Shane wielded his knife to halve the cherry to-matoes, a tight smile crossed his lips. He remembered the first time he'd met Audrey, still in her teens back then, during that summer in St. Thomas when he was doing a promotional stint as a guest chef.

She had been scared to death of him. Who could blame her? At twenty-four, with his heavy boots and impossi-ble standards, he must have cut a frightening figure. An-other sneer broke through as he realized that not much had changed since then.

Except for two massively successful restaurants that had made his name a household word. Although the world didn't know that the restaurants had ceased making the profits they used to. Had anyone noticed that he was no longer asked to make appearances on national morning TV talk shows? That the public had moved on to new culinary revelations, new rising-star chefs? One thing they did know was that Shane Murphy had lost his wife to a gruesome death.

He plated the tomatoes and crumbled cojita cheese on them. Yes, he still remembered Audrey Girard and that midnight ocean swim. He flicked the mint on top of the cheese. Drizzled on olive oil and finished with a dotting of manzanilla olives. He could do this salad in his sleep.

All afternoon, he had been alone in the kitchen, trying to come up with a fresh idea. Just one new recipe for the cookbook. A start.

But he'd only spun his wheels. Unable to summon a clear vision. Nothing was right.

A muse was nowhere to be found.

"Aha," Shane heard Reg call out as he entered the dining room with the salads he'd served tens of thousands of in his restaurants. "We were just talking about the cookbook."

"What about it?" Shane already knew where this conversation was going.

"That perhaps we'll shoot some photos of you on the patio," Reg said. "Fire up the grill out there, and you can do street tacos with a party crowd surrounding you."

Shane placed the salad plates on an empty table nearby so that he could clear Reg and Audrey's appetizers away before serving. Audrey had only eaten a few bites of the poblano.

"You didn't like it," he announced rather than inquired.

Audrey looked up at him with her big eyes. He hadn't remembered how light a brown they were. The color of honey. "It was delicious," she answered, as if she thought that was something she needed to say.

"I see."

Shane kept his connection with Audrey's seductive orbs while Reg asked, "Are you any closer to actually finishing the cookbook, brother? Or even beginning it?"

"Enjoy the salad," Shane uttered between clenched teeth.

Back in the kitchen, he dialed up his music even louder.

Even if he didn't like it, he could see how the pairing of Reg and Audrey would benefit business. That was an important consideration now that Murphy Brothers Restaurants needed to take a huge step forward. A soaring success here could lead to more Shane's Table restaurants in other Girard hotels.

Shane rocked his hips to the beat of a heavy metal song as he deveined the shrimp for the Guatemalan tapado.

And let's face it, his brother needed to get married. A woman's touch was going to be the only way to get Reg to lighten up. Plus their parents, now semiretired, longed for grandchildren. Shane would never marry again or have children. Reg was their only hope.

His dad and Daniel Girard used to joke around about matchmaking Reg and Audrey, but after Melina's death the talk became serious. Shane had made an impulsive marriage that ended in disaster. His father probably felt he needed to step in to insure his other son had a more controllable fate.

After a hand wash, Shane began sautéing the onions and peppers.

One marriage was quite enough for Shane, thank you very much. He was clearly not to be trusted with the well-being of another person. Not a day went by that he didn't think about the death that maybe he could have prevented. Had he been a different person. In fairness if Melina had been, too.

Shane added the coconut milk that was the basis of the sauce to the sauté pan. Mixed in a ladleful of stock. Stirred in his seasonings.

If a Murphy brother was to marry, it was definitely going to be Reg.

Then why did he picture Audrey, with those spectacular golden eyes smiling at him, while a voice to the side of them asked, "Shane Niall Murphy, do you take this woman…?" Why was he picturing lifting a white-dressed Audrey up into his arms and carrying her over a doorway threshold into a private suite?

Tossing the shrimp into his sauce, he reckoned that the prospect of anyone getting married probably brought up twisted wedding images for him. He was just having a distorted waking nightmare about Melina.

Swirling in a handful of chopped chard, he finished the dish. He portioned cooked rice onto two plates and spooned his stew on top of each. Another recipe he could cook with his eyes closed.

Coming out from the kitchen with his tapado de camaron, Shane noticed from twenty feet away that Audrey hadn't finished her salad. Was she one of *those* girls, who only pecked at food? He'd always noticed the seriously lush curves on that small frame of hers. She didn't look like a bird who didn't eat.

Were his flavors too unusual for her? Was she used to a blander palate?

He placed the dinner dishes down on the side table.

"You didn't like the salad, either." He hastily snatched Audrey's barely touched plate. "I sell a lot of them."

"It was lovely, I'm just not that hungry," Audrey sputtered like she was making an excuse.

Shane served his entrée.

"Have a seat with us," Reg instructed, gesturing for Shane to pull a chair over from one of the other tables. Reg refilled his own sangria glass and slid it into position for Shane to have it. Audrey's was barely touched.

For all of his brother's annoyances, Shane respected Reg more than anyone in the world. Reg had provided the necessary foresight and know-how to lift Shane's Table to fame. Shane could never have done any of it without him.

Reg had taught him that he had to play the game sometimes, had to make nice with people even when he'd rather be hiding in the kitchen. So he obeyed his brother, turned around a chair and straddled it backward to sit down with them.

"We need to have a discussion about the cookbook," Reg said with a concerned look. Had they been spending the whole dinner talking about him? "You know we've committed to a date with the publisher and they, in turn, agreed to create a mock-up so we can do marketing with it."

"If it's a mock-up, then it could be filled with empty pages—what's the difference?"

"Because you have a contract with them, saying that you're going to deliver a cookbook," Audrey added. "They're not going to go forward if you're not going to meet the deadline."

"The TV taping is going to bring you and the restaurant into the living room of millions of viewers," Reg said.

"We'll not only sell cookbooks," Audrey said, "but it will bring people to Vegas to eat at Shane's Table."

"You know we all need this," his brother added.

"The publicity could put us at capacity for a year," Audrey stressed.

Reg and Audrey both paused to take bites of their tapado. Reg gestured his approval while Audrey stayed straight-faced and chewed slowly. Reg asked, "Have you even started it?"

"Enough already. I get it. I have to deliver the cookbook." With that, Shane hitched up from the chair and stomped back into the kitchen.

Annoyed, he portioned the pastel de tres leches he had made this afternoon. He hated being ganged up on like that. Hated all of that aggressive sales-y behavior, even though he knew that was what it took to be successful. Just as he knew he wasn't at all cut out for it. And as for that smart-talking bombshell Audrey... He'd like to show her how actions spoke louder than words.

Shane, he reprimanded himself, *Audrey is going to be your sister-in-law. You do not kiss your sister-in-law. You do not even think about kissing your sister-in-law. For heaven's sake.*

Yet he lingered on a mental image of feeding her something delicious with his fingers.

After he and rock 'n' roll had cleaned up the kitchen, he'd blown off enough steam to go serve the pastel.

Assuming this would be the fourth dish Audrey picked at but didn't finish, he placed the plate in front of her without much enthusiasm even though he knew this dessert was always a hit.

She gawked at the cake. Took a small forkful. As she slipped it between lips that were as juicy as the plums Shane'd had for breakfast that morning, he could swear he saw her eyelashes flutter. After her bite, she managed, "Wow."

"It's called tres leches because it's got condensed milk, evaporated milk and cream," he said of the sponge cake soaked in the custardy milk mixture and topped with whipped cream to make it even richer.

She took another demure forkful. Which was quickly followed with another, not as ladylike in size as the previous. Both Shane and Reg couldn't help but watch as she devoured one bite after the next.

The three chitchatted a bit about a successful New York bakery chain and how they went about their expansion.

Shane hadn't seen Reg in a couple of weeks. Something more than his usual worries was bothering him. He'd thought his brother had been in favor of this friendly marriage to Audrey. Maybe something had changed. He needed to speak with him privately.

But in between snippets of conversation, Audrey took bite after bite of the cake. Until it was gone. She made a final swirl around the plate with her fork to capture any bits that might have been left behind.

Then she pointed to Reg's plate. "Are you going to finish yours?"

Gotcha! A pirate grin slashed across Shane's mouth. After she'd barely eaten the dinner, he finally had her. "Now we see what you like, Sugar."

Audrey swiped the key card to her bungalow, opened the door and immediately eyed the cardboard cutout of Shane she had removed from the restaurant entrance earlier. "What are you looking at?" she snapped at the photo, which seemed to have a raised eyebrow she didn't remember from earlier.

No sooner had she arrived in Vegas than three handsome men had overwhelmed her. One was her father. She knew Daniel wanted the best for her and his concern for her unmarried status was at least half of his motivation in the matchmaking. Two tall, dark and handsome brothers were the other players.

The idea of a marriage being arranged and handed to her in a neat organized file was a relief. At twenty-eight, she knew she had decades of work ahead of her to keep up the Girard legacy that her father, and his father before him, had worked so hard to build. Yet she knew that going it completely alone could be a hard path.

A distant and uncaring mother had cured her of any silly dreams about a love that takes a whole heart. She would never set herself up for that kind of hurt again. Words like *allegiance* and *devotion* had been removed from her dictionary. *Sensible* and *logical* were welcome.

Timing the wedding to coincide with the opening was a good move. Audrey hoped Reg felt the same way. He had never gotten around to telling her what he wanted to talk to her about tonight, partially because he became invisible every time his brother burst into the dining room.

Shane was a thunderstorm of a man, all mysterious dark skies and punishing rain. Obviously still not over the death of his wife, he hulked under a cloud. That obsession with what she was, and wasn't, eating had been so annoying. Audrey snarked at the photo of him in the corner. How smug he had become when she couldn't stop eating that unbelievably scrumptious tres leches cake.

Throwing one of her suitcases up on the bed, she started to unpack as she hadn't had time to earlier. In a month she'd be married to Reg. There was no reason to care what the other Murphy brother thought of her. Yet when she unzipped the interior, she almost convinced herself that she had to open the flap in a direction that blocked Shane's photo from seeing what was inside. Was she crazy?

Okay, Shane. Here it is, she thought defensively as she pulled the first item from the case. Cookies. Yes, she had brought package upon package of her favorite cookies from Philadelphia! She didn't know if they would carry them in Vegas stores so she had stuffed as many as she could into her luggage. And not just cookies. There were boxes of candy from a famous Philadelphia chocolatier, too. There was no way she could live without those. When she ran out, she'd order more online.

"I like sweets. So what?" she challenged Shane's disapproving expression. He had no business becoming the third man prying into her affairs. She should just get that six feet and two inches of cardboard out of the bungalow tonight and be done with it. Hopefully Reg would ask for it tomorrow.

Yet somehow she liked it right where it was. Those deep, dark eyes of Shane's were magnets that pulled her in and wouldn't let go. She wanted to dive into those eyes, to understand the complexity, agony and secrets she knew lay beneath them. As nice as the furnishings in the suite were, Shane was clearly the focal point.

Once she emptied her suitcases, she picked out a nightgown and went to change in the bathroom so as not to let Shane's photo see her naked. *Bonkers*, she confirmed to herself, but did it anyway.

After she pulled back the covers on the bed and climbed in, she realized she wasn't the slightest bit tired. So she didn't turn off the bedside lamp. She examined Shane's full lips. Wondered how that beard stubble would feel against the delicate skin of her neck. Scratchy and rough in the most divine way, she figured. And she pondered his tangle of dark hair, the snug fit of his jeans, those leather cord bracelets!

No, Audrey didn't lie down and go to sleep. Instead, she bolstered up her pillows. Leaned back and laced her fingers behind her head.

She was going to win this staredown with Shane.

Even if it took all night.

Shane leaned back against one of the archways in the wedding pavilion, an outdoor terrace space shaded by an awning and edged by long rectangular planters filled with desert succulents. The late afternoon sun had moved toward the mountains and he crossed one leg over the other and folded his arms across his chest to settle in for a gander at the spectacle at hand. The pain-in-the-behind photographer who had just tortured him through a session in the restaurant was now at work on Audrey and Reg.

The guy and his assistant buzzed around like bees. Positioning Reg's hand a couple of inches higher, repinning one lock of Audrey's glossy hair, patting Reg's face with a cloth.

Shane didn't like the way Audrey was fashioned today. Was that some stylist's idea of the blushing bride to be? The updo hair was far too prim for someone as sexy as Audrey. The floral-print dress and pink shoes looked too country club. That sweet image was pretty on some women. But it just wasn't Audrey. He wanted to smear that pink lipstick right off of her mouth.

He chuckled to himself as the bees swarmed around the happy couple, posing them this way or that. If it was up to him, he would have Audrey in a bloodred dress cut way down to there, fitted enough to hug every one of her tempting curves. He'd leave that exquisite blond hair unfastened and free. And he wouldn't allow a speck of makeup to come between her smoothness and his hands or mouth.

There he went again, conjuring up improper images about the woman who was betrothed to his brother! And even if she wasn't, he was never going to marry again so he didn't need to be fantasizing about what his fiancée would wear in their engagement photos. Ridiculous.

Daniel Girard appeared from the other end of the pavilion nicely dressed in a beige suit.

Shane had on his signature chef's coat and jeans.

"Daniel, Shane, we're ready to bring you in for a couple of shots," the head bee called.

With a roll of the eyes, Shane trudged over. The Murphy brothers with their partners in business, and now in life, the Girards. Shane was apparently about to become Audrey's brother-in-law.

He had burned the few photos of him and Melina that they had taken the day they went to a justice of the peace in New York to become a legally married couple. It had been a no-fuss ceremony. Afterward, they'd had lunch with Reg, Shane's parents and Melina's mother. Melina's estranged father was not in attendance.

When he looked back on it, Shane wasn't really sure why he had agreed to marry Melina. It was she who'd wanted to. As a young man with the level of fame the restaurants brought, Shane attracted more than his fair share of chef groupies. He supposed Melina pressured him into marriage to try to insure his fidelity. The truth was that he'd been so immersed in cooking and the restaurants at that point, she needn't have worried. Though he did seek acclaim, he had no interest in sexual dalliances.

Melina was an outcast blueblood. Her father, a wildly successful mogul overseas, had cut her off because of her party lifestyle, but that hadn't changed her ways. Shane met her at an art gallery opening after he had returned to New York once the LA restaurant was up and running.

She was an eccentric who sang in a band. As a young star chef, Shane had temporarily enjoyed the diversion of her rock 'n' roll crowd, who were in great contrast to the luminaries of New York who came into the restaurant.

But he'd tired of the superficiality of Melina's orbit. And had become acutely aware that they were not growing closer. They were not turning marriage into a foundation to stand on together. Their apartment was not a home.

It had been a reckless and immature decision to marry Melina. Even their nuptials were a spur-of-the-moment plan on a Tuesday afternoon. They had never been right together.

His four years with her were now comingled with memories regarding the horror of her death. The phone call from the highway patrol. Police officers who were gracious enough to come to the cabin to pick him up during the snowstorm and drive him to identify his wife's body.

Shane hadn't even been a guest at a wedding in many years, so he'd forgotten about all of the pomplike engagement photos. Now, the next wedding he'd attend would be his brother's. Studying Audrey again, whose mere being seemed to light something buried down inside of him, he simply couldn't picture her and his brother together.

Reg seemed ill at ease with this photo shoot, breaking frequently to text. They hadn't had a chance to talk privately last night, but Shane could tell his brother was bearing the weight of the world on his slim shoulders.

After the last photos were taken and the bees left, Reg's phone rang and he took the call. Shane didn't like the look of alarm that came over his face. "Rick in New York." Reg identified the caller. "Shane, take Audrey into the kitchen and show her the progress you've made on the cookbook so far."

"Alright, let's go." Shane took Audrey by her hand, which was even tinier and softer than he'd imagined it was going to be, and tugged her in his direction. There wasn't much to show her but maybe it was time he assessed what he had.

In the restaurant kitchen, Shane rifled through the papers on his desk, all of which needed his attention. From under them he pulled a tattered manila folder. He dumped its contents onto a countertop.

Audrey looked surprised but managed a pursed lip.

"This is how I work," he said.

Ideas for recipes were written on food-stained pieces of paper. On napkins where the ink had smeared. On sticky notes that were stuck together. On the backs of packing slips from food deliveries. On shards of cardboard he'd torn from a box. There was one written on a section of a dirty apron.

"O…kay," Audrey prompted, "tell me exactly what's here."

He glanced down to the front of the floral dress she was wearing for the photo shoot. The pattern of the fabric was relentless in its repetition of pink, yellow and orange flowers. Begonias, if he had to guess. The way she filled out the dress sent his mind wondering about what sweet scents and earthly miracles he might find beneath the thin material.

Shane wanted to know what was under the dress, both literally and figuratively. She was an accomplished woman yet he thought there was something untouched and undernurtured in her.

He admonished himself for again thinking of his brother's soon-to-be bride, although he took a strange reassurance in the fact that this was an arranged marriage between people who were not in love.

Still, it was nothing he had any business getting involved in.

What he needed to concentrate on were these scraps of paper that were to become one of those sleek and expensive cookbooks that people laid on their coffee table as a design accessory and never cooked from. A book whose pages held close-up pictures of glistening grapes and of Shane tossing a skillet of wild mushrooms.

"These are my notes." A scrap from the pile caught his eye. "Feijoada."

He'd scribbled that idea over a year ago. When Reg had asked him to think about how to make use of the lesser cuts of pork he had left over from other recipes. "I've seen Brazilians throw everything into this stew, the ears, the snout, all of it. The whole pot simmers with the black beans for a long time and you squeeze the flavor out of every morsel."

"Let's see what you have," Audrey offered. She leaned close to him to read the note together.

His tendons tightened at the sweet smell of her hair.

"There are no amounts for the ingredients," she observed.

"Obviously."

"How are we going to use these notes for recipes then?"

"I have no idea."

"How do you get the dishes to taste the same every time if you don't have the measurements written down?"

"I feel it. They don't come out exactly the same every time."

"You feel it." She bit her lip. "Then how would someone at home be able to cook them?"

"They wouldn't."

Shane watched Audrey's expression go from irritated to intelligent as she thought through what she should say next. "You're not at Shane's Table in New York and Los Angeles cooking every single dish. How does your staff prepare the food?"

"Of course the restaurant menu recipes are written down. We'll use a few Shane's Table guest favorites for the book. But it's supposed to be all new food. Reg promised we'd deliver fresh, rustic and regional, and I'm still working on the dishes. The measurements are the least of my problems."

Audrey took a big breath into her lungs and held it there.

She sure looked adorable when she was thinking.

"I'm trying to work with you here, Shane." She exhaled. He liked hearing her say his name. "The restaurant menu had to have been ideas in your head at the beginning. How did you develop the recipes for those?"

"That was a long time ago." Before Melina died. Before grief and frustration and anger clouded his mind and heart. Nowadays he went through the motions but stayed under the darkness. Which was how he wanted it. Or thought he did anyway.

Another Shane's Table was opening. Truthfully, so what? A cookbook as a publicity stunt Reg said would bring their brand to every corner of the world. So what? The Feed U Project with the kids was about all he cared about anymore. Just as he and his family had done in a dozen other locations, he'd turned a warehouse in downtown Vegas into a kitchen where he taught local kids how to cook.

Reg's call interrupted his musing. His brother wanted to meet right away.

"I gotta go, Sugar," he said to the five-foot-two ray of light.

"I thought we were supposed to achieve something on the cookbook today."

He turned to the pan he had cooling on a nearby rack. With his fingers, he broke off a taste of what he had baked earlier. From an old recipe that it had occurred to him to whip up this morning. With Audrey in mind, if he was being honest.

"Pan de dulce de leche. Caramel." Shane popped the chunk of still-warm cake into her delectable mouth.

CHAPTER THREE

"It's BAD," Reg told Shane as they reached the edge of the pool after a lap. "Much worse than we thought."

"Kitchen or front-of-the-house kind of worse?" Shane knew the New York and Los Angeles restaurants weren't making the profits they once were but, apparently, that wasn't the extent of it.

He shook some water from his hair.

When Reg had called while he was in the kitchen with Audrey half an hour ago, Shane suggested they meet for a swim in the employee pool. The Girards made a practice of building a private pool or gym at all of their hotels exclusively for the employees to enjoy. Though this pool was small and not at all like the deluxe rooftop pool area for guests, it was a handy, gated-off oasis that Shane had taken to using often.

"Both kinds of worse," Reg continued his report. Shane could tell from the tone in his brother's voice that this wasn't just going to be "the price of tablecloths went up" bad.

"What?"

"Lee quit." Their executive chef in New York. The man they had left in charge of running the kitchen while they kept their eye on LA and put their energies into getting this third restaurant off the ground.

Shane's jaw flexed in disbelief. "Why?"

He'd always had a good relationship with Lee, whose friendly disposition never wavered no matter how difficult Shane could be.

"He got a better offer. A full partnership in London. Doing Korean food."

Shane sighed. "That's what he always wanted."

"Effective immediately," Reg added.

"Effective immediately?"

"I don't have a lot of the details," Reg continued. "He apologized profusely. Said he'd call you."

"No executive chef in New York." This was devastating. Shane couldn't be in three places at once. He'd counted on Lee remaining a major part of the team. Still, he understood. Lee was a Korean American who longed to elevate the flavorful food he loved to a fine-dining clientele.

Shane dunked his head under the water and then popped back up.

"That's not all." With the setting sun casting a shadow over Reg's face, Shane could see the disquiet in his brother's eyes.

"Okay, what?" Shane didn't want to hear whatever it was Reg was going to say, but knew he needed to.

"Rick reviewed the monthlies in New York and there are big discrepancies in the cash receipts." Rick was their accountant in charge of balancing their books.

"Meaning what?"

"Meaning someone at the restaurant is stealing from us."

Not again. This had happened before. Unfortunately, when cash changed hands sometimes some of it disappeared. But it had never been a large enough amount to warrant the tightness currently in Reg's voice.

"How much money?"

Reg gave Shane a figure that set his pulse racing.

He pushed away from the side of the pool. This was everything he disliked about being in business. Dealing with staff and money and logistics was never his forte. All he'd ever wanted was just to cook and let his brother handle the rest of it. Yet now it was do or die. If Murphy Brothers Restaurants was going to have a future, he was going to have to extend himself past that comfort zone and start tackling these problems head-on.

Yet he wasn't sure he'd be able to. Knew that he, himself, was the biggest problem.

Shane dove deep underwater and swam the length of pool without coming up for air. Took a quick gulp at the other end and then did the same on the way back. When he emerged, Reg hadn't moved and was staring out at nothing in particular.

"Race." Shane challenged his brother to a lap across the pool. A slight grin crossed Reg's thin lips. Growing up, neither Murphy brother was a star athlete. Reg was more likely to have a book in his hand than a ball. But Shane would walk over to the playground in their Brooklyn neighborhood and shoot some basketball with whatever kids were hanging around.

"Go." The two brothers sprinted through the water. Shane narrowly edged Reg to the end of the pool. He felt nothing at his victory. It was just a stall tactic before continuing the conversation.

The problem was they were both spending so much time in Vegas. They'd been flying back and forth to the other restaurants as much as possible, but that was no substitute for being there night after night.

When they opened the Los Angeles restaurant, they had taken turns being on each coast. And opening the Las

Vegas location had been manageable because they had thought the New York restaurant was in capable hands. They were wrong.

"What are we going to do?" Shane looked straight at his brother.

"I don't think we have a choice. I'll have to go back to New York and be there every night to oversee operations."

"Reg, you know I can't run things on my own here."

No one knew better than Reg that, not only was Shane incapable of the minutia involved in operating the restaurants, but since Melina died his concentration and patience were at zero. Even the cookbook, which should have been a joy, eluded him.

"We've got Rachel in LA training Enrique to be general manager here." Reg was focusing on solutions, thank goodness. "We'll bring him to Vegas now and Rachel can talk him through whatever comes up."

Shane would feel better with Enrique here. Many of the new staff had been hired. Perhaps some could start earlier than agreed upon to provide extra help.

"I'll be back a few days before the opening," Reg continued. "We'll still talk every day."

Shane's brother was a smart man who could have had a career doing anything he wanted. The two grew up working in the Brooklyn diner that their grandmother started, and then in the Lolly's chain named after her.

Their predispositions started early. Shane was always at Grandma Lolly's apron, learning to cook the sturdy Irish dishes that she had learned from her own mother who'd brought them with her when she emigrated from Limerick. And young Reg kept his eye on the money, suggesting that they add a particular menu item or buy from certain vendors in order to maximize profit. When Shane proved to be a true culinary prodigy, Reg saw the business opportunity. They had a symmetry that had worked.

For a few years. Until Melina died. Until new chefs started grabbing the public's attention. Until the already reclusive Shane disappeared into himself.

"There's more," Reg continued.

Shane splashed water on his face and exhaled an extended breath through his nose. He didn't know how much more he could take in one night. "Okay, better to have it all dumped at once."

"It's about Brittany."

"Our assistant bar manager in New York?"

"Yes."

"What?"

Audrey fought with the zipper of the flowered dress she'd had on for the engagement shoot earlier. She hadn't been thrilled with it but they'd needed to take some practice publicity photos today. Without a minute to come back to change, she'd kept the dress on all day but now tugged it off and threw it across the room, narrowly missing Shane's face on the stand-up photo that was still propped in her bungalow. She had to rush to an appointment to pick a wedding gown. With only a month until the ceremony, there was barely time to have it ordered and altered.

Charging around the room in her white undies, she no longer cared what cardboard Shane thought of her. In her secret nightstand drawer, she reached for one of the stashed chocolates she had brought from Philadelphia. Which, although it was her absolute favorite kind, paled in comparison to the caramel cake Shane had teased her with a little while ago.

Her eyes rolled back in her head at the memory of that

warm and gooey concoction delighting her taste buds. And how he had fed it to her with his fingers. His fingers! His thick, insistent fingers. She should have been deeply offended by his informality. Yet instead she'd been so powerfully aroused she could hardly keep her eyes open.

Once again, she thanked her lucky stars that she was marrying this man's brother and not him. Around Shane, who could even concentrate on anything?

As she chewed the familiar nougat robed in the fine chocolate of her Philadelphia candy, she couldn't remember a day in months when she hadn't craved and then savored this exact flavor. Yet suddenly, there was something unsatisfying about it. It tasted fine. But ordinary. Not the embodiment of heaven on earth she'd once thought it was.

Not able to name what, she hankered for something different. For something she'd be surprised to know she wanted. She glowered at Shane's photo and indicted him, "You did this! It's your fault! With your *pan de dulce de leche* on your warm fingers. Leave me be!"

After buttoning up a cotton shirt and slipping on jeans, she walked out her door and over to the hotel's half-built spa and salon. There, the manager Natasha had set up a temporary dressing room for her. Audrey had also called on Jesse, one of their stylists, to select some sample dresses. He wheeled them in on a rack.

"These will be far too long on you but we just want to get the idea, yeah?" Jesse said as he lifted one of the gowns and hung it on a hook for Audrey to try.

She inspected the dress.

Wedding gowns. She was here to choose a wedding gown. There had never been a clear picture in her mind of the actual ceremony binding her to Reg. If it wasn't for their new concept of using the wedding for hotel publicity, she might have married him in a courthouse. A simple legal transaction. Perhaps she'd have worn a plain white business suit.

Now that her nuptials were going to be photographed for the public's enticement, a full-on fantasy wedding was called for. Was the dress in front of her *the one*, as a bride who'd thought about it for years and poured over magazines and websites might know? Audrey didn't have the slightest idea. But it was worth a try.

Jesse zipped her into the mermaid-style dress with its slim line from the bosom to the knee where it then flared out down to the floor. Audrey examined herself in the three-sided mirror he had carried in.

The look was only okay. With her own curves above and below her waist, the extra slant outward at the bottom of the dress seemed out of proportion. Too zigzaggy.

Standing behind her in the mirror, Jesse gave a hoist up from under the arms and then a tug at the knee. After thorough consideration from every angle he concluded, "Not our dress."

The next one he helped her into was a tea-length lacy dress with sleeves and a very full skirt. The under layers crunched with every move she made. Once she saw herself in the mirror, it was an easy vote. She was completely lost in all the volume. It even made her head look disproportionately large.

"All gussied up in big-girl clothes, yeah?" Jesse joked, in complete compliance with the veto.

After that came a cream-colored gown that fit her like a glove. It was a strapless silk shantung number with plenty of structure meant to hold all of a busty girl's parts in place. It cinched at the waist with a band of fabric, then hugged her round hips and fell straight to the floor. A thigh-high slit would allow for movement while dancing.

In keeping with that swinging early 1960s Vegas look the hotel evoked, the dress could have been worn by any of the va-va-voom movie stars of that era. Although Audrey guessed those great ladies had a little more height than she did at her shrimpy five-foot-two.

Still, she felt gorgeous in it.

"Now *that* is your dress." Jesse knew it, too.

"Aw," Natasha called over from the shelves where she was stocking salon products.

Jesse fluffed out Audrey's hair to give it some bounce. And a pair of pumps he brought perfectly matched the gown. Audrey couldn't take her eyes off her reflection in the mirror. Her heart banged against her chest, as if it was fighting to break out.

She'd helped when needed with weddings at the hotels, knew a little about everything from invitations to ring pillows to emergency shoe repair.

But now that it had finally come to her own? Would Audrey wear this spectacular dress to consecrate a marriage in which she'd never have to risk putting love and trust to the test?

That was what she wanted. Wasn't it?

"Shane showed me his heap of half-baked notes," she told her dad in his office before the Murphys arrived. She'd come over after the dress fitting. The brothers had asked for an evening meeting.

"Pun intended." Daniel couldn't resist, but quickly turned serious. "We need all of these pieces to come together."

Everything was riding on this hotel. They had sunk a lot more money than they had intended to into its overhaul. The Girards were in debt.

"We'll be on top again," Daniel said softly.

"I let you down." Audrey chewed her lower lip. "Three years ago when I was at the helm, a lot of things started to go wrong for us."

"No. I'm so proud of how much you handled. It was me. I neglected my personal relationships with some our investors. We lost good staff at the other properties because I wasn't on top of their needs. Then we got a later start on this project than we should have. It all added up."

The time leading up to Jill's death would always be a thorn in both Daniel and Audrey's sides. When his wife got sick, Daniel became unable to concentrate. He let deadlines pass on important decisions and abandoned the constant follow-up that kept the hotels at the high benchmarks Girard was known for.

Audrey had clearly seen what was happening and jumped in. She temporarily stepped into his shoes, even operating from his corner office at the Philadelphia headquarters. Knowing enough about each department to provide a stopgap, she kept the company afloat.

Running the company provided her a perfect excuse to distance herself from her dying mother, who had made it clear that she didn't want Audrey around. "I don't want you to see me like this," Jill had told Audrey during one of their few visits. That was ironic given that her mother had never let Audrey truly *see* her. Jill had spent most of her life in the top floor of their townhouse in Philadelphia's exclusive Rittenhouse Square, hiding behind a veil of alcohol and pills.

Daniel saw his wife in a different light. He had loved her so completely he always held on to the belief that he could *fix* her. As if she were one of the faded grand hotels they were able to revamp with enough care and repair. He never comprehended how unwanted Jill had made Audrey feel. But Audrey would always know. She'd carry it with her for the rest of her life. It had shaped her into the person she was. A person who wasn't going to love or expect to be loved by anyone.

Therefore, during those grueling months of Jill's demise, Daniel chose one path and Audrey chose another. Once Jill died, Daniel wallowed in grief for a few months, and then his enthusiasm for the hotels gradually returned.

"Regrets?" she asked her dad.

"Of course not." He nodded. "You?"

"A sky full."

She'd said the same thing to Shane last night when they shared a heart-to-heart talk that lasted into the wee hours. Granted, it was with cardboard Shane. But he really seemed to understand her.

The brothers arrived. Reg told them about the turmoil in New York and his decision to leave the next day.

Then he confessed his feelings about his assistant bar manager, Brittany. "I'm in love with her. I am so sorry, Audrey."

What? Who was Brittany? He was calling the marriage off?

Blood palpitated through every vein in Audrey's body. She had just picked out a wedding gown! Worked day and night to tie up loose ends in Philadelphia so that she could shift her operations to Las Vegas in time to not only open the hotel but to plan a lavish wedding! And he was in love with someone else?

"I flew out here with an open mind to seeing the plan through with you." Reg rubbed his palms back and forth. "But I can't go through with it. It wouldn't be fair to either of us. I seem to have only just realized that I was missing something important in my life. Something I want to make room for."

"Lo-ove. You want love. You fell in love." Stunned, Audrey repeated herself like a babbling idiot.

Shane shifted in his armchair without taking his eyes off Audrey. He'd obviously already known what Reg had come to say. It was so humiliating to have Shane in the room while this bombshell was being dropped on her! She directed a piercing stare right back at him.

Once she wrapped her mind around it, the news provoked a confusing mix of emotions in her. Rejection. More rejection for her to endure. But also liberation. In reality, Reg had been off-kilter since he'd arrived, and Audrey had sensed that something was amiss. Their fathers had agreed on this match a long time ago but she didn't know Reg all that well. She'd assumed they were kindred spirits in their desire for pragmatic companionship and nothing more.

Perhaps he was committed to fulfilling his family duty. But had secretly longed for love and for children all along. He was entitled to that, which he surely wasn't going to find with her. Ever.

She wouldn't want to be responsible for holding him back from what he wanted.

Audrey could no longer deny that the agreement had been like a safety net that she had been relying on. In the back of her mind she'd had a long-standing engagement to a pleasant man and she hadn't had to give her personal life any further thought. Her heart belonged to the hotels. Audrey had it in her plans for so long that she was going to end up with Reg, she hardly knew who she would be without this pact.

Yet, returning Shane's penetrating stare, she was suddenly, oddly, keen to find out.

Maybe Vegas was where she would discover herself.

After all, she was out here in the boundless new frontier, in the Wild West.

Daniel uttered the same words to Reg as she would have. "I wish you every happiness. We can't wait to meet Brittany." After all, she no longer had claims to him.

"Thank you, sir. I'll bring her back with me for the opening."

"Forgive me for sounding callous—" Daniel looked to Reg and then to Shane "—but the plans we had for the hoopla and engagement events to open the property were critical to bringing in bookings. That leaves a big hole in our promotional campaigns. I know you need a strong launch as much as we do."

Shane remained silent, elbows on the arms of the chair and his legs spread wide apart. Still looking at Audrey. She felt naked under his gaze, having to remind herself that it was only his photo and not he who had seen her flitting around her bungalow in her undies earlier. His attention was unrelenting. Was he pitying her now that she'd essentially been jilted at the altar?

And now everyone was on to the next piece of business? She couldn't catch up.

"What about a substitute fiancé?" Reg suggested.

"Hmm…" Daniel weighed the idea. "Even though it wouldn't tie the hotel to the restaurant, it would still generate buzz about the property and we could show off how much we have to offer for special occasions."

"Then you can just break the engagement off after a year or so when it has faded in the public's memory."

"Who then? Befitting hotel royalty, it would be ideal if it was someone in the industry." Daniel rubbed his chin as if massaging a pretend beard.

Reg rubbed his own chin the same way. "What about

Dean Ryder, the catering manager at the Bellagio? He's single."

"I think he's gay," Daniel answered.

"Does that matter in this setup?" Reg asked.

"Brian Haywood, maître d' at Scallops is single," Daniel suggested.

"But, then again, would it behoove us to partner with someone from another hotel?" Reg questioned.

"It should be someone in house," Daniel agreed.

"I'm right here, folks!" Audrey finally erupted. "Don't talk about me like I'm not in the room!" First her arranged marriage was called off and then, within minutes, they were talking about a replacement.

Shane let out a huge belly laugh, the first sound out of him.

He winked at Audrey. Then rested his hand on the inside of his thigh.

The sight of which halted her breathing and caused her lower jaw to drop open.

Just as Daniel and Reg both froze and stared at Shane.

"What about…?" Daniel mused.

"Nah," Reg rejected the thought.

"Think about it," Daniel insisted.

"It might work…" Reg slowly nodded at the possibility.

"You couldn't ask for a spicier publicity match-up," Daniel pressed.

"The beautiful hotelier and the sexy chef," Reg continued.

"No way!" Shane and Audrey both shouted in unison when they realized what the other two were devising.

Even if it was just for publicity, she couldn't pose alongside Shane Murphy as the happy couple. He was far too moody and complicated. She couldn't possibly handle the way he made her feel. He made her *feel*. Always had.

Reg didn't make her *feel* anything. Audrey wasn't ever going to take a chance again on feeling. She'd let herself go from a hurt child to a wounded adult. Any more pain and she might not be able to get out of bed in the morning. The "no feel" principle was her trump card.

Finally Shane leaned forward in his chair and spoke up. "Absolutely not. I don't have the time to get into shenanigans surrounding a phony engagement." He was clearly as against the idea as she was, thank goodness. "Look, we're going to have to turn the cookbook project into our prime strategy. That's going to be the focal point of the campaigns. My first book. International distribution. Promoted with TV tapings at the new restaurant and all over the property. Hotel Girard Las Vegas as the place to be!"

They were all surprised to hear Shane talk about things from such a businessman's point of view.

"Let's be honest," Reg said, "The editor quit. You fired our public relations coordinator as well as your literary agent. You've been struggling with the book all along."

Shane exchanged a heartfelt unspoken moment with his brother. "Well I'm going to have to change my tune, aren't I?"

"Thank you," Reg said softly, obviously knowing how hard this was likely to be for Shane.

"I'm here to help," Audrey chimed in.

"You're going to do more than help, Sugar." Shane pointed his finger at her. "Clearly, I can't direct and manage this by myself. We're doing this together. As a matter of fact, you're in charge!"

CHAPTER FOUR

INTRODUCING MR. AND MRS. Shane Murphy. Yes, Audrey and Shane Murphy will attend. Hello, have you met my husband, Shane Murphy?

Whaaaaat?

The following day, Audrey couldn't stop playing images in her head as she skirted from meeting to meeting. What if she had agreed to a fake marriage with Shane?

The toasts of Las Vegas, the Murphys returning to town and descending the steps of their private jet after a quick weekend in Geneva where Shane received an award for restaurant excellence. The Murphys partying the night away at Vegas's newest exclusive club, Shane graciously allowing handsome movie stars to salsa dance with his wife. The Murphys sailing around the Greek Islands on their second wedding anniversary. Is Mrs. Murphy sporting a baby bump above the teeny triangle of designer bikini she wears?

That's publicity and public relations for you. Even Audrey's fantasy mind knew how to put a spin on everything.

The reality wasn't as pretty. First, her riskless and sane arranged engagement had fallen apart. Second, she was set to work closely with a man who made the ground she stood on shaky every time she was near him.

Shane ignited her, gave her a sense of something spontaneous and out of her control. She worried he could blow her "no feel" policy to smithereens.

But they were both professionals and this was critical business. All she had to do was get him through the cookbook and publicity needed for a successful opening. Then she could back away from him. Easy peasy.

The evening was spent in her bungalow toiling on her laptop, finishing up work on the summer events she had planned at Hotel Girard Cape Cod. Looking at photos of the Atlantic Ocean shoreline gave her a bit of a shiver, replaying again that brush with Shane ten years ago in the Caribbean Sea at St. Thomas.

It was almost midnight when she powered down her computer. Her dad knew that Audrey liked to swim and had mentioned that the employee pool was in operation. It was late, but the idea sounded too refreshing to pass up. Quickly changing into her bathing suit, she stuck her tongue out at cardboard Shane as she left her bungalow.

The pool area was completely empty. No lights had been left on so Audrey treaded carefully. She put her towel down on a chair and removed her bathing suit cover-up and flip-flops. With a brave plunge, she dove straight into the deep end. The water felt divine as she sank into it, cool but not cold. In Philadelphia, she swam indoors, so it was a treat to be out under the bright moon. The midnight desert winds were strong and warm.

Swimming was an activity Audrey did as often as she could, both for exercise and as meditation. While her arms and legs rotated rhythmically through the water, lap after lap, one after the next, she could contemplate her day. Set goals for the next. And, occasionally, she could get a glimpse into the bigger pictures of life.

Each time she reached the edge of the pool, she turned

and pushed off with both feet to start in the next direction. Back and forth. Back and forth.

Reg, she contemplated, was not the slightest bit attractive to her. That would have been good. Not sexy would rank as the number one quality she'd be looking for in a man if she ever did decide to wed. In the meantime, she'd have to steer clear of men like Shane, who stoked the fires she kept contained inside of her.

He was gorgeous. She spelled out each letter in time with an arm stroke as she swam. *G*, stroke, *o*, stroke, *r*, stroke, *g-e-o-u-s*.

Although her laps were smooth, she seemed to be cutting a lot of water because she felt waves of vibration moving across the pool.

She could see one day getting married to a man who could accept her limitations. No love. No trust. No need. She'd been down that road. Just because it was with her mother and not a romance didn't change the blackness in her heart. Anything more was out of the question.

Her past had shaped her into the person she was now, and her future was determined. Audrey wasn't going to care for someone or expect to be cared for in return. If a man even hinted at wanting that, he'd be off the list immediately.

It had seemed like it was going to be so easy with Reg. Darn.

As she swam, she thought about a time a decade earlier in St. Thomas. It had been the summer before she started college. Celebrity chef Shane, only twenty-four then and not yet married, had been contracted to cook a special seasonal menu in the dining room for two weeks while the Murphys were opening their Lolly's outlet. There had been huge hype for his appearance. The hotel was at capacity, the kitchen bustling with activity and food deliveries.

Shane was not only a hotshot, he was a hothead. She'd never heard a voice so loud it could rattle stacks of dishes in the kitchen. A boom that overpowered the clamor of pots and pans, of chopping and frying and grilling. Eighteen-year-old Audrey had somewhat understood that he was volatile because he was a perfectionist, uncompromising, expecting excellence in himself and others.

At the time, though, to her Shane was downright daunting. Scary, yet utterly thrilling in the way he'd hulk into the kitchen and throw down his motorcycle helmet and leather jacket. How he refused to don the Hotel Girard chef's coat, instead wearing T-shirts bearing the names of heavy-metal rock bands. His impossibly broad shoulders leading the eyes to a solid wall of chest and muscular arms. He was raw manpower, something young Audrey had never been exposed to so nakedly.

She pushed off into another lap in the pool. For a minute she thought she heard splashing, but she didn't see anything around her.

In St. Thomas, Reg had always been there somewhere in the background, holding up a file for his brother to review or soothing egos after one of Shane's outbursts. Wiry and calculating, Reg could slip in or out of a room without anyone noticing. Whereas Shane was a tidal wave whose undertow was always felt both before his arrival and after his departure. Shane had stolen all the air in her lungs every time she was near him.

Audrey felt a whoosh of water so strong it almost veered her off her straight lap. Maybe the pump system in the pool needed to be adjusted.

Then there had been that last night on the island. After the resounding success of those two weeks, the Murphy brothers were packing up to jet back to New York. The summer was ending and Audrey would be heading to college later that week.

As she often liked to do at night, she'd walked barefoot in the soft island sand down to the beach. The sky was dark blue as she waded into the sparkling water and then launched herself into a swim. Her young brain was swimming, as well, with mental images of that powerful dark chef who she wondered when she'd see again given their families' business dealings.

While she was swimming farther into the sea, she felt something slide up along her leg. At first she was frightened that it might be a shark, or another marine predator. But a human head poked out from under the water. She'd have recognized him anywhere, even in the darkness. Those long crazy locks of hair were a wet and wild tangle framing his unshaven face. His lips glistened with moisture. Shane had come out for a swim, as well.

"Well, what do we have here?" he called to her with surprise, their heads bobbing above the water and the sound of the waves making it difficult to hear. "Why it's little Audrey Girard."

She'd felt so light-headed, she thought she might drown. The way he had slithered up beside her. Unintentionally, of course, but nonetheless he'd shocked her half to death. And then when she found it was him, a screaming awakening coursed through her. The mixture of attraction, fascination and fear was like nothing she'd ever felt before.

Or since.

No words had come out of her mouth. All she could do was summon all of her might to paddle herself back to shore as quickly as possible and run away in the sand.

A split second in the Caribbean Sea. A moment that she was never able to forget.

Why it's little Audrey Girard.

"We meet underwater again," came a low voice from the other side of the pool.

Audrey thought she might be hallucinating. Shane's words from a decade ago had just been looping over and over again in her head.

"What?" she stuttered into the Vegas night, blinking her eyes to try to focus.

He plied a few strokes and was quickly by her side. Shane. A decade later. "You discovered the pool. That you kindly built for the staff."

Get out of the water immediately, Audrey's mind directed. Yes, their fates were inexorably linked now in commercial partnerships. Yes, she'd be at his side working on the cookbook tomorrow. But there was no reason why she should be with him in a swimming pool at midnight.

"I'm glad you're making use of it," she stammered, her chest knocking so loud she thought she could hear it.

"Some turn of events, huh? I only just found out myself about Reg's change of heart."

"Yes." Move away from him. Audrey wasn't exactly sure what she was scared of, but terrified she was. Did she think that now because she was no longer engaged to Shane's brother, he might touch her? Or worse still, that she wouldn't be able to resist touching him? Many years may have passed but her gravitational pull toward Shane Murphy was as strong as ever. And, just like last time in the water, escape seemed the only option.

"I'm going to get some sleep." She had to get away from him. Tomorrow was another day. Best to take them one at a time. "I'll meet you at your kitchen. At noon."

Audrey hoisted herself out of the pool using the stepladder in the deep end. Which was nowhere near her towel. Just as she knew he would, Shane stayed in the water and watched her in what was enough moonlight for him to get a full outline of her body. Thankfully, she wasn't wearing a bikini. But, still, the athletic one-piece bathing suit didn't leave anything to the imagination.

As she crossed the length of the pool toward her things, he used both hands to rake back his long wet hair. "Sugar—" he smiled up from the shimmering water "—you sure grew up."

A glistening flesh-and-blood Shane in the moonlit water an hour ago. Ten-year-old memories of Shane in the Caribbean Sea. Now she was back to cardboard Shane in her bungalow. Everywhere Audrey turned, she found him.

After a hot shower, Audrey was still flustered by the interaction at the pool. He'd really gotten under her skin. All of a sudden she was no longer attached to the man she was to marry, yet it was his brother she couldn't stop thinking about.

Tossing and turning in bed, she was wide-awake and aware. Giving up on sleep, she switched on the lamps, propped herself up in bed and opened her laptop.

She'd promoted a date for the press to tour the hotel, but she needed to get to the nuts and bolts of the event. After welcoming them at the rooftop pool, they'd be taken on a guided tour of the property. She'd have the spa staff treat them to mini massages and give them goody bags filled with samples of the hotel's signature body care products. Then they'd reconvene on the roof for a reception.

"What should we serve for a light brunch?" Audrey

asked cardboard Shane as matter of factly as she might have if her dad had been in the room.

Weirder still, she received an answer. "Right, morning pastries and fruit kebobs would be easier than something they have to sit down to eat with a fork," she said aloud, typing in Shane's recommendation, knowing that she had gone insane.

"That would be great." She complimented Shane's idea of a station serving flavored coffees. "Okay, we'll do a dark chocolate, a hazelnut and an orange."

His suggestions for mini smoothies and for the buffet setup were all noted. "Thank you for your help."

When she couldn't keep her eyes open any longer, she ended the meeting by flicking off the light.

Shane's photo said, "Good night, Sugar."

The next day, Audrey arrived in the kitchen. She expected to find Shane at work on the cookbook recipes. The lights were on. Yet the kitchen was silent, save for the hum of the refrigeration system.

"Shane?" she called out in case he was in one of the nooks or walk-in cabinets within the large space. "Shane?"

There was no reply.

Audrey had been in here with him yesterday when he unceremoniously dumped his pile of recipe ideas out onto his desk. And the day before when he'd ushered her and Reg out. She'd yet to have a quiet moment to really take in the scale of the kitchen. It, like the dining room, was by far the largest at any of the Girard hotels.

Zones were designated for cleaning, cutting, frying, sautéing, baking, grilling, plating and so on. Boxes of state-of-the-art equipment, appliances and tools were marked for their station. There were food prep tables, dishwashing stations, freezers, ice makers, storage areas. There appeared to be a place for everything. Based on what she'd seen of how Shane functioned, this level of organization seemed impossible.

She looked to the spot where Shane had popped that divine dulce de leche cake into her mouth. Sadly, the pan was no longer there. Who had eaten it, she wondered? With envy.

"What are you doing here?" Shane's voice stunned her as he charged in wearing a motorcycle helmet, each of his big hands lugging half a dozen grocery bags. He plopped them all onto a prep table.

"We had an appointment for noon. To work on the cookbook."

Shane peeled off his helmet and laid it on the counter. He finger-combed his long hair away from his face. Audrey wondered what it would be like to do that for him.

"You're right, we did."

"What would be a good way to get started? Should we look at your idea file again?" Audrey asked, referring to that collection of notes scrawled on napkins and pieces of cardboard. If that was all Shane had to go from, it would have to do.

"Those are just scribbles. I haven't given them much thought."

"Well, did you jot them down because you were hoping they might be right for the cookbook? Didn't you work with an editor on it already?"

"He was a moron," Shane shot back. He dug into the grocery bags he had tossed onto the counter.

"But did you…"

"Let's make a ceviche," he interrupted. "I got some lovely red snapper filets I want to play around with."

He quickly washed his hands, unwrapped the fish

from its paper and laid it on a cutting board. With a knife selected from a drawer, he swiftly sliced the fish into bite-sized chunks. They were dispatched into a bowl.

Reaching in another bag for limes, he halved and squeezed the juice of five of them over the fish. He reached for a disposable glove to mix in the lime with his fingers. Then he placed the bowl in a refrigerated drawer.

"Is this for the cookbook?"

"Sugar, I don't know at this point. This is how I work. Let's just try some things."

"Stop calling me Sugar."

The used glove was tossed in the trash, and the cutting board and knife deposited into a sink.

Next, he pulled out a clean cutting board and knife. Swung around to locate the tomatoes in his grocery bags, and rinsed them under a sink. With breakneck speed and precision, they were diced.

He opened another drawer for a clean spoon to scoop up a pile of the ruby-red tomatoes and feed them to Audrey.

They were surely the juiciest, most flavorful she'd ever tasted.

"Beautiful, right?"

Audrey knew he was talking about food. There was no rationale for the jealousy she felt when he called the tomatoes beautiful and the red snapper lovely. Was she competing with a fish? And why would she care anyway?

"Get me the jalapeño peppers. They're in a plastic bag," he directed her. What was she now, his kitchen assistant? She supposed she could be, and should be, if that would help get the cookbook done.

But Shane's style was hard to take. He was too quick. Too forceful. Too impulsive. Too right up in her face.

Feeding her yesterday with his fingers and today with a spoon. For heaven's sake!

Yet all of that spontaneity jostled her to the core. He was hypnotizing. Making her want to be part of whatever he was doing.

When she handed him the jalapeños their fingers touched, and flickers flew up her arm.

"If you ever work with these, be careful not to touch your eyes until your hands are clean," he cautioned about the peppers. Because their heat might burn her, just as Shane was doing with his very being?

He chopped the peppers into tiny minces.

"Are we keeping a measurement?" she reminded herself of the task at hand. "In order duplicate the recipe?"

"We don't know if we have a recipe yet."

"But if we change it later, at least we'll know where we started from."

Shane's nostrils flared. As if in slow motion, his jaw tensed and then twitched. He shot her a scowl so scornful it made her take a step backward. Her mere suggestion of a method to accomplish one recipe for the cookbook upset him.

"I think I know what I'm doing in my own kitchen."

Yet she could tell from the lost look in his eyes that his reaction was a heartbreaking combination of pain and frustration. Half of her wanted to run away while the other half wished she could hug him.

She cast her eyes downward for a momentary respite.

Shane put his knife down and busied himself at another station unpacking a box. Leaving Audrey standing with a lump in her throat.

What kind of monster had he become? Shane asked himself the question as he arranged and rearranged jars of spices he had ordered. He wished he hadn't quit smoking years ago because a lungful of tar was just what he was really craving right now.

Yes, he did want this new Shane's Table restaurant to bring him back to the short list of best chefs in the world. Yes, he did know that an internationally distributed cookbook and TV special would put his name back in the limelight. Yes, he did understand that this was do or die for the Murphy Brothers Restaurants company.

Then why was he being such an ass?

He looked over to Audrey as if she held the answer.

Down inside, he knew.

A man doesn't just snap back from a wrong marriage that ends in his wife's death. An awful death that he might have been able to prevent had he taken action. He would always blame himself. He still wanted to scream, to cry, to shout his truth. That he felt responsible for Melina's death and perhaps he always would. That he should wear a sign around his neck that read Don't Get Close. That he was never to be trusted. He tried to issue Audrey a silent warning.

Two years had passed since Melina's death and Shane hadn't shaken off any of it. He'd sat wordlessly through appointments with grief counselors. Taken a soul-searching trip to Europe. Spent lots of time with his parents. Gotten back to swimming every day. None of it had helped. Setting up the Las Vegas location for the Feed U Project, the charitable organization his family oversaw, was one positive thing he had accomplished. There was purpose in working with kids who might otherwise fall victim to poor nutrition.

But he surely didn't have a clear plan for the future of his restaurants, nor the energy and enthusiasm he'd need to see it come to fruition. He'd run on Reg's fumes.

Nothing was ever going to move forward unless he created some steam of his own.

For starters, he wished he could undo having just gotten annoyed with Audrey.

He finished inventorying the jars just as a delivery of equipment arrived. Shane shook the driver's hand and instructed him where to place the order.

Audrey was still standing exactly where he had left her a few minutes ago, though she was on her phone. Her time was valuable. She was here to work. How could he explain to her that it was a calling beyond his own will that had steered him to create the original, innovative dishes that made him a success? And that he didn't know how to get his inspiration back.

Her blond hair looked like spun silk. He guessed that her sensual body would be soft in his hands. Like he could take a trip to heaven by exploring every supple inch. He'd seen many inches indeed by the pool last night. His center had wrung with an ache he didn't know he could feel anymore.

Great, the only woman in years to remind him that he still had a pulse was completely off-limits! He might be ready now to satisfy carnal desires with a female, but it certainly wouldn't be with a corporate partner he'd known for years and would be working with for many to come. Who was supposed to have become his sister-in-law! That was all kinds of wrong.

If Shane was ready, perhaps he could start thinking about dating again. But nothing ongoing, of course. He'd never be in a long-term relationship again. Not after what he'd done, or failed to do, with Melina. It had cost them the highest price imaginable. He'd lost the right to a relationship where he would be counted on.

He had always figured that's why his dad and Daniel's

royal match up for Reg and Audrey had taken shape in the first place. After Shane's catastrophe of a marriage, the dads got spooked and decided to step in. He could hardly blame them.

So it's Brittany in New York, huh, Reg? She was a former drug addict who had been clean and sober for years and was a hard-working employee they valued. Shane was happy for his brother. Why shouldn't Reg fall in love if that's what he wanted? His brother had only dated a few women, but never for longer than a few months because he'd always been so preoccupied with the business. What a stable, serious man his brother was. It was touching to see the light in Reg's eyes as he spoke of Brittany and this unexpected turn of events. If for no other reason but for Reg's sake, Shane had to pull himself together to accomplish what he'd told his brother he would here in Vegas.

He couldn't gauge whether Audrey was devastated or relieved that her wedding was called off. In any case, he wished he hadn't been such a jerk a few minutes ago.

After the deliveryman unloaded the order in the kitchen, Audrey and Shane faced each other at an impasse.

"What's going to get you motivated again?" she asked in earnest.

"I don't know." Shane had an impulse and grabbed Audrey by the hand. "Let's go."

"Go where?" she protested. "We need to work."

He snatched up his keys and helmet, and tugged her toward the door. "Come on. I can at least show you something that's become important to me."

Outside, he freed the spare helmet he had locked in his motorcycle. He couldn't remember the last time he'd had a rider with him. And had to admit to himself that he was turned on by the idea of Audrey's arms around his waist and her breasts pressing into his back while they zoomed along city streets.

"Oh, no. No. I can't." Audrey shook her head as Shane tried to hand her the helmet. She fumbled for words. "I mean, look at what I'm wearing."

She gestured to her black business dress and heels. True, not appropriate for a ride on a motorbike.

"Why don't you run over to your bungalow and change clothes?" he suggested.

She shook her head even more adamantly. "No."

"Why not?"

"Because I'm afraid. Okay? Are you happy now? You got me to admit it. I don't want to ride on your motorcycle."

Her honesty pulled at his heart. His lips gravitated forward, compelled to kiss her.

Almost.

Thankfully, he pulled back in time.

"Alright, Sugar." He twisted his nose and locked both helmets onto the bike. "We'll take the Jeep."

She let out a whoosh of relief, making him realize how scared she had been. "Where are we going?"

CHAPTER FIVE

EVEN THOUGH SHE wouldn't get on his motorcycle, Shane liked having Audrey next to him in his Jeep while he drove away from the Strip. In the months he'd been in Vegas, he couldn't think of a time he'd had anyone besides his brother in the vehicle with him.

With the roof retracted, they motored in the open air. Audrey's hair bounced every ray of sunlight as it whooshed around her face, and her dark sunglasses gave her a fashion that harkened back to movie stars of yesteryear. As they passed the intersection where he'd make a turn if he was going to his apartment, it tortured him to imagine the multiple activities he'd like to engage in with her if they were going there.

Instead, he continued on toward their destination. It never ceased to amaze him that just a few blocks away from the Strip, away from the lights and the jumbotrons, the endless procession of people and the clanking of the casinos, Las Vegas was an actual city. The streets were lined with gas stations, fast food restaurants, medical offices and shopping centers. Residents had jobs and kids. There was suburban wealth and the slums of poverty. Most tourists never saw any of it. The whole point of their visit was the total escape from real life that the Strip offered.

When he pulled into the parking lot of the nondescript industrial building, Audrey gave him a questioning look.

He sprang out of the Jeep and went around to the other side to open her door and lead her to the entrance. With a turn of his key, the metal door in the front of the building unlatched and he pushed it open.

The cavernous space was set up as one enormous kitchen, equipped with many work stations in stainless steel. The walls were redbrick and unfussy lighting hung from the ceiling.

"What is this?" Audrey asked.

"We teach kids to cook here," Shane said as he pointed to the plastic banner that hung from a wall-to-wall shelf. It read Welcome to Feed U.

"Feed U," Audrey repeated. "Is this what you do in your spare time?"

"I set this one up a few months ago," Shane explained, "My family is overseeing about a dozen of these kitchens. You know, a lot of kids are at risk of malnutrition. Maybe they don't have a parent around during the day to supervise their eating. Or parents are passing on bad habits to their kids. We try to help as many as we can learn about healthy eating."

At the far end of the space, sun-weathered Lois sat working at her desk. "Hey, Shane," she called.

"Hi, Lois," he returned, and then told Audrey, "she's our kitchen manager. Don't mess with Miss Lois."

"I heard that," Lois yelled over.

"My man," teenage Santiago called as he came through the side door with a half dozen six-year-olds in tow. Each kid held a herb or vegetable in their hand.

"Ah, you've been out to the garden," Shane said to them.

No matter what was going on in his life, as soon as

Shane was with the kids he started to relax. The pressure was off. He didn't have to be a big, fancy chef. In a way, Feed U had nothing at all to do with his distinguished career or running the restaurants. But because his family lent their famous name to it, the Feed U Project was growing. Plans for even more locations worldwide were in the works.

Santiago and Shane did their four-part handshake. Shane high-fived each of the kids.

"I want you all to meet my friend Audrey," Shane said. "Santiago here is our teen supervisor."

Audrey fumbled trying to follow Santiago's handshake. She raised her palm toward the kids in a tentative hello.

"What's everybody cooking today?" Shane asked.

"Salad with matos," one of the kids answered.

"Tomatoes," Shane corrected. "Cool."

"And kooky-umbers," another kid added.

"Yeah, cucumbers." Shane nodded. "What else are you making?"

"We're baking bread," piped up a living doll with curly blond hair.

Although he was sure he'd never have kids, couldn't be trusted with that kind of responsibility, he loved working with them. There was never anything fake with children. Everything was alive. Nothing else existed except the honesty of the moment. That little cutie who'd just announced they were baking bread was receptive and radiant with pure optimism.

Shane could vaguely remember how that felt. A happy, if impatient, kid himself, his parents and Grandma Lolly had paid attention to him. They were able to see that his intuition in the kitchen as a child was something unique.

It was their belief in him that had propelled Shane's rise to such a high level at such a young age.

And he'd rewarded their faith and nurturance by becoming a burned-out grouch. Who'd made a rash marriage that had led to a horrifying conclusion. All of which brought him to almost burying himself alive.

Had he succeeded, or could he find his way home from *almost*?

What had made him just smile wistfully at Audrey?

"Okay." He summoned his attention back to the kids. "What are the three rules we always have to remember in the kitchen?"

"Learn the safe way," the kids all chanted. Which was followed by "Always cook with an adult."

"That's right," Shane affirmed. "And what's the third important thing to remember?"

The kids shouted, "Rock 'n' roll!"

Audrey giggled.

With that, Shane flicked a switch on the wall and music played from several speakers scattered around the room. He wiggled his hips and the kids followed suit.

"You work with Santiago and help the kids knead the bread dough," Shane said to Audrey. "I'm going to cut the vegetables and then they can compose their salads."

"Oh, no. I'll just watch." Audrey seemed uncomfortable. In fact, she looked at the kids like the precious and fragile miracles they were.

"Why?" Shane probed.

"I'm, uh, I'm not used to being around children," she whispered.

"Here's your opportunity. They won't break."

"I wouldn't want to take any chances," she said with her chin pointed downward.

"Chances of what?"

"That I couldn't protect them."

Not a day went by that Shane didn't have a thought like that. He wondered where Audrey's fear of herself originated.

"I don't think there's much danger in kneading bread dough," he tried to reassure her. She was acting very out of character. Not the spunky and confident go-getter she was at the hotel. "Did your mom have you help in the kitchen when you were growing up?"

"No," she said quickly, "my mother wouldn't let me come in the kitchen. She said that it wasn't a place for children."

Those words stung Shane. The kitchen was for everyone. It was a place where love could be passed from generation to generation. Food could mean care. Or rejuvenation. Or bonding. He wished there had been someone to teach Audrey those lessons when she was a kid. No wonder she liked sweets. She found the pleasure of food that way. He'd have to work on her.

A life in restaurants had shown him a lot of crazy eating habits that had nothing to do with food. Women so thin he could see their bones right through their skin who dined with powerful men yet never ate a morsel themselves. He'd learned that sometimes they didn't eat as a way of exercising control over food when they didn't have control in other areas of their lives.

Or those rich and important men who'd stuff so much food in their faces they'd become red and sweaty. Maybe they'd been criticized by their parents and now they were showing the world they deserved opulence because they had made something of their lives.

Shane had dozens of stories about the role of food in people's lives. That's why Feed U's mission was to help young people foster healthy relationships with eating.

"Come here, munchkin, what's your name?" He called the girl with the ringlets over.

"Mia."

"Mia, my friend Audrey here doesn't know anything about making bread. Can you help her?"

"It's easy," the little girl said. Then she lifted up her hand to take Audrey's and guided her to the work station. Audrey swallowed hard. Shane almost thought he saw her biting back tears. He fought an urge to go hold her, to wrap her in his arms and tell her everything was going to be okay no matter what it was she was carrying around in her soul. He wanted to right her wrongs. Release her from them.

But that wasn't his place. Nothing about their association with each other entitled him to really get to know her.

He couldn't help but visualize Audrey looking like little Mia when she was that age. The blond hair, the brown eyes, the determined set of their shoulders. Seeing them together pulled at Shane's heart. There was something unspeakably beautiful about how the young girl gave Audrey a ball of dough and showed her how to press it with the heels of her teeny hands.

Audrey glanced up and her eyes met Shane's. "I can see why this means a lot to you," she said to him. "It would have to me when I was a kid."

"Yeah, Shane's cool," Mia said.

"Yes. He is."

Shane scratched his beard stubble, humbled.

Tonight he and Audrey were attending their first strategic event. To show him off. She wanted him seen in public, to become a glittering fixture on the Strip. Something he'd completed avoided, hovering in his kitchen day and night.

They were going to a new nightclub at Caesars Palace.

As his publicist, she'd escort him. Soon they'd head back to the hotel to get ready. It'd be an evening of limos, nice clothes, razzle-dazzle.

Fine, Shane thought. He'd play the game, after all, they were betting high to win. One thing he knew was that, secretly, he was looking forward to spending the evening with Audrey.

Just to keep her company, of course.

And it made good sense to at least get out of the kitchen and be seen around Vegas. He'd cut himself off from almost everyone except his family. He had chef friends here. His old-kitchen mates Tino and Loke were cooking on the Strip, yet he hadn't seen them in all the months he'd been coming into town to supervise the construction of the restaurant. Worse still, he hadn't gone out to see Josefina, the grandmotherly friend that he considered a mentor. He'd talked to her on the phone but hadn't been able to face the look she'd give him, knowing in an instant how much of himself he'd let slip away.

He watched Santiago move around from kid to kid to be sure they were able to do the kneading. Shane liked the sixteen-year-old aspiring chef, who was earning high school service credits for helping the little ones. Santiago made his way over to Shane at the salad station.

"Shane, man, like, how do you create a recipe? Like, how do you know what ingredients to put together?"

A good question. One Shane had, apparently, forgotten how to answer. "I think one recipe kind of leads to the next," he managed. "You taste some dish you like. You figure out what's in it. That this tastes good with that. And then it occurs to you how you could make it better."

"Yeah but, like, how does that actually happen?"

Oh, if he only knew. Here he was opening up a high-profile restaurant in one of the top food destinations in the world, yet he couldn't find his way back to the imagination and originality that had brought him his initial acclaim. Where was the magic that his family had seen in him even as a young boy? Who had he become?

"Patience. Focus. Concentration." Shane tried to answer Santiago's question with what came to mind. His stomach wrenched into a knot, his fists balled involuntarily until his fingernails were digging into his flesh.

Why on earth couldn't he follow his own advice?

Audrey modeled in front of the mirror in her bungalow. She didn't like the fifth dress, either. Why she objected tonight to all of these dresses that she usually enjoyed wearing, she didn't know. The perfect one just wasn't jumping out.

Nix on the black fitted dress with the cap sleeves. Too somber.

With the many dressy occasions at the hotels, Audrey owned a substantial wardrobe. It was what the job demanded. Her dad, and her grandfather back when he was still alive, only had to choose from tuxedos and tailored suits when they represented the company at events. Men had it easy. Audrey owned clothes for black-tie affairs, celebrations, civic functions and sportswear, along with the conservative business dresses and skirts she wore most of the time.

No to the red dress with the ruffles down the front. Too froufrou.

When packing up in Philadelphia for her stay out here, she figured ball gowns were not going to be required and left those behind. Vegas nights would call for party frocks and cocktail dresses. She'd need to straddle the line between tasteful, the Girard brand promise, and current, so as to present herself as on top of trends. She'd packed a few suitcases full, along with shoes and accessories, knowing that someone at headquarters could send more of her things if she needed them.

The emerald green with the ruching at the waist? Better for a wedding guest.

It wasn't lack of selection that was prohibiting her from deciding on a dress for tonight. The truth was that she wanted to look good for Shane. Although she told herself that shouldn't matter one iota, it did. She was going out to a nightclub on the Las Vegas Strip with a devastatingly handsome and charismatic man. She hadn't done anything like that in…she couldn't even remember the last time. If an event she attended called for her to bring a *plus one*, it was always her dad. That duty was to have switched to Reg. Tonight it was Shane who needed the date.

Veto on the geometric pattern wrap dress. Too casual.

So while Audrey traveled the globe and certainly lived a life of culture and even luxury, for the moment she was a nervous teenager going out on a first date with her crush. "Whoosh," she said aloud. Better push those feelings out of the picture right now. They had no place in her world. This was not that kind of date.

Even though she had thought of Shane almost every day since she'd first laid eyes on him in St. Thomas ten years ago. How he skidded up to the entrance of the hotel on his motorcycle, yanked off his helmet and shook his hair out in the sea breeze. He'd spotted her, *little Audrey Girard*, that day in tennis whites holding her racquet as she crossed the valet station. He'd winked at her and she'd been mortified with embarrassment at his attention. Yet she'd never forgot it. Nor the chaos in the kitchen and especially not the late-night encounter in the sea.

That was then. This was business. It couldn't be anything more. She simply needed to put on clothes for the evening. The first dress she had tried on was the best. Copper-colored and satiny, it had a halter neck with a deep V in front and a slim bodice that gave way to a full skirt. The style was a bit retro 1950s, which suited her hourglass figure. The dress also had a modern edge with its length, which ended well above the knee, making her legs look longer than they really were. She paired it with metallic high-heeled sandals and an evening purse. Earlier, she'd begged Natasha at the salon to blow out her hair and do evening makeup on her face.

With her ensemble complete, she headed for the door. Giddiness and apprehension about seeing Shane competed within her despite her attempts to shut them down. Cardboard cutout Shane gave her an appreciated boost of confidence when he complimented her with "You look hot."

She blushed as she thanked him.

"You look hot," real Shane seconded with his seal of approval as he ushered her into the limo. He spiked her temperature, as well, in his slim-fitting black suit with a dress shirt and no tie. How did it happen that he chose a brown shirt that perfectly complemented the copper of her dress? Kismet. He slid in next to her, much closer than was necessary, before the chauffeur shut the car door.

Shane settled back against the leather seat. Whether he meant to or not, his trouser-clad leg brushed against her bare thigh. Acting on the urge to shift away would have been too obvious, so Audrey froze in place. Her skin tickled at the fresh smell of his wild hair, which brushed incongruously against the jacket of the fine suit he had on.

"Champagne?" Shane asked although he didn't wait for an answer as he expertly and cleanly popped the bottle's cork. He poured the bubbly into the two crystal flutes that had been set up for them. Caesars Palace wasn't far away from the Hotel Girard. Drinks weren't even in order, and Audrey never took more than a bit, but it was a fun touch. And traffic moved notoriously slow on Las Vegas Boulevard.

"To our new venture." Audrey proposed a toast. They clinked glasses and sipped.

Shane gave her a small smile. It wasn't one of his sexy smirks. This one was intimate and knowing, as if he saw right through to her soul. Its focus tormented her.

"Why are you examining me like that?" she asked after the silence stretched too long yet his fix on her didn't waver.

"Wondering who you are," he rejoined quickly. "We've been acquainted for a long time but I don't really know a thing about you."

"I like movies and long walks on the beach," she kidded in a monotone about the typical get-to-know-you answers.

"Me, too!" Shane played along.

"And cuddling with puppies."

"And world peace." Then he let the joking subside. "I mean, I don't know anything *real* about you."

"What do you want to know?"

"You strut around the hotel with your conferences and your high-heeled shoes, yet today at Feed U you looked like a scared little girl who couldn't find her mommy."

Her neck flushed. He was right. He'd seen her naked today. Not in a bathing suit at the pool under the moonlight where he might have been able to make out the shape of her body. No, she'd been exposed when she freaked out about being around the children and wasn't quick enough to cover up her emotional scars.

An only child, she didn't have nieces or nephews.

Her work had her dashing from one of the Girard properties to the next, and their brand of boutique hotels tended to attract adults rather than families. She simply wasn't around kids very often and was uncomfortable in their presence. How odd, that as a twenty-eight-year-old woman she'd had almost no contact with children.

Part of her had wanted to go play in the garden with those kids today. To sing silly songs in the sunshine and cheer them on while they picked their "matos" and "kooky-umbers."

She'd almost come completely unglued when Shane asked if she'd ever cooked with her mother. Not only didn't Jill cook or let Audrey in the kitchen, but his question had brought back a particularly telling memory.

Audrey was not much older than the kids at Feed U when a girl at school had told her that her mother had baked her a birthday cake and that they had decorated it together. Already having a sweet tooth, that sounded like the most fun Audrey could imagine, to decorate a cake exactly how she wanted to. She mentioned it to Jill during her five-minute visit one night before bed.

When Audrey's birthday came around a couple of weeks later, Jill drove her to their hotel in Philadelphia. There, the pastry chef had laid out all of the necessary components for a birthday cake. Several flavors of cake to choose from, and icing with various colors to mix in, piping bags, candy sprinkles and sugar beads in every shape and variety.

But since Daniel was out of town and Jill had merely dropped Audrey off with the hotel's bell captain, it was with a kitchen assistant that the birthday girl decorated and ate her cake. A smile never once crossing her lips.

That was Jill in a nutshell. She'd administrated Audrey's upbringing rather than participating in it.

Being around the children at Feed U earlier that day had made her wonder, and not for the first time, what it would be like to have a child herself. Yet that seemed impossible, unthinkable. With the kind of lessons she'd learned from Jill, she'd have no clue how to properly parent and would no doubt fail miserably at it. No way she'd let that happen!

Shane had pushed the wrong button and Audrey retaliated, knowing she was being defensive but unable to bite her tongue. "I could say the same about you. You skulk around your own kitchen seemingly lost, yet you give kids you don't even know that incredible experience. If you can teach them to cook, how come you can't write down a recipe?"

Shane's teeth clenched; he turned his gaze away from her and directed it forward out the limo's front windshield. Colored lights reflecting from the giant advertisements on the Strip played shadows across his face.

Yikes, she shouldn't have picked at his wound like that, but he'd riled her up. Rolling around in her own old hurts hadn't helped her move forward any. All it had served to do was hold her back and limit her world.

"Shane, I'm sorry I said that," she begged. "I had a really difficult relationship with my mother and when I saw those kids—"

"It's none of my business," Shane interrupted, but he kept his eyes forward. His jaw ticked.

"Exactly," she agreed. "Let's just have a fun evening as colleagues and we don't have to talk about anything serious."

"How long do we have to stay?"

How did this evening get off to such a sour start so fast? Audrey answered her own question. Unlike everyone she'd ever known in her life, including herself, Shane Murphy wasn't someone who pretended everything was okay.

Alright, Shane thought as he helped Audrey out of the limo at Caesars Palace. She wanted a fun evening…he'd give her a fun evening. He could use one himself. But what constituted fun? He didn't know anymore. Did she?

As they were ushered onto the night's red carpet, he didn't have time to ponder the question. A solid wall of arms aiming camera lenses stretched for yard upon yard toward the new club's entrance. The camera flashes were like endless exploding fireworks blinding guests as they promenaded down the long carpet.

Shane spotted some film actors, musicians and sports stars among the lineup. Each grouping stopped at a few interview stations set up for reporters to try to grab a sound bite that news outlets could use with the photos.

"This is a big whoop," Shane said as he leaned down toward Audrey by his side while they took slow steps to keep pace with the crowd. He knew that with her job, she'd probably been involved with extravaganzas like these many times. "Have you orchestrated high-rolling shindigs like this?"

"Well, you know loud and glitzy isn't Girard style," she replied, both of them having to raise their voices to be heard over the festivities. "But we've done red carpets on a smaller scale. Like for charity fundraisers. You?"

"The opening in LA was all-out glam. In New York, we built ourselves up slowly with invitation-only nights. But to have an impact on Los Angeles, we figured we'd better go full tilt. A lot of press. Not that I did anything but get out of the kitchen to put my arms around people for photos."

Conversation was coming easier than he'd thought it

would with Audrey after that brisk exchange in the limo. Small talk was hardly Shane's specialty but he had to admit it was nice to get out and Audrey looked killer in that shiny dress. He was tempted to reach out and run his fingers along the fabric. And what was underneath it.

"What do we have planned for *our* opening?" He continued their chat between the two coworkers who were not the slightest bit attracted to each other.

"We're doing a number of what I'm calling parties." She looked up to him in the shoulder-to-shoulder throng on the carpet. "An opening night at the restaurant with invited guests. Another opening for investors. A late-night bash for our social media followers. Brunch for the press. A dance party at the pool."

"Shane Murphy!" A reporter thrust her microphone in his face. "What can you tell us about the new Shane's Table opening at the Girard?"

He turned on the hundred-watt smile he only took out of his back pocket when it was absolutely necessary. "Fresh food. Craft cocktails. A fiesta every night."

"Shane, who are you with tonight?" another reporter probed as the cameras pointed at them.

"This is Audrey Girard, director of public relations for the Girard hotels." The Girard family had a renowned name but, apparently, her face wasn't as instantly recognizable to the press as his was.

"Are you two a couple?" the first reporter interrogated with glee while the photographers went at them.

"Nah, she's out of my league," Shane quickly retorted.

Audrey blushed.

Which was, of course, so out-of-control cute he wanted to scoop her up and demand Caesars Palace's best suite. There he'd lay her down on a bed fit for a Roman emperor and do things to her that would certainly make her blush some more.

"Come on Shane, you look smitten!" the second reporter persisted. Shane suddenly realized he hadn't been hiding his pull toward Audrey as well as he'd thought he had.

Audrey stepped in with, "The Murphy family of restaurants and the Girard family of hotels are excited to continue our professional collaboration here in the great city of Las Vegas." She stretched her hand out toward Shane in an exaggerated gesture of a professional handshake. He took hers and they pivoted to the cameras for a perfect shot that the photographers gobbled up.

"Mission accomplished." She lifted on tiptoe to whisper this in his ear as they proceeded through the nightclub's tall entrance doors.

Shane and Audrey took in the totality of Big Top, a circus-themed nightclub. They looked up to the swaths of heavy red and gold fabrics draped across the ceiling to make the enormous space look more like a circus tent and less like the arena its size could accommodate.

The entrance had led them to an elevated level of the club. Down on the ground floor, thousands of revelers danced to a pounding rhythm. From a center booth that shot yellow, pink and green light beams in every direction, a deejay commanded the crowd though his microphone, "Let's get this party started, Las Vegaaaas!"

It was rhetorical, because he need only glance around to see that the revelry was well underway.

Gigantic cages hung by chains from the ceiling held dancers whose bodies were painted to look like circus animals. A tall lioness in one cage, a muscular tiger in another, and two painted as parrots in a third swayed to the music, deeply into their own rhythms.

Right beside where Audrey and Shane were standing, a trapeze artist clad in a black-and-white polka-dot leotard swung past them on her way to the other end of the cavernous space where she perched on a landing. At the same time, a male counterpart swung back toward Audrey and Shane. Audrey gawked as he flew by them. "Fantastic."

"Who has a vision for a club like this?" Shane nodded in amazement. "This is astonishing creativity."

Somebody conceived of this, and these days he couldn't even put together a simple ceviche.

A hostess dressed like a lion tamer in a top hat, red tailcoat, tiny shorts and lace-up boots showed them to one of the plush booths that ringed this level of the club. "Run away and join the circus," she said as she handed them a cocktail menu.

A waitress, in the same top hat plus bra and shorty shorts took their order for the "lion juice" that Shane picked for them, a multi-liquored concoction they'd feel awful from the next day if they drank more than one. Shane wasn't much of a drinker and he noticed Audrey wasn't, either. He'd keep an especially close watch on himself tonight. Drunken unwanted advances toward Audrey would be a big no-no.

After sipping and people-watching, Shane suggested they explore the rest of the club. One level down, photo booths captured guests wearing costumes and props that had been provided. Audrey put on a clown's red nose and curly orange wig while Shane mimed swallowing a pretend flaming sword made of plastic.

They walked away giggling at the instant photos they were handed.

"Let's dance," he suggested when they reached the ground floor.

He maneuvered them into the belly of the dance floor, which was jam-packed with partyers.

The deejay boomed out his directive, "Las Vegaaaas! Fists up, hearts open!" The crowd obeyed as everyone lifted an arm in the air and they undulated as one to the throbbing beat. *Fists up, hearts open.*

Shane and Audrey danced. And danced. And danced some more, until they were sweating. There were some seriously good-looking people in the mass around them. Buff guys in tight shirts and women in dresses the size of postage stamps. But Shane's eyes were only interested in Audrey. How stunning she looked with her hair loose and tousled, sweat glistening on her skin, her golden eyes that gazed up at him.

They writhed and wriggled against each other in uninhibited dancing that almost ought to be called something else. Sobriety notwithstanding, it still took every fiber of Shane's being not to steal Audrey into an embrace, not to claim her lips. Which wasn't allowed.

But in that moment he experienced a freedom, one he'd never felt with Melina nor since. *Hearts open*, the deejay had commanded.

A sudden clearing in Shane's personal raincloud allowed him to see light in a way he hadn't in a long, long time.

CHAPTER SIX

"I DON'T KNOW if it's a good idea for me to take charge of Shane's publicity," Audrey confessed to her dad as they inspected one of the newly finished guest rooms. The various crews would be coming through to give their okays on everything, but Daniel liked to take a look at each of his rooms himself. As he'd taught Audrey, even the tiniest detail can bring a guest back for another stay or make them choose never to return.

"Why?" Daniel asked as he jimmied the windows and checked the sills to make sure they were completed to the specifications.

"I'm uncomfortable around him. He's so…intense." Audrey lay down on one of the beds as a Las Vegas visitor might after a full night on the town. Which was exactly what she'd had. Staying out until almost dawn last night at Big Top with Shane, it was no wonder she was groggy today. In any case, she enjoyed the comfortable mattress for a moment under the guise of quality control.

"You and Shane did great last night," Daniel said, "with your appearance at Caesars Palace."

"How would you know how *we* did, or didn't, do?" Audrey propped up on her elbows while continuing her sprawl on the bed. "He's the celebrity."

Daniel took his phone out of his pocket and tapped in.

"It was on the gossip sites this morning." He read from his phone, "'Formerly reclusive star chef Shane Murphy seems to have come out from hiding, tearing up the town with petite hotel powerhouse Audrey Girard. Though they insisted their dealings were of a professional nature only, the pair were their own three-ring circus dirty dancing the night away at Big Top. From the way they had eyes only for each other, we see a unification that might go past the contracts.'"

"Dirty dancing? Eek." Audrey sat up, and opened and shut the drawers in the nightstand that, like the headboard, were finished in a shiny black veneer. It wasn't a lie, though. She and Shane did dance, booty shake, twerk, gyrate, rub up against each other and do every still-legal thing people could do on a dancefloor last night, lost in the music and the crowd.

And therein lay the issue. Of course, they looked like a couple to an outside eye. It was a struggle even for *her* to believe they weren't more than professional partners after the whole magical evening.

"The point was to get Shane photographed out in the nightlife. Not to start gossip about his dating life."

"What's that old saying—any publicity is good publicity?" Daniel chimed in.

"I guess it's all good for the bottom line," she reasoned.

Had she seen attractive widower Shane Murphy out in Las Vegas with a young woman she, too, would have assumed they were out on a date.

In reality, they were both unattached. Audrey hadn't thought of her status as single for a long time. She'd settled into this vague vision of a future with Reg, one that demanded nothing of her. A future she could play out in her mind before it had even begun.

Last night wouldn't have been a problem if she'd been out with Reg. They'd look like a couple, pretend to be in love if it was for the cameras and then get right back to their agreed-upon friendly companionship. All previously plotted and outlined and tied up with a ribbon.

Whereas, with Shane, even being in the same room with him set her off questioning the limitations she had carefully defined for her life.

Daniel inspected the teal and hunter green fabric of the curtains, drawing them open and closed to make sure they slid properly.

There was so much her sweet dad didn't know. He wasn't aware that his wife's pregnancy was accidental. Wasn't aware just how much Jill never wanted to have a child, because she'd never told him. Or that when she did become pregnant and Daniel's happiness prevented her from any option other than having the baby, she didn't know what to do with Audrey once she was born.

Jill had treated Audrey like a chore. She would make sure the nanny gave Audrey a bath at night, she'd take her to the doctor if she was sick and sought out good schools for her. In other words, she fulfilled the job requirements of a mother.

Her mother had *managed* her daughter's upbringing. But she had never been a part of it. Like the time with the birthday cake. She had never let Audrey need her. Daniel had tried his best to fill in the gaps, which Audrey was grateful for, but there was no substitute for a mother's love and involvement.

It was only years later that Audrey would come to understand that her mother had suffered from crippling depression. And that the pills and alcohol she'd used to numb her pain only took her even further away.

A distant mother who wasn't warm or watchful, Jill

had died without letting her daughter love and dote on her, either.

It was no surprise, then, that Audrey was committed to spending her adulthood with her walls firmly erected.

Argh, she wished Shane Murphy would stop complicating matters by putting those convictions to the test!

Audrey slid open the room's clothes closet to make sure everything was in order. "I just wonder if we shouldn't hire someone to work with Shane. You know, not get ourselves so mixed up in his personal business." That dancing last night surely felt, uh, personal.

"I think we're down to the wire here. And he's comfortable with you. It's what he wants."

"Yeah but…"

"Listen, I don't want to worry you, but I met with Wayne and Suzanne this morning." The building contractor and the hotel general manager. "Because of the teardown and rebuild we had to do in the north corridor, the zeroes to the twelves on all four floors aren't going to be ready in time for the opening."

Audrey's eyes widened in alarm. "For our grand opening, the whole hotel won't be fully opened?"

"Our other guests won't be inconvenienced, but it does mean we can't take reservations to capacity."

"But the first quarter of revenues isn't going to be what we hoped it would be."

"Which is why I don't think this is the time to let anything out of our hands. Who knows what we'd really get if we hire someone to handle Shane. We know you'll do the job right."

Now her concerns seemed trivial. That with Reg it would be easy to pretend there was something between them. And that with Shane, even though there was nothing, it felt like something. Because when she was with him, there was definitely not nothing.

She'd confessed the same thing to Shane earlier. Not the real Shane, of course, with whom she'd had an electrifying evening with at the club. No, it had been daybreak this morning in her bungalow over a cup of herbal tea when she was having that conversation with cardboard Shane. Who was so easy to talk to.

After that, she was disgusted with herself for having yet another tête-à-tête with a photograph, and actually got out of bed and turned the display around so that she didn't have to see his expressive eyes or look at the powerful hands that had traveled down her back when they were dancing last night. Or notice those solid thighs that she had boogied around and between as the dancing got more and more wild. With the photo turned around, all she had to see was a white cardboard outline of the enthralling man she couldn't stop thinking about.

Then the weirdest thing happened. When she woke up after conking out for a few hours' sleep, the cutout had turned around. She opened her eyes to Shane's welcoming face wishing her a good morning. Either she'd been sleepwalking and turned the photo around during the night, or the display was possessed with demonic abilities.

In any case, with this bad news about the construction delays, Audrey couldn't back down. She'd have to go through with the plans. She could handle it. Absolutely. As long as she didn't let it occur to her that she might want to spend every moment of the rest of her life with Shane Murphy.

Making a quick mental list, firstly she'd definitely need to keep her recollections away from yesterday afternoon at Feed U. How when she witnessed the smiles he brought to the faces of the kids, she thought sincerely for the very first time about what the joys of having a child might be. His praise for them made her ponder what it would be like to encourage someone, and to find pleasure in their achievement.

Second, it would not be her problem to figure out how to yank Shane out from the shadow he'd been under since his wife's death. Hitting a nightclub and playing around with the kids was fine, but most of his time seemed to be spent in his own personal prison. He needed to live fully again, to unlock the inventiveness and skill he'd bound in chains. But that was another task that would categorically *not* be on her to-do list.

Third, to make this work, she most certainly wouldn't be participating in evenings like last night again. Like when he ever-so-slowly slid his enormous hands down the bare spine her halter dress revealed, which was a sensation that would now rank in her personal hall of fame greatest moments of her life. Possibly even surpassing his slither against her in the sea ten years ago.

As long as there was none of *any* of that, she'd be fine.

Shane was already at the rooftop pool complex when Audrey and Daniel came up to meet him. This was where they'd tape one of the segments for Shane's TV special and also where they'd hold the press brunch. The area was quite a contrast to the no-frills employee pool. Audrey loved the grandeur of what was dubbed Maurice's Club, named after her grandfather who began the Girard hotel business.

This massive rooftop pool area was to be one of the highlights of Hotel Girard Las Vegas and she hoped it would be a big draw for guests. The day club pool scene in Vegas was a major part of the visit for the under thirty-five crowd. A day in the fresh air with cocktails, music and lots and lots of barely clad flesh brought people out in droves. And especially as a boutique hotel with no casino, many other events would take place at the pool, as well. She and her father had known that they would have to create a truly spectacular daytime venue to compete with what their giant neighbors had already established. And they had.

Audrey was thrilled to see the superb designs come to life. The area utilized a full L-shape of two sides of the roof of the square property. Glass guard rails enclosed the entire perimeter, which allowed a fun fifth-story view of Las Vegas Boulevard and the Strip.

The two swimming pools mirrored each other, both a sensuous pear shape. The narrower ends of the pools were linked together with a bridge. Guests would be able to walk over the bridge and interact with people in the water while swimmers could coast underneath to move from pool to pool. A crew was at work tiling both of the pools with turquoise glass mosaic.

As was the custom for pool clubs, a stage for well-known deejays and guest performers was under construction.

The landscapers had already planted rows of palm trees to define the club space. On the roof, round concrete platforms with two steps up to each level formed a staircase of patios where plush lounge chairs and small tables would be utilized by sun worshippers. Turquoise and fuchsia pink were the base colors for the pool decor. Coordinating umbrellas would provide shelter.

Six hot tubs were dotted across the roof. At the corner where the two sides of the roof met sat a section of pod-like structures, each of which had three walls and a canvas roof. These were the poolside cabanas for those seeking a luxury experience. With a curtain to draw for privacy, the interiors were to be equipped with a refrigerator to keep refreshments cold all day and wiring for electronics. Waitstaff would be shuttling in buckets of icy beers, tiered towers of seafood, silver trays of deserts. In essence, whatever the guest wanted, Hotel Girard would be able to provide. And charge for.

"Fabulous, sir." Shane reached to shake Daniel's hand after he had taken in the scope of this important hotel feature. "I walked through a couple of months ago, but now it's really taken shape."

"I've sent an eblast to our loyalty club members with an exclusive offer," Audrey announced. "Two nights in a suite and two days of cabanas and cocktails at an attractive price."

"Let's hope we've got a winner here on all fronts," Daniel said. "Audrey, fill us in on the press brunch."

One of the events for the grand opening was to be a full press tour of the hotel followed by mini massages from the spa staff and concluding with a brunch.

"We'll do the buffet here." Audrey pointed to the outer corner of the L, "that way everyone gets a great view."

"Good," Daniel approved.

"Shane had some helpful recommendations that we do fruit kebobs and breakfast pastries so that guests can eat standing or sitting on loungers, rather than food that needs tables or a fork and knife."

Shane lowered his aviator sunglasses and aimed his dark eyes at her, "I never said that."

"Yeah, you did," Audrey insisted. "When you also suggested we do a flavored-coffee bar and mini smoothies."

"Those are good ideas. Not mine."

Oops, Audrey winced. She hadn't had that conversation with *this* Shane! That was from a late-night brainstorming session she'd had with clever cardboard Shane.

"Great, that's what we'll go with," she quickly tried to cover. Shane wrinkled his eyebrows at her and then used one finger to secure his sunglasses back in place.

"What about the TV taping? You're shooting part of it up here?" Daniel asked.

"Can I snap a few pictures of you on my phone just to think about placement?" Audrey asked Shane. Photo shoots and TV segments with Shane at different locations in the hotel would showcase the property and help promote his iconic image.

Right now in his aviators, chef's coat and with those leather cords wrapped around his wrist, he had image to spare. He was so downright sexy she almost couldn't believe what her eyes saw through the phone's camera. Yes, photos of him would appeal to everyone on earth. Women would want to be *with* him and men would want to *be* him.

This was the man she had rubbed up against in the club last night. She couldn't have had a premonition of what it would feel like to be out in public with him. She had no way of knowing that he'd swirl her into a vortex where the rest of the world disappeared.

But she was not about to let any true feelings for Shane find an opening in the barricade she had built. Feelings could only lead to pain. Feelings only got a person into trouble.

"Were you thinking of doing a segment from the stage?" Daniel pointed to the raised area still being constructed.

"I was." Audrey snapped back to business. "But now I wonder if we shouldn't do it on the bridge between the pools."

"I'm not wearing a bathing suit." Shane made a slicing motion with his hand to indicate his limits. Daniel and Audrey laughed.

"Although, come on, that would be funny if we had you rise up from the pool like a god of the sea," Audrey bounced back. A sliver shot up her spine remembering that swish of wet Shane against wet Audrey in St. Thomas. "Seriously though, let's do get you out of the chef's coat for some of this. Maybe crisp white casual clothes. It will be perfect framing with you on the bridge, the pools gleaming, the Strip in the background."

Daniel elbowed his daughter affectionately. "Nice."

Shane nodded, too.

Audrey fixated on the bridge. On crossing a bridge. Passing from one reality in space and time. Into another.

"I had a nice time last night," Shane's voice called out to Audrey when she was on her third lap of the evening.

No! Not again! With twenty-four hours in a day, why were she and Shane in the employee pool at the exact same time again?

She asked the black sky for an answer but didn't receive one.

Tonight, Audrey was so tired she didn't even have the energy to run away from him. She just wanted to do her laps in peace, but he swam to meet her as she reached the edge of the pool.

"I had a really, really, really nice time last night at Big Top," he repeated.

Audrey squeezed some water out of her hair. "I did, too." Surely there was no harm in admitting that.

"I've been thinking all day about the imagination it took to conceive of that nightclub. While I'm beating my head against the wall in an empty kitchen, waiting for something to happen that just isn't coming."

"Would you be better off in the hustle and bustle of one of your restaurants?" she inquired with genuine concern. For people who didn't know each other very well, she and Shane seemed to cut to the quick with some brutally honest conversations. Which filled her with a mix of terror and emancipation she didn't know how to process. Her connection with him was unlike anything she'd ever experienced before.

"I'm sure you've been in one of your hotel restaurants during the dinner service?"

Audrey nodded. It was like a hospital emergency room.

"Everything happens so fast," he said, "you're firing on all cylinders. Orders are being barked, dishes are being finished and sent out. Cooks and waiters are yelling. Dishes are clattering. It's blistering hot and ear-splittingly loud. It can be the greatest rush in the world, but it can drain the life out of you."

"It must be very hectic."

"I used to thrive on it."

He pushed off the side and swam a lap. Audrey followed. With him a foot taller than her, she finished well behind.

"I've fizzled out. Nothing sparks me up anymore." They each held on to the edge of the pool.

He used two fingers on his free hand to move some strands of wet hair off her face. The tender touch across her forehead was in stark contrast to what he was saying to her.

She wasn't sure if he was asking for advice. "The ecstasy is gone." The pain in his eyes lasered toward her and struck at her heart. "I'm dead to it. I don't know how to reclaim it."

"But at Feed U, with the kids…"

"Oh, come on. Cutting up kooky-umbers for a bunch of cute munchkins who think I'm a rock star. How hard is that?"

It was impossible to reconcile the two Shanes. How could he deny the twinkle in his eye and the enthusiasm in his voice when he made salad with those kids and told them about the vitamins and minerals in leafy greens? That didn't mesh with the imprisoned man who couldn't break out of his own shackles.

"What would inspire you?" Audrey chastised herself for having thoughts on how to solve his problems. It wasn't her job to get involved, although if he was going to finish the cookbook, he needed to confront what was holding him back. "You mentioned some old friends you know in Vegas that you haven't been to see. Do you think that might help?"

"Maybe." She could tell he wanted to tell her something else. He started to speak and then stopped himself. "There's something I've only just figured out."

"Do you want to tell me what it is?"

The pool water became still as they remained in place. He stalled.

Exhaled.

Raked his hair.

Eyes darted out to the distance. Left to right as if he were defending his territory.

Then he looked to her.

But couldn't bear it so he returned to surveying nothingness.

"I didn't…"

Without finishing the thought, he took off for another lap across the pool. Audrey noticed the speed and ferocity with which he swam.

When he returned, his voice was tight and low.

"I didn't love her."

"Who?"

"My wife." Shane shook his head back and forth as if he himself was in total disbelief. His words were like bullets. "I. Didn't. Love. Her."

Suffering poured out of his eyes as they met hers.

Audrey instantly wanted to reach out and hold him while he cried out all the agony he had inside. Which was strange because that wasn't a gift anyone had ever extended to her. She'd always felt the need to hold herself together in front of other people. Any tears Audrey shed had been when she was alone. But she wanted to feel Shane's teardrops on her skin.

At the moment, though, he looked untouchable so she didn't dare move. Muscles spasmed in his arms and shoulders. Which convinced her that they weren't having a conversation. She just happened to be in the pool while he was having an emotional breakthrough.

But she *was* here. "Do you want to talk about it?"

Silence.

He pushed off for another lap. She followed and met him at the other side. Squinting, he said, "We had gone to her mother's cabin in upstate New York for a couple of days. To me, the trip was a sort of last ditch effort to make it better with her."

"Did it help?"

"No." He bristled as if arrows of memory were attacking him from every angle. "We were not a fit. We were just living out the whim we had acted on. It was growing more obvious with every day that we had nothing substantial between us."

"And?" Audrey encouraged him to keep talking.

"A torrential storm blew through and we were snowed

in," he said as if he was seeing the blizzard right in front of him. "Instead of that being romantic and cozy, it only pointed out the chasm between us even more clearly. I really couldn't take it anymore."

He stopped abruptly, working something through in his own mind.

"What happened after that?"

His lower jaw jutted out as he continued processing his thoughts.

"I told her that as soon as the weather cleared and we could get back to the city I was going to move out of our apartment." He squeezed his eyes shut and swallowed back a breath. "I'm sure she wasn't surprised. But she put on a jacket and went out the cabin's door. I thought she was just going out to the porch for air until I heard the car engine."

Audrey wrapped her hand around the leather cording that enveloped Shane's wrist, unable to censor herself from wanting to offer some tangible support. He violently shook her hand off.

"Visibility was terrible," he said as his head fell forward toward his chest. "I don't know how she even pulled the car out of the driveway. Sheer will, I suppose. I sat staring into my cup of coffee, lost in thought. And sadness. I'd intended to make it work with her. I thought I had tried."

"I'm so sorry," Audrey muttered. She'd had no idea that Shane had been unhappy in his marriage. How many times had he told this story, and when he did, what got included and what got left out? What was he editing out now?

"By the time I comprehended what she was doing, I ran to the front door to stop her, but she was gone. I'd been so caught up in my own head, I'd let her go. Within a few miles of the cabin she crashed into a telephone pole."

"You couldn't have predicted what would happen," Audrey interjected.

He leaned his elbows on the ledge of the pool and held his face in his hands. Sheer sorrow poured out of him. "The highway patrol had advised staying off the roads. I should have chased after her. I couldn't protect her from the mistake of our marriage, but I should have shielded her from harm. I was her husband."

"It doesn't sound like she would have listened at that moment."

"I was her *husband*. Who didn't love her." He gulped in some air. Jutted out his chin again and then retracted it. Anguish roiled through his voice. "I didn't love her. I've never said that out loud."

Drops of water trickled down from his hair onto his back. His voice rose. "I DIDN'T LOVE HER!"

CHAPTER SEVEN

"LET'S GO FOR a ride," Shane said to Audrey when she arrived at the kitchen's delivery dock. He'd texted her early this morning and asked her to meet him.

"Where are we going this time?"

"You want to take the bike?" he pointed to his nearby motorcycle.

"I most certainly do not want to take the bike," she scrunched up her nose.

"I know, I know, you're not dressed for it." He repeated what she had said the last time when she wouldn't put the helmet on. Indeed, in yet another prim business dress, today in navy, and her high heels, Audrey was not going to straddle his Yamaha. That was okay. He was only teasing her. With a wave, he opened the passenger door of the Jeep for her to get in.

"Where are you taking me?" She tried again as she swung into the seat and put on her dark sunglasses.

"Somewhere that worked for me in the past," he closed the car door.

"Okay," she kindly agreed.

Shane cranked up his rock 'n' roll and took off. They traveled far away from the Strip and the center of the town. Soon the gorgeous Spring Mountains of the Mojave Desert didn't have to compete with the pizzazz of the city. He hadn't taken this drive in a long time but it was one he knew by heart. It was good to be out on the open road, silent but for his music, with Audrey beside him.

It was true about getting things off your chest.

After last night in the pool with Audrey, when Shane had said aloud for the first time that he had never loved Melina, he drove home with agonizing remembrances banging through his head.

As soon as he got to his apartment, he'd crashed face-down on his bed. He'd punched his pillows, screamed and even wept. Cried for the first time since Melina's death, until he finally emptied what had seemed a bottomless well of grief.

Then, much to his surprise, he felt lighter. His outpouring didn't minimize the tragedy of Melina's death. It did nothing to alleviate his guilt, either about not preventing her accident or about not loving her. Yet it had never before occurred to him that he hadn't been able to get it all said.

Taking the words from inside his brain and putting them into his mouth gave them a perimeter. The words had a beginning and they had an end. It was his horror to face head-on, but it was much better than carrying it around in his gut like a lead weight.

The last thing he could remember thinking about before he finally fell asleep was Audrey in the pool placing her hand on his arm to offer comfort. It was somehow because of her that he was able to face his truth.

The first thing he thought of when he woke up this morning was seeing her again as soon as possible.

The second thought was of Josefina, his longtime pal who reminded him of his grandmother Lolly. It was shameful that he'd been spending this much time in Vegas and hadn't gone out to see her yet. Previously, if he'd been anywhere near the American Southwest he'd made a point to connect with her. If there was any hope for him, he needed to stop cutting himself off from what might help set him straight.

After letting out his secret about Melina, Josefina was the next bridge to cross.

Eventually, they reached the left turn at the corner Laundromat. Everything looked exactly the same as it had when he was here last. Children played ball in the street. Small houses were painted in pastel colors. Then it was a right at the local *mercado*. A banner hung from an old church building advertising worship services in Spanish. With another right turn, he pulled into the parking lot of Casa Josefina.

"What's this?" Audrey asked while unbuckling her seat belt. She smoothed down her hair, which had been swirling in the open-topped Jeep. Navigating the graveled parking lot was no easy maneuver for her in her work heels. Shane dashed to her side to provide a stable arm, which she gratefully grabbed hold of. His chest swelled with a sort of pride as he helped her into the small adobe building.

"Remember how you suggested that I reach out to important people in my life who I've been cut off from? I'm taking your advice."

"Shane, *mi amor*!" Josefina noticed them as soon as they came through the restaurant's door. She rushed over. "I am so happy to see you. Why has it taken you so long to visit me?"

Was the answer that shame and regret had kept him from those he cared about?

All he could do now was try to move forward. Shane embraced Josefina, wrapping his arms around her slim body. Josefina had been something of a mentor, and she was certainly a true friend. They kissed each other on both cheeks.

"How are the grandbabies?"

"Paulo is riding his tricycle day and night. Olivia is learning to walk."

"If there's anything Josefina loves more than cooking, it's her family," Shane said to Audrey by way of introduction. "This is my friend Audrey."

That sounded awkward the minute it came out of his mouth. Audrey wasn't exactly his friend.

His introduction didn't matter to Josefina, who sized Audrey up with a sparkle in her eyes and a toothy grin that told Shane she was thinking the obvious. That Audrey was a love interest he had brought to her restaurant.

"Que linda," she complimented Audrey. Pretty, she surely was. Then Josefina murmured under her breath to Shane, *"Finalmente."*

"No, Josefina," Shane protested with a chuckle. "Audrey is actually a coworker." He realized he should have asked Audrey ahead of time if she wanted to be introduced with her last name. Everyone in Vegas knew the Girards had purchased the old Royal Neva. Maybe Audrey wasn't in the mood for a barrage of questions, so he didn't mention it.

"Coworker? I see." Josefina shot him a mischievous smile of disbelief. "You have come to eat? Please." She gestured into her small restaurant.

The dining room was dark but strung with Christmas lights that blinked year-round. Half of the dark wood booths were filled with midafternoon diners. Come dinnertime, people would be waiting an hour for a table to sample Josefina's Oaxacan specialties. Attracting a mix of locals and tourists, the restaurant was both a neighborhood joint and a foodie pilgrimage.

With the raised dais in the corner decorated with hanging piñatas and streams of Mexican flags, the restaurant also sometimes served as a wedding chapel. Josefina was an ordained marriage officiant. After all, this was Vegas and that designation had been known to come in handy.

"I need to take a call." Audrey swiped her phone.

Meanwhile, everything Shane wanted to say to Josefina spilled out. About being stymied in his efforts to nail down the cookbook recipes. How blocked in general he was. The disconnection and isolation he'd been feeling.

Josefina patted him on the back. "Now you have come to see me. And you are with this magical woman. Change is in the wind."

Just what he'd been thinking on the car ride over.

"Come, *chicos*, I am starting a pot of mole negro. Mole is so complicated it takes your mind off of your troubles." She took Shane by the arm and turned to Audrey. "You put your phone away, *linda*, and come to my kitchen."

Josefina gave them aprons, which they tied on. Audrey couldn't do anything about her business garb but pulled her hair back into a ponytail with a band she found in her purse. "Toast the onions and garlic in the frying pan," Josefina instructed her. "Shane, the chilies have been soaking. Now we puree them."

Her small kitchen with its well-worn supplies and equipment was nothing like the huge operation Shane was running at his restaurants. Everything that came out of this kitchen was flavored with love, something he needed to remember if he wanted to stay sincere to his own mission of treating each diner as if the meal had been prepared just for them.

He enjoyed the heavy crank of Josefina's old-fashioned food mill as he used it to separate the skins from the flesh of the chilies.

Grandma Lolly had had one just like it. Shane wondered if it was in the stack of old pots and pans of hers he had under his desk at the restaurant. He hadn't worked with Lolly's things in a long time. Maybe that would help him get back what he'd lost.

Audrey dutifully moved the chopped onion and minced garlic around the scorching hot skillet. She'd told Shane she didn't know how to cook. But she was a hard worker, he could tell that from all she did for her family's company.

And he couldn't help gawking at how lovely she looked as she performed the task with a determined concentration.

"Josefina is from Oaxaca in Southwestern Mexico," Shane explained to Audrey over the sizzle of her pan. "The area is known for some of the most complex food in that country. Moles are sauces that have dozens of ingredients."

Josefina continued to give them small steps working toward the completion of her mole. Pan fry the sesame seeds. Then the pecans. When they have cooled down, pulverize them in a spice grinder. "That's right, *mijo*." She caressed Shane's back with the endearment used for a son. "This is what we do. We get absorbed in the work. The miracle is in the work."

Fry the raisins. Fry the plantains. Shane did appreciate the meditation of the tasks.

Josefina's two staff cooks filled orders for diners in the same small space with them while upbeat Spanish music played from an old radio. When the sauce had reached the point where it needed to simmer, Josefina served Shane and Audrey a plate of chicken topped with the last of her mole negro from the previous batch. "It is still my top seller," Josefina said, talking shop to Shane.

He and Audrey stood in a corner of the kitchen, two forks digging into the same plate.

Audrey's eyes lit up at the flavor of the dense, spicy, almost black sauce atop the simple grilled chicken.

"What do I taste that's familiar?" she asked.

"I'll give you three guesses," Shane teased. He tilted his head to Josefina, "Sugar here has got a big-time sweet tooth. Maybe this is the way we'll get her to eat chicken."

"Chocolate!" Audrey exclaimed. "Wow, is that good. Chocolate on chicken. But it's not really sweet, is it? It has layers of flavor. Brilliant."

"This girl is full of life, yes, Shane?" Josefina arched her eyebrows knowingly at him.

"I told you—" Shane gently squeezed Josefina's shoulder "—she and I are business partners."

Josefina flashed her playful grin. "Maybe it's a different kind of partner you need, *mijo*."

After Josefina packed them some food to take, it was time to go. In the dining room, Shane hugged her. Then Josefina embraced Audrey as if she'd known her for her entire life. "When my Xavier died," she murmured to Audrey, although Shane was able to hear, "I could not come back to myself. It took a lot of time and a lot of patience to heal."

Shane knew Josefina was talking about him. Audrey looked Josefina in the eyes, unsure what to make of the unexpected intimacy. Then Audrey blurted, "My mother died three years ago. She was fifty-three."

"Ah, so you and Shane have your tragedies to bind you."

Audrey blinked heavily, not having been prepared for Josefina's quick analysis.

"These two want to get married." Josefina pointed to a couple waiting on the dais who were dressed in jeans but adorned with feather boas, sequined bowler hats and neon-plastic sunglasses. "Vegas, baby."

In the Jeep on the way back, Shane had a crystal-clear thought.

The pace he'd been keeping coupled with Melina's death had removed him from the only alchemy he'd ever known. By combining ingredients the way a painter would mix paints, he used to be able to find a new color. A holy formation that wasn't on the earth before.

After the devastation of Melina's death and the self-reproach that tore pieces of his flesh away day by day, those brushes with divinity stopped coming. Really the process had been shutting down for years. His relationship with Melina had been a chore. The lust, if that's what it would be called, that drew them together had long since faded. Pretending to keep up the relationship with someone who was essentially a stranger had done nothing more than wear him out.

His business had already been sagging before her death. He had lost steam. Too much fame, too many accolades, too many projects at too young an age to handle them. A lightbulb that burned too brightly. The restaurants had gotten to the point where they were running themselves, but he wasn't doing anything to keep them fresh and vital. He'd turned the kitchens over to his executive chefs, who were inventing the specials and new menu ideas that he should have been. When he crept into the New York or LA restaurants, it was usually to cook for an event or a group of VIPs that Reg had courted. Perhaps the Murphy brothers had gone as far as they could without that next insight into the future.

Then Reg was approached by the Girards with this Vegas idea. Which seemed like an ideal location with Shane's predilection for Spanish cooking and Vegas's world-class dining. Maybe this could be it. Las Vegas could turn everything around. Great food was available here. And Audrey was right—he needed to reconnect with people who knew him when he was at his best, like Josefina and his old kitchen mates from Paris, Tino and Loke.

Vegas could be where he found the good luck charm he had misplaced. It could not only revive, but catapult his career. Could he open up his soul again and reunite with the spirit that used to run through him? Was he capable of new heights?

As they sped down the open road away from Josefina's, both Shane and Audrey were absorbed in their own thoughts. She was rerunning Josefina's words to her about how she and Shane had loss to tie them together. Did having something like that in common *really* make people more compatible? Did it define who they were?

What she and Shane seemed to share was a commitment to *not* getting into a relationship after what their pasts had dealt them. Audrey hoped that important similarity itself would carry them through their dealings together.

The sun was beginning to set behind the mountains. "Wow—" Audrey pointed ahead to the horizon "—that's incredibly beautiful."

"Do you have to get back to the hotel? Let's take a longer look," Shane stated rather than asked. At the next turnoff, he drove them farther from the city along a flat road paved through dirt, cactus and other desert flora. Closer to the foot of the mountains, he pulled the car over and shut off the engine. In the peaceful silence of nowhere, Audrey vaguely remembered scenes from mafia movies where thugs would take wise guys out here never to return.

The view of the sunset was otherworldly. Nature was putting on one of her best shows. The noble red mountains with their voluptuous slopes rested calm and proud as darkness descended on them. Beneath the clusters of billowy clouds, the colors in the sky presented stunning layers of blue, purple, orange and yellow.

"That is something, isn't it?" Shane marveled.

"What a strange place Las Vegas is. All that man-made light and sound right in the center of all of this," she swept her arm left to right at the spectacular scenery in front of them.

Las Vegas, *the Meadows* in Spanish, had begun to attract visitors with legalized gambling, and loose requirements for marriage and divorce, in the 1930s. It grew, and continued to grow, into a one-of-a-kind oasis in the desert that the whole world flocked to. A place where people left their troubles at home, and came to play and indulge. As a restaurateur and hotelier, Shane and Audrey were trying to get their own pieces of that promise.

Shane unbuckled his seat belt and leaned back to enjoy the panorama. Audrey did the same. Out of the corner of her eye, she studied him. His striking face with its distinct jawline and beard stubble could almost give the sunset a run for its money. She stiffened at the realization that she hadn't sat in a parked car with a man in years. Not only hadn't she sat with a man in a parked car, she hadn't been anywhere with a man.

What had she become? Just a work bunny who pattered around all day long until she was exhausted enough to go to sleep, only to wake up and do it again? What kind of life was that? What was the end game?

A part of her was very disappointed to lose Reg.

Maybe it would have worked out nicely to have the less challenging Murphy as a companion. With Reg, she wouldn't have had to risk getting hurt. Wouldn't have had to ask herself any questions like the ones about authentic love that had begun scrolling through her mind since she'd been spending time with Shane.

But Reg was no longer an option. He'd flown off to share sunsets filled with real feelings.

And here she sat with this red-hot man beside her now. Who was dynamite and could blow her into pieces. His mere being already held too great a power over her. They'd experienced too much together already.

It wasn't only her mind that asked questions when she was around Shane. It was her very essence, her identity, her womanhood, her soul. Those were supposed to be off-limits.

Shane stretched his shoulders back and let out a sigh. The reverberation of his voice made every hair on her body stand on end.

"How do you know Josefina?" Audrey asked to distract herself from the dangerous places her insides were taking her.

Shane smiled while he kept his eyes on the sunset. "Through Diego Reyes, a madman chef in Mexico City. He brought Josefina and me together years ago to create a banquet for his daughter's wedding and we became fast friends."

"She's very loving."

He agreed, "She reminds me of my grandmother Lolly, who taught me how to cook and serve food in the first place."

"What's something you remember learning to cook with Lolly?" Was she putting on her micromanaging hat, as if trying to solve Shane's problems was a way of distancing herself from her own? Every move Shane made and every move she made around him seemed to be calling her out on her own facades, on the lies she'd told herself too many times.

Shane's mouth tipped into a half smile. "Coddle. An old Irish dish she learned from *her* mother. Which can be dull as old shoes but, of course, Great-grandma Peg's recipe was delicious."

"What was her secret?"

"Sorry, Sugar, I'll never tell that one."

Audrey shifted in her seat. It made her itch every time he called her Sugar. She hated it. She loved it.

"When we drove out to Josefina's, you told me that cooking with her had helped you in the past. What did you mean?"

"The way she cooks reminds me that there aren't any shortcuts. Yeah, there's inspiration, but it's only slogging through that gets you where you're going. I'm waiting for a lightbulb to go off in my brain. I've lost my perseverance for the sheer work."

Audrey felt the opposite. All she could do was work, lose herself in detail. In the absence of toil, there was only emptiness.

Idle time was an aching reminder of what she was missing. What she had always been lacking. Deep down, that love she'd never received from her mother was something she'd never stop yearning for.

Her heart spiraled downward in sputters until it reached despair. Then she set her intention and pulled herself back up to the surface as she'd done so many times before.

Asking Shane another question, she threw herself a rope.

"How does a recipe get created?"

"An idea starts to come together in your mind. And then you try it out. And it's not right. You change it around. A little less this, a little more that, let's add in something else. Then you try it again. And again. And again. Eventually, if you're lucky, you find something that's only yours."

"You'll find your way back." She was sure of it.

Apparently having had enough of that conversation, Shane opened his car door. "Let's get out."

He came around to her side of the car and helped her out. There were no other cars anywhere. They were miles away from town, under the sunset and the hush of nightfall.

With no warning whatsoever, Shane rested one hand on each of Audrey's shoulders. He leaned down and kissed her. His lips pressed against hers with closed-mouthed but adamant force.

Her neck flushed instantly. Having him close to her was a little bit familiar now after their bodies had writhed together with their sexy dancing at Big Top. But he hadn't kissed her that night, and this new intimacy set off alarms in her system.

It was a shock she missed with all of her might when he took his lips away.

Shane let loose a laugh that echoed in the quiet of the desert. "My apologies. I don't know what the heck I did there."

Audrey's lungs ceased functioning. She was furious at him for having taken his lips from her. All she could seem to want was for him to kiss her again. Oxygen in, carbon dioxide out—she reminded herself of the basic breathing process.

"Come here," he said, filling her with the hope that

his mouth would graze hers again. Her eyelids fluttered uncontrollably.

But no. He lifted her up and sat her on the hood of his Jeep. Then hoisted himself onto it, as well. He maneuvered backward so that he could lean back against the glass of the windshield with his legs outstretched on the hood. Then he helped shimmy Audrey backward so that she could do the same.

She somehow didn't care that she was wearing a business dress and heels. His spontaneity was liberating.

Now they were able to continue to watch nature's spectacle with a warm breeze gliding across their faces.

Audrey had to settle herself down. He'd obviously kissed her by mistake. Out of some kind of urge that probably had nothing to do with her. She shouldn't read anything into it.

Maybe sensing Audrey's discomfort, Shane thankfully broke the quiet. "What was Josefina saying to you about tragedies?"

She creased her forehead, not sure what or how much was appropriate to tell Shane. "I told her that my mother died three years ago. Josefina thought that loss was a similarity to share."

Shane chuckled wistfully. "Does it work that way?"

Audrey shook her head. "I was wondering the same thing."

They took in the majesty of the sunset again. The sides of their bodies pressed into each other.

"You didn't love your wife," Audrey mused, "and my mother didn't love me."

"What do you mean your mother didn't love you?"

"She didn't. She suffered from a debilitating depression. I wasn't wanted and she never let me get close." Three or four tears broke their way out of hiding and dripped down Audrey's cheek. "When she was dying of cirrhosis of the liver, she didn't let me near then, either. And I didn't push. I let my dad watch her die while I studied market share statements."

"I let Melina die. I didn't protect her."

"I let my mother die without forcing her to let me care."

"We're quite a pair then."

"So we do have something in common, like Josefina said."

Shane turned himself until he was facing her. He kissed the tears on her face, one by one, ever so lightly. A sigh slipped through her lips.

"So soft," he murmured as he dotted kisses all over her face.

His beard stubble felt exactly as she imagined it would, rasping across her cheeks with a welcome harshness. Filling her with the wholly biological need for contact with something that was wholly male. Something that she'd dared not think of in years.

When his mouth inched down her neck, her head fell backward.

With a flattened palm, he caressed the length of her throat from behind her ear to the swerve of her shoulder. His lips moved under the collar of her dress. In a beat, her back arched to meet him.

Flowering with anticipation, her parted lips waited for him to return upward. As if he knew she couldn't delay a moment longer, his open mouth rejoined hers. A quick succession of kisses was followed by a longer one that melded them into each other.

Her arms reached around his neck. His mouth possessed hers, communicating what she had to hear. She met his every sensation, the kisses swirling deeper, further, quaking both of them at their epicenters.

"What are we doing?" Audrey muttered against his lips as Shane's kisses obscured the purple and orange sky from her view.

He whispered, "Sharing loss."

CHAPTER EIGHT

SHANE SHOVED HIS blanket off and rubbed his bare chest and belly. He knew he needed to get out of bed but the blackout shades had done their job of shielding him from the Nevada morning sun and he was just that comfortable. Soft, soft, soft. Audrey's face. Audrey's hands. Audrey's hair. Audrey's mouth. The word *soft* could be applied to so many of the images that played like a video in his mind.

The sun had set and risen again yet he couldn't concentrate on anything other than the memory of kissing Audrey on the hood of his Jeep yesterday.

Of course, it was totally inappropriate. It was all wrong the way their lips explored each other's like they did. It wasn't thought through. It wasn't smart. It wasn't professional.

But, man, was it a mind-blower.

He hadn't had the desire to kiss a woman that way in ages. The long, long, slow dance with Audrey's mouth had been totally unexpected. And left him certain that he'd never enjoyed kissing anyone that much.

His kisses with Melina had been different. Their physical encounters had begun with an aggressive hunger that was satisfied only too quickly. No time was taken for savoring.

With Audrey, all Shane could envision was the opposite. Were he to make love with her, which he was not going to do, he'd take all the time in the world. He'd bring her waters from warm to hot, and then keep them at a simmer long before he'd let them reach the boiling point. If he ever got her into his bed, he'd...well, that was never, ever, to happen.

Sure, maybe the time had come for him to start dating again. Though he'd never let a woman all the way back into his life. He couldn't be counted on and wouldn't bestow that unreliability on anybody. No one deserved that. Look what had happened with Melina.

If he did decide to fulfill primitive needs, there were billions of women in the world. Audrey was not an option. She was the most precious creature he'd ever encountered and she deserved the kind of dedication and protection he could never offer. Safeguarding was indeed what she needed after what sounded like a childhood filled with dashed hopes and disappointment. He would deny himself anything not to risk injuring her further.

Not to mention the fact that they were corporate partners and, with any luck, would be for many years to come. Messing with that wasn't a gamble to be taken. Business never mixed with pleasure, and with the stakes as high as they were for both families, no unnecessary chances should be taken.

In fact, he couldn't risk any more brushes with her like yesterday's kissing, or even the other night's dancing. Anything further would take him past the point of no return.

Into the stuff of dreams.

Which could too easily turn to nightmares.

But soaping himself up in the shower, he couldn't help riding on the high of those kisses.

* * *

After the drive to the restaurant's kitchen, Shane flipped on the lights with one clear intention. Moving aside the jumble of odds and ends and files that had been shoved under his desk as they set up the office, Shane found what he was looking for. A big packing box that he had sent himself from New York.

Grandma Lolly's pots and pans were easily his most treasured possessions. An instant smile crossed his lips as he opened the box. Like old friends, those pots and pans were his grounding on this earth. He'd let far too much time go by without visiting these beacons.

"Knock, knock." Audrey's voice called out from the back entrance of the kitchen.

"In here," Shane yelled from his office, which was separated from the kitchen with a smoked-glass partition. She found him sitting in the middle of the floor with the box open in front of him.

How was she always so beautiful? She was the personification of the sunny morning. Her blond hair was shiny and clean, and her pink blouse accentuated her creamy skin. His belly lurched with the appetite to pull her down to the floor and pick up where they left off yesterday at sunset.

"What are you doing down there?"

"These were my Grandma's." He pointed inside the box. "These cooking tools are like someone else's childhood teddy bear. I don't have a memory that goes back further than these do."

He lifted out a skillet. It was crusty and rusted but he caressed it as gently as he had Audrey's glossy hair yesterday. "She taught me my first recipe with this pan."

"What was it?"

"Just fried bread and eggs, but what she taught me was

how to not fear fire. How to control it. That's the most basic mastery a cook needs."

Audrey stood in the doorway, listening. His impulse to talk to her about things that were important to him was growing every day. Maybe it was just that he'd cut himself off from everyone for so long, he was relearning how to articulate what was inside.

An internal voice corrected him. It was Audrey in particular Shane wanted to talk to.

"My grandma never had old-lady hands," he continued. "Her skin stayed taut until the day she died."

Now Audrey moved toward him. And even though she was in one of her work outfits, she sat down on the floor next to him.

"She had her fair share of burn scars," he chuckled. "You can't spend a life in the kitchen without those."

He displayed the inside of his right arm for Audrey to see. "That was from buquerones fritos." He used his left hand to point to the biggest welt, which was a good inch and a half. Then he switched to his left arm to show her another choice one. Two, actually, that formed a V shape. "And thank you, coliflor rebozada."

"That's a doozy."

"But for all the cooking and dishwashing and running her diner in Brooklyn, Grandma Lolly had the nicest hands."

Shane took one of Audrey's small hands into his. Maybe his grandma had the second nicest hands. Audrey's were pure. They were pink and rounded rather than bony. The orange nail polish was the only thing that revealed they weren't the hands of a small child.

Without thinking twice, he brought her hand up toward his mouth, about to deliver a light kiss to each finger. He stopped himself in time.

No more kissing her, he chastised his urge. He must keep things only professional with her. Why was he finding that difficult to remember?

Shane returned Audrey's hand to her lap without a word about his actions. Reaching into the box, he hoisted out Lolly's large cast-iron pot.

"Ah, she taught me so many recipes with this Dutch oven. It was her favorite. Soups and mashes. Summer stews. Winter braises for cold nights." He rubbed the bottom of the pot like it could appreciate his affection. "You know, this pot is really why I'm a chef. This is the first one I used to try to create my own recipes."

He'd ask his grandma if thyme might add a good layer of flavor for mushrooms, or if the sweetness of carrots might enhance a potato puree. She'd lean down and give him a pat on the back with approval when he'd come up with something that tasted good. Years later, when he grew tall, she'd have to stretch up to pat the same spot on him.

And although the Brooklyn diner led to the Lolly's chain and a formidable restaurant business for the family, it was Grandma Lolly's special cash jar, which she diligently added to every week, that sent Shane to culinary school. She'd wanted it that way.

He owed so much to her. She'd hate what he'd turned into. Bitter and washed up at thirty-four years old. Lolly would expect him to dust himself off no matter how great his fall and pull himself back together.

Her small sauce pot was almost warm in his hands. He reached into the box for her knife roll. Which he spread out, and then he touched each blade. They were all dull, but a good sharpening could resurrect them.

Here he was in this humongous state-of-the-art kitchen with every tool and gadget at his disposal, his own equipment and knives the finest in the world, yet he knew that he needed to sharpen his grandmother's knives and pretend he was a young boy in the safe haven of her home kitchen.

He stretched one arm up to his desk and grabbed a pencil and scrap of paper, which he pulled down and handed to Audrey.

"Can you write this down? I'll start with the holy trinity of green peppers, onions and celery. But not with andouille, we'll use chorizo. And lux it up with lobster..."

Four hours later, Shane finished his sixth version of a Cajun-style paella. "Taste," he said to Audrey, who had been coming and going while she took care of other matters on the property but kept popping in to check his progress.

He spooned some of it into her mouth, noting that feeding her had become his new favorite hobby. She nodded her approval and circled the recipe on the piece of paper that was now covered in scribbles. "It's roasting the garlic that works, and less of it?"

"I think I nailed it." He did a shimmy with his shoulders that made Audrey giggle. He grabbed her arm and pulled her to him for a waltz around the kitchen even though the music was better suited to head banging. He kissed two fingers on his own hand and raised them up toward the ceiling. "Thank you, Grandma."

"You've got it?" Audrey wanted to be certain.

"Ladies and gentlemen, Shane Murphy has finally developed a new recipe."

If Audrey ever wondered who Shane Murphy was before he lost himself, she had her answer. To watch today as the creative juices flowed back into his hands was something to behold. To experience his earnest sense of hospitality, the way he cared to determine whether every single dash of salt would be pleasing to his diner, was magnificent.

She had been watching a painter at his easel. A composer at the piano. It was inspiring the way a resounding "crap" at any failure was quickly followed by the sizzle of oil in a clean skillet or the dice of a new onion. Labor was how he passed the time while waiting for the muse to tell him how to solve the next problem.

"You, sir, are poetry in motion," she gushed to Shane. Cardboard Shane, that is.

Back in the shelter of her bungalow she could let out what she'd managed to hold in all day. Namely, her wish against wishes that Shane would hold her, kiss her and dance with her again. When part of her yearning came true and he waltzed her around the kitchen after confirming that his paella was finally perfected, Shane fed her body a lifeblood she was sure she would have perished without.

Now, being totally honest, sitting on her bed with her shoes kicked off, gawking at that cutout that she was so enamored of, she wondered if every suite shouldn't be adorned with one of them, and she could admit her revelation.

She wanted to make love with Shane. The prolonged, slow, "lasts all night" type of love. She wanted to do things with him she'd never experienced. The kind of lovemaking that leaves you exhilarated and sweaty and spent on the bed, unable to get up for work the next day.

Through watching Shane in action today, she could tell that he knew deep things about passion and about satisfaction, about modulation and temperance. She wanted him to teach her.

"Hello…" She almost blushed with embarrassment when she answered Daniel's phone call.

She had a flashing moment of fury at her dad. What she was specifically angry about, she didn't know. About her mother. About the twisted person Audrey had become, who told herself she didn't want to be loved. And didn't want to love in return.

Nothing was really her father's fault. Back when her mother was alive, he had been so focused on just putting one foot in front of the next. Trying to take over the hotels from his own father, who had worked for decades to build their name and reputation. Directing and growing the brand. She couldn't really blame anything on her dad. There was something so innocent about him. He'd never known how bad it had gotten for her, the loneliness and the isolation of day after day with a mother who stayed upstairs in a bedroom that was off-limits to Audrey.

The sound of her dad's voice on the other end of the phone was a perfect reminder that she had no reason to be daydreaming about making love with Shane.

They were, and would remain, colleagues and nothing more. She wouldn't even be spending this much time with him if not for the cookbook and the publicity campaigns. Which were necessary for both families. Time to zip it up, rein it in and put her steely face on. She was more than capable of that. That was classic Audrey Girard.

"Do you want to come by my office for dinner?" Daniel asked her.

"Sorry, I can't. Shane asked me to go out with some chef buddies of his."

"Hmm…" Daniel's voice rose an octave. "Have you leaked it to the press?"

Audrey laughed in surprise that she hadn't thought of that. And why hadn't she? Everything Shane did was supposed to be toward a goal.

But when Shane asked her after his victory in the

kitchen if she wanted to meet some old friends of his, she knew it was sincere. That he really wanted her to come along. She just needed to keep on guard.

After her now-customary fashion show in the mirror before she decided on what outfit to wear, a fitted black blouse with a deep scoop neck paired with a full lacy white skirt seemed right for what Shane said would be a chefs' night off. She was just slipping on her heels when there was a knock at the bungalow's door.

"Ready," Audrey called as she grabbed her purse and unlatched the lock to find Shane standing in her doorway.

It seemed the most natural thing in the world to lean into him and kiss hello. Fortunately, she caught herself swerving toward him and pulled back in the nick of time. Those kisses under the sunset last night were a beginner's mistake. Not to be repeated. Let yesterday be a lesson to her.

First and foremost, business partners do not shower each other with kisses. Fine, they got carried away yesterday, but now it was time to back up and get on the correct track. Second, kisses like the ones she had with Shane, the kind that made you crave more and more and more of them, were not on her menu. Kisses could lead to feelings. Feelings might lead to hope. And hope led to heartbreak. She knew that connect-the-dots only too well.

Shane placed his hand on the door in an attempt to open it farther. "Can I look at your bungalow? I haven't seen the interior of a finished one."

"Yeah sure." She gestured him in. But as he lifted his foot over the threshold, she suddenly remembered the cardboard cutout of him that had become part of her decor. She surely didn't want him to see that she had it in her room. Propped directly facing her bed no less! Reg had left town so hastily, he never followed up on what

Audrey had done with the display after she removed it from the front of the restaurant. And knowing Shane, it wasn't something that ever occurred to him to ask about.

"Oh, actually, it's really too much of a mess right now." Audrey tried to shove Shane aside and get the door closed behind them as quickly as possible. "Why don't you come back tomorrow after Housekeeping has been through?"

"I don't care about a mess." He pushed on the door as Audrey tried to pull on the door handle.

"I'd rather you didn't," she protested with a tug.

"What's the big deal?" His strength made this a losing battle for her.

"Personal items, okay?" Her eyes defied him. And won.

He lifted his palms in surrender. "Alright, Sugar. Let's go. I've got to stop by Feed U first."

Audrey bit her lip in relief.

Shane drove them to the parking lot at the warehouse kitchen and they went in. Teen helper Santiago was the only one inside.

Santiago gave Shane his four-part handshake. When he turned to Audrey to do the same, she fumbled less than she had when they met the first time. She remembered the other day here, the guileless faces of the young children with their salad and their bread dough, gazing up at Shane as if he was a superhero. If only she'd had a superhero to look up to when she was a kid.

"What are you cooking?" Shane asked Santiago.

"Me and my cousins are going to try to make tamales like our great-grandma used to do."

Audrey noticed the bags of groceries on the counter.

"Okay, you know I can't let you cook without an adult here. You'll wait until Lois comes?"

"Yeah, man, no problem."

"And you'll lock everything down if she wants to leave and you stay to clean up?"

"Yeah, no problem. Thanks."

"Alright. Have fun." Shane handed him the keys.

"Man, it's good to see you," Tino said as he pulled Shane in for a bear hug.

"Been too long," Loke followed with a clinch for his old kitchen mate.

"Audrey, I want you to meet Tino and Loke." Shane introduced her to his two friends who were also cooking in Las Vegas. "The three of us go all the way back to apprenticing in Paris with Pierre."

Shane had been in and out of Vegas for months as he readied the restaurant but had made excuses to avoid hanging out with these guys. They were from a different time in his life. When he had been full of ideas and dreams.

Funny, but he felt some of those old feelings of hope and possibility coming back now.

Tonight, just like when he went to visit Josefina, he was very happy to have Audrey there with him, seeing these pals from the old days. The way she made him feel seemed to give him courage. Drive him forward. Finally.

"Oh, yeah, we'll never forget Paris," said Loke, a short but solid wall of muscle who hailed from Osaka. He shook Audrey's hand. With a perfect French accent, Loke mimicked their old instructor to a T. "Zee pate a choux muz be creesp ahn hallo."

Tino, a lanky Italian American, and Shane nodded in memory. "You muz slap zee dough aginst zee saucepan," Tino chimed in with his pretty good impersonation. He shook Audrey's hand, as well.

Shane added, "The guy was a major pill, but darn if we didn't learn how to make profiteroles in our sleep."

"I'm hungry. Let's eat," Tino urged.

The four left the entrance where they had met and strutted through the casino floor at the MGM Grand. The night was hopping with its herds of people who had fled their normal lives to come to the mirage that was Las Vegas.

The lights and sounds of the slot machines permeated the casino. Clangs signifying jackpots came from every direction even though, in reality, it was the casinos that gained win after win.

Cocktail waitresses in skimpy costumes hoisted trays of drinks while maneuvering through the rows of gaming tables. Blackjack, roulette and craps games were all in play. High rollers puffed on cigars while women who'd had too much cosmetic surgery sat beside them, some dragging on cigarettes in designated smoking areas and others looking around, hoping to be noticed. Poker tournaments and high-stakes games like baccarat were being played in areas partitioned off to the sides of the main gaming floor.

Besides the gamblers, people crossed the casino floor headed in every direction. The masses were from every corner of the earth, comprised of all colors, all ages, all sizes, all socio-economic classes.

Tourists in sneakers snapped photos. Older people walked slowly or used motor scooters or wheelchairs. Travel group chaperones pointed out casino features in several languages.

Groups of people in their twenties moved in packs this way or that. Many held cocktails. Among them, all of the young women wore a uniform of little dresses cut way up to there and sky-high heels. Of the men who accompanied them, some wore dress shirts and slacks while others looked incongruous with their dates in T-shirts and baseball hats, and some even in sports shorts.

Audrey and her curves looked hotter than any other woman around in her fitted black top tucked into a tasteful skirt. That body of hers was a true hourglass shape and Shane was starting to catch himself on far too many occasions imagining what all those inclines and angles might feel like without clothes to cover them. He'd held her during that crazy kissing on top of his car but, even in the throes of that, he'd censored himself from letting his hands wander too much.

The back of his mind lectured the front lobes that good things came to those who waited. Although, really, he shouldn't be waiting to experience her naked flesh because that was not going to happen. Never. Ever.

Nonetheless, when he was with her he was unable to direct his eyes anywhere else.

The end of the enormous casino gave way to the promenade of shops and restaurants. It was here that Loke was cooking at Shinrin, a small plates and sushi bar favored by the younger set as the cocktail menu was longer than the one for the food.

"Look at this place," Audrey said to Shane as they entered the restaurant.

"Vegas, baby." Shane placed his hand on Audrey's back as Loke escorted them in.

Shane remembered how impressed he and Audrey had been at the Big Top nightclub with its high-concept circus design, perfectly implemented. In fact, Shane had lain awake thinking about every tiny detail of that night at the club. It was that night, the magnificence of Big Top mingled with his heady memories of sensually dancing in a frenzy with Audrey that had served to crack his internal shutters open a little bit. Every step that had led him to be able to come up with a new recipe today was connected to Audrey.

The theme of Shinrin was that of a forest. Miniature fir trees stood in clusters that divided the space into semi-private areas of couches covered in checkered fabric to give them a picnic look. Patrons ate from low tables made of tree trunk slices where communal plates for sharing were served.

Loke gestured for them to take a seat at two small couches facing each other with a table in between. Shane helped Audrey to one and Tino took the other. While they settled in, Loke dashed away and returned with a ceramic flask of sake and four matching cups. "My cohorts are going to bring us some nibbles," he said and sat beside Tino.

"I stayed at your hotel in Key West," Tino said to Audrey as they sipped their rice wine.

"Ooh—" Audrey smiled "—I hope everything was good?"

"Yeah, first class. I like those huge wooden and brass fans in the front lobby."

"Thanks. We had the blades hand carved."

Loke pointed to Shane and asked Audrey, "Where did you get the idea to partner with this pain in the butt in Vegas?"

"We've been in business with the Murphys for a decade with the Lolly's casual eateries. But when we bought the old Royal Neva here, we knew we needed a big restaurant."

"Reg had been thinking about an expansion to Vegas, anyway. Who wouldn't want to showcase here, where you can pull out all of the stops? When the Girards asked us to consider venturing in, the pieces fit."

Much as he loved these guys, he wasn't going to tell them how much he needed Vegas. Just like he didn't want to acknowledge how much he was beginning to need Audrey.

Tino lifted his sake cup in a toast and the others followed suit. "To the Murphy brothers in Vegas. Long may you reign."

Shane looked over to Audrey, at the smooth cheeks he had enjoyed running his lips across. How cute she was sitting there with one leg crossed over the other, both shapely legs on view.

"Thank you, Emi," Loke said to the pretty waitress who delivered some plates. He pointed to one of them. "Ankimo sushi. Monkfish liver."

Tino and Shane laughed as they battled each other for what they thought was the choicest piece on the plate. Loke lifted one, as well. Audrey didn't. Shane wasn't surprised but wondered how to handle what food might be arriving, knowing that she wasn't an adventurous eater. He didn't want to embarrass her.

"Unagi." Loke pointed to another plate.

"You'll like that one," Shane said to Audrey, knowing it was cooked eel brushed with a sweet glaze. "Trust me on that."

She lifted a piece on rice and took a tentative bite. And shot a sly smile at him that went straight to his heart. If this was a different world, he might like to spend his life figuring out things he could do for her that would earn him that kind of smile.

Emi delivered more dishes. Loke pointed, "Karaage."

"Fried chicken," Shane translated.

"I want some," Audrey said quickly. In his zeal, Shane reached for a morsel and fed it to Audrey. Then immediately wished he hadn't in front of Tino and Loke.

When Audrey excused herself to the ladies' room, Shane knew he was going to get grilled.

Tino started, "What's going on there?"

"A corporate partnership." Shane put up his palm as if to shut Tino down.

"Uh-huh." Loke bent in to take another piece of unagi. "I'd like to see what Fat Riku in the kitchen would do if I tried to feed him a bite with my fingers."

"I know, I shouldn't have done that." Shane chuckled, still shocked at his own lack of censorship. Although he shouldn't be surprised. Whenever he got anywhere near Audrey's succulent mouth, he didn't do his most prudent thinking.

"Been a long time for you, man," Loke said. "You dated anyone since Melina died?"

"I'm not dating Audrey!"

"I'll tell you," Tino persisted, "the way you hardly take your eyes off of her looks like a different kind of merger to me."

Loke picked up a piece of ankimo and, with fluttering eyelashes and a quivering mouth, fed it to Tino. The two busted out laughing.

Shane flared his nostrils like he was a bull about to charge at them. But then he cracked up, too. It was about time he laughed at himself.

These guys were really fun to be around. He wished he hadn't waited so long to see them.

After dinner, they decided to play some blackjack in the casino. They were able to find a table with four stools available. None of them were planning to gamble big—it was just to have some fun. Bets were placed and the dealer doled out the cards.

"Eighteen, Loke, you're good," Tino said. "Argh, what do I do on fifteen?"

"Hit," Audrey said without missing a beat.

"Ah ha, the lady is a gambler?" Tino raised an eyebrow.

Audrey smiled at Tino.

Then she turned to Shane.

Then Shane fastened his eyes on her.

Then time stood still.

Then the lights and sounds of the casino faded into a foggy distance.

Then talk of Audrey as a gambler had nothing to do with blackjack anymore.

CHAPTER NINE

"OH, NO," Shane exclaimed when he checked his phone while he and Audrey, Tino and Loke were wrapping up their blackjack session at the MGM. He shoved his and Audrey's gambling chips over to Tino, grabbed Audrey by the hand and pulled her up from her seat. "There's a fire at Feed U. We'll talk to you guys later."

Audrey ran to keep up with him as he tugged her across the casino and out to the valet station. "What happened?" she asked as they waited for his car to be retrieved.

"I don't know. Darn it, I missed three calls from Santiago before he texted." And attempts to return the teenager's calls were going unanswered. Shane tabbed to another phone number and explained to Audrey, "Lois.

"She doesn't know anything about it…" He kept Audrey updated as he talked to Lois. "She went home two hours ago. Santiago's family had finished cooking and they were cleaning up when she left."

"Should we call the fire department?"

"We're close by. We'd better go see what's going on."

Shane swung into the driver's seat of the Jeep as one of the valets helped Audrey in. He palmed the guy a tip, gunned the gas pedal and pulled a sharp left to get away from the Strip as quickly as possible.

When they careened into Feed U Santiago and two other teenagers were in the parking lot, trying to get their phones to work.

"What's happening?" Shane charged out of the car and toward them.

"Fire! Our phones aren't working." Santiago was distraught as he cried out. "Two of my cousins are still inside!"

Shane raced over to the door, which was ajar, and he was able to kick it open farther. Once he saw the blaze inside, he turned back to Audrey and yelled, "Call the fire department!"

Putting an arm in front of his face as a shield, Shane entered. Smoke engulfed the kitchen from flames centered around the stove. He remembered that he had a blanket in the back of the Jeep so he stepped back out to call to Audrey, "Bring me the blanket."

She quickly met him at the door and he used the blanket as a cape and hood to protect himself as he went back in.

"What are your cousins' names?" Audrey yelled behind her to Santiago.

"Denise is twelve and Celia is eight."

Audrey joined Shane inside as he was moving toward the fire.

"Go back!" he shouted to her.

"I'll help. Let me under the blanket."

Not wanting to take the time to argue, Shane threw a piece of the blanket over her and they charged forward.

"Denise!" Audrey called out. Flames crackled and visibility was low.

Smoke and ash burned Shane's eyes. He commanded Audrey, "Shield your eyes.

"Celia!" she yelled.

"Denise!"

"Celia!"

Shane and Audrey moved farther toward the flames. Stacks of kitchen towels succumbed to the fire's reach. Boxes of dry goods on another surface were burning to dust.

"Celia!"

"Denise!"

Shane's heart beat double time as more seconds elapsed without a response from the girls. Anxiety nearly overtook him. He looked over to Audrey who, like him, had begun to choke on the smoke. Taking a few steps farther into the raging heat, they heard a rustling from under one of the worktables. And both girls rolled toward them.

Audrey picked up the smaller girl and yelled to Shane to take the larger. He did his best to cloak them all in the blanket and they ran out the door. Once outside, Audrey and Shane placed the girls gently on the ground. Santiago and the other cousins rallied around them. Everyone was covered in smoke and soot.

A fire truck arrived and several firefighters dashed into the building. One met with the group to ask questions. Santiago was able to confirm that there was no one else inside and explained what had happened.

The cooking had gone well. After they had finished and were cleaning up, Lois went home. Santiago hadn't noticed that one of the younger kids had tossed an apron on the stove where it ignited. The greasy frying pans on the burners made matters worse when one of the other guys tried to douse the fire with water. By the time he could get to the fire extinguisher on the wall, the flames had spread too wide for him to contain the blaze.

Santiago, shaken to the bone, turned to Shane. "I'm so sorry, man."

"Look, all that matters is that everyone is okay." Shane blew out a breath. He laid his hand across his chest while he took in huge gasps of air.

As the paperwork was logged, Shane and Audrey stood in their ruined clothes. They used the blanket as best they could to wipe their blackened and sweat-soaked faces, after which Shane called his insurance company.

After the firefighters finished and Santiago's parents and aunts and uncles had picked up their kids, it was finally quiet at Feed U. Audrey and Shane were alone in the parking lot, exhausted, filthy and thirsty.

"My apartment isn't far from here. Do you want to go there and get cleaned up?" he asked her, glassy-eyed and stunned.

"Sure." She didn't dawdle to answer.

Shane drove them there quickly and steered the car into his underground garage. They rode the elevator to the nineteenth floor of the modern apartment building. With a swipe of his entry fob, Shane opened the door and let Audrey in.

It was a bachelor pad just as she might have imagined it would be. Minimal man-furniture was contemporary and clean, and did its job of not distracting from the floor-to-ceiling windows, which offered a city view. The tops of the large hotels on the Strip stood triumphant in the background. Closer in, offices and university buildings were a reminder that Las Vegas was a thriving metropolis.

Shane rushed into his dark kitchen and returned with two waters. They popped the caps and both drank their entire bottle in one go.

"There's a half bathroom right there." He pointed to

a door off the dining area. "Or do you want to take a shower in the master bath?"

Audrey gulped even though she'd finished drinking her water. The immediacy of the fire and the danger to the kids had triggered an agitated state and her lungs were still pumping faster than normal. But when she thought about entering Shane's bedroom to get naked in his en-suite shower, her heart thumped at a pace so rapid she was worried it was going to burst through her body and race out the door on its own.

Yet the idea of getting out of the burned clothes and washing her grimy hair and skin sounded too good to pass up, and this was hardly a time to be thinking about her inappropriate attraction to Shane. She decided to brave her hesitation. "A shower would be great."

Flipping on the bedroom lights, Shane showed Audrey in. Picture windows looked out to the same view as in the living room. "Sorry about the mess."

It wasn't much of a mess but she appreciated his awareness. Some clothes were strewn on the floor and over a chair. Magazines, an iPad, stacks of paperwork, empty drinking glasses and a couple of books peppered the nightstands. But the sheets and blankets on the bed looked crisp and clean. She couldn't help taking pause at the idea that she was inches away from Shane's bed.

Bed.

Where things besides sleep sometimes happened. For some people. Not her, but some people.

Handing her fresh towels he retrieved from a closet, Shane let her enter the bathroom and then closed the door.

Audrey tossed her ruined clothes into a corner. The heel was broken on one of her shoes and the leather on both was shredded. She stepped into the all-glass shower and blasted the taps. As hot water cascaded down her body, it turned gray and swirled into the drain. She rinsed until the water ran clear and then used the musky-scented soap and shampoo that sat on a shelf.

As the last whoosh of clean water rolled down her, her body quivered at an involuntary memory of Shane sliding against her on St. Thomas. Would she ever be free of that moment? She thought the other night dancing and writhing against him at Big Top nightclub might have eclipsed that split second in the Caribbean, but it hadn't. Perhaps because that brush in the ocean had come at such a young age, and from someone who had made such a strong impact on her.

Tonight, a decade later and most unpredictably, she and that very same influential person had saved lives together. Saved lives! Perhaps the Las Vegas Fire Department would have arrived in time to free Santiago's cousins Denise and Celia from the burning kitchen. But she and Shane were able to do it themselves. They got the girls to safety without harm.

Another memory that Audrey would live with for the rest of her life was lifting petrified eight-year-old Celia and carrying her out to the parking lot. Celia had clutched her around the neck with all of her might, the child feverishly hot and screaming for help even though she was already in Audrey's arms.

Instinct had told Audrey what to do. In that moment, she'd never felt more protective, reliable and capable. Audrey had held the child as if she were her own.

When Audrey stepped out of the shower to dry herself with the fluffy yellow towels Shane had provided, she had one immediate problem. Looking over to the pile of near-ashes that were her clothes, she had nothing to put on. There was no choice but to ask Shane to borrow something.

"Shane," she called as she opened the bathroom door and stuck her head out. When there was no reply, she yelled louder. "Shane!"

With still no answer, she wrapped one of the towels tightly around her, toed out of the bathroom and across his bedroom.

She found him in the kitchen.

"I'm starved. I thought you might be, too," Shane said over the sputtering bacon he was flipping in the skillet. He popped slices of bread into the nearby toaster.

Only then did he look up and see that Audrey was dressed in nothing more than a towel. The look on his face was almost that of a cartoon character whose eyes literally boinged out of their head attached by springs. Audrey would have giggled except Shane's expression swiftly changed to something darker. His eyes slit. His Adam's apple jumped.

Wet hair draped across her still-dewy shoulders. Her lips parted ever so slightly as their eyes froze for a moment in which what wasn't said was a lot. Sizzles ran up and down her body, mimicking the sound of the bacon.

"I need to borrow something to wear," she rasped.

"You certainly do," he concurred while clearing his throat. "And quick."

He fought a smile trying to break through.

If she were a different person, she might have let the towel drop to the floor then and there. Done something crazy and impulsive that she would have regretted later. But that wasn't her. Was it?

"Top drawer of the dresser." Shane returned her to practicality. "There are T-shirt or sweats. Whatever you think will fit you best." His eyes dropped to her bare legs.

She turned away and returned to his bedroom, somehow a little disappointed in herself.

All of his sweatpants were impossibly long on her so she settled for a big T-shirt that hung halfway down her thighs. That was greeted with another look-see from Shane that she interpreted as lustful.

As to the matter at hand, Shane laid out a much-appreciated meal of bacon, eggs and toast on square Asian-inspired plates.

"Do you have any jam?" Audrey asked as she took a seat at the dining table.

"Of course. How could I forget, Sugar?"

He fetched her a pot of what looked like homemade jam. "You go ahead and eat. It's my turn for the shower."

As welcome as the food tasted, all of Audrey's attention was alert to the fact that Shane was taking a shower in the next room.

She recalled that this day had started with Shane's success in the restaurant kitchen using his grandma's pots and pans. It then progressed to the casino night with his friends at the MGM before the fire at Feed U. And now to here. It wasn't just the smoke that made her eyes feel heavy.

"My phone battery died. What time is it?" she asked when he returned wearing a pair of sweatpants that rode low on his hips and a white T-shirt that kept nothing of his muscled torso a mystery.

"It's 4:00 a.m."

While Shane ate, they discussed the fire. "We have so many safety checks in place, nothing like that has ever happened in any of our kitchens," he explained.

"And, of course, you have staff who are trained in emergency procedures," she agreed and took a sip of the tea he had prepared. "We had a dryer fire in a laundry room once. Certain oils and products the spa uses can be highly flammable. But it was quickly contained and no one was hurt."

"Kids. I'll chew the heck out of Santiago later, but I wasn't going to say anything tonight when he was scared half to death." Shane chomped on a slice of bacon.

"As well he should have been. I shudder to think what would have happened if we hadn't got there when we did."

"Those little munchkins' faces…" Shane blinked his eyes in distress. "Heartbreaking."

Audrey forked up the last of her eggs. "You like kids, huh?"

"Hmm. Yeah. I guess I do. I like how they just tell it as it is. And they always see the best in things."

"Do you think you'll ever have any of your own?"

Shane filled his cheeks with air like a balloon and then deflated them. "Absolutely not."

Audrey wasn't sure why the space between her shoulder blades tightened.

"I couldn't even be responsible for the safety of a grown woman," Shane said with a frown. "I sure as heck couldn't be trusted with the well-being of a munchkin. Look at tonight. Thank heavens none of them were hurt, but I shouldn't have agreed to let Santiago close up the kitchen."

"Lois was there until she thought they were done."

"Doesn't matter. My kitchen. My problem." He bit into a piece of toast. "What about you? Little Girards in your future?"

She quickly nodded. "No way. I'd have absolutely no idea what to do with a child."

"Why do you always talk about kids as if they were a separate species?"

"Do I?"

"And when I took you to cook with them you seemed so uneasy."

Audrey stuck her knife in the jar of jam and began spreading some on her toast. Tears threatened from behind her eyes. But this was no time to cry. Children's lives had been at stake tonight. There was no room at the moment for self-pity.

Yet she wanted to confide in Shane.

More than wanted to.

Needed to.

"That's how my mother made me feel," she said softly with her focus still on her toast.

"How?"

"You said it exactly right. Like I was a different species." She put the toast down, suddenly not hungry for it. "I guess the apple doesn't fall far from the tree. My mother was uncomfortable around kids. Around me."

"Why do you think that was?"

"She was afraid of me. Because she never understood my needs and didn't believe she was up to the task of parenting."

"Didn't she have anyone around her to help her be a mother? In my big Irish family there were my grandmas and four aunts, and they were all always meddling in each other's parenting."

Audrey shook her head. "She cut herself off from everybody." Her lip trembled. "Depression ran my mom's life. Alcohol and pills were her only friends."

"Where was your dad in all of this?"

"He saw what he wanted to see. He had the hotels to run. His response was to make the hotels my home away from home and my playground. And then to teach me the business. Not a bad way to go, under the circumstances."

Daniel Girard was like a big kid himself. Always optimistic. Assuming the next day would be even better than the last. He probably thought he was sheltering Audrey by letting her grow up around hotel staff who watched over her.

Still, there was nothing to replace a mother's love. The hole in her heart that nothing would ever fill.

Audrey looked out Shane's windows overlooking the city. She mashed her lips, attempting to seal in the emotions that were trying to overflow. She'd said enough.

Shane sensed that she was deep in her own pain. He reached a hand over and put it on top of hers. Her head tilted slightly toward him.

"Alright, two people who think they are completely unsuitable to be parents put themselves in danger to protect some children tonight anyway."

The irony brought a curve to her lips.

Shane shifted his chair closer to her. He moved his thumb across her piece of toast to get a swipe of jam.

"You didn't taste my jam yet, Sugar. Blackberry." He brought his thumb close to her mouth, daring her to lick it.

Which she was unable to resist. The fruit was especially sweet from the pad of his fingertip.

He thumbed another smear of jam and spread it across her bottom lip. "I'd like to try it myself," he said in a low, gravelly voice.

Taking her face in both hands, he pulled her to him. With the tip of his tongue he flicked the jam from the soft pillow of her lip.

"Mmm," he moaned his approval. The timbre of the sound coursed like an infusion straight through Audrey's veins. She'd give the world just to hear it once more. Shane obliged by again licking her lip and again moaning with pleasure.

One of his hands moved to the back of her head, threading his fingers through her hair. The other hand remained on her face, caressing her cheekbone.

This wasn't supposed to be happening again. Kissing him. The episode on top of his car had arisen spontaneously. The sunset had been beautiful and they were curious. But this time they knew better.

Yet the back of Shane's big hand stroking her cheeks, one then the other, over and over, rendered her utterly powerless to stop him.

He'd enjoyed the jam kiss so much that he spread the purple sweetness on her lips for another. This time his warm tongue made an ever-so-slow circle all the way around her mouth before that sound roiled up from his belly, and then surged through her body. Her lower back arched inward.

In a sudden move, he gathered all of her hair in one hand. With the other, he used a finger to paint a line of jam from behind her ear down to the base of her neck. He made her anticipation build toward the inevitable, leaning over to let his hot breath settle against her tender skin before he gradually licked away his marking.

Then he took her mouth fully, joining it to his. Her lips rose up to him. He kissed her over and over, each meeting delivering more urgency than the one before.

He reached under the table and slid his hand beneath the T-shirt she had borrowed, feeling only bare skin underneath. Audrey gasped. His sure fingers clutched pieces of her. Her thigh. Her hip. All the way up to her waist.

In one fell swoop, he pushed his chair back to lift her into his arms and stood up. Her hands draped around his neck of their own volition, as if they knew they were supposed to go there, knew that was where they belonged.

Fear tried desperately to grip hold of her as he carried her to his bedroom. She shouldn't do this. It would be a mistake. But if she knew it was wrong, why did she have a box of condoms in her purse that she had bought this morning when she stopped at the store for toothpaste?

Shane sat her down on his bed and slid off the thin T-shirt that had concealed her body. He laid her down and began to explore every inch of her. His curious hands were closely followed by his mouth, causing tiny pinpoints of sensation to bring her higher and then higher still. Yet he modulated his pace so that she lifted when he wanted her to, carrying her up slowly. When he let her glide free, she flew into the air on a cloud of ecstasy he never wanted her to come down from. Moments later, her earlier purchase was put to good use as their bodies soared together through the dawn skies, where they crested in each other's arms. Until the sun rose across the desert.

When the bright morning light hit his eyes, Shane rolled over for the remote control atop his nightstand that lowered the blinds on his bedroom windows. He had only slept for a couple of hours. Exhaustion weighed heavy in his bones. Beside him was glorious Audrey. With her spun-sleek hair and her velvety skin and her luxurious flesh reminding him of the exquisite pleasures they had just shared.

He wanted to wake her up with easy kisses down the entire length of her body. His own solid core let him know that's exactly what he ached to do.

Yet his brain told him something else entirely.

As he watched exquisite Audrey take in the gentle breaths of peaceful sleep, Shane's chest thundered with panic and regret.

CHAPTER TEN

CONSTRUCTION WAS NOT yet complete at the back of the hotel, so no one saw Shane drop Audrey off. With her burned and torn clothes now in Shane's trash can, she was suited up in a ridiculous outfit of his belted overcoat and a pair of his flip-flops that were twice the size of her feet. Key card in hand, she hurried to her bungalow and slipped inside.

Cardboard Shane pinged his tongue against his top lip as she entered. A silly grin broke out on her face as she plopped backward down on the bed. She lifted the collar of Shane's coat to find a faint smell of him.

Being wrong had never felt this right. Every inch of her body tingled as she recalled snippets of what they had just shared. His strong body entwined with hers in every possible configuration. Taut muscles presenting firm walls for her bonelessness to wrap around. The hypnotism of his kisses that robbed her mind of any past or any future.

Audrey had only been intimate with a couple of men. Both experiences were a long time ago and nothing like the heights she'd just climbed to with Shane. It shouldn't have come as a surprise to her that he held more passion in the crook of his finger than most of the people she'd ever met in her life had combined. Lying on her bed in his coat, she swooned.

They'd be reuniting in four hours to tape a segment of the cooking special. Two hundred and forty minutes until she would be back together with him. She painstakingly set her phone to alert her every half hour so that the time she had to wait to see him would be broken down into manageable stretches of time.

What?

Had she gone crazy? They got lost in the moment and had sex last night. It had no long-term meaning. They were still only business partners, not open to becoming involved with anyone, and last night was not going to change a thing.

Nevermind that her emotions after the fire at Feed U had led her to tell him more about what she'd bottled up inside than she'd ever told anyone. And nevermind that they had shared a lovemaking so poignant he had reached down into her and grabbed hold of her very being. Nevermind that in his arms she started to have new insights into something beyond arranged marriages and workaholic companionship.

Reality gnawed. Those were all silly daydreams. She knew all too well not to confuse them with reality.

But what if?

Audrey dressed for the appointment she had before the taping, a visit with a former Girard employee who was now a wedding coordinator at The Venetian. After kisses on both cheeks, Grace showed Audrey the wedding chapel at the stylish hotel. Grace lifted a slender finger up to her lips to let Audrey know that they should be quiet because a ceremony was taking place.

The bride was a fairy princess in a short-sleeved gown with a sweetheart neckline and a ballroom skirt that must have been constructed with yards upon yards of tulle to create its shape. Her dark skin glowed while her short curly hair was enhanced by a pearly headband attached to her veil. The slim groom stood tall in his traditional tuxedo, the bow tie and cummerbund a sky blue that matched his three groomsmen and the dresses of the three bridesmaids who stood in their designated places. A small group of guests filled the front pews.

Audrey couldn't hear what the officiant was saying to the couple in a muffled voice meant only for them, nor did she need to. The classic scene was profound and pastoral. She blinked repeatedly as a way of keeping tears from spilling down her face.

The way the bride and groom gazed at each other, she doubted they heard a word that was said, either. To each, there was nothing in the room but the other. Immeasurable happiness, pure love and total certainty emanated from both of them. Audrey mused on what plans they may have made and what they were looking forward to in their lives. Hopefully nothing but death would take them from each other and maybe not even that.

Audrey had been completely sure that nothing like that was ever in her future. That would involve trust, and she surely wasn't going to fall for that one again. If you couldn't trust your mother, your own flesh and blood, you surely couldn't count on someone who fundamentally came to you as a stranger. Love could only turn to disappointment and setback.

But when she was with Shane, anything seemed possible. Really, it had been building all along. From watching him cook with the little kids at Feed U to his friendship with Josefina to his warm memories of his own grandmother. With his insistence on perfection in his work. From his willingness to show her his vulnerable side in admitting that he hadn't loved his wife. And from the sunset kisses that were more than just physical attraction. Kissing him was an act of two spirits meeting. And what passed between them in his bed carried stories for all the ages.

Here she was in a predicament she was hardly expecting. Reg had fallen for someone else and her safety net had been pulled out from beneath her. Someone with lesser moral standards might have gone through with the arranged marriage and continued to see his true love at the same time. But Reg was a fair enough man not to allow any deception and had come forward straight away. Reg hadn't foreseen this, and Audrey did wish him well.

After that change of track, she'd returned all of her focus to her work. Which, bizarrely, entailed being at Shane's side much of the time. And now, for the good of all, not the least of whom was Shane himself, it seemed that he had been able to reclaim his magic.

Little could Audrey have known that along the way she'd find some of her own.

Shane was adamant that he'd never be in another relationship. Audrey herself had been decided, too. She still clutched a hurt that would never stop bleeding.

So why was it that now she wanted more than anything in the world to wear a white dress and hear Shane say words like *for better or for worse* and *as long as we both shall live*? Words that caused a couple to stare at one another like the pair she watched right now in the chapel. In each other's eyes, and in the promises they spoke, the past could be healed and the future was limitless. Yes, there would be disappointments and mistakes and tears, but they would weather the lows and embrace the highs. Together.

She wanted that with Shane.

More than anything she'd ever wanted in this world.

What was he feeling after last night? Had the flood-gates been opened for him, too? He was cooking again. More important still, he was conceiving again, tapping into that divinity that worked through him to create. Had he crossed over? Were they ready for each other?

Grace whispered to snap her out of her turmoil, "Audrey!"

She took in the panorama of the chapel and returned to earth. "Sorry, lost in thought."

Graced smiled. "What's his name?"

Later in Grace's office over cappuccinos they discussed event planning in Vegas. From there, Audrey returned to Hotel Girard and popped into her dad's office.

"'Yummy chef Shane Murphy was spotted on the Strip again last night with delicious hotelier Audrey Girard and a couple of other friends,'" Daniel read from his phone. "'While they may have been hooting and hollering at the blackjack table, it looked like these two were ready to place a bet on each other.'"

"Dad, you wouldn't believe what happened last night after that," she exclaimed. And proceeded to tell him all about the fire. And nothing at all about the fireworks.

"Hi." Audrey offered Shane a flirty smile when he came up to the swanky rooftop pool for the TV taping.

She bit her lower lip in order not to faint at the sight of him in the outfit she had worked through with the stylist. He'd wear his cook's coat for a later shoot in the restaurant and she was even considering having him in a tuxedo while he talked about food during a cocktail party segment. She had the feeling Shane would look good wearing anything. Last night, he looked mighty good wearing nothing. But for the rooftop it was white jeans, white button-down shirt, tan shoes and belt, and his own aviator sunglasses. Casual elegance that was pure crazy, in a great way, with his wild long curls and nicely groomed beard stubble.

Audrey's spine vibrated as her brain replayed that stubble awakening every part of her it touched last night. Those scratchy hairs demanded her full attention. And received it without a fight.

"Hi," he clipped in a tight voice and looked away. No doubt he was dreading this taping. At the height of his stardom a few years ago, he was on talk shows presenting cooking demonstrations left and right, so he knew how it was done. Maybe the process had probably become unfamiliar to him now.

Or perhaps he was tired today. They surely hadn't used his bed for much sleeping.

What sleeping they did do may have been as profound to her as the lovemaking. It had been years since she'd shared a bed with anything but a pillow.

Busy career gal, husbandless and childless, gives her all to the family legacy.

Nothing wrong with that. It was what she'd thought she'd wanted.

Now, suddenly, she coveted more. She wanted the whole shebang. To lie every night in a big bed with Shane's long arms around her. To yawn during sleepytime chitchat about their days, the successes, the failures. And she wanted to stand beside him as together they showered little Girard-Murphys with all the love she had to give, which lately had grown to infinitely more than she thought she had. She wanted to work hard, play hard, love hard.

Everything her dad told her she might feel some day was right. Because of Shane. She'd never have opened up to anyone like she did with him. Maybe Josefina had been right when she said that tragedy would bind them together. Could it be what would set them free, as well?

The TV crew had created a small set for Shane to cook from on the bridge between the swimming pools. Everything was in its place. Just as Audrey had visualized it. On the chic rooftop pool area of Hotel Girard with the Las Vegas Strip visible in the background, this opening segment of the TV special would create instant appeal for the property and its location. It was the Vegas fantasy come true. Stylish fun in the sun, great food and drink, gaming and entertainment at every turn.

"This is going to look fabulous on camera," she said as she ushered Shane to his spot at the makeshift kitchen. "Everything okay?"

"Are we ready?" Phil, the director, called over.

"Just dandy," Shane snapped at Audrey, taking her back a little. She knew he'd rather be almost anywhere else but he could be a bit more pleasant. Wasn't the memory of last night enough to put him in a good mood?

"Let's try a take, Shane," Phil instructed. Audrey moved to the side of the bridge to be out of the shot. "Places, please. And we go in five, four, three, two, one, cue Shane."

Shane turned on his electric smile. "Shane Murphy here on the rooftop of the Hotel Girard Las Vegas, site of my newest Shane's Table restaurant..." He continued to read from the teleprompter and kept on his camera face for a couple of minutes before asking for a break.

"All good, Shane?" Phil asked. "You look great."

"Delightful." Shane shot the answer at Audrey in a voice that suggested he was anything but.

Don't take it personally, she coached herself.

"I'm sorry we're taking up your time," Audrey said

to him by way of apology because he seemed so uncomfortable. Although, obviously, all of this was meant to benefit both of their interests. This morning he had said that he was anxious to try out a couple of recipe ideas so, she reasoned, maybe he was impatient because he would rather be in his kitchen. Where his heart was. In his think tank. His kingdom. Ultimately, the place where he felt at home.

If he didn't want to be shooting the show right now, she wished with all of her might that they weren't. But they had a job to do.

"Picking up where we left off," Phil called, "in three, two, one."

Shane flipped on his dazzle switch again. "We're going to do a refreshing first course for a poolside gathering. Watermelon gazpacho. Gazpacho refers to a cold, raw soup and there are hundreds of different preparations. It's classic to use a tomato base, and we're going to put a Mediterranean spin on it with watermelon and a finish of feta cheese. You'll be surprised how great the pairing of the acid in the tomato plays against the super-sweet melon."

Audrey watched Shane do his thing as he began explaining the ingredients and method. The way he managed to be authoritative but warm and friendly at the same time filled her with admiration. Were this formidable and complex man to be hers, she'd treasure every facet of him because they added up to who he was. She'd have to learn to back off when he wanted to be left alone. Not to read into it a rejection of her. Not everyone was her mother.

"Gazpacho is thought to have originated in Andalusia," Shane continued, the absolute professional. "Some recipes pulverize a piece of bread and blend that in to create a thickness that is hard to achieve in an uncooked soup. It was probably the ancient Romans who brought that concept over to Spain."

Shane completed the gazpacho, showing his would-be audience a variety of attractive serving suggestions. He poured the soup into small clear glasses, which he arranged on a wooden tray. In heavy blue margarita glasses with stems, the mixture resembled a refreshing cocktail. And ladled into small porcelain bowls with long slices of green bell peppers as a garnish, the gazpacho looked more traditional. Concluding, he said to the camera, "We'll see you over at the restaurant where we're doing tacos on the patio."

"And...cut." Phil ended the session.

Audrey rushed onto the bridge. "Perfect. It couldn't have gone better."

"Yep, it was a good segment." Shane didn't look at her but busied himself stacking up some plates.

Actually, were they to be together, she was going to need some practice weathering his moods. At the moment, she couldn't understand why he didn't seem to want her near. Was it because of the taping? Something he'd probably rather not have been doing? But both families had agreed this kind of big push was needed to get the hotel and restaurant off to a successful start. He must have known that the segment was flawless and that he'd done his duty.

When people saw this cooking special on TV, Audrey was sure the seed would be planted in their minds that, when in Vegas, a stop at Shane's Table at the Hotel Girard would be an experience in modern fine dining they wouldn't want to miss.

"How was it—" she decided to test the waters

"—being in front of the cameras again? I know it's been a long time for you."

"It was fun. I actually enjoyed it." Shane answered her yet kept his eyes on the workspace in front of him.

"Shane?" Audrey couldn't stand him not looking at her.

Without a word, he roped one arm around her waist and brought her close. He took hold of her hair with the other hand and kissed her mouth violently. She responded to his force and met his power as best she could.

After kissing him on the hood of his car and then a thousand ways last night, she knew his kisses. This one was different. It was defiant. It was contemptuous. There was fury in it.

Despite how much she had been trying to convince herself that Shane was merely out of his element in front of the cameras, she had to admit that what was bothering him had something to do with her.

After a long evening of solitary work in the empty kitchen, Shane amped his music even louder to keep him company while he cleaned up. He was pleased with his progress tonight. The tlayudas would fit well in the antojitos, snacks, section of the cookbook. Wanting to offer a vegetarian option, he hadn't yet found the perfect substitute for the chewy tasajo beef. Maybe shiitake mushrooms?

As he dunked some sponges into hot soapy water and began scouring the worktables, the thought he had pushed away for the last few hours fought for its rightful place. The five-foot two-inch intrusion would wait no longer. He'd used the lengthy cooking session to avoid concentrating on one thing. One "she" thing. Audrey.

That kiss earlier at the rooftop pool had almost done

him in, and from it he came running into the kitchen to hide and retreat.

All of his emotions had built up. At first, he'd tried to keep Audrey at arm's distance and just get through the taping. He'd said he would do the TV show and he needed to give it all he had. Which he did. But Audrey kept coming closer until he'd snapped and kissed her with a power he didn't like. Because it was a mixture of love and rage. Fortunately, the crew had been taking a break so no one saw him lose his restraint.

Darn her. For having those honey-colored eyes. For letting him trace jam down her neck and taste her sweetness mixed with the fruit. For being alive and responsive in his bed.

For making him abandon all the vows he took after Melina's death.

That he was never again going to care about a woman. Definitely not going to feel accountable to her. He'd loused that up in the most crucial way and he couldn't put someone in that kind of danger again. For their own safety.

His phone vibrated in his pocket. Why did he have a fleeting thrill that it might be Audrey?

It was Reg.

"Hey, did you talk to that guy Eli about the executive chef position? I video called him. He might be alright." Shane and his departing executive chef Lee had made dozens of calls to try to find a replacement. One prospect emerged, a friend of a friend who had the appropriate past experience.

"We're going to give him a try. Lee renegotiated his new deal to stay with us for a couple of weeks longer and train him."

"Thank goodness. What else?"

"It was Hammett who was stealing from us." A barback who had been with them less than a year.

"Jeez." Shane crooked the phone between his ear and shoulder so that he could continue his cleanup.

"We fired him."

"Man, you never know about people. How's it going with Brittany?"

"Risk and potential," Shane's ever-logical brother answered. "What's new there?"

Shane wanted to tell Reg something about Audrey. But his throat blocked. He felt excruciating remorse at having made love with her last night. That was a line that was profoundly unfair to cross. He knew she hadn't been physical with anyone in a long time. Maybe as long as it had been for him, maybe even longer. But they had no business doing that.

They had been partly spurred on by the fire at Feed U, all the adrenaline from the drama and danger surging through them. But he was wrong to have allowed himself to get swept up by emotion. Something he did far too often around Audrey. Acting without thinking was always a mistake. He could hardly face her today.

Audrey had been through her own personal wringer with a mother who hadn't wanted her. Audrey shouldn't take any kind of chance on him, he was not a safe wager. She'd have better odds at the casino.

He could only hurt her. He would hurt her. He probably already had.

"We're on schedule out here." Shane could at least report that much to Reg. "I'll see you soon, bro."

Shane quickly ended the call, too restless to talk. He scrubbed the kitchen from top to bottom until it glistened but still couldn't work out his growing discomfort.

Glad he kept a pair of swim trunks in his desk, he decided to hit the employee pool for a late-night swim to try to blow off his anxiety.

He heard splashing as he entered the pool area. Sure enough, there was Audrey, her petite length gliding from one end of the water to the other.

What an amazing creature she was, gliding through the pool. He thought of the fire. How sure and brave she was, marching into the flames if it meant saving the lives of those two children. It was moments like that in life that showed what a person was truly made of.

She proved how much she could care. And she should have that kind of care in return. Even though it wasn't something she was open to receiving, it was something he could never give. Not now. Not ever.

Tempted to leave unnoticed, he decided to confront her. She was entitled to the truth. He dove in and matched his laps to hers so that they reached the end of the pool at the same time.

"What is it with us?" Audrey half smiled. "We're in some kind of sync."

They both noticed a flash of light coming from behind the fence that enclosed the pool area.

"I need to say something, and I'm just going to come right out and say it." Shane commanded her to look him in the eye.

Her eyes opened wide, making Shane want to cower from the words he was about to speak. But he pressed on.

"I don't take sex casually and I'm guessing you don't, either."

She bit her plump bottom lip.

"But what happened between us was a one-off. A mistake."

Was it the pool water, or did her eyes mist with tears?

He knew that he'd make her cry at some point. Best, he thought, sooner rather than later.

She whispered, "I see."

"I can't afford to have anything like that happen ever again."

"You can't afford it?"

"I can't take the chance."

"What chance?"

"That I'll hurt you."

"Shouldn't that be my decision, not yours?"

They both turned to follow the distracting light that flashed above the top of the fence again.

"Please let me finish." Shane gritted his teeth. "I can't let anything develop between us. Maybe if I were a different man. But I'm not. You already mean too much to me, Audrey. My heart can't take it."

"But…"

Whatever she was going to say would be too painful, so he covered her mouth with a kiss. It would be the last one. With his kiss, he gave her all he had inside so he'd always know that deep in her heart, she would remember this moment. It was a kiss that would have to last a lifetime.

There was no question that it would for him. Audrey, Audrey. In such a short time, she'd changed him forever. Brought him back to life, as a matter of fact. Through her, he'd reached up and clutched a bit of hope above the rubble he was buried under. Through her, he believed in himself again.

And only without her could he continue.

When you really love something, you have to let it go. Wasn't that how the saying went? He loved her so much that he had to protect her from him, from what he was, and wasn't, capable or deserving of. As much as it would damage both of them, he had to do what was in her best interest. He didn't merit something as precious as her heart.

He broke from their last kiss and said with finality. "I can finish the cookbook on my own. Because I can't be that close to you. I can't have you spending time in my kitchen. Business partners is all we're meant to be."

Tears streamed down Audrey's face.

"Shane! Audrey!" A voice came over the fence. Their eyes darted toward it. A paparazzo popped up and began flashing his camera at them again and again.

CHAPTER ELEVEN

*Hotel Heiress Can't Choose Between
Restaurant Brothers!*

THAT WAS THE caption above the two photos that were released to every gossip site on earth. In one photo, taken last night Shane and Audrey were caught kissing in the employee pool under the moonlight. The second photo was of Reg and Audrey posed in the wedding pavilion two weeks ago. When Audrey was wearing that flowered dress she hated. They were supposed to be taking engagement photos just for practice. Before Reg changed the plan and returned to New York.

Audrey stood in her dad's office and shook her head back and forth. "We saw the camera flashes last night."

Daniel sat at his desk while Shane leaned back in his chair, leg spread apart, eyes downcast.

Reg joined them via Skype. "I can't imagine how those first photos of you and me were leaked," he said to Audrey.

"One of the photographer's crew," Daniel said. "Anyone who had access to the photographer's files. Or maybe the guy himself."

"I'll call our lawyer," Reg added, "Although that doesn't help us figure out what to do now."

"Nothing," Audrey said definitively. "We do nothing. Just let it blow over. There will be a different hot story by the next news cycle in a few hours."

Shane gave her half of a smile and then looked back down to the floor.

After the paparazzo had startled them in the pool last night, Shane yelled at the guy. He and Audrey stood dripping wet poolside. She was reeling both from the unexpected intrusion of the photographer, and from Shane's declaration that he no longer wanted her help. That he wouldn't pursue anything personal with her. Which, of course, stung worse than any of the other blows.

After Shane chased the pap away, Audrey did her best to hide the heartbreak that speared through her at his statement of finality. She mumbled a quick good-night and retreated to her bungalow.

Even though they had shared so much together already, he was very clear. He no longer wanted her involved in his life.

He'd made breakthroughs in his cooking. She didn't know if she'd really had anything to do with that other than providing a sounding board. But something seemed to have clicked and he was moving forward at last.

It hadn't been just one-sided. Night after night, she told him everything about her day. Every work challenge she faced or decision she had to make. It gave her focus and clarity to share all of her thoughts. She was doing her best work in years.

Granted, it was a Shane Murphy made out of cardboard she divulged her thoughts to, but without the effect the real Shane had on her, it wouldn't have meant anything.

Which is why she tried to ignore her four-hundred-pound heart and flushed neck as they held this meeting to discuss damage control about the photos. Everything was happening too fast—she really hadn't had a chance to understand or process her disappointment. They were in business together so avoiding Shane wasn't an option, although it's the one she would have chosen if she could have.

Once the meeting was over and Shane left Daniel's office, Audrey sank into a chair by the window. Her dad could tell she was upset and joined her in the chair at her side. They looked out to the action on the Strip. Even during the day, plenty of revelers had drinks in their hands and, probably empty pockets too.

She spotted a group of young women all wearing bridal veils that were attached to red headbands with cat ears. They giggled their way down the boulevard. Must have been an all-night bachelorette party.

Las Vegas, real and fake. The Eiffel Tower. New York skyline. Roman statue. Medieval castle. Ancient pyramid. Shane and Audrey.

Audrey told Daniel that Shane had excused her from her duties. She hadn't spoken to her dad about what had passed between them on a personal level. Since nothing was going to come of it, she saw no reason to now.

Yet he guessed at it. "You have feelings for Shane."

"Never." She pressed her lips together.

"Daughter," Daniel said, reaching over to take Audrey's hand. "I know you had it rough growing up. I was consumed with running the hotels but I wasn't blind. Your mother was a very unusual woman."

"That's one way of putting it."

"I did my best to compensate but I know that for a daughter there's no substitute for a mother. In her own way, though, she did love you. When I'd see her late in the evening after you'd gone to sleep, she'd tell me all about your accomplishments at school."

"After she'd heard about them from the nanny?" A tear slipped from Audrey's eye.

"Yes, but there was pride in her eyes as she listed your achievements."

"Wish I'd been allowed to see that." At least five more tears leaked out.

"Audrey, you're twenty-eight. You have to open some doors and let love in. Set the past to the side. Move forward."

She clutched her father's hand as dozens of fresh tears dropped down her cheeks. He'd never know that she had opened the door a sliver, only to have it slammed shut in her face.

The rest of Audrey's day was another blur of meetings and decisions. She went out to a local golf course to work on some incentives the hotel would offer. A limo would pick guests up at the Girard where they'd be sent off with a boxed breakfast and hot coffee. At the golf course, they'd have a desirable early-morning tee time before the sun got too blistering. A brunch with mimosas at the eighteenth hole would cap off the morning. Upon returning to the hotel, guests would be welcomed back with a basket full of after-sun products and icy packs for aching muscles plus a nice assortment of fruit, nuts and green juices for the afternoon. All well thought out. An impeccable Girard promotion. The kind of thing Audrey took the most pride in.

Audrey's joke of a dinner was comprised of hummus and pita plus loads of cookies leftover from an earlier meeting with Housekeeping when they discussed press

releases about the hotel's energy efficient laundry prac-
tices. Afterward, Audrey was restless. She paced her
empty bungalow, for the first time not wanting to even
look in cardboard Shane's direction. It occurred to her
to go out.

It being Vegas, she could participate in any of a hundred different activities. She might see an elaborate show.
Or a comedian or a piano-lounge singer. While away
some time placing bets on a low-stakes slot machine at
one of the big casinos. Drive off the Strip to go to a shopping mall or neighborhood restaurant and spend the evening like a resident Las Vegan.

But none of those options sounded good to her. Unable
to inspire herself for anything unfamiliar, she changed
into her bathing suit, threw on a cover-up and went to
the employee pool.

The sky was especially black. Audrey inched into the
pool and then pushed off to begin her methodical laps.
She thought of how many laps she had swum in her lifetime. How much she enjoyed the feeling of herself buoy-
ant and fast through the water. Here she often did her
best thinking.

Shane. Shane was her best thinking. No one could
have planned the unlikely sequence of events that had
played out here in Vegas. That once Reg was out the
door, her feelings for Shane would creep in the window.
The idea of an arranged companionship was usurped by
a love so real it decimated all of the pillars Audrey had
built and surrounded herself with. Like an innocent ape,
one man demolished her blockades with the loping sweep
of his mighty arm. And then ran away into the jungle.

Shane had made her fall in love with him. Yet he didn't
love her in return. Could there be a more ironic twist of
fate in this city of chance?

Audrey swam, kicking off from turns, using measured strokes, taking rhythmic breaths. Back and forth, shallow end of the pool to the deep and then to the shallow again. Was she wishing through every second of it that Shane would appear at the pool like he had every time she'd been swimming since she arrived in Vegas? To tell her he couldn't live without her and everything he had said to her was a mistake? Absolutely.

With every lap, she looked over to check if the gate was opening.

He never came.

Two weeks later...

"Shane, can we get some shots with you and Reg?" one of the invited guests at the press brunch called out.

As he had been for the past two hours, Shane continued to make the rounds at the rooftop event. Reg was flagged over and the two Murphys put on their glittering restaurant brothers act as the photos were snapped. Rail-thin and short-haired, Brittany watched from the sidelines, clearly proud of her man. Reg had on a smart suit, uncharacteristically without a tie to be appropriate for the poolside. Shane wore his chef's coat with black jeans.

"Get the cookbook," Reg, ever practical, instructed as he blotted under his nose with a napkin.

Shane reached for the mock-up he had placed on the stool beside him. *Shane's Table at Home* bore its cover art of him smiling up from the salad he tossed in a big wooden bowl. Pieces of lettuce were miraculously caught in flight. Shane had no idea how a shot like that was achieved. He and Reg had reviewed at least a hundred photos of him for the cover, until they found one that best upheld Shane's brand of rock 'n' roll meets world-class chef.

As he and Reg and the cookbook posed, out of the corner of his eye Shane spotted Audrey with a small circle of interested people surrounding her. Holding up a spa product or something, she seemed to be promoting it to her attentive audience.

His belly contracted at the sight of her, as spectacular as the late-morning sun. If there was ever an electrical outage, her smile could power the Strip.

She looked *brunchalicious* in white slacks, which he could tell were long enough to conceal the very high heels that she favored because she liked to look taller than her petite, yet perfect, height. A gold blouse that crossed in front flattered her marvelous femininity. And her shiny hair in loose waves was that kind of effortless look that probably took a lot of effort.

Sugar.

Indeed.

Over the past two weeks, not an hour had gone by that her stunning face hadn't popped its way front and center into Shane's mind. He'd felt certain that he couldn't pursue anything with her, not the completion of the cookbook nor what had passed between them personally. That when you loved something, you had to protect it even if that meant shielding it from yourself. If it meant denying himself the one thing he realized he most wanted, so be it. He'd sworn he'd never again be a hindrance to someone's well-being, he just couldn't risk having the power to hurt Audrey. The woman he loved.

The woman he loved.

The past two weeks had been busy from morning to night but Shane had still found time to agonize about Audrey and what he was turning his back on. It didn't help that he was involved with her in this business venture that was vitally important to both of their families. Normally, if you decided against a relationship, you could simply walk away and not have to see that person again.

In the months that turned to years after Melina's death, he'd been asleep in his own trauma. Audrey had woken him up, spun his wheels in a new direction. He'd always be grateful to her for that after years of stalling out.

He glanced over and saw his parents, Connor and Tara, talking to Daniel. They had flown in for the opening. He'd had dinner and a heart-to-heart talk with them last night. They knew the next move he'd decided on.

Always one for extremes, in the last two weeks Shane had done nothing but work. Locking himself in the kitchen from dawn to midnight, he focused solely on creating new recipes for the cookbook. He was forced to dig lower into his own well of inventiveness, his knowledge of flavors and of technique. He'd researched foods native to the area, something he always enjoyed. He'd driven to off-the-beaten-track ethnic grocery stores and farmers' markets. In the past two weeks, he'd come up with some of the greatest recipes of his career.

He looked over to the reason. Of course it was because of her. She had reintroduced him to himself.

"Come over here and take a few shots for *Vegas Food and Wine*." Reg guided his brother to do another smile show.

They invited their new manager Enrique over for photos. Shane couldn't have readied the restaurant for opening without his competent service. Rachel in LA had trained him well. After a handshake, Enrique returned to supervising the brunch buffet.

"Mom, Dad, Daniel, can we do some shots?" Shane rounded them up. He beckoned with his hand to the woman he loved who had been watching the grouping. "Audrey, join us please."

After a glance down to the ground, she strode over, shook Brittany's hand on the sidelines and then took her place next to her dad for the photo.

Shane had seen precious little of Audrey in person for the past two weeks. Which was probably for the best, since any time he smelled her perfume or was in proximity of her warm skin, he'd had to rein himself in from breaking his resolve.

After the photo, Shane moved toward the other end of the pool for some hellos. His feet stepped forward but his eyes were glued on Audrey as she shook hands and charmed another grouping of people. The woman he loved in her native habitat, being fabulous at her job.

The woman he loved.

She'd obviously kept her distance from him, as well, these past weeks as email became her preferred method to notify him of business matters. And by including Daniel and Reg in all correspondence, she further professionalized their communications.

Shane had completed the TV show, working through four other segments with Phil. Audrey came by each set to nod her approval but didn't stay for the tapings.

The woman he loved.

Yesterday, Shane had made up his mind. Once and for all. What he carried in his pocket was proof.

The cookbook, the TV show, the restaurants. As important as they were, he'd finally learned what he needed. What mattered the most.

Shane made nice with another cluster of guests enjoying the coffee bar but scanned the pool area until he located Daniel. When he could break away, Shane moved toward him.

As soon as he could budge Daniel away from the woman who was talking his ear off, Shane pulled him over to a quiet area against the railing overlooking the Strip and asked him the question that had been bubbling up inside him and could no longer be contained.

Shane caught Audrey observing them as they talked.

When Shane took a break from another round of schmoozing, he found Audrey who had also paused for a glass of water. "I need to speak with you in private," Shane whispered in her ear.

The game face she'd worn through the entire brunch disappeared.

"I don't think that's a good idea," she eked out in a constricted voice.

As she started to walk away, Shane reached out and took hold of her arm. He'd made a mistake two weeks ago. He wasn't going to make another.

Her body winced at his touch and she froze. Then turned to face him.

"Let's go out to the desert to watch the sunset after everything wraps up today," he said. "Like we did that day we went to see Josefina."

That sunset when they'd sat on the hood of his car and kissed and kissed together until darkness blanketed the mountains.

"I won't, Shane. You said your piece two weeks ago. I can't. You can't."

"I was wrong." His hand slid up her arm.

"You weren't wrong. You know yourself. Just like I know myself."

"Come to the desert with me."

"Shane, let me go. People are going to start to talk," she surveyed the crowd. "After all the photos and the gossip."

"We're business partners, people are going to see us together. Come out with me later."

"No," she insisted. But as his mouth cracked into a tiny smile, so did hers.

His spirit rose up and across every inch his body, cloaking him in a tingling aura of anticipation. That little hint of a smile told him everything he needed to know for the moment. "Audrey!" A voice from the other side of the rooftop called her. She looked over.

"I have to go."

"Say you'll take a drive with me, Sugar."

"Don't call me that."

"Say it."

"No."

"Say it." His smile grew wider. Despite how much he wanted to, he knew he couldn't kiss her now in front of all of these people. But that was sure as heck what he was going to do later. For starters.

"Okay!"

"Okay." He beamed. "I'll come for you at your bungalow."

"You're nuts, you know?"

"But that's what you love about me, isn't it?"

"I don't lo—" She didn't finish what she was saying but scrunched her face in an adorable way and hurried away.

His heart beat triple fast as he watched her go.

When the day was finally done, Shane couldn't believe what he was about to make happen. But he prickled with excitement as he pulled out his phone. *"¿Como estas, amiga?"* he greeted his old friend.

After the call, the spring in his step hurried him to Audrey's bungalow.

"Oops, not quite ready," Audrey said by way of a hello as she opened the door.

Shane leaned in on the door and it opened farther. He presented the bag he had prepared earlier. "I made you a zucchini lemon basil loaf. Notice how I put vegetables into cake? Can I come in?"

"Of course," she answered over her shoulder but then remembered something. "Oh, I mean, um, can you just wait outside? I'll just be one second."

"Huh?" he asked, having already entered and closed the door behind him. And then he saw the last thing he'd ever expect to see in her bungalow.

Him.

The cardboard cutout of him that Reg had ordered a month ago stood facing Audrey's bed. He'd hated the darn thing but Reg had insisted on putting it up in front of the restaurant. He hadn't seen it since, but with everything that had been going on, he hadn't remembered to ask Reg about its whereabouts.

What on earth was it doing in Audrey's room? Partially, he saw, it was being used for practical purposes. While he stood brooding and serious in his chef's coat, bandanna across his forehead and holding his knife like he meant business, now he also wore Audrey's floppy sunhat on top of his cardboard head. Several necklaces were roped around his neck. A purse with a long strap was balanced on one shoulder. Another two purses hung from the other one. And a few scarfs were tied around his waist.

Audrey's mouth dropped open in shock when she headed toward him and saw him inspecting the cutout.

"And you said *I* was nuts?"

"I can explain."

"Uh-huh, Sugar." He grinned. "You can tell me all about it in the car."

* * *

As Shane ushered Audrey into the Jeep, she knew her cheeks were pink from the embarrassment of his discovering the cardboard cutout.

"It was the first day I was here and I meant to bring it to my room just to get it out of the view of the public because I hated it so much," Audrey yammered nervously as Shane cut through side streets until he got them out on the open road. "And then Reg left and I kind of forgot it was there."

Shane glanced sideways at her with hitched eyebrows.

"I mean, before I knew it, it became part of the decor," she continued.

"I like that I've gotten to see you naked every night since you've been here." He smiled but straightened his focus to the road.

She wasn't about to tell him that it wasn't just her nude body but her naked soul that the cutout had been seeing every night. That the cardboard had become her best friend. She relied on it for feedback and for counsel; in fact, it had become her closest confidante. It never judged her, always had a sense of humor and was fiercely on her side. That cutout was good people.

Ten minutes ago, she was trying to get the cutout to talk her out of going on this ride with Shane. After all that had transpired, going out to the spot where they had shared life-altering kisses hardly seemed like a good idea.

Yet she couldn't resist. There wasn't anything she'd rather be doing after a hectic day of overseeing an important event and being *on* with everyone she encountered than driving out of the city to the tranquility of the mountains. With Shane.

Doing anything. With Shane.

"What were you and my dad talking about at the party?" she asked him.

He hesitated, started to say something but then pulled it back. "Just a question I needed to ask him."

"About what?"

He didn't answer.

She loved how once they left the boundaries of the city center, Nevada became vast and unknowable. It was land that held the promise of the West, of exploration and of opportunity. Something in her knew it was important to take this drive with Shane, although she couldn't put her finger on why. Maybe it was for closure. To get them to the next phase they needed to reach in order to work together.

Silence fell upon them for a few minutes. Shane didn't turn up the music as he usually did.

At the most unexpected moment, without taking his eyes off the road, he stated simply, "I love you."

A flush rose across her neck. Her throat parched. A dry murmur pushed through. "I love you, too."

Her eyes welled with tears. Her heart sputtered rather than beat. Welcome to love.

With one hand adequate to maneuver the steering wheel, Shane rested his other on Audrey's thigh. He squeezed it gently and then left his palm there.

For the moment, they were unable to look at each other, and both watched intently as that familiar purple began to descend over the orange and yellow shades of the setting sun.

Everything that had happened between them paraded across Audrey's mind like a slideshow.

"You couldn't have known Melina was going to get into an accident," she said after thinking about it for a long time.

"I'd upset her."

"She was a grown woman. Who should have known better than to drive in unsafe weather conditions."

"I had to identify her dead body. I'd never seen that much blood. I vomited."

"It wasn't your fault."

Again the hush of the wide-open desert became the only sound between them.

"She failed you," he finally said. "You deserved to have a caring mother."

Audrey took in several measured breaths.

"I should have been the stronger one at the end. It would have been good for me. Given me closure."

"You'll be an amazing mother someday."

"I know."

While they both kept their eyes forward, she stretched her arm to him and ran her fingers through the jet curls at the back of his neck.

Shane pulled off the road toward the vantage point where they had watched nature's display the first time. When they got there, two other cars were parked. Which seemed odd. That in such a full expanse of desert, two cars would also be at that very spot. Their spot.

He parked, hopped out, opened the door on her side and helped her out of the car.

A door opened on one of the other parked cars. Reg stepped out from behind the wheel. And from the passenger door Daniel emerged. Connor, Tara and Brittany exited from the backseat.

"What's going on?" Audrey asked, stunned.

Out of the second car, Shane's friend Josefina swung her small frame out. Audrey gave Shane a confused look.

"I asked your father at the brunch today. He said yes."

They looked to Daniel, who was beaming. As were Connor and Tara.

Shane took something from his pocket and then went down on one knee. He held up a simple gold wedding band that glistened under the setting sun. "Audrey Girard, will you marry me?"

"Right here? Right now?"

Her first response was shock but, in a way, hadn't she known all along that by getting in the car with him she was signing on for something?

"Yeah, right now. Will you roll the dice with me, Audrey? Can we ask Lady Luck to give our hearts a fighting chance?"

She couldn't form words. But she could nod her head. *Yes.*

Josefina approached. Audrey remembered that she was a wedding officiant.

It was happening.

Not a moment too soon. Shane was to be hers. To walk with. To laugh with. To fail with. To have and to hold.

Josefina gestured to bring everyone close. "*Mijos,* we gather today to celebrate the merger of Audrey and Shane." They all giggled a little bit. "A joint venture. A collaboration. The word *collaborate* means to work with one with another, to coproduce, to join together..."

After the ring was on Audrey's finger and they had shared their first kiss as man and wife, Daniel joked, "Are we working this for a publicity angle?"

Reg pulled out his phone. "Let's take a selfie."

Together, with the open sky and benevolent mountains behind them, they documented the moment.

"That'll give them something to talk about," Daniel said.

"Audrey, my wife… I like the sound of that," Shane mused. "Where would you like to go for our honeymoon?"

"I know," she answered big-eyed, pretending to have a brilliant idea. "How about Vegas?"

EPILOGUE

"WELCOME TO MY dining room." Audrey's husband said hello to guests enjoying his Midnight Cakes and Coffee service at Shane's Table Las Vegas. Since the restaurant opened a year ago, a dinner reservation had become nearly impossible to obtain as they were fully booked months in advance.

Audrey had the idea to keep the restaurant open until the wee hours on the weekends for an experience that would let patrons who couldn't get in for dinner indulge in Shane's recipes from his second cookbook, *Dulces Para Mi Dulce*, Sweets for My Sweet. He'd created the collection with Audrey in mind, of course. The hip young crowd that was also filling up rooms at Hotel Girard Las Vegas flocked to the late-night decadence of exotic desserts.

Audrey smiled to herself as she couldn't resist a bite of the piping hot cinnamon-flecked fried churro a waiter brought her to sample. She dipped it into the small cup of accompanying thick hot chocolate while she watched her breathtaking husband charm the entire room. Guests' faces lit up when Shane Murphy, who had reclaimed his rightful place as one the world's finest chefs, stopped at their table to chat.

With the kinks worked out at all of the hotels and restaurants, the Girard and Murphy families had their businesses firmly on course. Reg was back in New York at the moment, moving into a Midtown apartment with his girlfriend Brittany. And Audrey's dad was overseeing a landscaping project at Hotel Girard Key West.

Reg and Daniel were both expected back in Vegas at the end of the month, which is when Audrey and Shane intended to share what they had thus far kept secret.

"The atole is good?" Shane took a break from his hosting duties to make sure his wife liked the rich warm chocolate she was sipping.

"Delicioso," Audrey approved.

"How's our little gamble?" he asked and flattened his palm against Audrey's belly.

"I think we hit the jackpot."

"You know, if her eyes are like yours we're going to have to call her Honey." Shane gave his wife a kiss. "Because you'll always be my Sugar. And life is pretty sweet."

* * * * *

A BRIDE FOR THE ITALIAN BOSS

SUSAN MEIER

I want to thank the lovely editors at Mills & Boon for creating such a great continuity!

Everyone involved LOVED this idea. Thank you!

CHAPTER ONE

ITALY HAD TO BE the most beautiful place in the world.

Daniella Tate glanced around in awe at the cobblestone streets and blue skies of Florence. She'd taken a train here, but now had to board a bus for the village of Monte Calanetti.

After purchasing her ticket, she strolled to a wooden bench. But as she sat, she noticed a woman a few rows over, with white-blond hair and a slim build. The woman stared out into space; the faraway look in her eyes triggered Daniella's empathy. Having grown up a foster child, she knew what it felt like to be alone, sometimes scared, usually confused. And she saw all three of those emotions in the woman's pretty blue eyes.

An announcement for boarding the next bus came over the public address system. An older woman sitting beside the blonde rose and slid her fingers around the bag sitting at her feet. The pretty blonde rose, too.

"Excuse me. That's my bag."

The older woman spoke in angry, rapid-fire Italian and the blonde, speaking American English, said, "I'm sorry. I don't understand a word of what you're saying."

But the older woman clutched the bag to her and very clearly told the American that it was her carry-on.

Daniella bounced from her seat and scurried over. She faced the American. "I speak Italian, perhaps I can help?"

Then she turned to the older woman. In flawless Italian, she asked if she was sure the black bag was hers, because there was a similar bag on the floor on the other side.

The older woman flushed with embarrassment. She apologetically gave the bag to the American, grabbed her carry-on and scampered off to catch her bus.

The pretty blonde sighed with relief and turned her blue eyes to Daniella. "Thank you."

"No problem. When you responded in English it wasn't a great leap to assume you didn't speak the language."

The woman's eyes clouded. "I don't."

"Do you have a friend coming to meet you?"

"No."

Dani winced. "Then I hope you have a good English-to-Italian dictionary."

The American pointed to a small listening device. "I've downloaded the 'best' language system." She smiled slightly. "It promises I'll be fluent in five weeks."

Dani laughed. "It could be a long five weeks." She smiled and offered her hand. "I'm Daniella, by the way."

The pretty American hesitated, but finally shook Daniella's hand and said, "Louisa."

"It's my first trip to Italy. I've been teaching English in Rome, but my foster mother was from Tuscany. I'm going to use this final month of my trip to find her home."

Louisa tilted her head. "Your foster mother?"

Dani winced. "Sorry. I'm oversharing."

Louisa smiled.

"It's just that I'm so excited to be here. I've always wanted to visit Italy." She didn't mention that her long-time boyfriend had proposed the day before she left for her teaching post in Rome. That truly would be oversharing, but also she hadn't known what to make of Paul's request to marry him. Had he proposed before her trip to tie her to him? Or had they hit the place in their relationship where marriage really was the next step? Were they ready? Was marriage right for them?

Too many questions came with his offer of marriage. So she hadn't accepted. She'd told him she would answer him when she returned from Italy. She'd planned this February side trip to be a nice, uncomplicated space of time before she settled down to life as a teacher in the New York City school system. Paul had ruined it with a proposal she should have eagerly accepted, but had stumbled over. So her best option was not to think about it until she had to.

Next month.

"I extended my trip so I could have some time to bum around. See the village my foster mother came from, and hopefully meet her family."

To Daniella's surprise, Louisa laughed. "That sounds like fun."

The understanding in Louisa's voice caused Danielle to brighten again, thinking they had something in common. "So you're a tourist, too?"

"No."

Dani frowned. Louisa's tone in that one simple word suddenly made her feel as if she'd crossed a line. "I'm sorry. I don't mean to pry."

Louisa sighed. "It's okay. I'm just a bit nervous. You were kind to come to my rescue. I don't mean to be such a ninny. I'm on my way to Monte Calanetti."

Daniella's mouth fell open. "So am I."

The announcement that their bus was boarding came over the loudspeaker. Danielle faced the gate. Louisa did, too.

Dani smiled. "Looks like we're off."

"Yes." Louisa's mysterious smile formed again.

They boarded the bus and Daniella chose a spot in the middle, believing that was the best place to see the sights on the drive to the quaint village. After tucking her backpack away, she took her seat.

To her surprise, Louisa paused beside her. "Do you mind if I sit with you?"

Daniella happily said, "Of course, I don't mind! That would be great."

But as Louisa sat, Daniella took note again that something seemed off about her. Everything Louisa did had a sense of hesitancy about it. Everything she said seemed incomplete.

"So you have a month before you go home?"

"All of February." Daniella took a deep breath. "And I intend to enjoy every minute of it. Even if I do have to find work."

"Work?"

"A waitressing job. Or maybe part-time shop clerk. That kind of thing. New York is a very expensive place to live. I don't want to blow every cent I made teaching on a vacation. I'll need that money when I get back home. So I intend to earn my spending money while I see the sights."

As the bus eased out of the station, Louisa said, "That's smart."

Dani sat up, not wanting to miss anything. Louisa laughed. "Your foster mother should have come with you."

Pain squeezed Daniella's heart. Just when she thought she was adjusted to her loss, the reality would swoop in and remind her that the sweet, loving woman who'd saved her was gone. She swallowed hard. "She passed a few months ago. She left me the money for my plane ticket to Italy in her will."

Louisa's beautiful face blossomed with sympathy. "I'm so sorry. That was careless of me."

Daniella shook her head. "No. You had no way of knowing."

Louisa studied her. "So you have no set plans? No schedule of things you want to see and do? No places you've already scouted out to potentially get a job?"

"No schedule. I want to wing it. I've done a bit of research about Rosa's family and I know the language. So I think I'll be okay."

Louisa laughed. "Better off than I'll be since I don't know the language." She held up her listening device. "At least not for another five weeks."

The bus made several slow turns, getting them out of the station and onto the street.

Taking a final look at Florence, Dani breathed, "Isn't this whole country gorgeous?" Even in winter with barren trees, the scene was idyllic. Blue skies. Rolling hills.

"Yes." Louisa bit her lip, then hesitantly said, "I'm here because I inherited something, too."

"Really?"

"Yes." She paused, studied Daniella's face as if assessing if she could trust her before continuing, "A villa."

"Oh, my God! A *villa!*"

Louisa glanced away. "I know. It's pretty amazing. The place is called Palazzo di Comparino."

"Do you have pictures?"

"Yes." She pulled out a picture of a tall, graceful house. Rich green vines grew in rows in the background beneath a blue sky.

It was everything Dani could do not to gape in awe. "It's beautiful."

Louisa laughed. "Yes. But so far I haven't seen anything in Italy that isn't gorgeous." She winced. "I hate to admit it, but I'm excited."

"I'd be beyond excited."

"I'm told Monte Calanetti developed around Palazzo Chianti because of the vineyard which is part of the villa I inherited. Back then, they would have needed lots of help picking grapes, making the wine. Those people are the ancestors of the people who live there now."

"That is so cool."

"Yes, except I know nothing about running a vineyard."

Daniella batted a hand. "With the internet these days, you can learn anything."

Louisa sucked in a breath. "I hope so."

Daniella laid her hand on Louisa's in a show of encouragement. "You'll be fine."

Louise's face formed another of her enigmatic smiles and Daniella's sixth sense perked up again. Louisa appeared to want to be happy, but behind her smile was something…

Louisa brought her gaze back to Daniella's. "You know, I could probably use a little help when I get there."

"Help?"

"I don't think I'm just going to move into a villa without somebody coming to question me."

"Ah."

"And I'm going to be at a loss if they're speaking Italian."

Dani winced. "Especially if it's the sheriff."

Louisa laughed. "I don't even know if they have sheriffs here. My letter is in English, but the officials are probably Italian. It could turn out to be a mess. So, I'd be happy to put you up for a while." She caught Dani's gaze. "Even all four weeks you're looking for your foster mom's relatives— if you'd be my translator."

Overwhelmed by the generous offer, Daniella said, "That would be fantastic. But I wouldn't want to put you out."

"You'll certainly earn your keep if somebody comes to check my story."

Daniella grinned. "I'd be staying in a villa."

Louisa laughed. "I *own* a villa."

"Okay, then. I'd be happy to be your translator while I'm here."

"Thank you."

Glad for the friendship forming between them, Daniella engaged Louisa in conversation as miles of hills and blue, blue sky rolled past them. Then suddenly a walled village appeared to the right. The bus turned in.

Aged, but well-maintained stucco, brick and stone buildings greeted them. Cobblestone streets were filled with
happy, chatting people. Through the large front windows
of the establishments, Dani could see the coffee drinkers
or diners inside while outdoor dining areas sat empty because of the chilly temperatures.

The center circle of the town came into view. The bus
made the wide turn but Dani suddenly saw a sign that read
Palazzo di Comparino. The old, worn wood planks had a
thick black line painted through them as if to cancel out
the offer of vineyard tours.

Daniella grabbed Louisa's arm and pointed out the window. "Look!"

"Oh, my gosh!" Louisa jumped out of her seat and
yelled, "Stop!"

Daniella rose, too. She said, *"Fermi qui, per favore."*

It took a minute for the bus driver to hear and finally
halt the bus. After gathering their belongings, Louisa and
Daniella faced the lane that led to Louisa's villa. Because
Dani had only a backpack and Louisa had two suitcases and
a carry-on bag, Daniella said, "Let me take your suitcase."

Louisa smiled. "Having you around is turning out to
be very handy."

Daniella laughed as they walked down the long lane that
took them to the villa. The pale brown brick house soon became visible. The closer they got, the bigger it seemed to be.

Louisa reverently whispered, "Holy cow."

Daniella licked her suddenly dry lips. "It's huge."

The main house sprawled before them. Several stories
tall, and long and deep, like a house with suites not bedrooms, Louisa's new home could only be described as a
mansion.

They silently walked up the stone path to the front door.
When they reached it, Louisa pulled out a key and manipu-
lated the lock. As the door opened, the stale, musty scent
of a building that had been locked up for years assaulted

them. Dust and cobwebs covered the crystal chandelier in the huge marble-floored foyer as well as the paintings on the walls and the curved stairway.

Daniella cautiously stepped inside. "Is your family royalty?"

Louisa gazed around in awe. "I didn't think so."

"Meaning they could be?"

"I don't know." Louisa turned to the right and walked into a sitting room. Again, dust covered everything. A teacup sat on a table by a dusty chair. Passing through that room, they entered another that appeared to be a library or study. From there, they found a dining room.

Watermarks on the ceiling spoke of damage from a second-floor bathroom or maybe even the roof. The kitchen was old and in need of remodeling. The first-floor bathrooms were outdated, as was every bathroom in the suites upstairs.

After only getting as far as the second floor, Louisa turned to Daniella with tears in her eyes. "I'm so sorry. I didn't realize the house would be in such disrepair. From the picture, it looked perfect. If you want to get a hotel room in town, I'll understand."

"Are you kidding?" Daniella rolled Louisa's big suitcase to a stop and walked into the incredibly dusty, cobweb-covered bedroom. She spun around and facèd Louisa. "I love it. With a dust rag, some cleanser for the bathroom and a window washing, this room will be perfect."

Louisa hesitantly followed Daniella into the bedroom. "You're an optimist."

Daniella laughed. "I didn't say you wouldn't need to call a contractor about a few things. But we can clean our rooms and the kitchen."

Raffaele Mancini stared at Gino Scarpetti, a tall, stiff man, who worked as the maître d' for Mancini's, Rafe's very exclusive, upscale, Michelin-starred restaurant located in the heart of wine country.

Mancini's had been carefully crafted to charm customers. The stone and wood walls of the renovated farmhouse gave the place the feel of days long gone. Shutters on the windows blocked the light of the evening sun, but also added to the Old World charisma. Rows of bottles of Merlot and Chianti reminded diners that this area was the home of the best vineyards, the finest wines.

Gino ripped off the Mancini's name tag pinned to his white shirt. "You, sir, are now without a maître d'."

A hush fell over the dining room. Even the usual clink and clatter of silverware and the tinkle of good crystal wineglasses halted.

Gino slapped the name tag into Rafe's hand. Before Rafe could comment or argue, the man was out the door.

Someone began to clap. Then another person. And another. Within seconds the sophisticated Tuscany restaurant dining room filled with the sounds of applause and laughter.

Laughter!

They were enjoying his misery!

He looked at the line of customers forming beside the podium just inside the door, then the chattering diners laughing about his temper and his inability to keep good help. He tossed his hands in the air before he marched back to the big ultramodern stainless-steel restaurant kitchen.

"You!"

He pointed at the thin boy who'd begun apprenticing at Mancini's the week before. "Take off your smock and get to the maître d' stand. You are seating people."

The boy's brown eyes grew round with fear. "I…I…"

Rafe raised a brow. "You can't take names and seat customers?"

"I can…"

"But you don't want to." Rafe didn't have to say anything beyond that. He didn't need to say, "If you can't obey orders, you're fired." He didn't need to remind anyone in *his* kitchen that he was boss or that anyone working in the restaurant needed to be able to do *anything* that needed to be done to assure the absolute best dining experience for the customers. Everyone knew he was not a chef to be trifled with.

Except right now, in the dining room, they were laughing at him.

The boy whipped off his smock, threw it to a laundry bin and headed out to the dining room.

Seeing the white-smocked staff gaping at him, Rafe shook his head. "Get to work!"

Knives instantly rose. The clatter of chopping and the sizzle of sautéing filled the kitchen.

He sucked in a breath. Not only was his restaurant plagued by troubles, but now it seemed the diners had no sympathy.

"You shouldn't have fired Gino." Emory Danoto, Rafe's sous-chef, spoke as he worked. Short and bald with a happy face and nearly as much talent as Rafe in the kitchen, Emory was also Rafe's mentor.

Rafe glanced around, inspecting the food prep, pretending he was fine. Damn it. He *was* fine. He did not want a frightened rabbit working for him. Not even outside the kitchen. And the response of the diners? That was a fluke. Somebody apparently believed it was funny to see a world-renowned chef tortured by incompetents.

"I didn't fire Gino. He quit."

Emory cast him a condemning look. "You yelled at him."

Rafe yelled, "I yell at everybody." Then he calmed himself and shook his head. "I am the chef. I *am* Mancini's."

"And you must be obeyed."

"Don't make me sound like a prima donna. I am doing what's best for the restaurant."

"Well, Mr. I'm-Doing-What's-Best-for-the-Restaurant, have you forgotten about our upcoming visit from the Michelin people?"

"A rumor."

Emory sniffed a laugh. "Since when have we ever ignored a rumor that we were to be visited? Your star rating could be in jeopardy. You're the one who says chefs who ignore rumors get caught with their pants down. If we want to keep our stars, we have to be ready for this visit."

Rafe stifled a sigh. Emory was right, of course. His trusted friend only reminded him of what he already knew. Having located his business in the countryside, instead of in town, he'd made it even more exclusive. But that also meant he didn't get street traffic. He needed word of mouth. He needed every diner to recommend him to their friends. He needed to be in travel brochures. To be a stop for tour buses. To be recommended by travel agents. He couldn't lose a star.

The lunch crowd left. Day quickly became night. Before Rafe could draw a steady breath the restaurant filled again. Wasn't that the way of it when everything was falling apart around you? With work to be done, there was no time to think things through. When the last patron finally departed and the staff dispersed after the kitchen cleaning, Rafe walked behind the shiny wood bar, pulled a bottle of whiskey from the shelf, along with a glass, and slid onto a tall, black, wrought iron stool.

Hearing the sound of the door opening, he yelled, "We're closed." Then grimaced. Was he trying to get a reputation for being grouchy rather than exacting?

"Good thing I'm not a customer, then."

He swiveled around at the sound of his friend Nico Amatucci's voice.

Tall, dark-haired Nico glanced at the whiskey bottle, then sat on a stool beside Rafe. "Is there a reason you're drinking alone?"

Rafe rose, got another glass and set it on the bar. He poured whiskey into the glass and slid it to Nico. "I'm not drinking alone."

"But you were going to."

"I lost my maître d'."

Nico raised his glass in salute and drank the shot. "You're surprised?"

"I'm an artist."

"You're a pain in the ass."

"That, too." He sighed. "But I don't want to be. I just want things done correctly. I'll spread the word tomorrow that I'm looking for someone. Not a big deal." He made the statement casually, but deep down he knew he was wrong. It was a big deal. "Oh, who am I kidding? I don't have the week or two it'll take to collect résumés and interview people. I need somebody tomorrow."

Nico raised his glass to toast. "Then, you, my friend, are in trouble."

Didn't Rafe know it.

CHAPTER TWO

THE NEXT MORNING, Daniella and Louisa found a tin of tea and some frozen waffles in a freezer. "We're so lucky no one had the electricity shut off."

"Not lucky. The place runs off a generator. We turn it on in winter to keep the pipes from freezing."

Daniella and Louisa gasped and spun around at the male voice behind them.

A handsome dark-haired man stood in the kitchen doorway, frowning at them. Though he appeared to be Italian, he spoke flawless English. "I'm going to have to ask you to leave. I'll let you finish your breakfast, but this is private property."

Louisa's chin lifted. "I know it's private property. I'm Louisa Harrison. I inherited this villa."

The man's dark eyes narrowed. "I don't suppose you have proof of that?"

"Actually, I do. A letter from my solicitor." She straightened her shoulders. "I think the better question is, who are you?"

"I'm Nico Amatucci." He pointed behind him. "I live next door. I've been watching over this place." He smiled thinly. "I'd like to see the letter from your solicitor. Or—" he pulled out his cell phone "—should I call the police?"

Louisa brushed her hands down her blue jeans to remove the dust they'd collected when she and Daniella had searched for tea. "No need."

Not wanting any part of the discussion, Daniella began preparing the tea.

"And who are you?"

She shrugged. "Just a friend of Louisa's."

He sniffed as if he didn't believe her. Not accustomed to being under such scrutiny, Daniella focused all her attention on getting water into the teapot.

Louisa returned with the letter. When Nico reached for it, she held it back. "Not so fast. I'll need the key you used to get in."

He held Louisa's gaze. Even from across the room, Daniella felt the heat of it.

"Only if your papers check out." His frosty smile could have frozen water. "Palazzo di Comparino has been empty for years. Yet, suddenly here you are."

"With a letter," she said, handing it to Nico.

He didn't release her gaze as he took the letter from her hands, and then he scanned it and peered at Louisa again. "Welcome to Palazzo di Comparino."

Daniella let out her pent-up breath.

Louisa held his gaze. "Just like that? How do you know I didn't fake this letter?"

Giving the paper back to her, he said, "First, I knew the name of the solicitor handling the estate. Second, there are a couple of details in the letter that an outsider wouldn't know. You're legit."

Though Daniella would have loved to have known the details, Louisa didn't even seem slightly curious. She tucked the sheet of paper into her jeans pocket.

Nico handed his key to Louisa as he glanced around the kitchen. "Being empty so long, the place is in disrepair. So if there's anything I can do to help—"

Louisa cut him off with a curt "I'm fine."

Nico's eyes narrowed. Daniella didn't know if he was

unaccustomed to his offers of assistance being ignored, or if something else was happening here, but the kitchen became awkwardly quiet.

When Daniella's teapot whistled, her heart jumped. Always polite, she asked, "Can I get anyone tea?"

Watching Louisa warily, Nico said, "I'd love a cup."

Drat. He was staying. Darn the sense of etiquette her foster mother had drilled into her.

"I'll make some later," Louisa said as she turned and walked out of the kitchen, presumably to put the letter and the key away.

As the door swung closed behind her, Nico said, "She's a friendly one."

Daniella winced. She'd like to point out to Mr. Nico Amatucci that he'd been a tad rude when he'd demanded to see the letter from the solicitor, but she held her tongue. This argument wasn't any of her business. She had enough troubles of her own.

"Have you known Ms. Harrison long?"

"We just met. I saw someone mistakenly take her bag and helped because Louisa doesn't speak Italian. Then we were on the same bus."

"Oh, so you hit the jackpot when you could find someone to stay with."

Daniella's eyes widened. The man was insufferable. "I'm not taking advantage of her! I just finished a teaching job in Rome. Louisa needs an interpreter for a few weeks." She put her shoulders back. "And today I intend to go into town to look for temporary work to finance a few weeks of sightseeing."

He took the cup of tea from her hands. "What kind of work?"

His softened voice took some of the wind out of her sails. She shrugged. "Anything really. Temp jobs are temp jobs."

"Would you be willing to be a hostess at a restaurant?"

Confused, she said, "Sure."

"I have a friend who needs someone to fill in while he hires a permanent replacement for a maître d' who just quit."

Her feelings for the mysterious Nico warmed a bit. Maybe he wasn't so bad after all? "Sounds perfect."

"Do you have a pen?"

She nodded, pulling one from her purse.

He scribbled down the address on a business card he took from his pocket. "Go here. Don't call. Just go at lunchtime and tell Rafe that Nico sent you." He nodded at the card he'd handed to her. "Show him that and he'll know you're not lying."

He set his tea on the table. "Tell Ms. Harrison I said goodbye."

With that, he left.

Glad he was gone, Daniella glanced at the card in her hands. How could a guy who'd so easily helped her have such a difficult time getting along with Louisa?

She blew her breath out on a long sigh. She supposed it didn't matter. Eventually they'd become friends. They were neighbors after all.

Daniella finished her tea, but Louisa never returned to the kitchen. Excited to tell Louisa of her job prospect, Dani searched the downstairs for her, but didn't find her.

The night before they'd tidied two bedrooms enough that they could sleep in them, so she climbed the stairs and headed for the room Louisa had chosen. She found her new friend wrestling with some bedding.

"What are you doing?"

"I saw a washer and dryer. I thought I'd wash the bedclothes so our rooms really will be habitable tonight."

She raced to help Louisa with the huge comforter. "Our rooms were fine. We don't need these comforters, and the sheets had been protected from the dust by the comforters so they were clean. Besides, these won't fit in a typical washer."

Louisa dropped the comforter. "I know." Her face fell in dismay. "I just need to do something to make the place more livable." Her gaze met Daniella's. "There's dust and clutter…and watermarks that mean some of the bathrooms and maybe even the roof need to be repaired." She sat on the bed. "What am I going to do?"

Dani sat beside her. "We're going to take things one step at a time." She tucked Nico's business card into her pocket. "This morning, we'll clean the kitchen and finish our bedrooms. Tomorrow, we'll pick a room and clean it, and every day after that we'll just keep cleaning one room at a time."

"What about the roof?"

"We'll hope it doesn't rain?"

Louisa laughed. "I'm serious."

"Well, I have a chance for a job at a restaurant."

"You do?"

She smiled. "Yes. Nico knows someone who needs a hostess."

"Oh."

She ignored the dislike in her friend's voice. "What better way to find a good contractor than by chitchatting with the locals?"

Louisa smiled and shook her head. "If anybody can chitchat her way into finding a good contractor, it's you."

"Which is also going to make me a good hostess."

"What time's your appointment?"

"Lunchtime." She winced. "From the address on this card, I think we're going to have to hope there's a car in that big, fancy garage out back."

Standing behind the podium in the entry to Mancini's, Rafe struggled with the urge to throw his hands in the air and storm off. On his left, two American couples spoke broken, ill-attempted Italian in an effort to make reservations for that night. In front of him, a businessman demanded to be seated immediately. To his right, a couple kissed. And behind them, what seemed to be a sea of diners groused and grumbled as he tried to figure out a computer system with a seating chart superimposed with reservations.

How could no one in his kitchen staff be familiar with this computer software?

"Everybody just give me a minute!"

He hit a button and the screen disappeared. After a second of shock, he cursed. He expected the crowd to groan. Instead they laughed. *Laughed. Again, laughter!*

How was it that everybody seemed to be happy that he was suffering? These people—customers—were the people he loved, the people he worked so hard to please. How could they laugh at him?

He tried to get the screen to reappear, but it stayed dark.

"Excuse me. Excuse me. Excuse me."

He glanced up to see an American, clearly forgetting she was in Italy because she spoke English as she made her way through the crowd. Cut in an angled, modern style, her pretty blond hair stopped at her chin. Her blue eyes were determined. The buttons of her black coat had been left open, revealing jeans and pale blue sweater.

When she reached the podium, she didn't even look at Rafe. She addressed the gathered crowd.

"Ladies and gentlemen," she said in flawless Italian. "Give me two minutes and everyone will be seated."

His eyebrows rose. She was a cheeky little thing.

When she finally faced him, her blue eyes locked on his. Rich with color and bright with enthusiasm, they didn't merely display her confidence, they caused his heart to give a little bounce.

She smiled and stuck out her hand. "Daniella Tate. Your friend Nico sent me." When he didn't take her hand, her smile drooped as she tucked a strand of yellow hair behind her ear. But her face brightened again. She rifled in her jeans pocket, pulled out a business card and offered it to him. "See?"

He glanced at Nico's card. "So he believes you are right to be my hostess?"

"Temporarily." She winced. "I just finished a teaching position in Rome. For the next four weeks I'm sightseeing, but I'm trying to supplement my extended stay with a temp job. I think he thinks we can help each other—at least while you interview candidates."

The sweet, melodious tone of her voice caused something warm and soft to thrum through Rafe, something he'd never felt before—undoubtedly relief that his friend had solved his problem.

"I see."

"Hey, buddy, come on. We're hungry! If you're not going to seat us we'll go somewhere else."

Not waiting for him to reply, Daniella nudged Rafe out of the way, stooped down to find a tablet on the maître d' stand shelf and faced the dining area. She quickly drew squares and circles representing all the tables and wrote the number of chairs around each one. She put an X over the tables that were taken.

Had he thought she was cheeky? Apparently that was just the tip of the iceberg.

She faced the Americans. "How many in your party?"

"Four. We want reservations for tonight."

"Time?"

"Seven."

Flipping the tablet page, she wrote their name and the time on the next piece of paper. As the Americans walked out, she said, "Next?"

Awestruck at her audacity, Rafe almost yelled.

Almost.

He could easily give her the boot, but he needed a hostess. He had a growing suspicion about the customers laughing when he lost his temper, as if he was becoming some sort of sideshow. He didn't want his temper to be the reason people came to his restaurant. He wanted his food, the fantastic aromas, the succulent tastes, to be the draw. Wouldn't he be a fool to toss her out?

The businessman pushed his way over to her. "I have an appointment in an hour. I need to be served first."

Daniella Tate smiled at Rafe as if asking permission to seat the businessman, and his brain emptied. She really was as pretty as she was cheeky. Luckily, she took his blank stare as approval. She turned to the businessman and said, "Of course, we'll seat you."

She led the man to the back of the dining room, to a table for two, seated him with a smile and returned to the podium.

Forget about how cheeky she was. Forget about his brain that stalled when he looked at her. She was a very good hostess.

Rafe cleared his throat. "Talk to the waitresses and find out whose turn it is before you seat anyone else." He cleared his throat again. "They have a system."

She smiled at him. "Sure."

His heart did something funny in his chest, forcing his gaze to her pretty blue eyes again. Warmth whooshed through him.

Confused, he turned and marched away. With so much at stake in his restaurant, including, it seemed, his reputation, his funny feelings for an employee were irrelevant. Nothing. Whatever trickled through his bloodstream, it had to be more annoyance than attraction. After all, recommendation from Nico or not, she'd sort of walked in and taken over his restaurant.

Dani stared after the chef as he left. She wasn't expecting someone so young…or so gorgeous. At least six feet tall, with wavy brown hair so long he had it tied off his face and gray eyes, the guy could be a celebrity chef on television back home. Just looking at him had caused her breathing to stutter. She actually felt a rush of heat careen through her veins. He was *that* good-looking.

But it was also clear that he was in over his head without a maître d'. As she'd stood in the back of the long line to get into the restaurant, her good old-fashioned American common sense had kicked in, and she'd simply done what needed to be done: pushed her way to the front, grabbed some menus and seated customers. And he'd hired her.

Behind her someone said, "You'd better keep your hair behind your ears. He'll yell about it being in your face and potentially in his food once he gets over being happy you're here."

She turned to see one of the waitresses. Dressed in black trousers and a white blouse, she looked slim and professional.

"*That* was happy?"

Her pretty black ponytail bobbed as she nodded. "*Sì.* That was happy."

"Well, I'm going to hate seeing him upset."

"Prepare yourself for it. Because he gets upset every day. Several times a day. That's why Gino quit. I'm Allegra, by the way. The other two waitresses are Zola and Giovanna. And the chef is Chef Mancini. Everyone calls him Chef Rafe."

"He said you have a system of how you want people seated?"

Allegra took Daniella's seating chart and drew two lines dividing the tables into three sections. "Those are our stations. You seat one person in mine, one person in Zola's and one person in Gio's, then start all over again."

Daniella smiled. "Easy-peasy."

"*Scusi?*"

"That means 'no problem.'"

"Ah. *Sì.*" Allegra smiled and walked away. Daniella took two more menus and seated another couple.

The lunchtime crowd that had assembled at the door of

Mancini's settled quickly. Dani easily found a rhythm of dividing the customers up between the three waitresses. Zola and Gio introduced themselves, and she actually had a good time being hostess of the restaurant that looked like an Old World farmhouse and smelled like pure heaven. The aromas of onions and garlic, sweet peppers and spicy meats rolled through the air, making her confident she could talk up the food and promise diners a wonderful meal, even without having tasted it.

During the lull after lunch, Zola and Gio went home. The dining room grew quiet. Not sure if she should stay or leave, since Allegra remained to be available for the occasional tourist who ambled in, Daniella stayed, too.

In between customers, she helped clear and reset tables, checked silverware to make sure it sparkled, arranged chairs so that everything in the dining room was picture-perfect.

But soon even the stragglers stopped. Daniella stood by the podium, her elbow leaning against it, her chin on her closed fist, wondering what Louisa was doing.

"Why are you still here?"

The sound of Rafe's voice sent a surge of electricity through her.

She turned with a gasp. Her voice wobbled when she said, "I thought you'd need me for dinner."

"You were supposed to go home for the break. Or are you sneakily trying to get paid for hours you really don't work?"

Her eyes widened. Anger punched through her. What the hell was wrong with this guy? She'd done him a favor and he was questioning her motives?

Without thinking, she stormed over to him. Putting herself in his personal space, she looked up and caught his gaze. "And how was I supposed to know that, since you didn't tell me?"

She expected him to back down. At the very least to realize his mistake. Instead, he scoffed. "It's common sense."

"Well, in America—"

He cut her off with a harsh laugh. "You Americans.
Think you know everything. But you're not in America
now. You are in Italy." He pointed a finger at her nose.
"You will do what I say."

"Well, I'll be happy to do what you say as soon as you
say something!"

Allegra stopped dropping silverware onto linen-cov-
ered tables. The empty, quiet restaurant grew stone-cold
silent. Time seemed to crawl to a stop. The vein in Rafe's
temple pulsed.

Dani's body tingled. Every employee in the world knew
it wasn't wise to yell at the boss, but, technically, she wasn't
yelling. She was standing up to him. As a foster child, she'd
had to learn how to protect herself, when to stay quiet and
when to demand her rights. If she let him push her around
now, he'd push her around the entire month she worked
for him.

He threw his hands in the air, pivoted away from her
and headed to the kitchen. "Go the hell home and come
back for dinner."

Daniella blew out the breath she'd been holding. Her
heart pounded so hard it hurt, but the tingling in her blood
became a surge of power. He might not have said the words,
but she'd won that little battle of wills.

Still, she felt odd that their communication had come
down to a sort of yelling match and knew she had to get
the heck out of there.

She grabbed her purse and headed for the old green car
she and Louisa had found in the garage.

Ten minutes later, she was back in the kitchen of Palazzo di Comparino.

Though Louisa had sympathetically made her a cup of
tea, she laughed when Daniella told her the story.

"It's not funny," Dani insisted, but her lips rose into a smile when she thought about how she must have looked standing up to the big bad chef everybody seemed to be afraid of. She wouldn't tell her new friend that standing up to him had put fire in her blood and made her heart gallop like a prize stallion. She didn't know what that was all about, but she did know part of it, at least, stemmed from how good-looking he was.

"Okay. It was a little funny. But I like this job. It would be great to keep it for the four weeks I'm here. But he didn't tell me what time I was supposed to go back. So we're probably going to get into another fight."

"Or you could just go back at six. If he yells that you're late, calmly remind him that he didn't give you the time you were to return. Make it his fault."

"It is his fault."

Louisa beamed. "Exactly. If you don't stand up to him now, you'll either lose the job or spend the weeks you work for him under his thumb. You have to do this."

Dani sighed. "That's what I thought."

Taking Louisa's advice, she returned to the restaurant at six. A very small crowd had built by the maître d' podium, and when she entered, she noticed that most of the tables weren't filled. Rafe shoved a stack of menus at her and walked away.

She shook her head, but smiled at the next customers in line. He might have left without a word, but he hadn't engaged her in a fight and it appeared she still had her job.

Maybe the answer to this was to just stay out of his way?

The evening went smoothly. Again, the wonderful scents that filled the air prompted her to talk up the food, the waitstaff and the wine.

After an hour or so, Rafe called her into the kitchen. Absolutely positive he had nothing to yell at her about, she straightened her shoulders and walked into the stainless-steel room and over to the stove where he stood.

"You wanted to see me?"

He presented a fork filled with pasta to her. "This is my signature ravioli. I hear you talking about my dishes, so I want you to taste so you can honestly tell customers it is the best food you have ever eaten."

She swallowed back a laugh at his confidence, but when her lips wrapped around the fork and the flavor of the sweet sauce exploded on her tongue, she pulled the ravioli off the fork and into her mouth with a groan. "Oh, my God."

"It is perfect, *sì*?"

"You're right. It is probably the best food I've ever eaten."

Emory, the short, bald sous-chef, scrambled over. "Try this." He raised a fork full of meat to her lips.

She took the bite and again, she groaned. "What is that?"

"Beef *brasato*."

"Oh, my God, that's good."

A younger chef suddenly appeared before her with a spoon of soup. "Minestrone," he said, holding the spoon out to her.

She drank the soup and closed her eyes to savor. "You guys are the best cooks in the world."

Everyone in the kitchen stopped. The room fell silent.

But Emory laughed. "Chef Rafe is *one* of the best chefs in the world. These are his recipes."

She turned and smiled at Rafe. "You're amazing."

She'd meant his cooking was amazing. His recipes were amazing. Or maybe the way he could get the best out of his staff was amazing. But saying the words while looking into his silver-gray eyes, the simple sentence took on a totally different meaning.

The room grew quiet again. She felt her face reddening. Rafe held her gaze for a good twenty seconds before he finally pointed at the door. "Go tell that to customers."

She walked out of the kitchen, licking the remains of the fantastic food off her lips as she headed for the podium.

With the exception of that crazy little minute of eye contact, tasting the food had been fun. She loved how proud the entire kitchen staff seemed to be of the delicious dishes they prepared. And she saw the respect they had for their boss. Chef Rafe. Clearly a very talented man.

With two groups waiting to be seated, she grabbed menus and walked the first couple to a table. "Right this way."

"Any specialties tonight?"

She faced the man and woman behind her, saying, "I can honestly recommend the chef's signature ravioli." With the taste of the food still on her tongue, she smiled. "And the minestrone soup is to die for. But if you're in the mood for beef, there's a beef *brasato* that you'll never forget."

She said the words casually, but sampling the food had had the oddest effect on her. Suddenly she felt part of it. She didn't merely feel like a good hostess who could recommend the delicious dishes because she'd tasted them. She got an overwhelming sense that she was meant to be here. The feeling of destiny was so strong it nearly overwhelmed her. But she drew in a quiet breath, smiled at the couple and seated them.

Sense of destiny? That was almost funny. Children who grew up in foster care gave up on destiny early, and contented themselves with a sense of worth, confidence. It was better to educate yourself to be employable than to dally in daydreams.

As the night went on, Rafe and his staff continued to give her bites and tastes of the dishes they prepared. As she became familiar with the items on the menu, she tempted guests to try things. But she also listened to stories of the sights the tourists had seen that day, and soothed the egos of those who spoke broken Italian by telling stories of teaching English as a second language in Rome.

And the feeling that she was meant to be there grew, until her heart swelled with it.

* * *

Rafe watched her from the kitchen door. Behind him, Emory laughed. "She's pretty, right?"

Rafe faced him, concerned that his friend had seen their thirty seconds of eye contact over the ravioli and recognized that Rafe was having trouble seeing Daniella Tate as an employee because she was so beautiful. When she'd called him amazing, he'd struggled to keep his gaze off her lips, but that didn't stop the urge to kiss her. It blossomed to life in his chest and clutched the air going into and out of his lungs, making them stutter. He'd needed all of those thirty seconds to get ahold of himself.

But Emory's round face wore his usual smile. Nothing out of the ordinary. No light of recognition in his eyes. Rafe's unexpected reactions hadn't been noticed.

Rafe turned back to the crack between the doors again. "She's chatty."

"You did tell her to talk up the food." Emory sidled up to the slim opening. "Besides, the customers seem to love her."

"Bah!" He spun away from the door. "We don't need for customers to love her. They come here for the food."

Emory shrugged. "Maybe. But we're both aware Mancini's was getting to be a little more well-known for your temper than for its meals. A little attention from a pretty girl talking up *your* dishes might just cure your reputation problem. Put the food back in the spotlight instead of your temper."

"I still think she talks too much."

Emory shook his head. "Suit yourself."

Rafe crossed his arms on his chest. He would suit himself. He was *famous* for suiting himself. That was how he'd gotten to be a great chef. By learning and testing until he created great meals. And he wanted the focus on those meals.

The first chance he got, he intended to have a talk with Daniella Tate.

CHAPTER THREE

AT THE END of the night, when the prep tables were spotless, the kitchen staff raced out the back door. Rafe ambled into the dining room as the waitresses headed for the front door, Daniella in their ranks.

Stopping behind the bar, he called, "No. No. You…Daniella. You and I need to talk."

Her steps faltered and she paused. Eventually, she turned around. "Sure. Great."

Allegra and Gio tossed looks of sympathy at her as the door closed softly behind them.

Her shoulders straightened and she walked over to him. "What is it?"

"You are chatty."

She burst out laughing. "I know." As comfortable as an old friend, she slid onto a bar stool across from him. "Got myself into a lot of trouble in school for that."

"Then you will not be offended if I ask you to project a more professional demeanor with the customers?"

"Heck, no. I'm not offended. I think you're crazy for telling me not to be friendly. But I'm not offended."

Heat surged through Rafe's blood, the way it had when she'd nibbled the ravioli from his fork and called him amazing. But this time he was prepared for it. He didn't know what it was about this woman that got him going, why their arguments fired his blood and their pleasant encounters made him want to kiss her, but he did know he had to control it.

He pulled a bottle of wine from the rack beneath the bar and poured two glasses. Handing one of the glasses to her, he asked, "Do you think it's funny to argue with your boss?"

"I'm not arguing with you. I'm giving you my opinion."

He stayed behind the bar, across from her so he could see her face, her expressive blue eyes. "Ah. So, now I understand. You believe you have a right to an opinion."

She took a sip of the wine. "Maybe not a right. But it's kind of hard not to have an opinion."

He leaned against the smooth wooden surface between them, unintentionally getting closer, then finding that he liked it there because he could smell the hint of her perfume or shampoo. "Perhaps. But a smart employee learns to stifle them."

"As you said, I'm chatty."

"Do it anyway."

She sucked in a breath, pulling back slightly as if trying to put space between them. "Okay."

He laughed. "Okay? My chatty hostess is just saying okay?"

"It's your restaurant."

He saluted her with his wineglass. "At least we agree on something."

But when she set her glass on the bar, slid off the stool and headed for the door, his heart sank.

He shook his head, grabbed the open bottle of wine and went in the other direction, walking toward the kitchen where he would check the next day's menu. It was silly, foolish to be disappointed she was leaving. Not only did he barely know the woman, but he wasn't in the market for a girlfriend. His instincts might be thinking of things like kissing, but he hadn't dated in four years. He had affairs and one-night stands. And a smart employer didn't have a one-night stand with an employee. Unless he wanted trouble. And he did not.

He'd already had one relationship that had almost destroyed his dream. He'd fallen so hard for Kamila Troccoli that when she wasn't able to handle the demands of his schedule, he'd pared it back. Desperate to keep her, he'd refused plum apprenticeships, basically giving up his goal of being a master chef and owning a chain of restaurants.

But she'd left him anyway. After a year of building his life around her, he'd awakened one morning to find she'd simply gone. It had taken four weeks before he could go back to work, but his broken heart hadn't healed until he'd realized relationships were for other men. He had a dream that a romance had nearly stolen from him. A wise man didn't forget hard lessons, or throw them away because of a pretty girl.

Almost at the kitchen door, he stopped. "And, Daniella?"

She faced him.

"No jeans tomorrow. Black trousers and a white shirt."

Daniella raced to her car, her heart thumping in her chest. Having Rafe lean across the bar, so close to her, had been the oddest thing. Her blood pressure had risen. Her breathing had gone funny. And damned if she didn't want to run her fingers through his wavy hair. Unbound, it had fallen to his shoulders, giving him the look of a sexy pirate.

The desire to touch him had been so strong, she would have agreed to anything to be able to get away from him so she could sort this out.

And just when she'd thought she was free, he'd said her name. *Daniella.* The way it had rolled off his tongue had been so sexy, she'd shuddered.

Calling herself every kind of crazy, she got into Louisa's old car and headed home. A mile up the country road, she pulled through the opening in the stone wall that allowed entry to Monte Calanetti. Driving along the cobblestone street, lit only by streetlights, she marveled at the way her heart warmed at the quaint small town. She'd never felt so at peace as she did in Italy, and she couldn't wait to meet her foster mother's relatives. Positive they'd make a connection, she could see herself coming to Italy every year to visit them.

She followed the curve around the statue in the town square before she made the turn onto the lane for Palazzo di Comparino. She knew Louisa saw only decay and damage when she looked at the crumbling villa, but in her mind's eye Dani could see it as it was in its glory days. Vines heavy with grapes. The compound filled with happy employees. The owner, a proud man.

A lot like Rafe.

She squeezed her eyes shut when the familiar warmth whooshed through her at just the thought of his name. What was it about that guy that got to her? Sure, he was sexy. Really sexy. But she'd met sexy men before. Why did this one affect her like this?

Louisa was asleep, so she didn't have anyone to talk with about her strange feelings. But the next morning over tea, she told Louisa everything that had happened at the restaurant, especially her unwanted urge to touch Rafe when he leaned across the bar and was so close to her, and Louisa—again—laughed.

"This is Italy. Why are you so surprised you're feeling everything a hundred times more passionately?"

Dani's eyes narrowed. Remembering her thoughts about Monte Calanetti, the way she loved the quaint cobblestone streets, the statue fountain in the middle of the square, the happy, bustling people, she realized she did feel everything more powerfully in Italy.

"Do you think that's all it is?"

"Oh, sweetie, this is the land of passion. It's in the air. The water. Something. As long as you recognize what it is, you'll be fine."

"I hope so." She rose from the table. "I also hope there's a thrift shop in town. I have to find black trousers and a white blouse. Rafe doesn't like my jeans."

Louisa laughed as she, too, rose from the table. "I'll bet he likes your jeans just fine."

Daniella frowned.

Louisa slid her arm across her shoulder. "Your butt looks amazing in jeans."

"What does that have to do with anything?"

Louisa gave her a confused look, then shook her head. "Did you ever stop to think that maybe you're *both* reacting extremely to each other. That it's not just you feeling everything, and that's why it's so hard to ignore?"

"You think he's attracted to me?"

"Maybe. Dani, you're pretty and sexy." She laughed. "And Italian men like blondes."

Daniella frowned. "Oh, boy. That just makes things worse."

"Or more fun."

"No! I have a fiancé. Well, not a fiancé. My boyfriend asked me to marry him right before I left."

"You have a boyfriend?"

She winced. "Yeah."

"And he proposed right before you left?"

"Yes."

Louisa sighed. "I guess that rules out an affair with your sexy Italian boss."

Daniella's eyes widened. "I can't have an affair!"

"I know." Louisa laughed. "Come on. Let's go upstairs and see what's in my suitcases. I have to unpack anyway. I'm sure I have black pants and a white shirt."

"Okay."

Glad the subject had changed, Daniella walked with Louisa through the massive downstairs to the masterpiece stairway.

Louisa lovingly caressed the old, worn banister. "I feel

like this should be my first project. Sort of like a symbol that I intend to bring this place back to life."

"Other people might give the kitchen or bathrooms a priority."

Louisa shook her head. "The foyer is the first thing everyone sees when they walk in. I want people to know I'm committed and I'm staying."

"I get it."

It took ten minutes to find the black pants and white shirt in Louisa's suitcase, but Dani remained with Louisa another hour to sort through her clothes and hang them in the closet.

When it was time to leave, she said goodbye to Louisa and headed to the restaurant for the lunch crowd. She stashed her purse on the little shelf of the podium and waited for someone to unlock the door to customers so she could begin seating everyone.

Rafe himself came out. As he walked to the door, his gaze skimmed over her. Pinpricks of awareness rained down on her. Louisa's suggestion that he was attracted to her tiptoed into her brain. What would it be like to have this sexy, passionate man attracted to her?

She shook her head. What the heck was she thinking? He was only looking at her to make sure she had dressed appropriately. He was *not* attracted to her. Good grief. All they ever did was snipe at each other. That was not attraction.

Although, standing up to him did warm her blood…

After opening the door, Rafe strode away without even saying good morning, proving, at least to Dani, that he wasn't attracted to her. As she seated her first customers, he walked to the windows at the back of the old farmhouse and opened the wooden shutters, revealing the picturesque countryside.

The odd feeling of destiny brought Daniella up short again. This time she told herself it was simply an acknowledgment that the day was beautiful, the view perfect. There was no such thing as someone "belonging" somewhere. There was only hard work and planning.

An hour into the lunch shift, a customer called her over and asked to speak with the chef. Fear shuddered through her.

"Rafe?"

The older man nodded. "If he's the chef, yes."

She couldn't even picture the scene if she called Rafe out and this man, a sweet old man with gray hair, blue eyes and a cute little dimple, complained about the food. So she smiled. "Maybe I can help you?"

"Perhaps. But I would like to speak with the chef."

Officially out of options, she smiled and said, "Absolutely."

She turned to find Rafe only a few steps away, his eyes narrowed, his lips thin.

She made her smile as big as she could. "Chef Rafe…" She motioned him over. When he reached her, she politely said, "This gentleman would like to speak with you."

The dining room suddenly grew quiet. It seemed that everyone, including Daniella, held their breath.

Rafe addressed the man. "Yes? What can I do for you? I'm always happy to hear from my customers."

His voice wasn't just calm. It was warm. Dani took a step back. She'd expected him to bark. Instead, he was charming and receptive.

"This is the best ravioli I've ever eaten." The customer smiled broadly. "I wanted to convey my compliments to the chef personally."

Rafe put his hands together as if praying and bowed slightly. *"Grazie."*

"How did you come to pick such a lovely place for a restaurant?"

"The views mostly," Rafe said, smiling, and Dani stared at him. Those crazy feelings rolled through her again.

When it came to his customers he was humble, genuine. And very, very likable.

He turned to her and nodded toward the door. "Customers, Daniella?"

"Yes! Of course!" She pivoted and hurried away to seat the people at the door, her heart thrumming, her nerve endings shimmering. Telling herself she was simply responding to the happy way he chatted with a customer, glad he hadn't yelled at the poor man and glad everything was going so well, she refused to even consider that her appreciation of his good looks was tipping over into a genuine attraction.

She was so busy she didn't hear the rest of Rafe's conversation with the older couple. When they left, Rafe returned to the kitchen and Daniella went about her work. People arrived, she seated them, the staff served them and Rafe milled about the dining room, talking with customers. They gushed over the scene visible through the back windows. And he laughed.

He *laughed*. And the warmth of his love for his customers filled her. But that still didn't mean she was attracted to him. She appreciated him, yes. Respected him? Absolutely. But even though he was gorgeous, she refused to be attracted to him. Except maybe physically…the man *was* gorgeous. And having a boyfriend didn't mean she couldn't *notice* good-looking men… Did it?

When the lunch crowd emptied, and Gio and Zola left, Daniella turned to help Allegra tidy the dining room, but Rafe caught her arm. "Not so fast."

The touch of his hand on her biceps sent electricity straight to her heart. Which speeded up and sent a whoosh of heat through her blood.

Darn it. She *was* attracted to him.

But physically. Just physically.

She turned slowly.

Bright with anger, his gaze bored into her. "What in the hell did you think you were doing?"

With electricity careening through her, she pulled in a shaky breath. "When?"

"When the customer asked to speak with me!" He threw his hands in the air. "Did you think I did not see? I see everything! I heard that man ask to speak with me and heard you suggest that he talk to you."

She sucked in a breath to steady herself. "I was trying to head off a disaster."

"A disaster? He wanted to compliment the chef and you tried to dissuade him. Did you want the compliment for yourself?"

She gasped. "No! I was worried he was going to complain about the food." She took a step closer, now every bit as angry as he was. He was so concerned about his own agenda, he couldn't even tell when somebody was trying to save his sorry butt. "And that you'd scream at him and the whole dining room would hear."

He matched the step she took. "Oh, really? You saw how I spoke to him. I love my customers."

She held her ground. Her gaze narrowed on him. Her heart raced. "Yeah, well I know that now, but I didn't know it when he asked to speak with you."

"You overstepped your boundaries." He took another step, and put them so close her whole body felt energized—

Oh, no.

Now she knew what was going on. She didn't just think Rafe was handsome. She wasn't just *physically* attracted to him. She was completely attracted to him. And she wasn't yelling at him because she was defending herself. She was yelling because it was how he communicated with her. Because he was a stubborn, passionate man, was this how she flirted with him?

Not at all happy with these feelings, she stepped away

from him. Softening her voice, she said, "It won't happen again."

He laughed. "What? You suddenly back down?"

She peered over at him. Why hadn't he simply said, "Thank you," and walked away? That's what he usually did.

Unless Louisa was right and he was attracted to her, too?

The mere thought made her breathless. She sneaked a peek at him—he was distinguished looking with his long hair tied back and his white smock still crisp and clean after hours of work. The memory of his laughter with the customer fluttered through her, stealing her breath again. He was a handsome man, very, very good at what he did and dedicated to his customers. He could have his pick of women. And he was attracted to her?

Preposterous. She didn't for a second believe it, but she was definitely attracted to him. And she was going to have to watch her step.

She cleared her throat. "Unless you want me to hang out until the dinner crowd, I'll be going home now."

He shook his head. "Do not overstep your boundaries again."

She licked her suddenly dry lips. "Oh, believe me, I'll be very, very careful from here on out."

Rafe watched her walk away. His racing heart had stilled. The fire in his blood had fizzled. Disappointment rattled through him. He shook his head and walked back into the kitchen.

"Done yelling at Daniella?"

Rafe scowled at Emory. "She oversteps her place."

"She's trying to keep the peace. To keep the customers happy. And, in case you haven't noticed, they are happy. Today they were particularly happy."

He sniffed in disdain. "I opened the dining room to the view from the back windows."

Emory laughed. "Seriously? You're going with that?"

"All right! So customers like her."

"And no one seems to be hanging around hoping you'll lose your temper."

He scowled.

"She did exactly what we needed to have done. She shifted the temperament in the dining room. Customers are enjoying your food. You should be thrilled to have her around."

Rafe turned away with a "Bah." But deep down inside he *was* thrilled to have her around.

And maybe that wasn't as much of a good thing as Emory thought it was. Because the whole time he was yelling at her, he could also picture himself kissing her.

Worse, the part of him that usually toed the line wasn't behaving. That part kept reminding him she was temporary. She might be an employee, but she wasn't staying forever. He *could* have an affair with this beautiful, passionate woman and not have to worry about repercussions because in a few weeks, she'd be gone. No scene. No broken heart. No expectations. They could have a delicious affair.

CHAPTER FOUR

DANIELLA RETURNED HOME that night exhausted. Louisa hadn't waited up for her, but from the open cabinet doors and trash bags sitting by the door, it was apparent she'd begun cleaning the kitchen.

She dragged herself up the stairs, showered and crawled into bed, refusing to think about the possibility that Rafe might be attracted to her. Not only did she have a marriage proposal waiting at home, but, seriously? Her with Rafe? Mr. Unstable with the former foster child who needed stability? That was insanity.

She woke early the next morning and, after breakfast, she and Louisa loaded outdated food from the pantry into even more trash bags.

Wiping sweat from her brow, Louisa shook her head at the bag of garbage she'd just hauled to the growing pile by the door. "We don't even know what day to set out the trash."

Busy sweeping the now-empty pantry, Dani said, "You could always ask Nico."

Louisa rolled her eyes. "I'm not tromping over to his villa to ask about trash."

"You could call him. I have his card." She frowned. "Or Rafe has his card. I could ask for it back tonight."

"No, thanks. I'll figure this out."

"Or maybe I could ask the girls at the restaurant? Given

that we're so close to Monte Calanetti, one of them probably lives in the village. She'll know what day the trash truck comes by."

Louisa brightened. "Yes. Thank you. That would be great."

But Dani frowned as she swept the last of the dirt onto her dustpan. Louisa's refusal to have anything to do with Nico had gone from unusual to impractical. Still, it wasn't her place to say anything.

She dressed for work in the dark trousers and white shirt Rafe required and drove to the restaurant. Walking in, she noticed that two of the chefs were different, and two of the chefs she was accustomed to seeing weren't there. The same was true in the dining room. Allegra was nowhere to be seen and in her place was a tall, slim waitress named Mila, short for Milana, who told Daniella it was simply Allegra's day off and probably the chefs', too.

"Did you think they'd been fired?" Mila asked with a laugh.

Dani shrugged. "With our boss, you never know."

Mila laughed again. "Only Chef Rafe works twelve hours a day, seven days a week."

"I guess I should ask for a schedule, then."

She turned toward the kitchen but Mila stopped her. "Do yourself a favor and ask Emory about it."

Thinking that sounded like good advice, she nodded and walked into the kitchen. Emory stood at a stainless-steel prep table in the back of the huge, noisy, delicious-smelling room. Grateful that Rafe wasn't anywhere in sight, she approached the sous-chef.

"Cara!" he said, opening his arms. "What can I do for you?"

"I was wondering if there was a schedule."

The short, bald man smiled. "Schedule?"

"I'm never really sure when I'm supposed to come in."

"A maître d' works all shifts."

At the sound of Rafe's voice behind her, she winced, sucked in a breath and faced him. "I can't work seven days a week, twelve hours a day. I want this month to do some sightseeing. Otherwise, I could have just gone back to New York City."

He smiled and said, "Ah."

And Daniella's heart about tripped over itself in her chest. He had the most beautiful, sexy smile she had ever seen. Directed at her, it stole her breath, weakened her knees, scared her silly.

"You are correct. Emory will create a schedule."

Surprised at how easy that had been, and not about to hang around when his smile was bringing out feelings she knew were all wrong, she scampered out of the kitchen. Within minutes, Rafe came into the dining room to open Mancini's doors. As he passed her, he smiled at her again.

When he disappeared behind the kitchen doors, she blew out her breath and collapsed against the podium. What was he doing smiling at her? Dear God, was Louisa right? Was he interested in her?

She paused. No. Rafe was too business oriented to be attracted to an employee. This wasn't about attraction. It was about her finally finding her footing with him. He hadn't argued about getting her a schedule. He'd smiled because they were beginning to get along as employer and employee.

Guests began arriving and she went to work. There were enough customers that the restaurant felt busy, but not nearly as busy as they were for dinner. She seated an American couple and walked away but even before she reached the podium, they waved her back.

She smiled. "Having trouble with the Italian?"

The short dark-haired man laughed. "My wife teaches Italian at university. We actually visit every other year. Though this is our first time at Mancini's."

"Well, a very special welcome to you, then. What can I help you with?"

He winced. "Actually, we were kind of hoping to just have soup or a salad, but all you have is a full menu."

"Yes. The chef loves his drama."

The man's wife reached over and touched his arm. "I am sort of hungry for this delicious-sounding spaghetti. Maybe we can eat our big meal now and eat light at dinner."

Her husband laughed. "Fine by me."

Dani waved Gio over to take their orders, but a few minutes later, she had a similar conversation with a group of tourists who had reservations that night at a restaurant in Florence. They'd stopped at Mancini's looking for something light, but Rafe's menu only offered full-course meals.

With the lunchtime crowd thinned and two of the three waitresses gone until dinner, Dani stared at the kitchen door. If she and Rafe really had established a proper working relationship, shouldn't she tell him what customers told her?

Of course, she should. She shouldn't be afraid. She should be a good employee.

She headed for the kitchen. "May I speak with you, Chef Rafe?"

His silver-gray eyes met hers. "Yes?"

She swallowed. It was just plain impossible not to be attracted to this guy. "It's... I... Do you want to hear the things the customers tell me?"

Leaning against his prep table behind him, holding her gaze, he said, "Yes. I always want the opinions of customers."

She drank in a long breath. The soft, seductive tone of his voice, the way he wouldn't release her gaze, all reminded her of Louisa's contention that he was attracted to her. The prospect tied her tongue until she reminded herself that they were at work. And he was dedicated to his diners. In this kitchen, that was all that mattered.

"Okay. Today, I spoke with a couple from the US and a group of tourists, both of whom only wanted soup or salad for lunch."

"We serve soup and salad."

"As part of a meal."

"So they should eat a meal."

"That was actually their point. They didn't want a whole meal. Just soup and salad."

Rafe turned to Emory, his hands raised in question as if he didn't understand what she was saying.

She tried again. "Look. You want people to come in for both lunch and dinner but you only offer dinners on the menu. Who wants a five-course meal for lunch?"

The silver shimmer in Rafe's eyes disappeared and he gaped at her. "Any Italian."

"All right." So much for thinking he was attracted to her. The tone of his voice was now definitely all business and when it came to his business, he was clearly on a different page than she was. But this time she knew she was right. "Maybe Italians do like to eat that way. But half your patrons are tourists. If they want a big meal, they'll come at dinnertime. If they just want to experience the joy that is Mancini's, they'll be here for lunch. And they'll probably only want a salad. Or maybe a burger."

"A burger?" He whispered the word as if it were blasphemy.

"Sure. If they like it, they'll be back for dinner."

The kitchen suddenly got very quiet. Every chef in the room and both busboys had turned to face her.

Rafe quietly said, "This is Italy. Tourists want to experience the culture."

"Yes. You are correct. They do want to experience the culture. But that's only part of why tourists are here. Most tourists don't eat two huge meals a day. It couldn't hurt to put simple salads on the lunch menu, just in case a tourist or two doesn't want to eat five courses."

His gray eyes flared. When he spoke, it was slowly, deliberately. "Miss Daniella, you are a tourist playing hostess. I am a world-renowned chef."

This time the softness of his voice wasn't seductive. It was insulting and her defenses rose. "I know. But I'm the one in the dining room, talking with your customers—"

His eyes narrowed with anger and she stepped back, suddenly wondering what the hell she was doing. He was her boss. As he'd said, a world-renowned chef. Yet here she was questioning him. She couldn't seem to turn off the self-defense mechanisms she'd developed to protect herself in middle school when she was constantly teased about not having a home or questioned because her classmates thought being a foster kid meant she was stupid.

She sucked in a long, shaky breath. "I'm sorry. I don't know why I pushed."

He gave her a nod that more or less dismissed her and she raced out of the kitchen. But two minutes later a customer asked to speak with Rafe. Considering this her opportunity to be respectful to him, so hopefully they could both forget about their soup and salad disagreement, she walked into the kitchen.

But she didn't see Rafe.

She turned to a busboy. "Excuse me. Where's Chef Rafe?"

The young kid pointed at a closed door. "In the office with Emory."

She smiled. "Thanks."

She headed for the door. Just when she would have pushed it open, she heard Emory's voice.

"I'm not entirely sure why you argue with her."

"*I* argue with *her*? I was nothing but nice to that girl and she comes into my kitchen and tells me I don't know my own business."

Dani winced, realizing they were talking about her.

Emory said, "We need her."

And Rafe quickly countered with, "You are wrong. Had Nico not sent her, we would have hired someone else by now. Instead, because Nico told her I was desperate, we're stuck with a woman who thinks we need her, and thinks that gives her the right to make suggestions. Not only do we not need her, but I do not want her here—"

The rest of what Rafe said was lost on Dani as she backed away from the door.

Rafe saying that she wasn't wanted rolled through her, bringing up more of those memories from middle school before she'd found a permanent foster home with Rosa. The feeling of not being wanted, not having a home, rose in her as if she were still that teenage girl who'd been rejected so many times that her scars burrowed the whole way to her soul.

Tears welled in her eyes. But she fought them, telling herself he was right. She shouldn't argue with him. But seriously, this time she'd thought she was giving a valuable suggestion. And she'd stopped when she realized she'd pushed too far.

She just couldn't seem to get her bearings with this guy. And maybe it was time to realize this really wasn't the job for her and leave.

She pivoted away from the door, raced out of the kitchen and over to Gio. "Um, the guy on table three would like to talk with Rafe. Would you mind getting him?"

Gio studied her face, undoubtedly saw the tears shimmering on her eyelids and smiled kindly. "Sure."

Dani walked to the podium, intending to get her purse and her coat to leave, but a customer walked in.

Rafe shook his head as Emory left the office with a laugh. He'd needed to vent and Emory had listened for a few minutes, then he'd shut Rafe down. And that was good. He'd been annoyed that Dani challenged him in front of his staff. But venting to Emory was infinitely better than firing her.

Especially since they did need her. He hadn't even started interviewing for her replacement yet.

He walked into the kitchen at the same time that Gio did. "Chef Rafe, there's a customer who would like to speak with you."

He turned to the sink, rinsed his hands and grabbed his towel, before he motioned for Gio to lead him to the customer.

Stepping into the dining room, he didn't see Dani anywhere, but before he could take that thought any further, he was beside a happy customer who wanted to compliment him on his food.

He listened to the man, scanning the dining room for his hostess. When she finally walked into the dining room from the long hall that led to the restrooms, he sighed with relief. He accepted the praise of his customer, smiled and returned to his work.

An hour later, Dani came into the kitchen. "Chef Mancini, there's a customer who would like to speak with you."

Her voice was soft, meek. She'd also called him Chef Mancini, not Chef Rafe, but he didn't question it. A more businesslike demeanor between them was not a bad thing. Particularly considering that he'd actually wanted to have an affair with her and had been thinking about that all damned day—until they'd gotten into that argument about soup and salad.

Which was why the smile he gave her was nothing but professional. "It would be my pleasure."

He expected her to say, "Thank you." Instead, she nodded, turned and left the kitchen without him.

He rinsed his hands, dried them and headed out to the dining room. She waited by a table in the back. When she saw him she motioned for him to come to the table.

As he walked up, she smiled at the customers. She said, "This is Chef Mancini." Then she strode away.

He happily chatted with the customer for ten minutes, but his gaze continually found Daniella. She hadn't waited for him in the kitchen, hadn't looked at him when he came to the table—had only introduced him and left. Her usually sunny smile had been replaced by a stiff lift of her lips. Her bright blue eyes weren't filled with joy. They were dull. Lifeless.

A professional manner was one thing. But she seemed to be...hurt.

He analyzed their soup-and-salad conversation and couldn't find anything different about that little spat than any of their disagreements—except that he'd been smiling at her when she walked in, thinking about kissing her. Then they'd argued and he'd realized what a terrible idea kissing her was, and that had shoved even the thought of an affair out of his head.

But that was good. He should not want to get involved with an employee. No matter how pretty.

When the restaurant cleared at closing time, he left, too. He drove to his condo, showered and put on jeans and a cable-knit sweater. He hadn't been anywhere but Mancini's in weeks. Not since Christmas. And maybe that was why he was having these odd thoughts about his hostess? Maybe it was time to get out with people again? Maybe find a woman?

He shrugged into his black wool coat, took his private elevator to the building lobby and stepped outside.

His family lived in Florence, but he loved little Monte Calanetti. Rich with character and charm, the stone-and-stucco buildings on the main street housed shops run by open, friendly people. That was part of why he'd located Mancini's just outside of town. Tourists loved Monte Calanetti for its connections to the past, especially the vineyard of Palazzo di Comparino, which unfortunately had closed. But tourists still came, waiting for the day the vineyard would reopen.

Rafe's boots clicked on the cobblestone. The chill of the February night seeped into his bones. He put up the collar of his coat, trying to ward off the cold. It didn't help. When he reached Pia's Tavern, he stopped.

Inside it would be warm from a fire in the stone fireplace in the back. He could almost taste the beer from the tap. He turned and pushed open the door.

Because it was a weekday, the place was nearly empty. The television above the shelves of whiskey, gin and rum entertained the two locals sitting at the short shiny wood bar. The old squat bartender leaned against a cooler beside the four beer taps. Flames danced in the stone fireplace and warmed the small, hometown bar. As his eyes adjusted to the low lights, Rafe saw a pretty blonde girl sitting alone at a table in the back.

Dani.

He didn't know whether to shake his head or turn around and walk out. Still, when her blue eyes met his, he saw sadness that sent the heat of guilt lancing though him.

Before he could really think it through, he walked over to her table and sat across from her.

"Great. Just what every girl wants. To sit and have a drink with the boss who yells at her all day."

He frowned. "Is that why you grew so quiet today? Because I yelled at you? I didn't yell. I just didn't take your suggestion. And that is my right. I am your boss."

She sucked in a breath and reached for her beer. "Yes, I know."

"You've always known that. You ignore it, but you've always known. So this time, why are you so upset?"

She didn't reply. Instead, she reached for her coat and purse as if she intended to go. He caught her arm and stopped her.

Her gaze dropped to his hand, then met his.

Confused, he held her blue, blue eyes, as his fingers slid against her soft pink skin. The idea of having an affair with her popped into his head again. They were both incredibly passionate people and they'd probably set his bedroom on fire, if they could stop arguing long enough to kiss.

"Please. If I did something wrong, tell me—"

An unexpected memory shot through him. He hadn't cared what a woman thought since Kamila. The reminder of how he'd nearly given up his dream for her froze the rest of what he wanted to say on his tongue and forced him back to business mode.

"If you are gruff with customers I need to know why."

"I'm not gruff with customers." Her voice came out wispy and smoky.

"So it's just me, then?"

"Every time I try to be nice to you, you argue with me."

He laughed. "When did you try to be nice to me?"

"That suggestion about lunch wasn't a bad one. And I came to you politely—"

"And I listened until you wouldn't quit arguing. Then I had to stop you."

"Yes. But after that you told Emory I wasn't needed." She sniffed a laugh. "I heard you telling him you didn't even want me around."

His eyes narrowed on her face. "I tell Emory things like that all the time. I vent. It's how I get rid of stress."

"Maybe you should stop that."

He laughed, glad his feisty Dani was returning. "And maybe you should stop listening at the door?"

She shook her head and shrugged out of his hold. "I wasn't listening. You were talking loud enough that I could easily hear you through the door."

She rose to leave again. This time he had no intention of stopping her, but a wave of guilt sluiced through him. Her face was still sad. Her blue eyes dull. All because of his attempt to blow off steam.

She only got three steps before he said, "Wait! You are right. I shouldn't have said you weren't wanted. I rant to

Emory all the time. But usually no one hears me. So it doesn't matter."

She stopped but didn't return to her seat. Standing in the glow of the fireplace, she said, "If that's an apology, it's not a very good one."

No. He supposed it wasn't. But nobody ever took his rants so seriously. "Why did it upset you so much to hear you weren't wanted?"

She said nothing.

He rose and walked over to her. When she wouldn't look at him, he lifted her chin until her gaze met his. "There is a story there."

"Of course there's a story there."

He waited for her to explain, but she said nothing. The vision of her walking sadly around the restaurant filled his brain. He'd insulted hundreds of employees before, trying to get them to work harder, smarter, but from the look in her eyes he could see this was personal.

"Can you tell me?"

She shrugged away again. "So you can laugh at me?"

"I will not laugh!" He sighed, softened his voice. "Actually, I'm hoping that if you tell me it will keep me from hitting that nerve again."

"Really?"

"I'm not an idiot. I don't insult people to be cruel. When I vent to Emory it means nothing. When I yell at my employees I'm trying to get the best out of them. With you, everything's a bit different." He tossed his hands. He wouldn't tell her that part of the problem was his attraction. Especially since he went back and forth about pursuing it. Maybe if he'd just decide to take romance off the table, become her friend, things between them would get better? "It might be because you're American not European. Whatever the case, I'd like to at least know that I won't insult you again."

The bartender walked over. He gruffly threw a beer

coaster on the table, even though Dani and Rafe stood by the fireplace. "What'll it be?"

Rafe tugged Dani's hand. "Come. We'll get a nice Merlot. And talk."

She slid her hand out of his, but she did return to her seat. He named the wine he wanted from the bartender, and with a raise of his bushy brows, the bartender scrambled off to get it. When he returned with the bottle and two glasses, Rafe shooed him away, saying he'd pour.

Dani frowned. "No time for breathing?"

He chuckled. "Ah. So she thinks she knows wine?"

Her head lowered. "I don't."

His eyes narrowed as he studied her. The sad demeanor was back. The broken woman. "And all this rolls together with why I insulted you when I said you weren't wanted?"

She sighed. "Sort of. I don't know how to explain this so you'll understand, but the people I'm looking for aren't my relatives."

He smiled. "They're people who owe you money?"

She laughed. The first genuine laugh in hours and the tight ball of tension in Rafe's gut unwound.

"They are the family of the woman who was my foster mother."

"Foster mother?"

"I was taken from my mother when I was three. I don't remember her. In America, when a child has no home, he or she is placed with a family who has agreed to raise her." She sucked in a breath and took the wineglass he offered her. "Foster parents aren't required to keep you forever. So if something happens, they can give you back."

She tried to calmly give the explanation but the slight wobble of her voice when she said "give you back" caused the knot of tension to reform in Rafe's stomach. He imagined a little blue-eyed, blonde girl bouncing from home to home, hugging a scraggly brown teddy bear, and his throwaway comment about her not being wanted made his heart hurt.

"I'm sorry."

She sipped her wine. "And right about now, I'm feeling pretty stupid. You're a grouch. A perfectionist who yells at everyone. I should have realized you were venting." She met his gaze. "I'm the one who should be sorry."

"You do realize you just called me a grouch."

She took another sip of her wine. "And a perfectionist." She caught his gaze again. "See? You don't get offended."

He laughed.

She smiled.

Longing filled Rafe. For years he'd satisfied himself with one-night stands, but she made him yearn for the connection he'd had only once before. With her he wasn't Chef Rafe. She didn't treat him like a boss. She didn't talk to him like a boss...

Maybe because she had these feelings, too?

He sucked in a breath, met her gaze. "Tell me more."

"About my life?"

"About anything."

She set down her wineglass as little pinpricks of awareness sprung up on her arms.

She hadn't realized how much she'd longed for his apology until he'd made it. But now that he was asking to hear about her life, everything inside her stilled. How much to tell? How much to hold back? Why did he want to know? And why did she ache to tell him?

He offered his hand again and she glanced into his face. The lines and planes of his chin and cheeks made him classically handsome. His sexy unbound hair brought out urges in her she hadn't ever felt. She'd love to run her fingers through it while kissing him. Love to know what it would feel like to have his hair tumble to his face while they made love.

She stopped her thoughts. She had an almost fiancé at home, and Rafe wasn't the most sympathetic man in the world. He was bold and gruff, and he accepted no less than total honesty.

But maybe that's what appealed to her? She didn't want sympathy. She just wanted to talk to someone. To really be heard. To be understood.

"I had a good childhood," he said, breaking the awkward silence, again nudging his hand toward her.

She didn't take his hand, so he used it to inch her wine closer. She picked it up again.

"Even as a boy, I was fascinated by cooking."

She laughed, wondering why the hell she was tempting fate by sitting here with him when she should leave. She might not be engaged but she was close enough. And though she'd love to kiss Rafe, to run her fingers through that wild hair, Paul was stability. And she needed stability.

"My parents were initially put off, but because I also played soccer and roughhoused with my younger brother, they weren't worried."

She laughed again. He'd stopped trying to take her hand. And he really did seem to want to talk. "You make your childhood sound wonderful."

He winced. "Not intentionally."

"You don't have to worry about offending me. I don't get jealous of others' good lives. Once Rosa took me in, I had a good life."

"How old were you?"

"Sixteen."

"She was brave."

"Speaking from experience?"

"Let's just say I had a wild streak."

Looking at his hair, which curled haphazardly and made his gray eyes appear shiny and mysterious, Dani didn't doubt he had lots of women who'd helped his wild streak along.

Still, she ignored the potential to tease, to flirt, and said, "Rosa really was brave. I wasn't so much of a handful because I got into trouble, but because I was lost."

"You seem a little lost now, too."

Drat. She hadn't told him any of this for sympathy. She was just trying to keep the conversation innocent. "Seriously. You're not going to feel sorry for me, are you?"

"Not even a little bit. If you're lost now, it's your own doing. Something you need to fix yourself."

"That's exactly what I believe!"

He toasted. "To us. Two just slightly off-kilter people who make our own way."

She clinked her glass to his before taking another sip of wine. They finished their drinks in silence, which began to feel uncomfortable. If she were free, she probably would be flirting right now. But she wasn't.

Grabbing her jacket and purse, she rose from her seat. "I guess I should get going."

He rose, too. "I'll walk you to your car."

Her heart kicked against her ribs. The vision of a goodnight kiss formed in her brain. The knowledge that she'd be a cheat almost choked her. "There's no reason."

"I know. I know. It's a very peaceful little town. No reason to worry." He smiled. "Still, I've never let a woman walk to her car alone after dark."

Because that made sense, she said, "Okay." Side by side they ambled up the sidewalk to the old, battered green car Louisa had lent her.

When they reached it, she turned to him with a smile. "Thank you for listening to me. I actually feel better."

"Thank you for talking to me. Though I don't mind a little turmoil in the restaurant, I don't want real trouble."

She smiled up at him, caught the gaze of his pretty gray eyes, and felt a connection that warmed her. She didn't often tell anyone the story of her life, but he had really listened. Genuinely cared.

"So you're saying yelling is your way of creating the kind of chaos you want?"

"You make me sound like a control freak."

"You are."

He laughed. "I know."

They gazed into each other's eyes long enough for Dani's heart to begin to thrum. Knowing they were now crossing a line, she tried to pull away, but couldn't. Just when she was about to give one last shot at breaking their contact, he bent his head and kissed her.

Heat swooshed through her on a wave of surprise. Her hands slid up his arms, feeling the strength of him, and met at the back of his neck, where rich, thick hair tickled her knuckles. When he coaxed open her mouth, the taste of wine greeted her, along with a thrill so strong it spiraled through her like a tornado. The urge to press herself against him trembled through her. She'd never felt anything so powerful, so wanton. She stepped closer, enjoying sensations so intense they stole her breath.

His hands trailed from her shoulders, down her back to her bottom and that's when everything became real. What was she doing kissing someone when she had a marriage proposal waiting for her in New York?

CHAPTER FIVE

NOTHING IN RAFE'S life had prepared him for the feeling of his lips against Dani's. He told himself it was absurd for an experienced man to think one kiss different from another, but even as that thought floated to him, her lips moved, shifted, and need burst through him. She wasn't a weak woman, his Dani. She was strong, vital, and she kissed like a woman starving for the touch of a man. The kind of touch he longed to give her. And the affair was back on the table.

Suddenly, Dani jumped back, away from him. "You can't kiss me."

The wildness in her eyes mirrored the roar of need careening through him. The dew of her mouth was sprinkled on his lips. His heart pounded out an unexpected tattoo, and desire spilled through his blood.

He smiled, crossed his arms on his chest and leaned against the old car. "I think I just did."

"The point is you shouldn't kiss me."

"Because we work together?" He glanced to the right. "Bah! You Americans and your puritanical rules."

"Oh, you hate rules? What about commitments? I'm engaged!"

That stopped the need tumbling through him. That stopped the sweet swell of desire. That made him angry that she'd led him on, and feel stupid that he hadn't even suspected that a woman as pretty and cheerful as his Dani would have someone special waiting at home.

"I see."

She took three steps back, moving herself away from her own transportation. "I didn't mean to lead you on." She groaned and took another step back. "I didn't think I *was* leading you on. We were talking like friends."

He shoved off the car. "We were."

"So why'd you kiss me?"

He shrugged, as if totally unaffected, though a witch's brew of emotions careered through him like a runaway roller coaster. "It felt right." Everything about her felt right, which only annoyed him more.

She took another step away from him. "Well, it was wrong."

"If you don't stop your retreat, you're going to end up back in the tavern."

She sucked in a breath.

He opened her car door. "Get in. Go home. We're fine. I don't want you skittering around like some frightened mouse tomorrow. Let's just pretend that little kiss never happened."

He waited, holding open the door for her until he realized she wouldn't go anywhere near her car while he stood beside it. Anger punched up again. Still, keeping control, he moved away.

She sighed with relief and slid into her car.

He calmly started the walk to his condo, but when he got inside the private elevator he punched the closed door, not sure if he was angry with himself for kissing her or angry, *really angry*, that she was engaged. Taken.

He told himself not to care. Were they to have an affair, it would have been short because she was leaving, returning to America.

And even if she wasn't, even if they'd been perfect for

each other, he didn't do relationships. He knew their cost. He knew he couldn't pay it.

When the elevator doors opened again, he stepped out and tossed his keys on a convenient table in the foyer of his totally remodeled condo on the top floor of one of Monte Calanetti's most beautiful pale stone buildings. The quiet closed in on him, but he ignored it. Sometimes the price a man paid for success was his soul. He put everything he had into his meals, his restaurant, his success. He'd almost let one woman steal his dream—he wouldn't be so foolish as to even entertain the thought a second time.

The next day he worked his magic in the kitchen, confident his attraction to Dani had died with the words *I'm engaged*. He didn't stand around on pins and needles awaiting her arrival. He didn't think about her walking into the kitchen. He refused to wonder whether she'd be happy or angry. Or ponder the way he'd like to treat her to a full-course meal, watch the light in her eyes while she enjoyed the food he'd prepare especially for her...

Damn it.

What was he doing thinking about a woman who was engaged?

He walked through the dining room, checking on the tables, opening the shutters on the big windows to reveal the striking view, not at all concerned that she was late, except for how it would impact his restaurant. So when the sound of her bubbly laugher entered the dining room, and his heart stopped, he almost cursed.

Probably not seeing him in the back of the dining room, she teased with Allegra and Gio, a clear sign that the kiss hadn't affected her as much as it had affected him. He remembered the way she'd spoken to him the night before. One minute she was sad, confiding, the next she would say something like, "You should stop that." Putting him in his place. Telling him what to do. And he wondered, really, who had confided in whom the night before?

Walking to the kitchen, he ran his hand along the back of his neck. Had he really told her about his family? Not that it was any great secret, but his practice was to remain aloof. Yet, somehow, wanting to comfort her had bridged that divide and he'd talked about things he normally kept out of relationships with women.

As he approached a prep table, Emory waved a sheet of paper at him. "I've created the schedule for Daniella. I'm giving her two days off. Monday and Tuesday. Two days together, so she can sightsee."

His heart stuttered a bit, but he forced his brain to focus on work. "And just who will seat people on Monday and Tuesday?"

"Allegra has been asking for more hours. I think she'll be fine in the position as a stand-in until, as Daniella suggested, we hire two people to seat customers."

He ignored the comment about Daniella. "Allegra is willing to give up her tips?"

"She's happy with the hourly wage I suggested."

"Great. Fine. Wonderful. Maybe you should deal with staff from now on."

Emory laughed. "This was a one-time thing. A favor to Daniella. I'm a chef, too. I might play second to you, but I'm not a business manager. In fact, you're the one who's going to take this to Dani."

Ignoring the thump of his heart at having to talk to her, Rafe snatched the schedule sheet out of Emory's hands and walked out of the kitchen, into the dining room.

His gaze searched out Dani and when he found her, their eyes met. They'd shared a conversation. They'd shared a kiss. But she belonged to someone else. Any connection he felt to her stopped now.

He broke the eye contact and headed for Allegra.

"Emory tells me you're interested in earning some extra money and you're willing to be Dani's fill-in."

Her eyes brightened. *"Sì."*

"Excellent. You will come in Monday and Tuesday for Dani, then." He felt Dani's gaze burning into him, felt his face redden with color like a schoolboy in the same room with his crush. Ridiculous.

He sucked in a breath, pasted a professional smile on his face and walked over to Dani. He handed the sheet of paper to her. "You wanted a schedule. Here is your schedule."

Her blue eyes rose slowly to meet his. She said, "Thanks."

The blood in his veins slowed to a crawl. The noise in the dining room disappeared. Every nuance of their kiss flooded his memory. Along with profound disappointment that their first kiss would be their last.

He fought the urge to squeeze his eyes shut. Why was he thinking these things about a woman who was taken? All he'd wanted was an affair! Now that he knew they couldn't have one, he should just move on.

"You wanted time off. I am granting you time off."

He turned and walked away, satisfied that he sounded like his normal self. Because he was his normal self. No kiss…no *woman* would change him.

Lunch service began. Within minutes, he was caught up in the business of supervising meal prep. As course after course was served, an unexpected thought came to Rafe. An acknowledgment of something Dani had said. He didn't eat a multicourse lunch. He liked soup and salad. Was Dani right?

Dani worked her shift, struggling to ward off the tightness in her chest every time Rafe came out of the kitchen. Memories of his kiss flooded her. But the moment of pure pleasure had been darkened by the realization that she had a proposal at home…yet she'd kissed another man. And it had been a great kiss. The kind of kiss a woman loses herself in. The kind of kiss that could have swept her off her feet if she wasn't already committed.

She went home in between lunch and dinner and joined Louisa on a walk through the house as she mentally charted everything that needed to be repaired. The overwhelmed villa owner wasn't quite ready to do an actual list. It was as if Louisa needed to get her bearings or begin acclimating to the reality of the property she owned before she could do anything more than clean.

At five, Dani put on the black trousers and white blouse again and returned to the restaurant. The time went more smoothly than the lunch session, mostly because Rafe was too busy to come into the dining room, except when a customer specifically asked to speak with him. When she walked into the kitchen to get him, she kept their exchanges businesslike, and he complied, not straying into more personal chitchat. So when he asked for time with her at the end of the night again, she shivered.

She didn't think he intended to fire her. He'd just given her a schedule. He also wouldn't kiss her again. He seemed to respect the fact that there was another man in the picture, even if she had sort of stretched the truth about being *engaged*. But that was for both of their benefits. She had a proposal waiting. Her life was confusing enough already. There was no point muddying the waters with a fling. No point in leading Rafe on.

She had no idea why he wanted to talk to her, but she decided to be calm about it.

When he walked out of the kitchen, he indicated that she should sit at the bar, while he grabbed a bottle of wine.

After a sip, she smiled. "I like this one."

"So you are a fan of Chianti."

She looked at the wine in the glass, watched how the light wove through it. "I don't know if I'm a fan. But it's good." She took a quiet breath and glanced over at him. "You wanted to talk with me?"

"Today, I saw what you meant about lunch being too much food for some diners."

She turned on her seat, his reply easing her mind enough that she could be comfortable with him. "Really?"

"Yes. We should have a lunch menu. We should offer the customary meals diners expect in Italy, but we should also accommodate those who want smaller lunches."

"So I made a suggestion that you're going to use?"

He caught her gaze. "You're not a stupid woman, Dani. You know that. Otherwise, you wouldn't be so bold in your comments about the restaurant."

She grinned. "I am educated."

He shook his head. "And you have instincts." He picked up his wineglass. "I'd like you to work with me on the few selections we'll add."

Her heart sped up. "Really?"

"Yes. It was your suggestion. I believe you should have some say in the menu."

That made her laugh.

"And what is funny about that?" His voice dripped with incredulity, as if he had no idea how to follow her sometimes. His hazy gray eyes narrowed in annoyance.

She sipped her wine, delaying her answer to torment him. He was always so in control that he was cute when he was baffled. And it was fun to see him try to wrangle himself around it.

Finally she said, "You're not the big, bad wolf you want everybody to believe."

His eyes narrowed a little more as he ran his thumb along his chin. His face was perfect. Sharp angles, clean lines, accented by silvery eyes and dark, dark hair that gave him a dramatic, almost mysterious look.

"I don't mind suggestions to make the business better. Ask Emory. He's had a lot more say than you would think."

She smiled, not sure why he so desperately wanted to cling to his bossy image. "I still say you're not so bad."

* * *

Rafe's blood heated. The urge to flirt with Dani, and then seduce her, roiled like the sea before a storm. He genuinely believed she was too innocent to realize he could take her comments about his work demeanor as flirting, and shift the conversation into something personal. But he also knew they couldn't work together if she continued to be so free with him.

"Be careful what you say, little Dani, and how you take our conversations. Because I am bad. I am not the gentleman you might be accustomed to. Though I respect your engagement, if you don't, I'll take that as permission to do whatever I want. You can't have a fiancé at home and free rein to flirt here."

Her eyes widened. But he didn't give her a chance to comment. He grabbed the pad and pencil he'd brought to the bar and said, "So what should we add to this lunch menu you want?"

She licked her lips, took a slow breath as if shifting her thoughts to the task at hand and said, "Antipasto and minestrone soup. That's obvious. But you could add a garden salad, club sandwich, turkey sandwich and hamburgers." She slowly met his gaze. "That way you're serving a need without going overboard."

With the exception of the hamburger, which made him wince, he agreed. "I can put my own spin on all of these, use the ingredients we already have on hand, redo the menu tonight and we'll be ready to go tomorrow."

She gaped at him. "Tomorrow? Wow."

He rose. "This is my business, Dani. If a suggestion is good, there is no point waiting forever. I get things done. Go home. I will see you tomorrow."

She walked to the door, and he headed for the kitchen where he could watch her leave from the window above the sink, making sure nothing happened to her. No matter how hard he tried to stop it, disappointment rose up in him. At the very least, it would have been nice to finish a glass of wine with her.

But he couldn't.

Dani ran to her car, her blood simmering, her nerve endings taut. They might have had a normal conversation about his menu. She might have even left him believing she was okay with everything he'd said and they were back to normal. But she couldn't forget his declaration that he was bad. It should have scared her silly. Instead, it tempted her. She'd never been attracted to a man who was clearly all wrong for her, a man with whom she couldn't have a future. Everything she did was geared toward security. Everything about him spelled danger.

So why was he so tempting?

Walking into the kitchen of Louisa's run-down villa, she found her friend sitting at the table with a cup of tea.

Louisa smiled as she entered. "Can I get you a cup?"

She squeezed her eyes shut. "I don't know."

Louisa rose. "What's wrong? You're shaking."

She dropped to one of the chairs at the round table. "Rafe and I had a little chat after everyone was gone."

"Did he fire you?"

"I think I might have welcomed that."

Louisa laughed. "You need a cup of tea." She walked to the cupboard, retrieved the tin she'd bought in the village, along with enough groceries for the two of them, and ran water into the kettle. "So what did he say?"

"He told me to be careful where I took our conversations."

"Are you insulting him again?"

"He danced around it a bit, but he thinks I'm flirting with him."

Eyes wide, Louisa turned from the stove. "Are you?"

Dani pressed her lips together before she met Louisa's gaze. "Not intentionally. You know I have a fiancé."

"Sounds like you're going to have to change the way you act around Rafe, then. Treat him the way he wants to be treated, like a boss you respect. Mingle with the waitstaff. Enjoy your job. But stay away from him."

The next day, Rafe stacked twenty-five black leather folders containing the new menus on the podium for Dani to distribute when she seated customers.

An hour later, she entered the kitchen, carrying them. Her smile as radiant as the noonday sun, she said, "These look great."

Rafe nodded, moving away from her, reminding himself that she was engaged to another man. "As I told you last night, this is a business. Good ideas are always welcome."

Emory peeked around Rafe. "And, please, if you have any more ideas, don't hesitate to offer them."

Rafe said, "Bah," and walked away. But he saw his old, bald friend wink at Dani as if they were two conspirators. At first, he was comforted that Emory had also succumbed to Dani's charms, but he knew that was incorrect. Emory liked Dani as a person. While Rafe wanted to sleep with her. But as long as he reminded himself his desires were wrong, he could control them.

Customer response to the lunch menu was astounding. Dani took no credit for the new offerings and referred comments and compliments to him. Still, she was in the spotlight everywhere he went. Customers loved her. The waitstaff deferred to her. Her smile lit the dining room. Her laughter floated on the air. And he was glad when she said goodbye at the end of the day, if only so he could get some peace.

Monday morning, he arrived at the restaurant and breathed in the scent of the business he called home. Today would be a good day because Dani was off. For two glorious days he would not have to watch his words, watch where his eyes went or control hormones he didn't understand. Plus, her having two days off was a great way to transition his thoughts away from her as a person and to her as an employee.

And who knew? Maybe Allegra would work so well as a hostess that he could actually cut Dani's hours even more. Not in self-preservation over his unwanted attraction, but because this was a business. He was the boss. And the atmosphere of the restaurant would go back to normal.

As Emory supervised the kitchen, Rafe interviewed two older gentlemen for Dani's job. Neither was suitable, but he comforted himself with the knowledge that this was only his first attempt at finding her replacement. He had other interviews scheduled for that afternoon and the next day. He *would* replace her.

Allegra arrived on time to open for lunch. Because they were enjoying an unexpected warm spell, he opened the windows and let the breeze spill in. The scents of rich Tuscan foods drifted from the kitchen. And just as Rafe expected, suddenly, all became right with the world.

Until an hour later when he heard a clang and a clatter from the dining room. He set down his knife and stormed out. Gio had dropped a tray of food when Allegra had knocked into her.

"What is this?" he asked, his hands raised in confusion. "You navigate around each other every day. Now, today, you didn't see her?"

Allegra stooped to help Gio pick up the broken dishes. "I'm sorry. It's just nerves. I was turned away, talking to the customer and didn't watch where I was going."

"Bah! Nerves. Get your head on straight!"

Allegra nodded quickly and Rafe returned to the kitchen. He summoned the two busboys to the dining room to clean up the mess and everything went back to normal.

Except customers didn't take to Allegra. She was sweet, but she wasn't fun. She wasn't chatty. A lifelong resident, she didn't see Italy through the eyes of someone who loved it with the passion and intensity of a newcomer as Dani did.

One customer even asked for her. Rafe smiled and said she had a day off. The customer asked for the next shift she'd be working so he could return and tell her of his trip to Venice.

"She'll be back on Wednesday," Rafe said. He tried to pretend he didn't feel the little rise in his heart at the thought of her return, but he'd felt it. After only a few hours, he missed her.

CHAPTER SIX

AND SHE MISSED HIM.

The scribbled notes of things she remembered her foster mother telling her about her Italian relatives hadn't helped her to find them. But Dani discovered stepping stones to people who knew people who knew people who would ultimately get her to the ones she wanted.

Several times she found herself wondering how Rafe would handle the situation. Would he ask for help? What would he say? And she realized she missed him. She didn't mind his barking. He'd shown her a kinder side. She remembered the conversation in which he'd told her about his family. She loved that he'd taken her suggestion about a lunch menu. But most of all, she replayed that kiss over and over and over in her head, worried because she couldn't even remember her first kiss with Paul.

Steady, stable Paul hadn't ever kissed her like Rafe had. Ever. But he had qualities Rafe didn't have. Stability being number one. He was an accountant at a bank, for God's sake. A man did not get any more stable than that. She'd already had a life of confusion and adventure of a sort, when she was plucked from one foster home and dropped in another. She didn't want confusion or danger or adventure. She wanted stability.

That night when she called Paul, he immediately asked

when she was returning. Her heart lifted a bit hearing that. "I hate talking on the phone."

It was the most romantic thing he'd ever said to her. Until he added, "I'd rather just wait until you get home to talk."

"Oh."

"Now, don't get pouty. You know you have a tendency to talk too much."

She *was* chatty.

"Anyway, I'm at work. I've got to go."

"Oh. Okay."

"Call me from your apartment when you get home."

She frowned. Home? Did he not want to talk to her for an entire month? "Aren't you going to pick me up at the airport?"

"Maybe, but you'll probably be getting in at rush hour or something. Taking a taxi would be easier, wouldn't it? We'll see how the time works out."

"I guess that makes sense."

"Good. Gotta run."

Even as she disconnected the call, she thought of Rafe. She couldn't see him telling his almost fiancée to call when she arrived at her apartment after nearly seven months without seeing each other. He'd race to the airport, grab her in baggage claim and kiss her senseless.

Her breath vanished when she pictured the scene, and she squeezed her eyes shut. She really could not think like that. She absolutely couldn't start comparing Paul and Rafe. Especially not when it came to passion. Poor sensible Paul would always suffer by comparison.

Plus, her feelings for Rafe were connected to the rush of pleasure she got from finding a place in his restaurant, being more than useful, offering ideas a renowned chef had implemented. For a former foster child, having somebody give her a sense of worth and value was like gold.

And that's all it was. Attraction to his good looks and

appreciation that he recognized and told her she was doing a good job.

She did not want him.

Really.

She needed somebody like Paul.

Though she knew that was true, it didn't sit right. She couldn't stop thinking about the way he didn't want to pick her up at the airport, how he'd barely had two minutes to talk to her and how he'd told her not to call again.

She tried to read, tried to chat with Louisa about the house, but in the end, she knew she needed to get herself out of the house or she'd make herself crazy.

She told Louisa she was going for a drive and headed into town.

Antsy, unable to focus, and afraid he was going to royally screw something up and disappoint a customer, Rafe turned Mancini's over to Emory.

"It's not like you to leave so early."

"It's already eight o'clock." Rafe shrugged into his black wool coat. "Maybe too many back-to-back days have made me tired."

Emory smiled. "Ah, so maybe like Dani, you need a day off?"

Buttoning his coat, he ignored the dig and walked to the back door. "I'll see you tomorrow."

But as he was driving through town, he saw the ugly green car Dani drove sitting at the tavern again. The last time she'd been there had been the day he'd inadvertently insulted her. She didn't seem like the type to frequent taverns, so what if she was upset again?

His heart gave a kick and he whipped his SUV into a parking place, raced across the quiet street and entered the tavern to find her at the same table she'd been at before.

He walked over. She glanced up.

Hungrier for the sight of her than was wise, he held her

gaze as he slid onto the chair across from her. "So this is how you spend your precious time off."

She shook her head. "Don't start."

He hadn't meant to be argumentative. In fact that was part of their problem. There was no middle with them. They either argued or lusted after each other. Given that he was her boss and she was engaged, both were wrong.

The bartender ambled over. He set a coaster in front of Rafe with a sigh. "You want another bottle of that fancy wine?"

Rafe shook his head and named one of the beers on tap before he pointed to Dani's glass. "And another of whatever she's having."

As the bartender walked away, she said, "You don't have to buy me a beer."

"I'm being friendly because I think we need to find some kind of balance." He was tired of arguing, but he also couldn't go on thinking about her all the time. The best way to handle both would be to classify their relationship as a friendship. Tonight, he could get some questions answered, get to know her and see that she was just like everybody else. Not somebody special. Then they could both go back to normal.

"Balance?"

He shrugged. Leaning back, he anchored his arm across the empty chair beside him. "We're either confiding like people who want to become lovers, or we fight."

She turned her beer glass nervously. "That's true."

"So, we drink a beer together. We talk about inconsequential things, and Wednesday when you return to Mancini's, no one snipes."

She laughed.

He smiled. "What did you do today?"

"I went to the town where my foster mother's relatives lived."

His beer arrived. Waiting for her to elaborate, he took

a sip. Then another. When she didn't say anything else, he asked, "So did you find them?"

"Not yet. But I will."

Her smooth skin virtually glowed. Her blue eyes met his. Interest and longing swam through him. He ignored both in favor of what now seemed to be a good mission. Becoming friends. Finding a middle ground where they weren't fighting or lusting, but a place where they could coexist.

"What did you do today?"

"Today I created a lasagna that should have made customers die from pleasure."

She laughed. "Exaggerate much?"

He pointed a finger at her. "It's not an exaggeration. It's confidence."

"Ah."

"You don't like confidence?"

She studied his face. "Maybe it's more that I don't trust it."

"What's to trust? I love to cook, to make people happy, to surprise them with something wonderful. But I didn't just open a door to my kitchen and say, come eat this. I went to school. I did apprenticeships. My confidence is in my teachers' ability to take me to the next level as much as it is in my ability to learn, and then do."

Her head tilted. "So it's not all about you."

He laughed, shook his head. "Where do you get these ideas?"

"You're kind of arrogant."

He batted his hand. "Arrogant? Confident? Who cares as long as the end result is good?"

"I guess…"

"I know." He took another sip of beer, watching as she slid her first drink—which he assumed was warm—aside and reached for the second glass he'd bought for her. "Not much of a drinker?"

"No."

"So what are you?"

She laughed. "Is this how you become friends with someone?"

"Conversation is how everyone becomes friends."

"I thought it was shared experience."

"We don't have time for shared experience. If we want to become friends by Wednesday we need to take shortcuts."

She inclined her head as if agreeing.

He waited. When she said nothing, he reframed his question. "So you are happy teaching?"

"I'm a good teacher."

"But you are not happy?"

"I'm just not sure people are supposed to be happy."

He blinked. That was the very last thing he'd expected to hear from his bubbly hostess. "Seriously?"

She met his gaze. "Yeah. I think we're meant to be content. I think we're meant to find a spot and fill it. But happy? That's reserved for big events or holidays."

For thirty seconds, he wished she were staying in Italy. He wished he had time enough to show her the sights, teach her the basics of cooking, make her laugh, show her what happiness was. But that wasn't the mission. The mission was to get to know her just enough that they would stop arguing.

"This from my happy, upbeat hostess?"

She met his gaze again. "I thought we weren't going to talk about work."

"We're talking about you, not work."

She picked up her beer glass. "Maybe this isn't the best time to talk about me."

Which only filled him with a thousand questions. When she was at Mancini's she was usually joyful. After a day off, she was as sad as the day he'd hurt her feelings? It made no sense…unless he believed that she loved working in his restaurant enough that it filled her with joy.

That made his pulse jump, made his mind race with thoughts he wasn't supposed to have. So he rose.

"Okay. Talking is done. We'll try shared experience." He pointed behind her. "We'll play darts."

Clearly glad they'd no longer be talking, she laughed. "Good."

"So you play darts at home in New York?"

She rose and followed him to the board hung on a back wall. They passed the quiet pool table, and he pulled some darts from the corkboard beside the dartboard.

"No, I don't play darts."

"Great. So we play for money?"

She laughed again. "No! We'll play for fun."

He sighed as if put out. "Too bad."

But as they played, she began to talk about her search for her foster mother's family. Her voice relaxed. Her smile returned. And Rafe was suddenly glad he'd found her. Not for his mission to make her his friend. But because she was alone. And in spite of her contention that people weren't supposed to be happy, her normal state was happy. He'd seen that every day at the restaurant. But something had made her sad tonight.

Reminded of the way he had made her sad by saying she wasn't needed, he redoubled his efforts to make her smile.

It was easy for Dani to dismiss the significance of Rafe finding her in the bar. They lived in a small town. He didn't have a whole hell of a lot of choices for places to stop after work. So she wouldn't let her crazy brain tell her it was sweet that he'd found her. She'd call it what it was. Lack of options.

Playing darts with her, Rafe was kind and polite, but not sexy. At least not deliberately sexy. There were some things a really handsome man couldn't control. So she didn't think he was coming on to her when he swaggered over to pull the darts from the board after he threw them. She didn't think he was trying to entice her when he laughed at her poor attempts at hitting the board. And she absolutely made nothing of it when he stood behind her, took her arm and showed her the motion she needed to make to get the dart going in the right direction.

Even though she could smell him, feel the heat of his body as he brushed up against her back, and feel the vibrations of his warm whisper as he pulled her arm back and demonstrated how to aim, she knew he meant nothing by any of it. He just wanted to be friends.

When their third beer was gone and the hour had gotten late, she smiled at him. "Thank you. That was fun."

His silver eyes became serious. "You were happy?"

She shook her head at his dog-with-a-bone attitude. "Sort of. Yes. It was a happy experience."

He sniffed and walked back to their table to retrieve his coat. "Everyone is made to be happy."

She didn't believe that. Though she liked her life and genuinely liked people, she didn't believe her days were supposed to be one long party. But she knew it was best not to argue. She joined him at their table and slipped into her coat.

"I'll walk you to your car."

She shook her head. "No." Their gazes caught. "I'm fine."

He dipped his head in a quick nod, agreeing, and she walked out into the cold night. Back into the world where her stable fiancé wouldn't even pick her up at the airport.

CHAPTER SEVEN

WHEN DANI ENTERED the restaurant on Wednesday ten minutes before the start of her shift, Rafe stood by the bar, near
the kitchen. As if he'd sensed her arrival, he turned. Their
gazes caught. Dani's heart about pounded its way out of
her chest. She reminded herself that though they'd spent an
enjoyable evening together playing darts at the tavern, for
him it had been about becoming friends. He hadn't made
any passes at her—though he'd had plenty of chances—
and he'd made a very good argument for why being friends
was a wise move for them.

Still, when he walked toward her, her heart leaped. But
he passed the podium to unlock the front door. As he turned
to return to the kitchen, he said, "Good morning."

She cleared her throat, hoping to rid it of the fluttery
feeling floating through her at being in the same room with
him. Especially since they were supposed to be friends
now. Nothing more. "Good morning."

"How did your search go for your foster mother's relatives yesterday?"

She shook her head. "Still haven't found them, but I got
lots of information from people who had been their neighbors. Most believe they moved to Rome."

"Rome?" He shook his head. "No kidding."

"Their former neighbors said something about one of

their kids getting a job there and the whole family wanting to stay together."

"Nice. Family should stay together."

"I agree."

She turned to the podium. He walked to the kitchen. But she couldn't help thinking that while Paul hadn't said a word about her quest for Rosa's family, Rafe had immediately asked. Like someone who cared about her versus someone who didn't.

She squeezed her eyes shut and told herself not to think like that. They were *friends. Only friends.*

But all day, she was acutely aware of him. Anytime she retrieved him to escort him to a table, she felt him all around her. Her skin tingled. Everything inside her turned soft and feminine.

At the end of the night, the waitstaff and kitchen help disappeared like rats on a sinking ship. Rafe ambled to the bar, pulled a bottle of wine from the rack behind it.

The Chianti. The wine he'd ordered for them at the tavern.

Her heart trembled. She'd told him she liked that wine.

Was he asking her to stay now? To share another bottle of the wine she'd said she liked?

Longing filled her and she paused by the podium. When he didn't even look in her direction, she shuffled a bit, hoping the movement would cause him to see her and invite her to stay.

He kept his gaze on a piece of paper sitting on the bar in front of him. Still, she noticed a second glass by the bottle. He had poured wine in one glass but the other was empty—yet available.

She bit her lip. Was that glass an accident? An oversight? Or was that glass her invitation?

She didn't know. And things were going so well between

them professionally that she didn't want to make a mistake that took them back to an uncomfortable place.

Still, they'd decided to be friends. Wouldn't a friend want another friend to share a glass of wine at the end of the night?

She drew in a slow breath. She had one final way to get him to notice her and potentially invite her to sit with him. If he didn't take this hint, then she would leave.

Slowly, cautiously, she called, "Good night."

He looked over. He hesitated a second, but only a second, before he said, "Good night."

Disappointment stopped her breathing. Nonetheless, she smiled and headed for the door. She walked to Louisa's beat-up old car, got in, slid the key in the ignition...

And lowered her head to the steering wheel.

She wanted to talk to him. She wanted to tell him about the countryside she'd seen as she looked for Rosa's relatives. She longed to tell him about the meals she'd eaten. She yearned to ask him how the restaurant had been the two days she was gone. She needed to get not just the cursory answers he'd given her but the real in-depth stuff. Like a friend.

But she also couldn't lie to herself. She wanted that crazy feeling he inspired in her. Lust or love, hormones or genuine attraction, she had missed that feeling. She'd missed *him*. No matter how much she told herself she just wanted to be his friend, it was a lie.

A light tapping on her window had her head snapping up.

Rafe.

She quickly lowered the window to see what he wanted. "Are you okay?"

Her heart swelled, then shrank and swelled again. Everything he did confused her. Everything she felt around him confused her even more.

"Are you ill?"

She shook her head.

Damn it. She squeezed her eyes shut and decided to just go with the truth. "I saw you with the wine and thought I should have joined you." She caught the gaze of his smoky-gray eyes. "You said we were going to be friends. And I was hoping you sitting at the bar with a bottle of wine was an invitation."

He stepped back. She'd never particularly thought of a chef's uniform as being sexy, but he'd taken off the jacket, revealing a white T-shirt that outlined muscles and a flat stomach. Undoubtedly hot from working in the kitchen, he didn't seem bothered by the cold night air.

"I always have a glass of wine at the end of the night."

So, her instincts had been wrong. If she'd just started her car and driven off, she wouldn't be embarrassed right now. "Okay. Good."

He glanced down into the car at her. "But I wouldn't have minded company."

Embarrassment began to slide away, only to be replaced by the damnable confusion. "Oh."

"I simply don't steal women who belong to other men."

"It wouldn't be stealing if we were talking about work, becoming friends like you said we should."

"That night was a one-time thing. A way to get to know each other so we could stop aggravating each other."

"So we're really not friends?"

He laughed and glanced away at the beautiful starlit sky. "We're now friendly enough to work together. Men only try to become 'real' friends so that they can ultimately become lovers."

The way he said *lovers* sent a wave of yearning skittering along her nerve endings. It suddenly became difficult to breathe.

He caught her gaze again. "I've warned you before to be careful with me, Dani. I'm not a man who often walks away from what he wants."

"Wow. You are one honest guy."

He laughed. "Usually I wouldn't care. I'd muscle my way into your life and take what I wanted. But you're different. You're innocent."

"I sort of liked being different until you added the part about me being innocent."

"You are."

"Well, yeah. Sort of." She tossed her hands in exasperation, the confusion and longing getting the better of her. "But you make it sound like a disease."

"It's not. It's actually a quality men look for in a woman they want to keep."

Her heart fluttered again. "Oh?"

"Don't get excited about that. I'm not the kind of guy who commits. I like short-term relationships because I don't like complications. I'm attracted to you, yes, but I also know myself. My commitment to the restaurant comes before any woman." He forced her gaze to his again. "This thing I feel for you is wrong. So as much as I wanted you to take the hint tonight and share a bottle of wine with me, I also hoped you wouldn't. I don't want to hurt you."

"We could always talk about the restaurant."

"About how you were missed? How a customer actually asked for you?"

She laughed. "See? That's all great stuff. Neutral stuff."

"I suppose you also wouldn't be opposed to hearing that Emory thinks that after the success of your lunch menu, we should encourage you to make suggestions."

Pride flooded her. "Well, I'll do my best to think of new things."

He glanced at the stars again. Their conversation had run its course. He stood in the cold. She sat in a car that could be warm if she'd started the darn thing. But the air between them was anything but cool, and she suddenly realized they were kidding themselves if they believed they could be just friends.

He looked down and smiled slightly. "Good night, Dani."

He didn't wait for her to say good-night. He walked away.

She sat there for a few seconds, tingling, sort of breathless, but knowing he was right. They couldn't be friends and they couldn't have a fling. She *was* innocent and he would hurt her. And though technically she'd stretched the truth about being engaged, it was saving her heartbreak.

After starting her car, she pulled out, watching in the rearview mirror as he revved the engine of his big SUV and followed her to Monte Calanetti.

Though Dani dressed in her usual black trousers and white blouse the next morning, she took extra care when she ironed them, making them crisper, their creases sharper, so she looked more professional when she arrived at the restaurant.

Rafe spoke sparingly. It wasn't long before she realized that unless she had a new idea to discuss, they wouldn't interact beyond his thank-you when she introduced him to a customer who wanted to compliment the chef.

She understood. Running into each other at the tavern the first time and talking out their disagreement, then playing darts the second, had made them friendly enough that they no longer sniped. But having minimal contact with her was how he would ignore their attraction. They weren't right for each other and, older, wiser, he was sparing them both. But that didn't really stop her attraction to him.

To keep herself from thinking about Rafe on Friday, she studied the customer seating, the china and silverware, the interactions of the waitresses with the customers, but didn't come up with an improvement good enough to suggest to him.

A thrill ran through her at the knowledge that he took her ideas so seriously. Here she was, an educated but simple girl from Brooklyn, being taken seriously by a lauded European chef.

The sense of destiny filled her again, along with Rafe's comment about happiness. This time her thoughts made her gasp. What if this feeling of rightness wasn't about Rafe or Italy? What if this sense of being where she belonged was actually telling her the truth about her career choice? She loved teaching, but it didn't make her feel she belonged the way being a part of this restaurant did. And maybe this sense of destiny was simply trying to point her in the direction of a new career when she returned to the United States?

The thought relieved her. Life was so much simpler when the sense of destiny was something normal, like an instinct for the restaurant business, rather than longing for her boss—a guy she shouldn't even be flirting with when she had a marriage proposal waiting for her at home.

Emory came to the podium and interrupted her thoughts. "These are the employee phone numbers. Gio called off sick for tonight's shift. I'd like you to call in a replacement."

She glanced up at him. "Who should I call?"

He smiled. "Your choice. Being out here all the time, you know who works better with whom."

After calling Zola, she walked back to the kitchen to return the list.

Emory shook his head. "This is your responsibility now. A new job for you, while you're here, to make my life a little easier."

She smiled. "Okay."

Without looking at her, Rafe said, "We'd also like you to begin assigning tasks to the busboys. After you say goodbye to a guest, we'd like you to come in and get the busboys. That will free up the waitresses a bit."

The feeling of destiny swelled in her again. The new tasks felt like a promotion, and there wasn't a person in the world who didn't like being promoted.

When Rafe refused to look at her, she winked at Emory. "Okay."

Walking back to the dining room, she fought the feeling that her destiny, her gift, was for this particular restaurant. Especially since, when returning to New York, she'd start at the bottom of any dining establishment she chose to work, and that would be a problem since she'd only make minimum wage. At Mancini's, she only needed to earn extra cash. In New York, would a job as a hostess support her?

The next day, Lazare, one of the busboys, called her "Miss Daniella." The shift from Dani to Miss Daniella caught on in the kitchen and the show of respect had Daniella's shoulders straightening with confidence. When she brought Rafe out for a compliment from a customer, even he said, "Thank you, Miss Daniella," and her heart about popped out of her chest with pride.

That brought her back to the suspicion that her sense of destiny wasn't for the restaurant business, but for *this* restaurant and these people. If she actually got a job at a restaurant in New York, she couldn't expect the staff there to treat her this well.

Realizing all her good fortune would stop when she left Mancini's, her feeling of the "destiny" of belonging in the restaurant business fizzled. She would go home to a tiny apartment, a man whose marriage proposal had scared her and a teaching position that suddenly felt boring.

"Miss Daniella," Gio said as she approached the podium later that night. "The gentleman at table two would like to speak to the chef."

She said it calmly, but there was an undercurrent in her voice, as if subtly telling Daniella that this was a problem situation, not a compliment.

She smiled and said, "Thank you, Gio. I'll handle it."

She walked over to the table.

The short, stout man didn't wait for Dani to speak. He immediately said, "My manicotti was dry and tasteless."

Daniella inclined her head in acknowledgment of his comment. "I'm sorry. I'm not sure what happened. I'll tell the kitchen staff."

"I want to talk to the chef."

His loud, obnoxious voice carried to the tables around him. Daniella peeked behind her at the kitchen door, then glanced at the man again. The restaurant had finally freed itself of people curious about Rafe's temper. The seats had filled with customers eager to taste his food. She would not let his reputation be ruined by a beady-eyed little man who probably wanted a free dinner.

"We're extremely busy tonight," she told the gentleman as she looped her fingers around his biceps and gently urged him to stand. "So rather than a chat with the chef, what if I comp your dinner?"

His eyes widened, then returned to normal, as if he couldn't believe he was getting what he wanted so easily. "You'll pay my tab?"

She smiled. "The whole meal." A quick glance at the table told her that would probably be the entire day's wage, but it would be worth it to avoid a scene.

"I'd like dessert."

"We'll get it for you to go." She nodded to Gio, who quickly put two slices of cake into a take-out container and within seconds the man and his companion were gone.

Rafe watched from the sliver of a crack he created when he pushed open the kitchen door a notch. He couldn't hear what Dani said, but he could see her calm demeanor, her smiles, the gentle but effective way she removed the customer from Rafe's dining room without the other patrons being any the wiser.

He laughed and Emory walked over.

"What's funny?"

"Dani just kicked somebody out."

Emory's eyes widened. "We had a scene?"

"That's the beauty of it. Even though he started off yelling, she got him out without causing even a ripple of trouble. I'll bet the people at the adjoining tables weren't even aware of what was happening beyond his initial grousing."

"She is worth her weight in gold."

Rafe pondered that. "Gio made the choice to get her rather than come to me."

Emory said, "She trusts Dani."

He walked away, leaving Rafe with that simple but loaded thought.

At the end of the night, the waitstaff quickly finished their cleanup and began leaving before the kitchen staff. Rafe glanced at the bar, thought about a glass of wine and decided against it. Instead, he walked to the podium as Dani collected her purse.

He waited for the waitresses on duty to leave before he faced Dani.

"You did very well tonight."

"Thank you."

"I saw you get rid of the irate customer."

She winced. "I had to offer to pay for his meal."

"I'll take care of that."

Her gaze met his, tripping the weird feeling in his chest again.

"Really?"

"Yes." He sucked in a breath, reminding himself he didn't want the emotions she inspired in him. He wanted a good hostess. He didn't want a fling with another man's woman.

"I trust your judgment. If not charging for his food avoided a scene, I'm happy to absorb the cost."

"Thanks."

He glanced away, then looked back at her. "Your duties just keep growing."

"Is this your subtle way of telling me I overstepped?"

He shook his head. "You take work that Emory and I would have to do. Things we truly do not have time for."

"Which is good?"

"Yes. Very good." He gazed into her pretty blue eyes and fought the desire to kiss her that crept up before he could stop it. His restaurant was becoming exactly what he'd envisioned because of her. Because she knew how to direct diners' attention and mood. It was as if they were partners in his venture and though the businessman in him desperately fought his feelings for her, the passionate part of him wanted to lift her off the ground, swing her around and kiss her ardently.

But that was wrong for so many reasons that he got angry with himself for even considering it.

"I was thinking tonight that a differentiation between you and the waitresses would be good. It would be a show of authority."

"You want me to wear a hat?"

He laughed. Was it any wonder he was so drawn to her? No one could so easily catch him off guard. Make him laugh. Make him wish for a life that included a little more fun.

"I want you to wear something other than the dark trousers and white blouses the waitresses wear. Your choice," he said when her face turned down with a puzzled frown. "A dress. A suit. Anything that makes you look like you're in charge."

Her gaze rose to meet his. "In charge?"

"Of the dining room." He laughed lightly. "You still have a few weeks before I give you my job."

She laughed, too.

But when her laughter died, they were left gazing into each other's eyes. The mood shifted from happy and businesslike to something he couldn't define or describe. The click of connection he always felt with her filled him. It was hot and sweet, but pointless, leaving an emptiness in the pit of his stomach.

He said, "Good night, Dani," and walked away, into the kitchen and directly to the window over the sink. A minute later, he watched her amble across the parking lot to her car, start it and drive off, making sure she had no trouble.

Then he locked the restaurant and headed to his SUV.

He might forever remember the joy in her blue eyes when he told her that he wanted her to look like the person of authority in the dining room.

But as he climbed into his vehicle, his smile faded. Here he was making her happy, giving her promotions, authority, and just when he should have been able to kiss her to celebrate, he'd had to pull back…because she was taken.

Was he crazy to keep her on, to continually promote her, to need her for his business when it was clear that there was no chance of a relationship between them?

Was he being a sucker?

Was she using him?

Bah! What the hell was he doing? Thinking about things that didn't matter? The woman was leaving in a few weeks. And that was the real reason he should worry about depending on her. Soon she would be gone. So why were he and Emory leaning on her?

Glad he had more maître d' interviews scheduled for the following Monday, he started his car and roared out of the parking lot. He would use what he had learned about Dani's duties for his new maître d'. But he wouldn't give her any more authority.

And he absolutely would stop all thoughts about wanting to swing her around, kiss her and enjoy their success. It was not "their" success. It was his.

It was also her choice to have no part in it.

Sunday morning, Dani arrived at the restaurant in a slim cream-colored dress. She had curled her hair and pinned it in a bundle on top of her head. When Rafe saw her his jaw fell.

She looked regal, sophisticated. Perfect as the face of his business.

Emory whistled. "My goodness."

Rafe's breath stuttered into his lungs. He reminded himself of his thoughts from the night before. She was leaving. She wanted no part in his long-term success. He and Emory were depending on her too much for someone who had no plans to stay.

But most of all, leaving was her choice.

She didn't want him or his business in her life. She was here only for some money so she could find the relatives of her foster mother.

The waitresses tittered over how great she looked. Emory walked to the podium, took her hands and kissed both of her cheeks. The busboys blushed every time she was near.

She handled it with a cool grace that spoke of dignity and sophistication. Exactly what he wanted as the face of Mancini's. As if she'd read his mind.

Laughing with Allegra, she said, "I feel like I'm playing dress up. These are Louisa's clothes. I don't own anything so pretty."

Allegra sighed with appreciation. "Well, they're perfect for you and your new position."

She laughed again. "Rafe and Emory only promoted me because I have time on my hands in between customers. While you guys are hustling, I'm sort of looking around, figuring things out." She leaned in closer. "Besides, the extra authority doesn't come with more money."

As Allegra laughed, Rafe realized that was true. Unless Dani was a power junkie, she wasn't getting anything out of her new position except more work.

So why did she look so joyful in a position she'd be leaving in a few weeks?

Sunday lunch was busier than normal. Customers came in, ate, chatted with Dani and left happy.

Which relieved Rafe and also caused him to internally scold himself for distrusting her. He didn't know why she'd taken such an interest in his restaurant, but he should be glad she had.

She didn't leave for the space between the last lunch customer and the first dinner customer because the phone never stopped ringing.

Again, Rafe relaxed a bit. She had good instincts. Now that his restaurant was catching on, there were more dinner reservations. She stayed to take them. She was a good, smart employee. Any mistrust he had toward her had to be residual bad feelings over not being able to pursue her when he so desperately wanted to. His fault. Not hers.

In fact, part of him believed he should apologize. Or maybe not apologize. Since she couldn't see inside his brain and know the crazy thoughts he'd been thinking, a compliment would work better.

He walked out of the kitchen to the podium and smiled when he saw she was on the phone. Their reservations for that night would probably be their best ever.

"So we're talking about a hundred people."

Rafe's eyebrows rose. A hundred people? He certainly hoped that wasn't a single reservation for that night. Yes, there was a private room in which he could probably seat a hundred, but because that room was rarely used, those tables and chairs needed to be wiped down. Extra linens would have to be ordered from their vendor. Not to mention enough food. He needed advance warning to serve a hundred people over their normal customer rate.

He calmed himself. She didn't know that the room hadn't been used in months and would need a good dusting. Or about the linens. Or the extra food. Once he told her, they could discuss the limits on reservations.

When she finally replaced the receiver on the phone, her blue eyes glowed.

Need rose inside him. Once again he fought the unwanted urge to share the joy of success with her. No matter how he sliced it, she was a big part of building his clientele. And rather than worry about her leaving, a smart businessman would be working to entice her to stay. To make *his* business *her* career, and Italy her new home.

Romantic notions quickly replaced his business concerns. If she made Italy her home, she might just leave her fiancé in America, and he could—

Realizing he wasn't just getting ahead of himself, he was going in the wrong direction, he forced himself to be professional. "It sounds like you got us a huge reservation."

"Better."

He frowned. "Better? How does something get better than a hundred guests for dinner?"

She grinned. "By catering a wedding! They don't even need our dishes and utensils. The venue is providing that. All they want is food. And for you that's easy."

Rafe blinked. "What?"

"Okay, it's like this. A customer came in yesterday. The dinner they chose was what his wife wanted to be served for their daughter's wedding at the end of the month. When they ate your meal, they knew they wanted you to cook food for their daughter's wedding. The bride's dad called, I took down the info," she said, handing him a little slip. "And now we have a new arm of your business."

Anything romantic he felt for Dani shrank back against the rising tide of red-hot anger.

"I am not a caterer."

He controlled his voice, didn't yell, didn't pounce. But he saw recognition come to Dani's eyes. She might have only worked with him almost two weeks, but she knew him.

Her fingers fluttered to her throat. "I thought you'd be pleased."

"I have a business plan. I have Michelin stars to protect. I will not send my food out into the world for God knows who to do God knows what with it."

She swallowed. "You could go to the wedding—"

"And leave the restaurant?"

She sucked in a breath.

"Call them back and tell them you checked with me and we can't deliver."

"But…I…" She swallowed again. "They needed a commitment. Today. I gave our word."

He gaped at her. "You promised something without asking me?" It was the cardinal sin. The unforgivable sin. Promising something that hadn't been approved because she'd never consulted the boss. Every employee knew that. She hadn't merely overstepped. She'd gone that one step too far.

Her voice was a mere whisper when she said, "Yes."

Anger mixed with incredulity at her presumptuousness, and he didn't hesitate. With his dream in danger, he didn't even have to think about it. "You're fired."

CHAPTER EIGHT

"Leave now."

Dani's breaths came in quick, shallow puffs. No one wanted to be fired. But right at that moment she wasn't concerned about her loss. Her real upset came from failing Rafe. She'd thought he'd be happy with the added exposure. Instead, she'd totally misinterpreted the situation. Contrary to her success in the dining room, she wasn't a chef. She didn't know a chef's concerns. She had no real restaurant experience.

Still, she had instincts—

Didn't she?

"I'll fix this."

He turned away. "This isn't about fixing the problem. This is about you truly overstepping this time. I don't know if it's because we've had personal conversations or because to this point all of your ideas have been good. But no one, absolutely no one, makes such an important decision without my input. You are fired."

He walked into the kitchen without looking back. Dani could have followed him, maybe even should have followed him, but the way he walked away hurt so much she couldn't move. She could barely breathe. Not because she'd angered him over a mistake, but because he was so cool. So distant. So deliberate and so sure that he wanted her gone. As if their evenings at the tavern hadn't happened, as if all those stolen moments—that kiss—had meant nothing, he was tossing her out of his life.

Tears stung her eyes. The pain that gripped her hurt like a physical ache.

But common sense weaved its way into her thoughts. Why was she taking this personally? She didn't love him. She barely knew him. She had a fiancé—almost. A guy who might not be romantic, but who was certainly stable. She'd be going home in a little over two weeks. There could be nothing between her and Rafe. He was passion wrapped in electricity. Moody. Talented. Sweet but intense. Too sexy for his own good—or hers. And they weren't supposed to be attracted to each other, but they were.

Staying at Mancini's had been like tempting fate. Teasing both of them with something they couldn't have. Making them tense, and him moody. Hot one minute and cold the next.

So maybe it really was time to go?

She slammed the stack of menus into their shelf of the podium, grabbed her purse and raced out.

When she arrived at the villa, Louisa was on a ladder, staring at the watermarks as if she could divine how they got there.

"What are you doing home?"

Dani yanked the pins holding up her short curls and let them fall to her chin, as she kicked off Louisa's high, high heels.

"I was fired."

Louisa climbed off the ladder. "What?" She shook her head. "He told you to dress like the authority in the dining room and you were gorgeous. How could he not like how you looked?"

"Oh, I think he liked how I looked." Dani sucked in a breath, fully aware now that that was the problem. They were playing with fire. They liked each other. But neither of them wanted to. And she was done with it.

"Come to Rome with me."

"You're not going to try to get your job back?"

"It just all fell into place in my head. Rafe and I are attracted, but my boyfriend asked me to marry him. Though I didn't accept, I can't really be flirting with another guy. So Rafe—"

Louisa drew in a quick breath. "You know, I wasn't going to mention this because it's not my business, but now that you brought it up... Don't you think it's kind of telling that you hopped on a plane to Italy rather than accept your boyfriend's proposal?"

"I already had this trip scheduled."

"Do you love this guy?"

Dani hesitated, thinking of her last conversation with Paul and how he'd ordered her not to call him anymore. The real kicker wasn't his demand. It was that it hadn't affected her. She didn't miss their short, irrelevant conversations. In six months, she hadn't really missed *him*.

Oh, God. That was the thing her easy, intense attraction to Rafe was really pointing out. Her relationship to Paul might provide a measure of security, but she didn't love him.

She fell to a kitchen chair.

"Oh, sweetie. If you didn't jump up and down for joy when this guy proposed, and you find yourself attracted to another man, you do not want to accept that proposal."

Dani slumped even further in her seat. "I know."

"You should go back to Mancini's and tell Rafe that."

She shook her head fiercely. "No. *No!* He's way too much for me. Too intense. Too *everything*. He has me working twelve-hour days when I'm supposed to be on holiday finding my foster mother's relatives, enjoying some time with them before I go home."

"You're leaving me?"

Dani raised her eyes to meet Louisa's. "You've always known I was only here for a month. I have just over two weeks left. I need to start looking for the Felice family now." She smiled hopefully because she suddenly, fervently didn't want to be alone, didn't want the thoughts about Rafe that would undoubtedly haunt her now that she knew she couldn't accept Paul's proposal. "Come with me."

"To Rome?"

"You need a break from studying everything that's wrong with the villa. I have to pay for a room anyway. We can share it. Then we can come back and I'll still have time to help you catalog everything that needs to be fixed."

Louisa's face saddened. "And then you'll catch a plane and be gone for good."

Dani rose. "Not for good." She caught Louisa's hands. "We're friends. You'll stay with me when you have to come back to the States. I'll visit you here in Italy."

Louisa laughed. "I really could use a break from staring at so many things that need repairing and trying to figure out how I'm going to get it all done."

"So it's set. Let's pack now and go."

Within an hour, they were at the bus station. With Mancini's and Rafe off the list of conversation topics, they chit-chatted about the scenery that passed by as their bus made its way to Rome. Watching Louisa take it all in, as if trying to memorize the country in which she now owned property, a weird sense enveloped Dani. It was clear that everything was new, unique to Louisa. But it all seemed familiar to Dani, as if she knew the trees and grass and chilly February hills, and when she returned to the US she would miss them.

Which was preposterous. She was a New York girl. She needed the opportunities a big city provided. She'd never lived in the country. So why did every tree, every landmark, every winding road seem to fill a need inside her?

The feeling followed her to Rome. To the alleyways between the quaint buildings. To the sidewalk cafés and bistros. To the Colosseum, museums and fountains she took Louisa to see.

And suddenly the feeling named itself. *Home.* What she felt on every country road, at every landmark, gazing at every blue, blue sky and grassy hill was the sense that she was home.

She squeezed her eyes shut. She told herself she wasn't home. She was merely familiar with Italy now because she'd lived in Rome for months. Though that made her feel better for a few minutes, eventually she realized that being familiar with Rome didn't explain why she'd felt she belonged at Mancini's.

She shoved that thought away. She did not belong at Mancini's.

The next day, Dani and Louisa found Rosa's family and were invited to supper. The five-course meal began, reminding her of Rafe, of his big, elaborate dinners, the waitresses who were becoming her friends, the customers who loved her.The weepy sense that she had lost her home filled her. Rightly or wrongly, she'd become attached to Mancini's, but Rafe had fired her.

She had lost the place where she felt strong and smart and capable. The place where she was making friends who felt like family. The place where she—no matter how unwise—was falling for a guy who made her breath stutter and her knees weak.

Because the guy she felt so much for had fired her.

Her brave facade fell away and she excused herself. In the bathroom, she slid down the wall and let herself cry. She'd never been so confused in her life.

"Rafe, there's a customer who'd like to talk to you."

Rafe set down his knife and walked to Mila, who stood in front of the door that led to the dining room. "Great, let's go."

Pleased to be getting a compliment, he reached around

Mila and pushed open the door for her. Since Dani had gone, compliments had been fewer and farther between. He needed the boost.

Mila paused by a table with two twentysomething American girls. Wearing thick sweaters and tight jeans, they couldn't hide their tiny figures. Or their ages. Too old for college and too young to have amassed their own fortunes, they appeared to be the daughters of wealthy men, in Europe, spending their daddies' money. Undoubtedly, they'd heard of him. Bored and perhaps interested in playing with a celebrity chef, they might be looking for some fun. If he handled this right, one of them could be sharing Chianti with him that night.

Ignoring the tweak of a reminder of sharing that wine with Dani, her favorite, he smiled broadly. "What can I do for you ladies?"

"Your ravioli sucked."

That certainly was not what he'd expected.

He bowed slightly, having learned a thing or two from his former hostess. He ignored the sadness that shot through him at even the thought of her, and said, "Allow me to cover your bill."

"Cover our bill?" The tiny blonde lifted a ravioli with her fork and let it plop to her plate. "You should pay us for enduring even a bite of this drivel."

The dough of that ravioli had serenaded his palms as he worked it. The sweet sauce had kissed his tongue. The problem wasn't his food but the palates of the diners.

Still, remembering Dani, he held his temper as he gently reached down and took the biceps of the blonde. "My apologies." He subtly guided her toward the door. The woman was totally cooperative until they got to the podium, and then she squirmed as if he was hurting her, and made a hideous face. Her friend snapped a picture with her phone.

"Get it on Instagram!" the blonde said as they raced out the door. "Rafe Mancini sinks to new lows!"

Furious, Rafe ran after them, but they jumped into their car and peeled out of his parking lot before he could catch them.

After a few well-aimed curses, he counted to forty. Great. Just when he thought rumors of his temper had died, two spoiled little girls were about to resurrect them.

He returned to the quiet dining room. Taking another page from Dani's book, he said, "I'm sorry for the disturbance. Everyone, please, enjoy your meals."

A few diners glanced down. One woman winced. A couple or two pretended to be deep in conversation, as if trying to avoid his misery.

With a weak smile, he walked into the kitchen, over to his workstation and picked up a knife.

Emory scrambled over and whispered, "You're going to have to find her."

Facing the wall, so no one could see, Rafe squeezed his eyes shut. He didn't have to ask who *her* was. The shifts Daniella had been gone had been awful. This was their first encounter with someone trying to lure out his temper, but there had been other problems. Squabbles among the waitresses. Seating mishaps. Lost reservations.

"Things are going wrong, falling through the cracks," Emory continued.

"This is my restaurant. I will find and fix mistakes."

"No. If there's anything Dani taught us, it's that you're a chef. You are a businessman, yes. But you are not the guy who should be in the dining room. You are the guy who should be trotted out for compliments. You are the special chef made more special by the fact that you must be enticed out to the dining room."

He laughed, recognizing he liked the sound of that because he did like to feel special. Or maybe he liked feeling that his food was special.

"Did you ever stop to think that you don't have a temper with the customers or the staff when Dani's around?"

He didn't even try to deny it. With the exception of being on edge because of his attraction to her, his temperament had improved considerably. "Yes."

Emory chuckled as if surprised by his easy acquiescence. "Because she does the tasks that you aren't made to do, which frees you up to do the things you like to do. So, let's just bring her back."

Missing Dani was about so, so much more than Emory knew. Not just a loss of menial tasks but a comfort level. It was as if she brought sunshine into the room. Into his life. But she was engaged.

"Why should I go after her?" Rafe finally faced Emory. "She is returning to America in two weeks."

"Maybe we can persuade her to stay?"

He sniffed a laugh. Leaning down so that only Emory would hear, he said, "She has a fiancé in New York."

Emory's features twisted into a scowl. "And she's in Italy? For months? Without him? Doesn't sound like much of a fiancé to me."

That brought Rafe up short. There was no way in hell he'd let the woman he loved stay alone in Italy for *months*. Especially not if the woman he loved was Daniella.

He didn't tell Emory that. His reasoning was mixed up in feelings that he wasn't supposed to have. He'd gone the route of a relationship once. He'd given up apprenticeships to please Kamila. Which meant he'd given up his dream for her. And still they hadn't made it.

But he'd learned a lesson. Relationships only put the future of his restaurants at stake, so he satisfied himself with one-night stands.

Dani would not be a one-night stand.

But Mancini's really wasn't fine without her.

And Mancini's was his dream. He needed Daniella at his restaurant way too much to break his own rule about relationships. And that was the real bottom line. Getting involved with her would risk his dream as much as Kamila had. He needed her as an employee and he needed to put everything else out of his mind.

Emory caught Rafe's arm. "Maybe there is an opportunity here. If she's truly unhappy, especially with her fiancé, you might be able to convince her Mancini's should be her new career."

That was exactly what Rafe intended to do.

"But you can't have that discussion over the phone. You need to go to Palazzo di Comparino tomorrow. Talk to her personally. Make your case. Offer her money."

"Okay. I'll be out tomorrow morning, maybe all day if I need the time. You handle things while I'm gone."

Emory grinned. "That's my boy."

At the crack of dawn the next morning, Louisa woke Dani and said she was ready to take the bus back to Monte Calanetti. She was happy to have met Dani's foster mom's relatives, but she was nervous, antsy about Palazzo di Comparino. It was time to go back.

After grabbing coffee at a nearby bistro, Dani walked her friend to the bus station, then spent the day with her foster mother's family. By late afternoon, she left, also restless. Like Louisa, she'd loved meeting the Felice family, but they weren't *her* family. Her family was the little group of restaurant workers at Mancini's.

Saddened, she began the walk back to her hotel. A block before she reached it, she passed the bistro again. Though the day was crisp, it was sunny. Warm in the rays that poured down on a little table near the sidewalk, she sat.

She ordered coffee, telling herself it wasn't odd that she felt a connection to the staff at Mancini's. They were nice people. Personable. Passionate. Of course, she felt as if they were family. She'd mothered the waitresses, babied the customers and fallen for Emory like a favorite uncle.

But she'd never see any of them again. She'd been fired

from Mancini's. Rafe hated her. She wouldn't go home happy, satisfied to have met Rosa's relatives, because the connection she'd made had been to a totally different set of people. She would board her plane depressed. Saddened. Returning to a man who didn't even want to pick her up at the airport. A man whose marriage proposal she was going to have to refuse.

A street vendor caught her arm and handed her a red rose.

Surprised, she looked at him, then the rose, then back at him again. "*Grazie...* I think."

He grinned. "It's not from me. It's from that gentleman over there." He pointed behind him.

Dani's eyes widened when she saw Rafe leaning against a lamppost. Wearing jeans, a tight T-shirt and the waist-length black wool coat that he'd worn to the tavern, he looked sexy. But also alone. Very alone. The way she felt in the pit of her stomach when she thought about going back to New York.

Her gaze fell to the rose. Red. For passion. But with someone like Rafe who was a bundle of passion about his restaurant, about his food, about his customers, the color choice could mean anything.

Carrying the rose, she got up from her seat and walked over to him. "How did you find me?"

"Would you believe I guessed where you were?"

"That would have to be a very lucky guess."

He sighed. "I talked to your roommate, Louisa, this afternoon. She told me where you were staying, and I drove to Rome. Walking to your hotel, I saw you here, having coffee."

He glanced away. "Look, can we talk?" He shoved his hands tightly into the side pockets of his coat and returned his gaze to hers. "We've missed you."

"We?"

She almost cursed herself for the question. But she

needed to hear him say it so she'd know she wasn't crazy, getting feelings for a guy who found it so easy to fire her.

"*I've* missed you." He sighed. "Two trust-fund babies faked me out the other night. They insulted my food and when they couldn't get a rise out of me, they made it look like I was tossing one out on her ear to get a picture for Instagram."

She couldn't help it. She laughed. "Instagram?"

"It's the bane of my existence."

"But you hadn't lost your temper?"

He shook his head and glanced away. "No. I hadn't." He looked back at her. "I remembered some things you'd done." He smiled. "I learned."

Her heart picked up at the knowledge that he'd learned from her, and the thrill that he was here, that he'd missed her. "You're not a bad guy."

His face twisted around a smile he clearly tried to hide. "According to Emory, I'm just an overworked guy. And interviewing for a new maître d' isn't helping. Especially when no one I talk to fits. It's why I need you. You're the first person to take over the dining room well enough that I don't worry."

She counted to ten, breathlessly waiting for him to expand on that. When he didn't, she said, "And that's all it is?"

"I know you want there to be something romantic between us. But there are things that separate us. Not just your fiancé, but my temperament. Really? Could you see yourself happy with me? Or when you look at me, do you see a man who takes what he wants and walks away? Because that's the man I really am. I put my restaurant first. I have no time for a relationship."

Her heart wept at what he said. But her sensible self, the lonely foster child who didn't trust the wash of feelings that raced through her every time she got within two feet of him, understood. He was a gorgeous man, born for the limelight, looking to make a name for himself. She was a foster kid, looking for a home. Peace. Quiet. Security. They might be physically attracted, but, emotionally, they were totally wrong for each other. No matter how drawn she was to him, she knew the truth as well as he did.

"You can't commit?"

He shook his head. "My commitment is to Mancini's. To my career. My reputation. I want to be one of Europe's famed chefs. Mancini's is my stepping stone. I do not have time for what other men want. A woman on their arm. Fancy parties. Marriage. To me those are irrelevant. All I want is success. So I would hurt you. And I don't want to hurt you."

"Which makes anything between us just business?"

"Just business."

Her job at Mancini's had awakened feelings in Dani she'd never experienced. Self-worth. A sense of place. An unshakable belief that she belonged there. And the click of connection that made her feel she had a home. Something deep inside her needed Mancini's. But she wouldn't go back only to be fired again.

"And you need me?"

He rolled his eyes. "You Americans. Why must you be showered with accolades?"

Oh, he did love to be gruff.

She slid her hand into the crook of his elbow and pointed to her table at the bistro. "I don't need accolades. I need acknowledgment of my place at Mancini's...and my coffee. I'm freezing."

He pulled his arm away from her hand and wrapped it around her shoulders. She knew he meant it only as a gesture between friends, but she felt his warmth seep through to her. Longing tugged at her heart. A fierce yearning that clung and wouldn't let go.

"You should wear a heavier coat."

His voice was soft, intimate, sending the feeling of rightness through her again.

"It was warm when I came here."

"And now it is cold. So from here on I will make sure you wear a bigger coat." He paused. His head tilted. "Maybe you need me, too?"

She did. But not in the way he thought. She wanted him to love her. Really love her. But to be the man of her dreams, he would have to be different. To be warm and loving. To want her—

And he might. Today. But he'd warned her that anything he felt for her was temporary. He couldn't commit. He didn't want to commit. And unless she wanted to get her heart broken, she had to really hear what he was saying. If she was going to get the opportunity to go back to the first place in her life that felt like home, Mancini's, and the first people who genuinely felt like family, his staff, then a romance between them had to be out of the question.

"I need Mancini's. I like it there. I like the people."

"Ah. So we agree."

"I guess. All I know for sure is that I don't want to go back to New York yet."

He laughed. They reached her table and he pulled out her chair for her. "That doesn't speak well of your fiancé."

Hauling in a breath, she sat, but she said nothing. Her stretching of the truth to Rafe about Paul being her fiancé sat in her stomach like a brick. Still, even though she knew she was going to reject his marriage proposal, it protected her and Rafe. Rafe wouldn't go after another man's woman. Not even for a fling. And he was right. If they had a fling, she would be crushed when he moved on.

One of his eyebrows rose, as he waited for her reply.

She decided they needed her stretched truth. But she couldn't out-and-out lie. "All right. Paul is not the perfect guy."

"I'm not trying to ruin your relationship. I simply believe you should think all of this through. You have a place here in Italy. Mancini's needs you. I would like for you to stay in Italy and work for me permanently, and if you decide to, then maybe your fiancé should be coming here."

She laughed. Really? Paul move to Italy because of her? He wouldn't even drive to the airport for her.

Still, she didn't want Paul in the discussion of her returning to Mancini's. She'd already decided to refuse his proposal. If she stayed in Italy, it had to be for her reasons.

"I think we're getting ahead of ourselves. I have a few weeks before I have to make any decisions."

"Two weeks and two days."

"Yes."

He caught her hands. Kissed the knuckles. "So stay. Stay with me, Daniella. Be the face of Mancini's."

Her heart kicked against her ribs. The way he said "Stay with me, Daniella" froze her lungs, heated her blood. She glanced at the red rose sitting on the table, reminded herself it didn't mean anything but a way to break the ice when he found her. He wasn't asking her to stay for any reason other than her abilities in his restaurant. And she shouldn't want to stay for any reason other than the job. If she could prove herself in the next two weeks, she wouldn't be boarding a plane depressed. She wouldn't be boarding a plane at all. She'd be helping to run a thriving business. Her entire life would change.

She pulled her hands away. "I can't accept Louisa's hospitality forever. I need to be able to support myself. Hostessing doesn't pay much."

He growled.

She laughed. He was so strong and so handsome and so perfect that when he let his guard down and was himself, his real self, with her, everything inside her filled with crazy joy. And maybe if she just focused on making him her friend, a friend she could keep forever, working for him could be fun.

"I can't pay a hostess an exorbitant salary."

"So give me a title to justify the money."

He sighed. "A title?"

"Sure, something like general manager should warrant a raise big enough that I can afford my own place."

His eyes widened. "General manager?"

"Come on, Rafe. Let's get to the bottom line here. If things work out when we return to Mancini's, I'm going to be taking on a huge chunk of your work. I'm also going to be relocating to another *country*. You'll need to make it worth my while."

He shook his head. "Dear God, you are bossy."

"But I'm right."

He sighed. "Fine. But if you're getting that title, you will earn it."

She inclined her head. "Seems fair."

"You'll learn to order supplies, check deliveries, do the job of managing things Emory and I don't have time for."

"Makes perfect sense."

He sighed. His eyes narrowed. "Anything else?"

She laughed. "One more thing." Her laughter became a silly giggle when he scowled at her. "A ride back to Louisa's."

He rolled his eyes. "Yes. I will drive you back to Louisa's. If you wish, I will even help you find an apartment."

Leaving the rose, she stood and pushed away from the table. "You keep getting ahead of things. We have two weeks for me to figure out if staying at Mancini's is right for me." She turned to head back to the hotel to check out, but spun to face him again. "Were I you, I'd be on my best behavior."

The next morning, she called Paul. If staying in Italy was the rest of her life, the *real* rest of her life, she had to make things right.

"Do you know what time it is?"

She could hear the sleep in his voice and winced. "Yes. Sorry. But I wanted to catch you before work."

"That's fine."

She squeezed her eyes shut as she gathered her courage. It seemed so wrong to break up with someone over the phone and, yet, they'd barely spoken to each other in six months. This was the right thing to do.

"Look, Paul, I'm sorry to tell you this over the phone, but I can't accept your marriage proposal."

"What?"

She could almost picture him sitting up in bed, her bad news bringing him fully awake.

"I'm actually thinking of not coming back to New York at all, but staying in Italy."

"What? What about your job?"

"I have a new job."

"Where?"

"At a restaurant."

"So you're leaving teaching to be a waitress?"

"A hostess."

"Oh, there's a real step up."

"Actually, I'm general manager," she said, glad she'd talked Rafe into the title. She couldn't blame Paul for being confused or angry, and knew he deserved an honest explanation.

"And I love Italy. I feel like I belong here." She sucked in a breath. "We've barely talked in six months. I'm going to make a wild guess that you haven't even missed me. I think we were only together because it was convenient."

Another man's silence might have been interpreted as misery. Knowing Paul the way she did, she recognized it as more or less a confirmation that she was right.

"I'm sorry not to accept your proposal, but I'm very happy."

After a second, he said, "Okay, then. I'm glad."

The breath blew back into her lungs. "Really?"

"Yeah. I did think we'd make a good married couple,

but I knew when you didn't say yes immediately that you might have second thoughts."

"I'm sorry."

"Don't be sorry. This is just the way life works sometimes."

And that was her pragmatic Paul. His lack of emotion might have made her feel secure at one time, but now she knew she needed more.

They talked another minute and Dani disconnected the call, feeling as if a weight had been taken from her shoulders, only to have it quickly replaced by another one. She'd had to be fair to Paul, but now the only defense she'd have against Rafe's charms would be her own discipline and common sense.

She hoped that was enough.

CHAPTER NINE

HER RETURN TO the restaurant was as joyous as a celebration. Emory grinned. The waitresses fawned over her. The busboys grew red faced. The chefs breathed a sigh of relief.

Annoyance worked its way through Rafe. Not that he didn't want his staff to adore her. He did. That was why she was back. The problem was he couldn't stop reliving their meeting in Rome. He'd said everything that he'd wanted to say. That he'd missed her. That he wanted her back. But he'd kept it all in the context of business. He'd missed her help. He wanted her to become the face of Mancini's. He didn't want anything romantic with her because he didn't want to hurt her. He'd been all business. And it had worked.

But with her return playing out around him, his heart rumbled at the injustice. He hadn't lied when he said he didn't want her back for himself, that he didn't want something romantic between them. His fierce protection of Mancini's wouldn't let him get involved with an employee he needed. But here at the restaurant, with her looking so pretty, helping make his dream a reality, he just wanted to kiss her.

He reminded himself that she had a fiancé—

A fiancé she admitted was not the perfect guy.

Bah! That fiancé was supposed to be the key weapon in his arsenal of ways to keep himself away from her. Her admission that he wasn't perfect, even the fact that she was considering staying in Italy, called her whole engagement into question. And caused all his feelings for her to surface and swell.

She swept into the kitchen. Wearing a blue dress that highlighted her blue eyes and accented a figure so lush she was absolutely edible, she glided over to Emory. He took her hands and kissed the back of both.

"You look better than anything on the menu."

Rafe sucked in a breath, controlling the unwanted ripple of longing.

Dani unexpectedly stepped toward Emory, put her arms around him and hugged him. Emory closed his eyes as if to savor it, a smile lifted his lips.

Rafe's yearning intensified, but with it came a tidal wave of jealousy. He lowered his knife on an unsuspecting stalk of celery, chopping it with unnecessary force.

Dani faced him. "Why don't you give me the key and I'll open the front door for the lunch crowd?"

He rolled his gaze toward her slowly. Even as the businessman inside him cheered her return, the jealous man who was filled with need wondered if he wasn't trying to drive himself insane.

"Emory, give her your key."

The sous-chef instantly fished his key ring out of his pocket and dislodged the key for Mancini's. "Gladly."

"Don't be so joyful." He glanced at Dani again, at the soft yellow hair framing her face, her happy blue eyes. "Have a key made for yourself this afternoon and return Emory's to him."

She smiled. "Will do, boss."

She walked out of the kitchen, her high heels clicking on the tile floor, her bottom swaying with every step, all eyes of the kitchen staff watching her go.

Jealousy spewed through him. "Back to work!" he yelped, and everybody scrambled.

Emory sauntered over. "Something is wrong?"

He chopped the celery. "Everything is fine."

The sous-chef glanced at the door Dani had just walked through. "She's very happy to be back."

Rafe refused to answer that.

Emory turned to him again. "So did you talk her into staying? Is her fiancé joining her here? What's going on?"

Rafe chopped the celery. "I don't know."

"You don't know if she's staying?"

"She said her final two weeks here would be something like a trial run for her."

"Then we must be incredibly good to her."

"I gave her a raise, a title. If she doesn't like those, then we should be glad if she goes home to her *fiancé*." He all but spat the word *fiancé*, getting angrier by the moment, as he gave Dani everything she wanted but was denied everything he wanted.

Emory said, "I still say something is up with this fiancé of hers. If she didn't tell him she's considering staying in Italy, then there's trouble in paradise. If she did, and he isn't on the next flight to Florence, then I question his sanity."

Rafe laughed.

"Seriously, Rafe, has she talked to you about him? I just don't get an engaged vibe from her."

"Are you saying she's lying?"

Emory inclined his head. "I don't think she's lying as much as I think her fiancé might be a real dud, and her engagement as flat as a crepe."

Rafe said only, "Humph," but once again her statement that her fiancé wasn't the perfect guy rolled through his head.

"I only mention this because I think it works in our favor."

"How so?"

"If she's not really in love, if her fiancé doesn't really love her, we have the power of Italy on our side."

"To?"

"To coax her to stay. To seduce her away from a guy who doesn't deserve her."

Rafe chopped the celery. His dreams were filled with scenarios where he seduced Daniella. Except he had a feeling that kind of seducing wasn't what Emory meant.

"Somehow or another we have to be so good to her that she realizes what she has in New York isn't what she wants."

Sulking, Rafe scraped the celery into a bowl. Why did he have to be the one doing all the wooing? *He* was a catch. He wanted her eyelashes to flutter when he walked by and her eyes to warm with interest. He had some pride, too.

Emory shook his head. "Okay. Be stubborn. But you'll be sorry if some pasty office dweller from New York descends on us and scoops her back to America."

Rafe all but growled in frustration at the picture that formed in his head. Especially since she had said her fiancé wasn't perfect. Shouldn't a woman in love swoon for the man she's promised to marry?

Yes. Yes. She should.

Yet, here she was, considering staying. Not bringing her fiancé into the equation.

And he suddenly saw what Emory was saying.

She wasn't happy with her fiancé. She was searching for something. She'd gone to Rome looking for her foster mother's relatives—family! What Dani had been looking for in Rome was family! That was why she was getting so close to the staff at Mancini's.

Still, something was missing.

He tapped his index fingers against his lips, thinking, and when the answer came to him he smiled and turned to Emory. "I will need time off tomorrow."

Emory's face fell. "You're taking another day?"

"Just lunch. And Daniella will be out for lunch, too."

Emory caught his gaze. "Really?"

"Yes. Don't go thinking this is about funny business.

I'm taking her apartment hunting. Dani is a woman looking for a family. She thinks she's found it with us. But Mancini's isn't a home. It's a place of business. Once I help her get a house, somewhere to put down roots, it will all fall into place for her."

Rafe's first free minute, he called the real estate agent who'd sold him his penthouse. She told him she had some suitable listings in Monte Calanetti and he set up three appointments for Daniella.

When the lunch crowd cleared, he walked into the empty, quiet dining room.

Dani smiled as he approached. "You're not going to yell at me for not going home and costing you two hours' wages are you?"

"You are management now. I expect you here every hour the restaurant is open."

"Except my days off."

He groaned. "Except your days off. If you feel comfortable not being here two days every week, I am fine with it. But if something goes wrong, you will answer for it."

She laughed. "Whatever. I've been coaching Allegra. She'll be much better from here on out. No more catastrophes while I'm gone."

"Great. I've lined up three appointments for us tomorrow."

She turned from the podium. "With vendors?"

"With my friend who is a real estate agent."

"I told you we shouldn't get ahead of ourselves."

"Our market is tight. You must be on top of things to get a good place."

"I haven't—"

He interrupted her. "You haven't decided you're staying. I get that. But if you choose to stay, I don't want you panicking. Getting ahead of a problem is how a smart businessperson staves off disaster."

"Yeah, I know."

"Good. Tomorrow morning, Emory will take over lunch prep while you and I apartment hunt. We can be back for dinner."

Sun poured in through the huge window of the kitchen of the first unit Maria Salvetti showed Rafe and Dani the next morning. Unfortunately, cold air flowed in through the cracks between the window and the wall.

Dani eased her eyes away from the unwanted ventilation and watched as Rafe walked across a worn hardwood floor, his motorcycle boots clicking along, his jeans outlining an absolutely perfect behind and his black leather jacket, collar flipped up, giving him the look of a dangerous rebel.

For the second time that morning, she told herself she was grateful he'd been honest with her about his inability to commit. She didn't know a woman who wouldn't fall victim to his steel-gray eyes and his muscled body. She had to be strong. And her decision to stay at Mancini's had to be made for all the right reasons.

She faced Maria. "I'd have to fix this myself?"

"*Sì*. It is for sale. It is not a rental."

She turned to Rafe. "I wouldn't have time to work twelve-hour days and be my own general contractor."

"You could hire someone."

She winced as she ran her hand along the crack between the wall and window. "Oh, yeah? Just how big is my raise going to be?"

"Big enough."

She shook her head. "I still don't like it."

She also didn't like the second condo. She did have warm, fuzzy feelings for the old farmhouse a few miles away from the village, but that needed more work than the first condo she'd seen.

Maria's smile dipped a notch every time Dani rejected a prospective home. She'd tried to explain that she wasn't even sure she was staying in Italy, but Maria kept plugging along.

After Dani rejected the final option, Maria shook Rafe's hand, then Dani's and said, "I'll check our listings again and get back to you."

She slid into her car and Dani sighed, glad to be rid of her. Not that Maria wasn't nice, but with her decision about staying in Italy up in the air, looking for somewhere to live seemed premature. "Sorry."

"Don't apologize quite yet." He pulled his cell phone from his jacket and dialed a number. "Carlo, this is Rafe. Could you have a key for the empty condo at the front desk? *Grazie*." He slipped his phone into his jacket again.

She frowned at him. "You have a place to show me?"

He headed for his SUV, motioning for her to follow him. "Actually, I thought Maria would have taken you to his apartment first. It's a newly renovated condo in my building."

She stopped walking. "*Your* building?" She might be smart enough to realize she and Rafe were a bad bet, but all along she'd acknowledged that their spending too much time together was tempting fate. Now he wanted them to live in the same building?

"After Emory, you are my most valued employee. A huge part of Mancini's success. We need to be available for each other. Plus, there would be two floors between us. It's not like we'd even run into each other."

She still hesitated. "Your building's that big?"

"No. I value my privacy that much." He sighed. "Seriously. Just come with me to see the place and you will understand."

Dani glanced around as she entered the renovated old building, Rafe behind her. Black-and-white block tiles were accented by red sofas and chairs in a lounge area of the lobby. The desk for the doorman sat discreetly in a corner.

Leaning over her shoulder, Rafe said, "My home is the penthouse."

His warm breath tickled her ear and desire poured through her. She almost turned and yelled at him for flirting with her. Instead, she squelched the feeling. He probably wasn't flirting with her. This was just who he was. Gorgeous. Sinfully sexy. And naturally flirtatious. If she really intended to stay in Italy and work for him, she had to get accustomed to him. As she'd realized after she'd spoken to Paul, she would need discipline and common sense to keep her sanity.

He pointed at the side-by-side elevators. "I don't use those, and you can't use them to get to my apartment."

His breath tiptoed to her neck and trickled down her spine. Still, she kept her expression neutral when she turned and put them face-to-face, so close she could see the little flecks of silver in his eyes.

Just as her reactions couldn't matter, how he looked—his sexy face, his smoky eyes—also had to be irrelevant. If she didn't put all this into perspective now, this temptation could rule her life. Or ruin her life.

She gave him her most professional smile. "And I'd be a few floors away?"

"Not just a few floors, but also a locked elevator."

Dangling the apartment key, he motioned for her to enter the elevator when it arrived. They rode up in silence. He unlocked the door to the available unit and she gasped.

"Oh, my God." She spun to face him. "I can afford this?"

He laughed. "Yes."

From the look of the lobby, she'd expected the apartment to be ultramodern. The kind of place she would have killed to have in New York. Black-and-white. Sharp, but sterile. Something cool and sophisticated for her and distant Paul.

But warm beiges and yellows covered these walls. The

kitchen area was cozy, with a granite-topped breakfast bar where she could put three stools.

She saw it filled with people. Louisa. Coworkers from Mancini's. And neighbors she'd meet who could become like a family.

She caught that thought before it could take root. Something about Italy always caused her to see things through rose-colored glasses, and if she didn't stop, she was going to end up making this choice before she knew for certain that she could work with Rafe as a friend or a business associate, and forget about trying for anything more.

She turned to Rafe again. "Don't make me want something I can't have."

"I already told you that you can afford it."

"I know."

"So why do you think you can't have it?"

It was exactly what she'd dreamed of as a child, but she couldn't let herself fall in love with it. Or let Rafe see just how drawn she was to this place. If he knew her weakness, he'd easily lure her into staying before she was sure it was the right thing to do.

She pointed at the kitchen, which managed to look cozy even with sleek stainless-steel appliances, dark cabinets and shiny surfaces. "It's awfully modern."

"So you want to go back to the farmhouse with the holes in the wall?"

"No." She turned away again, though she lovingly ran her hand along the granite countertop, imagining herself rolling out dough to make cut-out cookies. She'd paint them with sugary frosting and serve them to friends at Christmas. "I want a homey kitchen that smells like heaven."

"You have that at Mancini's."

"I want a big fat sofa with a matching chair that feels like it swallows you up when you sit in it."

"You can buy whatever furniture you want."

"I want to turn my thermostat down to fifty-eight at night so I can snuggle under thick covers."

He stared at her as if she were crazy. "And you can do that here."

"Maybe."

"Undoubtedly." He sighed. "You have an idealized vision of home."

"Most foster kids do."

He leaned his shoulder against the wall near the kitchen. His smoky eyes filled with curiosity. She wasn't surprised when he said, "You've never really told me about your life. You mentioned getting shuffled from foster home to foster home, but you never explained how you got into foster care in the first place."

She shrugged. Every time she thought about being six years old, or eight years old, or ten years old—shifted every few months to the house of a stranger, trying unsuccessfully to mingle with the other kids—a flash of rejection froze her heart. She was an adult before she'd realized no one had rejected her, per se. Each child was only protecting himself. They'd all been hurt. They were all afraid. Not connecting was how they coped.

Nonetheless, the memories of crying herself to sleep and longing for something better still guided her. It was why she believed she could keep her distance from Rafe. Common sense and a longing for stability directed her decisions. Along with a brutal truth. The world was a difficult place. She knew that because she'd lived it.

"There's not much to tell. My mom was a drug addict."

He winced.

"There's no sense sugarcoating it."

"Of course there is. Everyone sugarcoats his or her past. It's how we deal."

She turned to him again, surprised by the observation. She'd always believed living in truth kept her sane. He seemed to believe exactly the opposite.

"Yeah. What did you sugarcoat?"

"I tell you that I'm not a good bet as a romantic partner."

She sniffed a laugh.

"What I should have said is that I'm a real bastard."

She laughed again. "Seriously, Rafe. I got the message the first time. You want nothing romantic between us."

"Mancini's needs you and I am not on speaking terms with any woman I've ever dated. So I keep you for Mancini's."

She looked around at the apartment, unable to stop the warm feeling that flooded her when he said he would keep her. Still, he didn't mean it the way her heart took it. So, remembering to use her common sense, she focused her attention on the apartment, envisioning it decorated to her taste. The picture that formed had her wrestling with the urge to tell him to get his landlord on the line so she could make an offer—then she realized something amazing.

"You knew I'd love this."

He had the good graces to look sheepish. "I assumed you would."

"No assuming about it, you *knew*."

"All right, I knew you would love it."

She walked over to him, as the strangest thought formed in her head. Maybe it wouldn't take a genius to realize the way to entice a former foster child would be with a home. But no one had ever wanted her around enough to figure that out.

"How did you know?"

He shrugged. His strong shoulders lifted the black leather of his jacket and ruffled the curls of his long, dark hair. "It didn't take much to realize that you'd probably lost your sense of home when your foster mother died."

She caught his gaze. "So?"

"So, I think you came to Italy hoping to find it with her relatives."

"They're nice people."

"Yes, but you didn't feel a connection to Rosa's nice relatives. Yet, you keep coming back to Mancini's, because you did connect with us."

Her heart stuttered. Even her almost fiancé hadn't understood why she so desperately wanted to find Rosa's family. But Rafe, a guy who had known her a little over two weeks, a guy she'd had a slim few personal conversations with, had seen it.

He'd also hit the nail on the head about Mancini's. She felt they were her family. The only thing she didn't have here in Italy was an actual, physical home.

And he'd found her one.

He cared about her enough to want to please her, to satisfy needs she kept close to her heart.

Afraid of the direction of her thoughts, she turned away and walked into the master bedroom. Seeing the huge space, her eyebrows rose. "Wow. Nice."

Rafe was right behind her. "Are you changing the subject on me?"

She pivoted and faced him. He seemed genuinely clueless about what he was doing. Not just giving her everything she wanted, but caring about her. He was getting to know her—the real her—in a way no one else in her life ever had. And the urge to fall into his arms, confess her fears, her hopes, her longings, was so strong, she had to walk away from him. If she fell into his arms now, she'd never come out. Especially if he comforted her. God help her if he whispered anything romantic.

"I think we need to change the subject."

"Why?"

She walked over to him again. For fifty cents, she'd answer him. She'd put her arms around his neck and tell him he was falling for her. The things he did—searching her out in Rome, making her general manager, helping her find a home—those weren't things a boss did. No matter how much he believed he needed her as an employee, he also had feelings for her.

But he didn't see it.

And she didn't trust it. He'd said he was a bastard? What if he really was? What if he liked her now, but didn't tomorrow?

"Because I'm afraid. Every time I put down roots, it fails." She said the words slowly, clearly, so there'd be no misunderstanding. Rafe was a smart guy. If she stayed in Italy, shared the joy of making Mancini's successful, no matter how strong she was, how much discipline she had, how much common sense she used, there was a chance she'd fall in love with him.

And then what?

Would she hang around his restaurant desperate for crumbs of affection from a guy who slept with her, then moved on?

That would be an epic fail. The very thought made her ill.

Because she couldn't tell him that, she stuck with the safe areas. The things they could discuss.

"For as good as I am at Mancini's, I can see us having a blowout fight and you firing me again. And for as much as I like the waitstaff, I can see them getting new jobs and moving on. This decision comes with risks for me. I know enough not to pretend things will be perfect. But I have to have at least a little security."

"You and your security. Maybe to hell with security and focus on a little bit of happiness."

Oh, she would love to focus on being happy. Touring Italy with him, stolen kisses, nights of passion. But he'd told her that wasn't in the cards and she believed him. Somehow she had to stop herself from getting those kinds of thoughts every time he said something that fell out of business mode and tipped over into the personal. That would be the only way she could stay at Mancini's.

When she didn't answer, he sighed. "I don't think it's an accident you found Mancini's."

"Of course not. Nico sent me."

"I am not talking about Nico. I'm talking about destiny."

She laughed lightly and walked away from him. It was almost funny the way he used the words and phrases of a lover to lure her to a job. It was no wonder her thoughts always went in the wrong direction. He took her there. Thank God she had ahold of herself enough to see his words for what they were. A very passionate man trying to get his own way. To fight for her sanity, she would always have to stand up to him.

"Foster kids don't get destinies. We get the knowledge that we need to educate ourselves so we can have security. If you really want me to stay, let me come to the decision for the right reasons. Because if I stay, you are not getting rid of me. I will make Mancini's my home." She caught his gaze. "Are you prepared for that?"

CHAPTER TEN

WAS HE PREPARED for that?

What the hell kind of question was that for her to ask?

He caught her arm when she turned to walk away. "Of course, I'm prepared for that! Good God, woman, I drove to Rome to bring you back."

She shook her head with an enigmatic laugh. "Okay. Just don't say I didn't warn you."

He rolled his eyes heavenward. Women. Who could figure them out? "I am warned." He motioned to the door. "Come. I'll drive you back to Louisa's."

But by the time they reached Louisa's villa and he drove back to his condo to change for work, her strange statement had rattled around in his head and made him crazy. Was he prepared for her staying? Idiocy. He'd all but made her a partner in his business. He *wanted* her to stay.

He changed his clothes and headed to Mancini's. Walking into the kitchen, he tried to shove her words out of his head but they wouldn't go—until he found the staff in unexpectedly good spirits. Then his focus fell to their silly grins.

"What's going on?"

Emory turned from the prep table. "Have you seen today's issue of *Tuscany Review*?"

In all the confusion over Daniella, he'd forgotten that today was the day the tourist magazine came out. He snatched it from Emory's hands.

"Page twenty-nine."

He flicked through the pages, getting to the one he wanted, and there was a picture of Dani. So many tourists had snapped pictures that someone from the magazine could have come in and taken this one without anyone in the restaurant paying any mind.

He read the headline. "Mancini's gets a fresh start."

"Read the whole article. It's fantastic."

As he began to skim the words, Emory said, "There's mention of the new hostess being pretty and personable."

Rafe inclined his head. "She is both."

"And mention of your food without mention of your temper."

His gaze jerked up to Emory. "No kidding."

"No kidding. It's as if your temper didn't exist."

He pressed the magazine to his chest. "Thank God I went to Rome and brought her back."

Daniella pushed open the door. Dressed in a sheath the color of ripe apricots, she smiled as she walked toward Rafe and Emory. "I heard something about a magazine."

Rafe silently handed it to her.

She glanced down and laughed. "Well, look at me."

"Yes. Look at you." He wanted to pull her close and hug her, but he crossed his arms on his chest. The very fact that he wanted to hug her was proof he needed to keep his distance. Even forgetting about the fiancé she had back home, she needed security enough that he wouldn't tempt her away from finding it. Her staying had to be about Mancini's and her desire for a place, a home. He had to make sure she got what she wanted out of this deal—without breaking her heart. Because if he broke her heart, she'd leave. And everything they'd accomplished up to now would have been for nothing.

"You realize that even if every chef and busboy cycles out, and every waitress quits after university, Emory and I will always be here."

Emory grinned at Daniella. Rafe nudged him. "Stop behaving like one of the Three Stooges. This is serious for her."

She looked up from the magazine with a smile for Rafe. "Yes. I know you will always be here." Her smile grew. "Did you ever stop to think that maybe that's part of the problem?"

With that she walked out of the kitchen and Rafe shook his head.

"She talks in riddles." But deep down he knew what was happening. He'd told her they'd never become lovers. She had feelings for him. Hell, he had feelings for her, but he intended to fight them. He'd told her anything between them was wrong, so she had to be sure she could work with him knowing there'd never be anything between them.

And maybe that's what she meant about being prepared.

Lately, it seemed he was fighting his feelings as much as she was fighting hers.

Two nights later, as the dinner service began to slow down, Rafe stepped out into the dining room to see his friend Nico walking into Mancini's. Nico's eyes lit when he saw Dani standing at the podium.

"Look at you!" He took her hand and gave her a little twirl to let her show off another pretty blue dress that hugged her figure.

Jealousy rippled through Rafe, but he squelched it. He put her needs ahead of his because that served Mancini's needs. It was a litany he repeated at least four times a day. After her comment about him being part of the reason her decision was so difficult, he'd known he had to get himself in line or lose her.

As he walked out of the kitchen, he heard Nico say, "Rafe tells me you're working out marvelously."

She smiled sheepishly. "I can't imagine anyone not loving working here."

Rafe sucked in a happy breath. She loved working at Mancini's. He knew that, of course, but it was good to hear her say it. It felt normal to hear her say it. As if she knew she belonged here. Clearly, keeping his distance the past two days had worked. Mancini's was warm and happy. The way he'd always envisioned it.

"We don't have reservations," Nico said when Dani glanced at the computer screen.

She smiled. "No worries. The night's winding down. We have plenty of space."

Seeing him approach, Nico said, "And here's the chef now."

"Nico!" Rafe grabbed him and gave him a bear hug. "What brings you here?"

"I saw your ravioli on Instagram and decided I had to try it."

"Bah! Damned trust-fund babies. I should—" He stopped suddenly. Half-hidden behind Nico was Marianna Amatucci, Nico's sister, who'd been traveling for the past year. Short with wild curly hair and honey skin, she was the picture of a natural Italian beauty.

"Marianna!" He nudged Nico out of the way and hugged her, too, lifting her up to swing her around. Rafe hadn't even seen her to say hello in months. Having her here put another piece of normalcy back in his life.

She giggled when he plopped her to the floor again.

"Daniella," he said, one hand around Marianna's waist, the other clasped on Nico's shoulder. "These are my friends. Nico and his baby sister, Marianna. They get the best table in the house."

She smiled her understanding, grabbed two menus and led Nico and Marianna into the dining room. "This way."

Rafe stopped her. "Not *there*. I want them by my kitchen." He took the menus from her hands. "I want to spoil them."

Nico chuckled and caught Dani's gaze. "What he really means is use us for guinea pigs."

She laughed, her gaze meeting Nico's and her cheeks turning pink.

An unexpected thought exploded in Rafe's brain. He'd told Dani he wanted nothing romantic between them. Her fiancé was a dud. Nico was a good-looking man. And Dani was a beautiful, personable woman. If she stayed, at some point, Dani and Nico could become lovers.

His gut tightened.

Still, shouldn't he be glad if Nico was interested in Daniella and that interest caused her to stay?

Of course he should. What he wanted from Daniella was a face for his business. If Nico could help get her to stay, then Rafe should help him woo her.

"You are lucky the night is nearly over," Rafe said as he pulled out Marianna's chair. He handed the menus to them both.

Smiling warmly at Nico, Dani said, "Can I take your drink orders?"

Nico put his elbow on the table and his chin on his fist as he contemplated Daniella, as if she were a puzzle he was trying to figure out.

Thinking of Dani and Nico together was one thing. Seeing his friend's eyes on her was quite another. The horrible black syrup of jealously poured through Rafe's veins like hot wax.

Unable to endure it, he waved Daniella away. "Go. I will take his drink order. You're needed at the door. The night isn't quite over yet."

She gave Nico one last smile and headed to her post.

Happier with her away from Nico, Rafe listened to his friend's wine choice.

Marianna said, "Just water for me."

Rafe gaped at her. "You need wine."

She shook her head. "I need water."

Rafe's jaw dropped. "You cannot be an Italian and refuse wine with dinner."

Nico waved a hand. "It's not a big deal. She's been weird ever since she came home. Just bring her the water."

Rafe called Allegra over so she could get Nico's wine from the bar and Marianna's water. All the while, Dani walked customers from the podium, past Nico, who would watch her amble by.

Rafe sucked in a breath, not understanding the feelings rumbling through him. He wanted Daniella to stay. Nico might give her a reason to do just that. He could not romance her himself. Yet he couldn't bear to have his friend even look at her?

"Give me ten minutes and I will make you the happiest man alive."

Nico laughed, his eyes on Daniella. "I sincerely doubt you can do that with food."

Jealousy sputtered through Rafe again. "Get your mind out of the gutter and off my hostess!"

Nico's eyes narrowed. "Why? Are you staking a claim?"

Rafe's chest froze and he couldn't speak. But Marianna shook her head. "Men. Does it always have to be about sex with you?"

Nico laughed.

Rafe spun away, rushing into the kitchen, angry with Nico but angrier with himself. He should celebrate Nico potentially being a reason for Daniella to stay. Instead, he was filled with blistering-hot rage. Toward his friend. It was insane.

To make up for his unwanted anger, he put together the best meals he'd ever created. Unfortunately, it didn't take ten minutes. It took forty.

Allegra took out antipasto and soups while he worked. When he returned to the dining room, there were no more people at the door. All customers had been seated. Tables that emptied weren't being refilled. Anticipating going home, the busboys cheerfully cleared away dishes.

And Dani sat with Nico and Marianna.

Forcing himself to be friendly—happy—Rafe set the plates of food in front of Nico and his sister.

Marianna said, "Oh, that smells heavenly."

Nico nodded. "Impressive, Rafe."

Dani inhaled deeply. "Mmm…"

Nico grinned, scooped up some pasta and offered it to Dani. "Would you like a bite?"

"Oh, I'd love a bite!"

Nico smiled.

Unwanted jealousy and an odd proprietary instinct rushed through Rafe. Before Daniella could take the bite Nico offered, Rafe grabbed the back of her chair and yanked her away from the table.

"I want her to eat that meal later tonight."

Nico laughed. "Really? What is this? A special occasion?"

Rafe knew Nico meant that as a joke, but he suddenly felt like an idiot as if Nico had caught his jealousy. He straightened to his full six-foot height. "Not a special occasion, part of the process. She's eaten bits of food to get our flavor, but tonight I had planned on treating her to an entire dinner."

Dani turned around on her chair to catch his gaze. "Really?"

Oh, Lord.

Something soft and earthy trembled through him, replacing his jealousy and feelings of being caught, as if they had never existed. Trapped in the gaze of her blue eyes, he quietly said, "Yes."

She rose, putting them face-to-face. "A private dinner?"

He shrugged, but everything male inside him shimmered. After days of only working together, being on his best behavior, he couldn't deny how badly he wanted time alone with her. He didn't want Nico to woo her. *He* wanted to woo her.

"Yes. A private dinner."

She smiled.

His breath froze. She was happy to be alone with him? He'd warned her…yet she still wanted to be alone with him? And what of her fiancé?

He pivoted and returned to the kitchen, not sure what he was doing. But as he worked, he slowed his pace. He rejected ravioli, spaghetti Bolognese. Both were too simple. Too common—

If he was going to feed her an entire meal, it would be his best. Pride the likes of which he'd never felt before rose in him. Only the best for his Dani.

He stopped, his finger poised above a pot, ready to sprinkle a pinch of salt.

His Dani?

He squeezed his eyes shut. Dear God. This wasn't just an attraction. He was head over heels crazy for her.

Dani alternated between standing nervously by the podium and sitting with Nico and Marianna.

The dining room had all but emptied, yet she couldn't seem to settle. Her fluttery stomach had her wondering if she'd even be able to eat what Rafe prepared for her.

A private dinner.

She had no idea what it meant, but when he emerged from the kitchen and walked to Nico's table, her breath stalled. He'd removed his smock and stood before the Amatuccis in dark trousers and a white T-shirt that outlined his taut stomach. Tight cotton sleeves rimmed impressive biceps and Dani saw a tattoo she'd never noticed before.

"I trust you enjoyed your dinners."

Nico blotted his mouth with a napkin, then said, "Rafe, you truly are gifted."

Rafe bowed graciously.

"And, Marianna." When Rafe turned to see her half-eaten meal, he frowned. "Why you not eat?"

She smiled slightly. "You give everyone enough to feed an army. Half was plenty."

"You'll take the rest home?"

She nodded and Rafe motioned for Allegra to get her plate and put her food in a take-out container.

Rafe chatted with Nico, calmly, much more calmly than Dani felt, but the second Allegra returned with the take-out container, Marianna jumped from her seat.

"I need to get home. I don't know what's wrong with me tonight, but I'm exhausted."

Nico rose, too. "It is late. Dinner was something of an afterthought. I promised Marianna I'd get her back at a decent hour. But I knew you'd want to see her after her year away, Rafe."

Rafe kissed her hand. "Absolutely. I'm just sorry she's too tired for us to catch up."

Dani frowned. Nico's little sister didn't look tired. She looked pale. Biting her lower lip, Dani realized she'd only known one other person who'd looked that way—

Rafe waved her over. "Say good-night to Nico and his sister."

Keeping her observations to herself, Dani smiled. "Good night, Marianna."

Marianna returned her smile. "I'm sure we'll be seeing more of you since Nico loves Rafe's food."

Nico laughed, took both her hands and kissed them. "Good night, Daniella. Tell your roomie I said hello."

Daniella's face reddened. Louisa had been the topic of most of Nico's questions when she'd sat with him and his sister, but there was no way in hell she'd tell Louisa Nico had mentioned her. Still, she smiled. Every time she talked to Nico, she liked him more. Which only made Louisa's dislike all the more curious.

"Good night, Nico."

After helping Marianna with her coat, Rafe walked his friends to their car. Dani busied herself helping the waitresses finish dining room cleanup. She didn't see Rafe return, but when a half hour went by, she assumed he'd come in through the back door to the kitchen.

Of course, he could be talking to beautiful Marianna. She might be with her brother, but that brother was a friend of Rafe's. And Nico had said he wanted to bring Marianna to Mancini's because he knew Rafe would want to see her. They probably had all kinds of stories to reminisce about. Marianna might be too young to have been his first kiss, his first love, but she was an adult now. A beautiful woman.

Realizing how possible it was that Rafe might be interested in Marianna, Dani swayed, but she quickly calmed herself. If she decided to stay, watching him with other women would be part of her life. She had to get used to this. She had to get accustomed to seeing him flirt, seeing beautiful women like Marianna look at him with interest.

She tossed a chair to the table with a little more force than was necessary.

Gio frowned. "Are you okay?"

She smiled. "Yes. Perfect."

"If you're not okay, Allegra and I can finish."

"I'm fine." She forced her smile to grow bigger. "Just eager to be done for the night."

As they finished the dining room, Rafe walked out of the kitchen to the bar. He got a bottle of wine and two glasses. As their private dinner became a reality, Dani's stomach tightened.

She squeezed her eyes shut, scolding herself. The dinner might be private for no other reason than the restaurant would be closed. Rafe probably didn't want to be alone with her as much as he wanted her to eat a meal, as hostess, so she could get the real experience of dining at Mancini's.

The waitresses left. The kitchen light went out, indicating Emory and his staff had gone.

Only she and Rafe remained.

He faced her, pointed at a chair. "Sit."

Okay. That was about as far from romantic as a man could get. This "private" dinner wasn't about the two of them having time together. It was about a chef who wanted his hostess to know his food.

She walked over, noticing again how his tight T-shirt accented a strong chest and his neat-as-a-pin trousers gave him a professional look. But as she got closer, Louisa's high, high heels clicking on the tile floor, she saw his gaze skim the apricot dress. His eyes warmed with interest. His lips lifted into a slow smile.

And her stomach fell to the floor. *This* was why she'd never quite been able to talk herself out of her attraction to him. He was every bit as attracted to her. He might try to hide it. He might fight it tooth and nail. But he liked her as more than an employee.

She reached the chair. He pulled it out, offering the seat to her.

As she sat, her back met his hands still on the chair. Rivers of tingles flowed from the spot where they touched. Her breath shuddered in and stuttered out. Nerves filled her.

He stepped away. "We're skipping soup and salad, since it's late." All business, he sat on the chair next to hers. He lifted the metal cover first from her plate, then his own. "I present beef *brasato* with pappardelle and mint."

When the scent hit her, her mouth watered. All thoughts of attraction fled as her stomach rumbled greedily. She closed her eyes and savored the aroma.

"You like?"

Unable to help herself, she caught his gaze. "I'm amazed."

"Wait till you taste."

He smiled encouragingly. She picked up her fork, filled it with pasta and slid it into her mouth. Knowing he'd made this just for her, the ritual seemed very decadent, very sensual. Their eyes met as flavor exploded on her tongue.

"Oh, God."

He grinned. "Is good?"

"You know you don't even have to ask."

He sat back with a laugh. "I was top of my class. I trained both in Europe and the United States so I could ascertain the key to satisfying both palates." He smiled slowly. "I am a master."

She sliced off a bit of the beef. It was so good she had to hold back a groan. "No argument here."

"Wait till you taste my tiramisu."

"No salad but you made dessert?"

He leaned in, studied her. "Are you watching your weight?"

She shook her head. "No."

"Then prepare to be taken to a world of decadence."

She laughed, expecting him to pick up his fork and eat his own meal. Instead, he stayed perfectly still, his warm eyes on her.

"You like it when people go bananas over your food."

"Of course."

But that wasn't why he was studying her. There was a huge difference between pride in one's work and curiosity about an attraction and she knew that curiosity when she saw it.

She put down her fork, caught in his gaze, the moment. "What are we really doing here, Rafe?"

He shook his head. "I'm not sure."

"You aren't staring at me like someone who wants to make sure I like his food."

"You are beautiful."

Her heart shivered. Her eyes clung to his. She wanted him to have said that because he liked her, because he was ready to do something about it. But a romance between them would be a disaster. She'd be hurt. She'd have to leave Monte Calanetti. She could not take anything he said romantically.

Forking another bite of food, she casually said, "Beauty doesn't pay the rent."

His voice a mere whisper, he said, "Why do you tease me?"

Her face fell. "I don't tease you!"

"Of course, you do. Every day you dress more beautifully, but you don't talk to me."

"I'm smart enough to stay away when a guy warns me off."

"Yet you tell me I must be prepared for you to stay."

"Because you…" *Like me.* She almost said it. But his admitting he liked her would be nothing but trouble. He might like her in the moment, but he wouldn't like her forever. It was stupid to even have that discussion.

She steered them away from it. "Because if I stay, no more firing me. You're getting me permanently."

"You keep saying that as if I should be afraid." He slid his arm to the back of her chair. His fingers rose to toy with the blunt line of her chin-length hair. "But your staying is not a bad thing."

The wash of awareness roaring through her disagreed. If she fell in love with him, her staying would be a very bad thing. His touching her did not help matters. With his fingers brushing her hair, tickling her nape, she couldn't move…could barely breathe.

His hand shifted from her hairline and wrapped around the back of her neck so he could pull her closer. She told herself to resist. To be smart. But something in his eyes wouldn't let her. As she drew nearer, he leaned in. Their gazes held until his lips met hers, then her eyelids dropped. Her breathing stopped.

Warm and sweet, his lips brushed her, and she knew why she hadn't resisted. She so rarely got what she wanted in life that when tempted she couldn't say no. It might be wrong to want him, but she did.

His hand slid from her neck to her back, twisting her to

sit sideways on her chair. Her arms lifted slowly, her hands hesitantly went to his shoulders. Then he deepened the kiss and her mind went blank.

It wasn't so much the physical sensations that robbed her of thought but the fact that he kissed her. He finally, finally kissed her the way he had the night he'd walked her to her car.

When he thought she was free.

When he wanted there to be something between them.

The kiss went on and on. Her senses combined to create a flood of need so strong that something unexpected suddenly became clear. She was already in love with Rafe. She didn't have to worry that someday she might fall in love. Innocent and needy as she was, she had genuinely fallen in love—

And he was nowhere near in love with her.

He was strong and stubborn, set in his ways. He said he didn't do relationships. He said he didn't have time. He'd told her he hurt women. And if he hurt her, she'd never be able to work for him.

Did she want to risk this job for a fling?

To risk her new friends?

Did she want to be hurt?

Hadn't she been hurt, rejected enough in her life already?

She jerked away from him.

He pulled away slowly and ran his hand across his forehead. "Oh, my God. I am so sorry."

"Sorry?" She was steeped in desire sprinkled with a healthy dose of fear, so his apology didn't quite penetrate.

"I told you before. I do not steal other men's women."

"Oh." She squeezed her eyes shut. Paul was such a done deal for her that she'd taken him out of the equation. But Rafe didn't know that. For a second she debated keeping up the charade, if only to protect herself. But they had hit the point where that wasn't fair. She couldn't let Rafe go on thinking he was romancing another man's woman. Especially not when she had been such a willing participant.

She sucked in a breath, caught his gaze and quietly said, "I'm not engaged."

Rafe sat up in his chair. "What?"

She felt her cheeks redden. "I'm not engaged."

His face twisted with incredulity. "You *lied*?"

"No." She bounced from her seat and paced away. "Not really. My boyfriend had asked me to marry him. I told him I needed time to think about it. I was leaving for Italy anyway—"

He interrupted her as if confused. "So your boyfriend asked you to marry him and you ran away?"

She swallowed. "No. I inherited the money for a plane ticket to come here to find Rosa's relatives and I immediately tacked extra time onto my teaching tour. All that had been done before Paul proposed."

"So his proposal was a stopgap measure."

She frowned. "Excuse me?"

"Not able to keep you from going to Italy, he tied you to himself enough that you would feel guilty if you got involved with another man while you were away." He caught her gaze. "But it didn't work, did it?"

She closed her eyes. "No."

"It shouldn't have worked. It was a ploy. And you shouldn't feel guilty about anything that happened while you were here since you're really not engaged."

"Well, it doesn't matter anyway. I called him after we returned from Rome and officially rejected his proposal."

"You told him no?"

She nodded. "And told him I might be staying in Italy." She sucked in a breath. "He wished me luck."

Rafe sat back in his chair. "And so you are free." He combed his fingers through his hair. Laughed slightly.

The laugh kind of scared her. She'd taken away the one barrier she knew would protect her. All she had now to keep her from acting on her love for him was her willpower. Which she'd just proven wasn't very strong.

"I should go."

His gaze slowly met hers. "You haven't finished eating."

His soulful eyes held hers and her stomach jumped. Everything about him called to her on some level. He listened when she talked, appreciated her work at his restaurant… was blisteringly attracted to her.

What the hell would have happened if she hadn't broken that kiss? What would happen if she stayed, finished her meal, let them have more private time? With Paul gone as protection, would he seduce her? And if she resisted… what would she say? Another lie? *I don't like you? I'm not interested? I don't want to be hurt?*

The last wasn't a lie. And it would work. But she didn't want to say it. She didn't want to hear him tell her one more time that he couldn't commit. She didn't want this night to end on a rejection.

"I want to go home."

His eyes on her, he rose slowly. "Let's go, then. I will clean up in the morning."

Finally breaking eye contact, she walked to the front of Mancini's to get her coat. Her legs shook. Her breaths hurt. Not because she knew she was probably escaping making love, but because he really was going to hurt her one day.

CHAPTER ELEVEN

THE NEXT MORNING, Rafe was in the dining room when Dani used her key to unlock the front door and enter Mancini's. Around him, the waitresses and busboys busily set up tables. The wonderful aromas of his cooking filled the air. But when she walked in, Dani brought the real life to the restaurant. Dressed in a red sweater with a black skirt and knee-high boots, she was just the right combination of sexy and sweet.

And she'd rejected him the night before.

Even though she'd broken up with her man in America.

Without saying good morning, without as much as meeting her gaze, he turned on his heel and walked into the kitchen to the prep tables where he inspected the handiwork of two chefs.

He waved his hand over the rolled-out dough for a batch of ravioli. "This is good."

He tasted some sauce, inclined his head, indicating it was acceptable and headed for his workstation.

Emory scrambled over behind him. "Is Daniella here?"

"Yes." But even before Rafe could finish the thought, she pushed open the swinging doors to the kitchen and entered. She strolled to his prep table, cool and nonchalant as if nothing had happened between them.

But lots had happened between them. He'd kissed her. And she'd told him she didn't have a fiancé. Then she'd run. Rejecting him.

"Good morning."

He forced his gaze to hers. His eyes held hers for a beat before he said, "Good morning."

Emory caught her hands. "Did you enjoy your dinner?"

She laughed. "It was excellent." She met Rafe's gaze again. "Our chef is extraordinary."

His heart punched against his ribs. How could a man not take that as a compliment? She hadn't just eaten his food the night before. She'd returned his kiss with as much passion and fervor as he'd put into it.

Emory glowed. "This we know. And we count on you to make sure every customer knows."

"Oh, believe me. I've always been able to talk up the food from the bites you've given me. But eating an entire serving has seared the taste of perfection in my brain."

Emory grinned. "Great!"

"I think our real problem will be that I'll start stealing more bites and end up fat as a barrel."

Emory laughed but Rafe looked away, remembering his question from the night before. *Are you watching your weight?* One memory took him back to the scene, the mood, the moment. How nervous she'd seemed. How she'd jumped when his hand had brushed her back. How her jitters had disappeared while they were kissing and didn't return until they'd stopped.

Because she had to tell him about her fiancé.

She wasn't engaged.

She *had* responded to him.

Emory laughed. "Occupational hazard."

Her gaze ambled to Rafe's again. All they'd had the night before was a taste of what could be between them. Yes, he knew he'd warned her off. But she'd still kissed him. He'd given her plenty of time to move away, but she'd stayed. Knowing his terms—that he didn't want a relationship—she'd accepted his kiss.

With their gazes locked, she couldn't deny it. He could see the heat in her blue eyes.

"From here on out, when we create a new dish or perfect an old one," Emory continued, oblivious to the nonverbal conversation she and Rafe were having, "you will sample."

"I want her to have more than a sample."

The words sprang from him without any thought. But he wouldn't take them back. He no longer *wanted* an affair with her. He now *longed* for it, yearned for it in the depths of his being. And they were adults. They weren't kids. Love affairs were part of life. She might get hurt, or because they were both lovers and coworkers, she might actually understand him. His life. His time constraints. His passion for his dream—

She might be the perfect lover.

The truth of that rippled through him. It might not be smart to gamble with losing her, but he didn't think he'd lose her. In fact, he suddenly, passionately believed a long-term affair was the answer to their attraction.

"And I know more than a sample would be bad for me." She shifted her gaze to Emory before smiling and walking out of the kitchen.

Rafe shook his head and went back to his cooking. He had no idea if she was talking about his food or the subtle suggestion of an affair he'd made, but if she thought that little statement of hers was a deterrent, she was sadly mistaken.

Never in his life had he walked away from something he really wanted and this would not be an exception. Especially since he finally saw how perfect their situation could be.

Dani walked out of the kitchen and pressed her hand to her jumpy stomach. Those silver-gray eyes could get more across in one steamy look than most men could in foreplay.

To bolster her confidence, which had flagged again, she

reminded herself of her final thoughts as she'd fallen asleep the night before. Rafe was a mercurial man. Hot one minute. Cold the next. And for all she knew, he could seduce her one day and dump her the next. She needed security. Mancini's could be that security. She would not risk that for an affair. No matter how sexy his eyes were when he said it. How deep his voice.

She walked to the podium. Two couples awaited. She escorted them to a table. As the day wore on, customer after customer chatted with her about their tours or, if they were locals, their homes and families. The waitstaff laughed and joked with each other. The flow of people coming in and going out, eating, serving, clearing tables surrounded her, reminded her that *this* was why she wanted to stay in Italy, at Mancini's. Not for a man, a romance, but for a life. The kind of interesting, fun, exciting life she'd never thought she'd get.

She wanted this much more than she wanted a fling that ended in a broken heart and took away the job she loved.

At the end of the night, Emory came out with the white pay envelopes. He passed them around and smiled when he gave one to Dani. "This will be better than last time."

"So my raise is in here?"

"Yes." He nodded once and strode away.

Dani tucked the envelope into her skirt pocket and helped the waitresses with cleanup. When they were done, she grabbed her coat, not wanting to tempt fate by being the only remaining employee when Rafe came out of the kitchen.

She walked to her car, aware that Rafe's estimation of her worth sat by her hip, half afraid to open it. He had to value her enough to pay her well or she couldn't stay. She would not leave the security of her teaching job and an apartment she could afford, just to be scraping by in a foreign country, no matter how much she loved the area, its people and especially her job.

After driving the car into a space in Louisa's huge ga-age, Dani entered the house through the kitchen.

Louisa sat at the table, enjoying her usual cup of tea before bedtime. "How did it go? Was he nice? Was he romantic? Or did he ignore you?"

Dani slipped off her coat. "He hinted that we should have an affair."

"That's not good."

"Don't worry. I'm not letting him change the rules he made in Rome. He said that for us to work together there could be nothing between us." She sucked in a breath. "So he can't suddenly decide it's okay for us to have an affair."

Louisa studied her. "I think you're smart to keep it that way, but are you sure it's what you want?"

"Yes. Today customers reminded me of why I love this job. Between lunch and dinner, I worked with Emory to organize the schedule for ordering supplies and streamline it. He showed me a lot of the behind-the-scenes jobs it takes to make Mancini's work. Every new thing I see about running a restaurant seems second nature to me."

"And?"

"And, as I've thought all along, I have instincts for the business. This could be more than a job for me. It could be a real career. If Rafe wants to risk that by making a pass at me, I think I have the reasoning set in my head to tell him no."

Louisa's questioning expression turned into a look of joy. "So you're staying?"

"Actually—" she waved the envelope "—it all depends on what's in here. If my salary doesn't pay me enough for my own house or condo, plus food and spending money, I can't stay."

Louisa crossed her fingers for luck. "Here's hoping."

Dani shook her head. "You know, you're so good to me I want to stay just for our friendship."

Louise groaned. "Open the darned thing already!"

She sliced a knife across the top of the envelope. When she saw the amount of her deposit, she sat on the chair across from Louisa. "Oh, my God."

Louisa winced. "That bad?"

"It's about twice what I expected." She took a breath. "What's he doing?"

Louisa laughed. "Trying to keep you?"

"The amount is so high that it's actually insulting." She rose from her seat, grabbed her coat and headed for the door. "Half this check would have been sufficient to keep me. This amount? It's—offensive." Almost as if he was paying her to sleep with him. She couldn't bring herself to say the words to Louisa. But how coincidental was it that he'd dropped hints that he wanted to have an affair, then paid her more money than she was worth?

The insult of it vibrated through her. The nerve of that man!

"Where are you going?"

"To toss this back in his face."

Yanking open the kitchen door, she bounded out into the cold, cold garage. She jumped into the old car and headed back to Monte Calanetti, parking on a side street near the building where Rafe had shown her the almost perfect condo.

But as she strode into the lobby, she remembered she needed a key to get into the elevator that would take her to the penthouse. Hoping to ask the doorman for help, she groaned when she saw the desk was empty.

Maybe she should take this as a sign that coming over here was a bad idea?

She sucked in a breath. No. Their situation was too personal to talk about at Mancini's. And she wanted to yell. She wanted to vent all her pent-up frustrations and maybe even throw a dish or two. She had to talk to him now. Alone.

She walked over to the desk and eyed the phone. Luck

ly, one of the marked buttons said Penthouse. She lifted
he receiver and hit the button.

After only one ring, Rafe answered. "Hello?"

She sucked in a breath. "It's me. Daniella. I'm in your
obby and don't know how to get up to your penthouse."

"Pass the bank of elevators we used to get to the condo
I showed you and turn right. I'll send my elevator down
or you."

"Don't I need a key?"

"I'll set it to return. You just get in."

She did as he said, walking past the first set of eleva-
ors and turning to find the one for the penthouse. She
stepped through the open doors and they swished closed
behind her.

Riding up in the elevator with its modern gray geomet-
ric-print wallpaper and black slate floors, she was suddenly overwhelmed by something she hadn't considered,
but should have guessed.

Rafe was a wealthy man.

Watching the doors open to an absolutely breathtaking
home, she tried to wrap her brain around this new facet
of Rafe Mancini. He wasn't just sexy, talented and mercurial. He was rich.

And she was about to yell at him? She, who'd always
been poor? Always three paychecks away from homeless-
ness? She'd never, ever considered that maybe the reason
he didn't think anything permanent would happen between
them might be because they were so different. They lived
in two different countries. They had two different belief
systems. And now she was seeing they came from two to-
ally different worlds.

Rafe walked around a corner, holding two glasses of
wine.

"Chianti." He handed one to her and motioned to the
black leather sofa in front of a stacked stone fireplace in
the sitting area.

Unable to help herself, she glanced around, trepidation filling her. Big windows in the back showcased the winking lights of the village. The black chairs around a long black dining room table had white upholstered backs and cushions. Plush geometric-patterned rugs sat on almost-black hardwood floors. The paintings on the pale gray walls looked ancient—valuable.

It was the home of a wealthy, wealthy man.

"Daniella?"

And maybe that's why he thought he could influence her with money? Because she came from nothing.

That made her even angrier.

She straightened her shoulders, caught his gaze. "Are you trying to buy me off?"

"Buy you off?"

"Get me to stop saying no to a relationship by bribing me with a big, fat salary?"

He laughed and fell to the black sofa. "Surely this is a first. An employee who complains about too much money." He shook his head with another laugh. "You said you wanted to be compensated for relocating. You said you wanted to be general manager. That is what a general manager makes."

"Oh." White-hot waves of heat suffused her. Up until this very second, everything that happened with reference to her job at Mancini's had been fun or challenging. He pushed. She pushed back. He wanted her for his restaurant. She made demands. But holding the check, hearing his explanation, everything took on a reality that had somehow eluded her. She was general manager of a restaurant. *This* was her salary.

He patted the sofa. "Come. Sit."

She took a few steps toward the sofa, but the lights of the village caught her attention and the feeling of being Alice in Wonderland swept through her.

"I never in my wildest dreams thought I'd make this much money."

"Well, teachers are notoriously underpaid in America, and though you'd studied a few things that might have steered you to a more lucrative profession, you chose to be a teacher."

Her head snapped up and she turned to face him. "How do you know?"

He batted a hand. "Do I look like an idiot? Not only did I do due diligence in investigating your work history, but also I took a look at your college transcripts. Do you really think I would have given you such an important job if you didn't have at least one university course in accounting?"

"No." Her gaze on him, she sat on the far edge of the sofa.

His voice became soft, indulgent. "Perhaps in the jumble of everything that's been happening I did not make myself clear. I've told you that I intend to be one of the most renowned chefs in Europe. I can't do that from one restaurant outside an obscure Tuscan village. My next restaurant will be in Rome. The next in Paris. The next in London. I will build slowly, but I will build."

"You'd leave Mancini's?" Oddly, the thought actually made her feel better.

"I will leave Mancini's in Tuscany when I move to Rome to build Mancini's Rome." He frowned. "I thought I told you this." His frown deepened. "I know for sure I told you that Mancini's was only a stepping stone."

"You might have mentioned it." But she'd forgotten. She forgot everything but her attraction to him when he was around. She'd accused him of using promotions to cover his feelings for her. But she'd used her feelings for him to block what was really going on with her job, and now, here she was, in a job so wonderful she thought she might faint from the joy of it.

"With you in place I can move to the next phase of my business plan. But there's a better reason for me to move on. You and I both worry that if we do something about our attraction, you will be hurt when it ends and Mancini's will lose you." He smiled. "So I fix."

"You fix?"

"I leave. Once I start my second restaurant, you will not have to deal with me on a day-to-day basis." His smile grew. "And we will understand each other because we'll both work in the same demanding profession. You will understand if I cancel plans at the last minute."

This time the heat that rained down on her had nothing to do with embarrassment. He'd really thought this through. Like a man willing to shift a few things because he liked her.

"Oh."

"There are catches."

Her gaze jumped to his. "Catches?"

"Yes. I will be using you for help creating the other restaurants. To scout sites. To hire staff. To teach them how to create our atmosphere. That is your real talent." He held her gaze. "That is also why your salary is so high. You are a big part of Mancini's success. You created that atmosphere. I want it not just in one restaurant, but all of them, and you will help me get it."

The foster child taught not to expect much out of life, the little girl who learned manners only by mimicking what she saw in school, the Italian tourist who borrowed Louisa's clothes and felt as though she was playing dress up every day she got ready for work, that girl quivered with happiness at the compliment.

The woman who'd been warned by him that he would hurt her struggled with fear.

"You didn't just create a great job for me. You cleared the way for us to have an affair."

Rafe sighed. "Why are you so surprised? You're beautiful. You're funny. You make me feel better about myself. My life. Yes, I want you. So I figured out a way I could have you."

She sucked in a breath. It was heady stuff to see the lengths he was willing to go to be with her. And she also saw the one thing he wasn't saying.

"You like me."

"What did you think? That I'd agonize this much over someone I just wanted to sleep with?"

She smiled. "You agonized?"

He batted a hand in dismissal. "You're a confusing woman, Daniella."

"And you've gone to some pretty great lengths to make sure we can…see each other."

His face turned down into his handsome pout. "And you should appreciate it."

She did. She just didn't know how to handle it.

"Is it so hard to believe I genuinely like you?"

"No." She just never expected he would say it. But he said it easily. And the day would probably come when those feelings would expand. He truly liked her and she was so in love with him that her head spun. This was not going to be an affair. He was talking about a relationship.

Happiness overwhelmed her and she couldn't resist. She set her wineglass on the coffee table and scooted beside him.

A warm, syrupy feeling slid through Rafe. But on its heels was the glorious ping of arousal. Before he realized what she was about to do, she kissed him. Quick and sweet, her lips met his. When she went to pull back, he slid his hand across her lower back and hauled her to him. He deepened their kiss, using his tongue to tempt her. Nibbling her lips. Opening his mouth over hers until she responded with the kind of passion he'd always known lived in her heart.

He pulled away. "You play with fire."

Her tongue darted out to moisten her lips. Temptation roared through him and all his good intentions to take it slowly with her melted like snow in April. He could have her now. In this minute. He could take what he greedily wanted.

She drew a breath. "How is it playing with fire if we really, really like each other?"

She was killing him. Sitting so warm and sweet beside him, tempting him with what he wanted before she was ready.

Still, though it pained him, he knew the right thing to do.

"So we will do this right. When you are ready, when you trust me, we will take the next step."

Her gaze held his. "When I trust you?"

"*Sì.* When I feel you trust me enough to understand why we can be lovers, you will come to my bed."

Her face scrunched as she seemed to think all that through. "Wait…this is just about becoming lovers?"

"Yes."

"But you just said you wouldn't worry that much about someone you wanted to sleep with." She caught his gaze. "You said you agonized."

"Because we will not be a one-night stand. We will be lovers. Besides, I told you. I don't do relationships."

"You also said that you'd never have a romance with an employee." She met his gaze. "But you changed that rule."

"I made accommodations. I made everything work."

"Not for me! I don't just want a fling! I want something that's going to last."

His eyebrows rose. "Something that will last?" He frowned. "Forever?"

"Forever!"

"I tried forever. It did not work for me."

"You tried?"

"*Sì.*"

"And?"

"And it ended badly." He couldn't bring himself to explain that he'd been shattered, that he'd almost given up his dream for a woman who had left him, that he'd been a ball f pain and confusion until he pulled himself together and ealized his dreams depended on him not trusting another voman with his heart or so much of his life.

"*Cara*, marriage is for other people. It's full of all kinds f things incompatible with the man I have to be to be a uccess."

"You *never* want to get married?"

"No!" He tossed his hands. "What I have been saying ll along? Do you not listen?"

She stood up. The pain on her face cut through him like knife. Though he suddenly wondered why. He'd always nown she wanted security. He'd always known he couldn't ive it to her. He couldn't believe he'd actually tried to get er to accept less than what she needed.

He rose, too. "Okay, let's forget this conversation hap-ened. It's been a long day. I'm tired. I also clearly misin-erpreted things. Come to Mancini's tomorrow as general nanager."

She took two steps back. "You're going to keep me, even hough I won't sleep with you?"

"Yes." But the sadness that filled him confused him. Ie'd had other women tell him no and he'd walked away inconcerned. Her *no* felt like the last page of a favorite ook, the end of something he didn't want to see end. And ret he knew she couldn't live with his terms and he couldn't ive with hers.

CHAPTER TWELVE

AGREEING THAT HE was right about at least one thing—she
was too tired, too spent, to continue this discussion—Dan
walked to the elevator. He followed her, hit the button that
would close the door and turned away.

She sucked in a breath and tried to still her hammer-
ing heart. But it was no use. They really couldn't find a
middle ground. It was sweet that he'd tried, but it was just
another painful reminder that she had fallen in love with
the wrong man.

She squeezed her eyes shut. She'd be okay—

No, she wouldn't. She'd fallen in love with him. Unless
he really stayed out of Mancini's, she'd always be in love
with him. Then she'd spend her life wishing he could fall for
her, too. Or maybe one day she'd succumb. She'd want him
so much she'd forget everything else, and she'd start the affair he wanted. With the strength of her feelings, that would
seal the deal for her. She'd love him forever. Then she'd
never have a home. Never have a family. Always be alone.

She thought of the plane ticket tucked away somewhere
in her bedroom in Louisa's house. Now that she knew he
wanted nothing but an affair, which was unacceptable, she
could go home.

But she didn't want to go home. She wanted to run Mancini's. He'd handed her the opportunity with her general
managership—

And he was leaving. Maybe not permanently, but for the next several years he wouldn't be around every day. Most of the time, he'd be in other cities, opening new restaurants.

Wouldn't she be a fool to leave now? Especially since she had a few days before she had to use that ticket. Maybe the wise thing to do would be to use this time to figure out if she could handle working with him as the boss she only saw a few times a month?

The next day when she walked in the door and felt the usual surge of rightness, she knew the job was worth fighting for. In her wildest dreams she'd never envisioned herself successful. Competent, making a living, getting a decent apartment? Yes. But never as one of the people at the top. Hiring employees. Creating atmosphere. Would she really let some feelings, one *man*, steal this from her?

No! No! She'd been searching for something her entire life. She believed she'd found it at Mancini's. It would take more than unrequited love to scare her away from that.

When Emory sat down with her in between lunch and dinner and showed her the human resources software, more of the things she'd learned in her university classes tumbled back.

"So I'll be doing all the admin?"

Emory nodded. "With Rafe gone, setting up Mancini's Rome, I'll be doing all the cooking. I won't have time to help."

"That's fine." She studied the software on the screen, simple stuff, really. Basically, it would do the accounting for her. And the rest? It was all common sense. Ordering. Managing the dining room. Hiring staff.

He squeezed her hand. "You and me…we make a good team."

Her smile grew and her heart lightened. She loved Emory.

Even tempered with the staff and well acquainted with

Rafe's recipes, he was the perfect chef. As long as Rafe wasn't around, she would be living her dream.

She returned his hand squeeze. "Yeah. We do."

When she and Emory were nearly finished going over the software programs, Rafe walked into the office. As always when he was around, she tingled. But knowing this was one of the things she was going to have to deal with, because he wasn't going away permanently, she simply ignored it.

"Have you taught her payroll?"

Emory rose from his seat. "Yes. In fact, she explained a thing or two to me."

Rafe frowned. "How so?"

"She understands the software. I'm a chef. I do not."

Dani also rose from her chair. "I've worked with software before to record grades. Essentially, most spreadsheet programs run on the same type of system, the same theories. My boyfriend—" She stopped when the word *boyfriend* caught in her throat. Emory's gaze slid over to her. But Rafe's eyes narrowed.

She took a slow, calming breath. "My ex-boyfriend Paul is a computer genius. I picked up a few things from him."

Rafe turned away. "Well, let us be glad for him, then."

He said the words calmly, but Dani heard the tension in his voice. There were feelings there. Not just lust. So it wouldn't be only her own feelings she'd be fighting. She'd also have to be able to handle his. And that might be a little trickier.

"I've been in touch with a Realtor in Rome. I go to see buildings tomorrow."

A look passed between him and Emory.

Emory tucked the software manual into the bottom bin of an in basket. "Good. It's time to get your second restaurant up and running." He slid from behind the desk. "But right now I have to supervise dinner."

He scampered out of the room and Rafe's gaze roamed over to hers again. "I'd like for you to come to Rome with me."

Heat suffused her and her tongue stuck to the roof of her mouth. "Me?"

"I want you to help me scout locations."

"Really?"

"I told you. You are the one who created the atmosphere of this Mancini's. If I want to re-create it, I think you need to be in on choosing the site."

Because that made sense and because she did have to learn to deal with him as a boss, owner of the restaurant for which she worked, she tucked away any inappropriate longings and smiled. "Okay."

She could be all business because that's what really worked for them.

The next day, after walking through an old, run-down building with their Realtor, Rafe and Dani stepped out into the bright end-of-February day.

"I could do with a coffee right now."

He glanced at her. In her sapphire-blue coat and white mittens, she looked cuddly, huggable. And very, very, very off-limits. Her smiles had been cool. Her conversations stilted. But she'd warmed up a bit when they actually began looking at buildings.

"Haven't you already had two cups of coffee?"

She slid her hand into the crook of his elbow, like a friend or a cousin, someone allowed innocent, meaning-less touches.

"Don't most Italians drink something like five cups a day?"

When he said, "Bah," she laughed.

All morning, their conversation at his apartment two nights ago had played over and over and over in his head. She wanted a commitment and he didn't. So he'd figured out a way they could be lovers and work together and she'd rejected it. He'd had to accept that.

But being with her this morning, without actually being allowed to touch her or even contemplate kissing her was making him think all kinds of insane things. Like how empty his life was. How much he would miss her when he stopped working at the original Mancini's and headquartered himself in Rome.

So though he knew her hand at his elbow meant nothing, he savored the simple gesture. It was a safe, nonthreatening way to touch her and have her touch him. Even if he did know it would lead to nothing.

"Besides, I love coffee. It makes me warm inside."

"True. And it is cold." He slid his arm around her shoulders. Her thick coat might keep her toasty, but it was another excuse to touch her.

They continued down the quiet street, but as they approached a shop specializing in infant clothing, the wheels of a baby stroller came flying out the door and straight for Daniella's leg. He caught her before she could as much as wobble and shifted her out of the way.

The apologetic mom said, *"Scusi!"*

Dani laughed. In flawless Italian she said, "No harm done." Then she bent and chucked the chin of the baby inside the stroller. "Isn't she adorable!"

The proud mom beamed. Rafe stole a quiet look at the kid and his lips involuntarily rose as a chuckle rumbled up from the deepest part of him. "She likes somebody's cooking."

The mom explained that the baby had her father's love of all things sweet, but Rafe's gaze stayed on the baby. She'd caught his eye and cooed at him, her voice a soft sound, almost a purr, and her eyes as shiny as a harvest moon.

A funny feeling invaded his chest.

Dani gave the baby a big, noisy kiss on the cheek, said

goodbye to the mom and took his arm so they could resume their walk down the street.

They ducked into a coffeehouse and she inhaled deeply. "Mmm...this reminds me of being back in the States."

He shook his head. "You Americans. You copy the idea of a coffeehouse from us, then come over here and act like we must meet your standards."

With a laugh, she ordered two cups of coffee, remembering his choice of brews from earlier that morning. She also ordered two scones.

"I hope you're hungry."

She shrugged out of her coat before sitting on the chair he pulled out for her at a table near a window. "I just need something to take the edge off my growling stomach. The second scone is for you."

"I don't eat pastries from a vendor who sells in bulk."

She pushed the second scone in front of him anyway. "Such a snob."

He laughed. "All right. Fine. I will taste." He bit into the thing and to his surprise it was very good. Even better with a sip or two of coffee. So tasty he ate the whole darned thing.

"Not quite the pastry snob anymore, are you?"

He sat back. He truly did not intend to pursue her. He respected her dreams, the way he respected his own. But that didn't stop his feelings for her. With his belly full of coffee and scone, and Daniella happy beside him, these quiet minutes suddenly felt like spun gold.

She glanced around. "I'll bet you've brought a woman or two here."

That broke the spell. "What?" He laughed as he shifted uncomfortably on his chair. "What makes you say that?"

"You're familiar with this coffeehouse. This street. You were even alert enough to pull me out of the way of the oncoming stroller at that baby shop." She shrugged. "You might not have come here precisely, but you've brought women to Rome."

"Every Italian man brings women to Rome." He toyed with his now-empty mug. He'd lived with Kamila just down the street. He'd dreamed of babies like the little girl in the stroller.

"I told you about Paul. I think you need to tell me about one of your women to even the score."

"You make me sound like I dated an army."

She tossed him an assessing look. "You might have."

Not about to lie, he drew a long breath and said, "There were many."

She grimaced. "Just pick one."

"Okay. How about Lisette?"

She put her elbow on the table, her eyes keen with interest. "Sounds French."

"She was."

"Ah."

"I met her when she was traveling through Italy…" But even as he spoke, he remembered that she was more driven than he was. *He* had taken second place to *her* career. At the time he hadn't minded, but remembering the situation correctly, he didn't feel bad about that breakup.

"So what happened?"

He waved a hand. "Nothing. She was just very married to her career."

"Like you?"

He laughed. "Two peas in a pod. But essentially we didn't have time for each other."

"You miss her?"

"No." He glanced up. "Honestly, I don't miss any of the women who came into and walked out of my life."

But he had missed Kamila and he would miss Dani if she left. He'd miss her insights at the restaurant and the way she made Mancini's come alive. But most of all he'd miss her smile. Miss the way she made *him* feel.

The unspoken truth sat between them. Their gazes caught, then clung. That was the problem with Dani. He felt for her the same things he had felt with Kamila. Except stronger. The emotions that raced through him had nothing to do with affairs, and everything to do with the kind of commitment he swore he'd never make again. That was why he'd worked so hard to figure out a way they could be together. It was why he also worked so hard to steer them away from a commitment. This woman, this Dani, was everything Kamila had been...and more.

And it only highlighted why he needed to be free.

He cleared his throat. "There was a woman."

Dani perked up.

"Kamila." He toyed with his mug again, realizing he was telling her about Kamila as much to remind himself as to explain to Dani. "She was sunshine when she was happy and a holy terror when she was not."

Dani laughed. "Sounds exciting."

He caught her gaze again. "It was perfect."

Her eyes softened with understanding. "Oh."

"You wonder how I know I'm not made for a relationship? Kamila taught me. First, she drew me away from my dream. To please her, I turned down apprenticeships. I took a permanent job as a sous-chef. I gave up the idea of being renowned and settled for being happy." Though it hurt, he held her gaze. "We talked about marriage. We talked about kids. And one day I came home from work and discovered her things were gone. *She* was gone. I'd given up everything for her and the life I thought I wanted, and she left without so much as an explanation of why."

"I'm sorry."

"Don't be." He sucked in a breath, pulled away from her, as his surety returned to him. "That loss taught me to be careful. But more than that it taught me never to do anything that jeopardizes who I am."

"So this Kamila really did a number on you."

"Were you not listening? There was no number. Yes, she broke my heart. But it taught me lessons. I'm fine."

"You're wounded." She caught his gaze. "Maybe even more wounded than I am."

He said, "That's absurd," but he felt the pangs of loss, the months of loneliness as if it were yesterday.

"At least I admit I need someone. You let one broken romance evolve into a belief that a few buildings and success are the answers to never being hurt. Do you think that when you're sixty you're going to look around and think 'I wish I'd started more Mancini's'? Or do you think you're going to envy your friends' relationships, wish for grandkids?"

"I told you I don't want those things." But even as he said the words, he knew they were a lie. Not a big pulsing lie, but a quiet whisper of doubt. Especially with the big eyes of the baby girl in the stroller pressed into his memory. With a world of work to do to get his chain of restaurants started, what she said should seem absurd. Instead, he saw himself old, his world done, his success unparalleled and his house empty.

He blinked away that foolish thought. He had family. He had friends. His life would never be empty. That was Dani's fear, not his.

"Let's go. Mario gave me the address of the next building where we're to meet him."

Quiet, they walked to his car, slid in and headed to the other side of the city. More residential than the site of the first property, this potential Mancini's had the look of a home, as did his old farmhouse outside Monte Calanetti.

He opened the door and she entered the aging building before him. Mario came over and shook his hand, but Dani walked to the far end of the huge, open first floor. She found the latch on the shutters that covered a big back window. When she flipped it, the shutters opened. Sunlight poured in.

Rafe actually *felt* the air change, the atmosphere shift. Though the building was empty and hollow, with her walking in, the sunlight pouring in through a back window, everything clicked.

This was his building. And she really was the person who brought life to his dining rooms. He'd had success of a sort without her, but she breathed the life into his vision, made it more, made it the vision he saw when he closed his eyes and dreamed.

Dani ambled to the center of the room. Pointing near the door, she said, "We'd put the bar over here."

He frowned. "Why not here?" He motioned to a far corner, out of the way.

"Not only can we give customers the chance to wait at the bar for their tables, but also we might get a little extra drink business." She smiled at him as she walked over. "Things will be just a tad different in a restaurant that's actually in a residential area of a city." Her smile grew. "But I think it could be fun to play around with it."

He crossed his arms on his chest to keep from touching her. He could almost feel the excitement radiating from her. While he envisioned a dining room, happy customers eating *his* food, he could tell she saw more. Much more. She saw things he couldn't bring into existence because all he cared about was the food.

"What would you play around with?"

Her gaze circled the room. "I'm not sure. We'd want to keep the atmosphere we've build up in Mancini's, but here we'd also have to become part of the community. You can get some really great customer relations by being involved with your neighbors." She tapped her finger on her lips. "I'll need to think about this."

Rafe's business instincts kicked in. He didn't know what she planned to do, but he did know whatever she decided, it would probably be good. Really good. Because she had the other half of the gift he'd been given.

He also knew she was happy. Happier than he'd ever seen her. Her blue eyes lit with joy. Her shoulders were back. Her steps purposeful. Confidence radiated from her.

"You want Mancini's to be successful as much as I want it to be successful."

She laughed. "I doubt that. But I do want it to be the best it can be." She glanced around, then faced him again. "In all the confusion between us, I don't think I've ever said thank-you."

"You wish to thank me?"

"For the job. For the fun of it." She shrugged. "I need this. I don't show it often but deep down inside me, there's a little girl who always wondered where she'd end up. *She* needed the chance to be successful. To prove her worth."

He smiled. "She'll certainly get that with Mancini's."

"And we're going to have a good time whipping this into shape."

He smiled. "That's the plan."

Her face glowed. "Good."

He said, "Good," but his voice quieted, his heart stilled, as he suddenly realized something he should have all along. Kamila had broken his heart. But Dani had wheedled her way into his soul. His dream.

If he and Dani got close and things didn't work out, he wouldn't just spend a month drinking himself silly. He'd lose everything.

CHAPTER THIRTEEN

THE NEXT DAY in the parking lot of Mancini's, Dani switched off the ignition of Louisa's little car, knowing that she was two days away from D-day. Decision day. The day she had to use her return ticket to New York City.

Being with Rafe in Rome had shown her he respected her opinion. Oh, hell, who was she kidding? Telling her about Kamila had been his way of putting the final nail in the coffin of her relationship dreams. It hurt, but she understood. In fact, in a way she was even glad. Now that she knew why he was so determined, she could filter her feelings for him away from her longing for a relationship with him and into his dream. He needed her opinion. He wanted to focus on food, on pleasing customer palates. She saw the ninety thousand other things that had to be taken care of. Granted, he'd chosen a great spot for the initial Mancini's. He'd fixed the building to perfection. But a restaurant in the city came with different challenges.

Having lived in New York and eaten at several different kinds of restaurants, she saw things from a customer's point of view. And she knew exactly how she'd set up Mancini's Rome restaurant.

She *knew*.

The confidence of it made her forget all about returning to New York, and stand tall. She entered the kitchen on her way to the office, carrying a satchel filled with pictures she'd printed off the internet the night before using Louisa's laptop.

This was her destiny.

Then she saw Rafe entering through the back door and her heart tumbled. He wore the black leather jacket. He hadn't pulled his hair into the tie yet and it curled around his collar. His eyes were cool, serious. When their gazes met, she swore she could feel the weight of his sadness.

She didn't understand what the hell he had to be sad about. He was getting everything he wanted. Except her heart. He didn't know that he already had her love, but their good trip the day before proved they could work together, even be friends, and he should appreciate that.

Everything would be perfect, as long as he didn't kiss her. Or tempt her. And yesterday he'd all but proven he needed her too much to risk losing her.

"I have pictures of things I'd like your opinion on."

Emory looked from one to the other. "Pictures?"

Rafe slowly ambled into the kitchen. "Dani has ideas for the restaurant in Rome."

Emory gaped at him. "Who cares? You have a hundred-person wedding tomorrow afternoon."

Dani's mouth fell open. Rafe's eyes widened. "We didn't cancel that?"

"We couldn't," Emory replied before Dani said anything, obviously taking the heat for it. "So I called the bride's mother yesterday and got the specifics. Tomorrow morning, we'll all come here early to get the food prepared. In the afternoon Dani and I will go to the wedding. I will watch your food, Chef Mancini. Your reputation will not suffer."

Rafe slowly walked over to Dani. "You know we cannot do this again!"

"Come on, Chef Rafe." She smiled slightly, hoping to dispel the tension, again confused over why he was so moody. "Put Mr. Mean Chef away. I got the message the day you fired me over this." With that she strode into the office, dumped her satchel on the desk and swung out again. She thought of the plane ticket in her pocket and reminded herself that in two days she wouldn't have that option. When he yelled, she'd have to handle it.

"I'll be in the dining room, checking with Allegra on how things went yesterday."

Rafe sagged with defeat as she stormed out. He shouldn't have yelled at her again about the catering, but everything in his life was spinning out of control. He saw babies in his sleep and woke up hugging his pillow, dreaming he was hugging Daniella. The logical part of him insisted they were a team, that a real relationship would enhance everything they did. They would own Mancini's together, build it together, build a life together.

The other part, the part that remembered Kamila, could only see disaster when the relationship ended. When Kamila left, he could return to his dream. If Dani left, she took half of his dream with her.

He faced Emory. "I appreciate how you have handled this. And I apologize for exploding." He sucked in a breath. "As penance, I will go to the wedding tomorrow."

Emory laughed. "If you're expecting me to argue, you're wrong. I don't want to be a caterer, either."

"As I said, this is penance."

"Then you really should be apologizing to Dani. It was her you screamed at."

He glanced at the door as he shrugged out of his jacket. She was too upset with him now. And she was busy. He would find a minute at the end of the night to apologize for his temper. If he was opting out of a romance because he needed her, he couldn't lose her over his temper.

But she didn't hang around after work that night. And the next morning, he couldn't apologize because they weren't alone. First, he'd cooked with a full staff. Then he'd had to bring Laz and Gino, two of the busboys, to the wedding to assist with setup and teardown. They drove to the vineyard in almost complete silence, every mile stretching Rafe's nerves.

Seeing the sign for 88 Vineyards, he turned down the winding lane. The top of a white tent shimmered in the winter sun. Thirty yards away, white folding chairs created two wide rows of seating for guests. He could see the bride and groom standing in front of the clergyman, holding hands, probably saying their vows.

He pulled the SUV beside the tent. "It looks like we'll need to move quickly to get everything set up for them to eat."

Dani opened her door of the SUV. "Not if there are pictures. I've known brides who've taken hours of pictures."

"Bah. Nonsense."

Ignoring him, she climbed out of the SUV.

Rafe opened his door and recessional music swelled around him. Still Dani said nothing. Her cold shoulder stung more than he wanted to admit.

A quick glance at the wedding ceremony netted him the sight of the bride and groom coming down the aisle. The sun cast them in a golden glow, but their smiles were even more radiant. He watched as the groom brought the bride's hand to his lips. Saw the worship in his eyes, the happiness, and immediately Rafe thought of Daniella. About the times he'd kissed her hand. Walked her to her car. Waited with bated breath for her arrival every morning.

He reached into his SUV to retrieve a tray of his signature ravioli. Handing it to Laz, he sneaked a peek at Daniella as she made her way to the parents of the bride, who'd walked out behind the happy couple. They smiled at her, the bride's mom talking a million words a second as she pointed inside the tent. Daniella set her hand on the mom's forearm and suddenly the nervous woman calmed.

He watched in heart-stealing silence. A lifetime of re-

jection had taught her to be kind. And one failed romance
had made him mean. Bitter.

As he pulled out the second ravioli tray, Dani walked
over.

"Apparently the ceremony was lovely."

"Peachy."

"Come on. I know you're mad at me for arranging this.
But at the time, I didn't know any better and in a few hours
all of this will be over."

He sucked in a breath. "I'm not mad at you. I'm angry
with myself—" *Because I finally understand I'm not worried about you leaving me, or even losing my dreams. I'm
disappointed in myself* "—for yelling at you yesterday."

"Oh." She smiled slowly. "Thanks."

The warm feeling he always got when she smiled invaded every inch of him. "You're welcome."

Not waiting for him to say anything else, she headed
inside the white tent where the dinner and reception would
be held. He followed her only to discover she was busy
setting up the table for the food. He and Laz worked their
magic on the warmers he'd brought to keep everything
the perfect temperature. Daniella and Gino brought in the
remaining food.

And nothing happened.

People milled around the tables in the tent, chatting, celebrating the marriage. Wine flowed from fancy bottles. The
mother of the bride socialized. The parents of the groom
walked from table to table. A breeze billowed around the
tent as everyone talked and laughed.

He stepped outside, nervous now. He'd never considered
himself wrong, except that he'd believed giving up apprenticeships for Kamila had made him weak. But setback after
setback had made Dani strong. It was humbling to realize
his master-chef act wasn't a sign of strength, but selfish-
ness. Even more humbling to realize he didn't know what
to do with the realization.

Wishing he still smoked, he ambled around the grounds, gazing at the blue sky, and then he turned to walk down a cobblestone path, only to find himself three feet away from the love-struck bride and groom.

He almost groaned, until he noticed the groom lift the bride's chin and tell her that everything was going to be okay.

His eyebrows rose. They hadn't even been married twenty minutes and there was trouble in paradise already?

She quietly said, "Everything is not going to be okay. My parents are getting a divorce."

Rafe thought of the woman in pink, standing with the guy in the tux as they'd chatted with Dani at the end of the ceremony, and he almost couldn't believe it.

The groom shook his head. "And they're both on their best behavior. Everything's fine."

"For now. What will I do when we get home from our honeymoon? I'll have to choose between the two of them for Christmas and Easter." She gasped. "I'll have to get all my stuff out of their house before they sell it." She sucked in a breath. "Oh, my God." Her eyes filled with tears. "I have no home."

Rafe's chest tightened. He heard every emotion Dani must feel in the bride's voice. No home. No place to call her own.

A thousand emotions buffeted him, but for the first time since he'd met Dani he suddenly felt what she felt. The emptiness of belonging to no one. The longing for a place to call her own. And he realized the insult he'd leveled when he'd told her he wanted to sleep with her, but not keep her.

"I'll be your home." The groom pulled his bride away from the tree. "It's us now. We'll make your home."

We'll make your home.

Rafe stepped back, away from the tree that hid him, the words vibrating through him. But the words themselves were nothing without the certainty behind them.

The strength of conviction in the groom's voice. The promise that wouldn't be broken.

We'll make your home.

"Let's go inside. We have a wedding to celebrate."

She smiled. "Yes. We do."

Rafe discreetly followed them into the tent. He watched them walk to the main table as if nothing was wrong, as the dining room staff scrambled to fill serving bowls with his food and get it onto tables.

The toast of the best man was short. Rafe's eyes strayed to Daniella. He desperately wanted to give her a home. A real one. A home like he'd grown up in with kids and a dog and noisy suppers.

This was what life had stolen from her and from him. When Kamila left, she hadn't taken his dream. She'd bruised him so badly, he'd lost his faith in real love. He'd lost his dream of a house and kids. And when it all suddenly popped up in the form of a woman so beautiful that she stole his breath, he hadn't seen it.

Dear God. He loved her. He loved her enough to give up everything he wanted, even Mancini's, to make her dreams come true. But he wouldn't have to give up anything. His dream was her dream. And her dream was now his dream.

Their meal eaten, the bride and groom rose from the table. The seating area was quickly dismantled by vineyard staff, who left a circle of chairs around the tent and a clear floor on which to dance.

The band introduced the bride and groom and he took her hand and kissed it before he led her in their dance.

Emotion choked Rafe. He'd spent the past years believing the best way to live his dream was to hold himself back, forget love, when the truth was he simply needed to meet the right woman to realize his dream would be hollow, empty without her.

"Hey." Daniella walked up beside him. "Dinner is

over. We can dismantle our warmers, take our trays and go home."

He faced her. Emotions churned inside him. Feelings for Dani that took root and held on. He'd found his one. He'd fired her, yelled at her, asked her to become his lover. And she'd held her ground. Stood up to him. Refused him. Forced him to work by her terms. And she had won him.

But he had absolutely no idea how to tell her that.

She picked up an empty tray and headed for his SUV. Grabbing up another empty tray, he scurried after her.

"I've been thinking about our choice."

She slid the tray into the SUV. "Our choice?"

"You know. Our choice not to—"

Before he could finish, the busboys came out of the tent with more trays. Frustration stiffened his back. With a quick glance at him, Dani walked back to the noisy reception for more pans. The busboys got the warmers.

Simmering with the need to talk, Rafe silently packed it all inside the back of his SUV.

Nerves filled him as he drove his empty pans, warmers and employees to Mancini's. When they arrived, the restaurant bustled with diners. Emory raced around the kitchen like a madman. Daniella pitched in to help Allegra. Rafe put on his smock, washed his hands and helped Emory.

Time flew, as it always did when he was busy, but Rafe kept watching Daniella. Something was on her mind. She smiled. She worked. She teased with staff. But he heard something in her voice. A catch? No it was more of an easing back. The click of connection he always heard when she spoke with staff was missing. It was as if she were distancing herself—

Oh, dear God.

In all the hustle and bustle that had taken place in the past four weeks, she'd never made the commitment to stay.

And she had a plane ticket for the following morning.

The night wound down. Emory headed for the office to

do some paperwork. Rafe casually ambled into the dining room. As the last of the waitstaff left, he pulled a bottle of Chianti from the rack and walked around the bar to a stool.

He watched Dani pause at the podium, as if torn between reaching for her coat and joining him. His heart chugged. Everything inside him froze.

Finally, she turned to him. Her lips lifted into a warm smile and she sashayed over.

Interpreting her coming to him as a good sign, he didn't give himself time to think twice. He caught her hands, lifted both to his lips and said, "Pick me."

Her brow furrowed. "What?"

"I know you're thinking about leaving. I see it on your face. Hear it in your voice. I know you think you have nothing here but a job, but that's not true. I need you for so much more. So pick me. Do not work for me. Pick me. Keep me. Take *me*."

Her breath hitched. "You're asking me to quit?"

"No." He licked his suddenly dry lips. He'd known this woman only twenty-four days. Yet what he felt was stronger than anything he'd ever felt before.

"Daniella, I think I want you to marry me."

Dani's heart bounced to a stop as she yanked her hands out of his.

"What?"

"I want you to marry me."

She couldn't stop the thrill that raced through her, but even through her shock she'd heard his words clearly. "You said *think*. You said you *think* you want to marry me."

He laughed a bit as he pulled his hand through his hair. "It's so fast for me. My God, I never even thought I'd want to get married. Now I can't imagine my life without you." He caught her hand again, caught her gaze. "Marry me."

His voice had become stronger. His conviction obvious.

"Oh." She wanted to say yes so bad it hurt to wrestle the

word back down her throat. But she had to. "For a month you've said you don't do relationships. Now suddenly you want to marry me?"

He laughed. "All these years, I thought I was weak because I gave Kamila what she wanted and she left me anyway. So I made myself strong. People saw me as selfish. I thought I was determined."

"I understand that."

"Now I see I *was* selfish. I did not want to lose my dream again."

"I understand that, too."

He shook his head fiercely. "You're missing what I'm telling you. I might have been broken by her loss, but Kamila was the wrong woman for me. I was never my real self with her. I was one compromise after another. With you, I am me. I see my temper and I rein it back. I see myself with kids. I see a house. I long to make you happy."

Oh, dear God, did the man have no heart? "Don't say things you don't mean."

"I never say things I don't mean. I love you, Daniella." He reached for her again. "Do not get on that plane tomorrow."

She stepped back, so far that he couldn't touch her, and pressed her fingers to her lips. Her heart so very desperately wanted to believe every word he said. Her brain had been around, though, for every time that same heart was broken. This man had called Paul's proposal a stopgap measure…yet, here he was doing the same thing.

"No."

His face fell. "No?"

"What did you tell me about Paul asking to marry me the day before I left New York?"

He frowned.

"You said it was a stopgap measure. A way to keep me." He walked toward her. "Daniella…"

She halted him with a wave of her hand. "Don't. I feel

foolish enough already. You're afraid I'm going to go home so you make a proposal that mocks everything I believe in."

She yearned to close her eyes at the horrible sense of how little he thought of her, but she held them open, held back her tears and made the hardest decision of her life.

"I'm going back to New York." Her heart splintered in two as she realized this really was the end. They'd never bump into each other at a coffee shop, never sit beside each other in the subway, never accidentally go to the same dry cleaner. He lived thousands of miles away from her and there'd be no chance for them to have the time they needed to really fall in love. He'd robbed them of that with his insulting proposal.

"Mancini's will be fine without me." She tried a smile. "*You* will be fine without me." She took another few steps back. "I've gotta go."

CHAPTER FOURTEEN

DANI RACED OUT of Mancini's, quickly started Louisa's little car and headed home. Her flight didn't leave until ten in the morning. But she had to pack. She had to say goodbye to Louisa. She had to give back the tons of clothes her new friend had let her borrow for her job at Mancini's.

She swiped at a tear as she turned down the lane to Palazzo di Comparino. Her brain told her she was smart to be going home. Her splintered heart reminded her she didn't have a home. No one to return to in the United States. No one to stay for in Italy.

The kitchen light was on and as was their practice, Louisa had waited up for Dani. As soon as she stepped in the kitchen door, Louisa handed her a cup of tea. Dani glanced up at her, knowing the sheen of tears sparkled on her eyelashes.

"What's wrong?"

"I'm going home."

Louisa blinked. "I thought this was settled."

"Nothing's ever settled with Rafe." She sucked in a breath. "The smart thing for me is to leave."

"What about the restaurant, your job, your destiny?"

She fell to a seat. "He asked me to marry him."

Louisa's eyes widened. "How is that bad? My God, Dani, even I can see you love the guy."

"I said no."

"Oh, sweetie! Sweetie! You love the guy. How the hell could you say no?"

"I've been here four weeks, Louisa. Rafe is a confirmed bachelor and he asked me to marry him. The day before I'm supposed to go home. You do the math."

"What math? You have a return ticket to the United States. He doesn't want you to go."

Dani slowly raised her eyes to meet Louisa's. "Exactly. The proposal was a stopgap measure. He told me all about it when we talked about Paul asking me to marry him. He said Paul didn't want to risk losing me, so the day before I left for Italy, he'd asked me to marry him."

"And you think that's what Rafe did?"

Her chin lifted. "You don't?"

Rafe was seated at the bar on his third shot of whiskey when Emory ambled out into the dining room.

"What are you doing here?"

He presented the shot glass. "What does it look like I'm doing?"

Emory frowned. "Getting drunk?"

Rafe saluted his correct answer.

"After a successful catering event that could have gone south, you're drinking?"

"I asked Daniella to marry me. And do you know what she told me?"

Looking totally confused, Emory slid onto the stool beside Rafe. "Obviously, she said no."

"She said no."

Emory laughed. Rafe scowled at him. "Why do you think this is funny?"

"The look on your face is funny."

"Thanks."

"Come on, Rafe, you've known the girl a month."

"So she doesn't trust me?"

Emory laughed. "Look at you. Look at how you've treated her. Would you trust you?"

"Yeah, well, she's leaving for New York tomorrow. I didn't want her to go."

Emory frowned. "Ah. So you asked her to marry you to keep her from going?"

"No. I asked her to marry me because I love her." He rubbed his hand along the back of his neck. "But I'd also told her that her boyfriend had asked her to marry him the day before she left for Italy as a stopgap measure. Wanting to tie her to him, without giving her a real commitment, he'd asked. But he hadn't really meant it. He just didn't want her to go."

Emory swatted him with a dish towel. "Why do you tell her these things?"

"At the time it made sense."

"Yeah, well, now she thinks you only asked her to marry you to keep her from going back to New York."

"No kidding."

Emory swatted him again. "Get the hell over to Palazzo di Comparino and fix this!"

"How?"

Emory's eyes narrowed. "You know what she wants… what she needs. Not just truth, proof. If you love her, and you'd better if you asked her to marry you, you have to give her proof."

He jumped off the stool, grabbed Emory's shoulders and noisily kissed the top of his head. "Yes. Yes! Proof! You are a hundred percent correct."

"You just make sure she doesn't get on that plane."

Dani's tears dried as she and Louisa packed her things. Neither one of them expected to sleep, so they spent the night talking. They talked of keeping in touch. Video chatting and texting made that much easier than it used to be. And

Louisa had promised to come to New York. They would be thousands of miles apart but they would be close.

Around five in the morning, Dani shoved off her kitchen chair and sadly made her way to the shower. She dressed in her own old raggedy jeans and a worn sweater, the glamour of her life in Tuscany, and Louisa's clothes behind her now.

When she came downstairs, Louisa had also dressed. She'd promised to take her to the airport and she'd gotten ready.

But there was an odd gleam in her eye when she said, "Shall we go?"

Dani sighed, knowing she'd miss this house but also realizing she'd found a friend who could be like a sister. The trip wasn't an entire waste after all.

She smiled at Louisa. "Yeah. Let's go."

They got into the ugly green car and rather than let Dani drive, Louisa got behind the wheel.

"I thought you refused to drive until you understood Italy's rules of the road better."

Stepping on the gas, Louisa shrugged. "I've gotta learn some time."

She drove them out of the vineyard and out of the village. Then the slow drive to Florence began. But even before they went a mile, Louisa turned down an old road.

"What are you doing?"

"I promised someone a favor."

Dani frowned. "Do we have time?"

"Plenty of time. You're fine."

"I know I'm fine. It's my flight I'm worried about."

"I promise you. I will pull into the driveway and be pulling out two minutes later."

Dani opened her mouth to answer but she snapped it closed when she realized they were at the old farmhouse Maria the real estate agent had shown her and Rafe. She faced Louisa. "Do you know the person who bought this?"

"Yes." She popped open her door. "Come in with me."

Dani pushed on her door. "I thought you said this would only take a minute."

"I said two minutes. What I actually said was I promise I will be pulling out of this driveway two minutes after I pull in."

Dani walked up the familiar path to the familiar door and sighed when it groaned as Louisa opened it. "Whoever bought this is in for about three years of renovations."

Louisa laughed before she called out, "Hello. We're here."

Rafe stepped out from behind a crumbling wall. Dani skittered back. "Louisa! *This* is your friend?"

"I didn't say he was my friend. I said I knew him." Louisa gave Dani's back a little shove. "He has some important things to say to you."

"I bought this house for you," Rafe said, not giving Dani a chance to reply to Louisa.

"I don't want a house."

He sighed. "Too bad. Because you now have a house." He motioned her forward. "I see a big kitchen here. Something that smells like heaven."

She stopped.

He motioned toward the huge room in the front. "And big, fat chairs that you can sink into in here."

"Very funny."

"I am not being funny. You," he said, pointing at her, "want a home. I want you. Therefore, I give you a home."

"What? Since a marriage proposal didn't keep me, you offer me a house?"

"I didn't say I was giving you a house. I said I was giving you a home." He walked toward the kitchen. "And you're going to marry me."

She scrambled after him. "Exactly how do you expect to make that happen?"

She rounded the turn and walked right into him. He caught her arms and hauled her to him, kissing her. She made a token protest, but, honestly, this was the man she couldn't resist.

He broke the kiss slowly, as if he didn't ever want to have to stop kissing her. "That's how I expect to make that happen."

"You're going to kiss me until I agree?"

"It's an idea with merit. But it won't be all kissing. We have a restaurant. You have a job. And there's a bedroom back here." He headed toward it.

Once again, she found herself running after him. Cold air leeched in from the window and she stopped dead in her tracks. "The window leaks."

"Then you're going to have to hire a general contractor."

"Me?"

He straightened to his full six-foot-three height. "I am a master. I cook."

"Oh, and I clean and make babies?"

He laughed. "We will hire someone to clean. Though I like the part about you making babies."

Her heart about pounded its way out of her chest. "You want kids?"

He walked toward her slowly. "*We* want kids. We want all that stuff you said about fat chairs and good-smelling kitchens and turning the thermostat down so that we can snuggle."

Her heart melted. "You don't look like a snuggler."

"I'll talk you into doing more than snuggling."

She laughed. Pieces of the ice around her heart began to melt. Her eyes clung to his. "You're serious?"

"I wouldn't have told Louisa to bring you here if I weren't. I don't do stupid things. I do impulsive things." He grinned. "You might have to get used to that."

She smiled. He motioned for her to come closer and when she did, he wrapped his arms around her.

"I could not bear to see you go."

"You said Paul only asked me to marry him as a stop-gap measure."

"Yes, but Paul is an idiot. I am not."

She laughed again and it felt so good that she paused to revel in it. To memorize the feeling of his arms around her. To glance around at their house.

"Oh, my God, this is a mess."

"We'll be fine."

She laid her head on his chest and breathed in his scent. She counted to ten, waited for him to say something that would drive her away, then realized what she was really waiting for.

She glanced up at him. "I'm so afraid you're going to hurt me."

"I know. And I'm going to spend our entire lives proving to you that you have no need to worry."

She laughed and sank against him again. "I love you."

"After only four weeks?"

She peeked up again. "Yes."

"So this time you'll believe me when I say it."

She swallowed. Years of fear faded away. "Yes."

"Good." He shifted back, just slightly, so he could pull a small jewelry box from the pocket of his jeans. He opened it and revealed a two-carat diamond. "I love you. So you will marry me?"

She gaped at the ring, then brought her gaze to his hopeful face. When he smiled, she hugged him fiercely. "Yes!"

He slipped the ring onto her finger. "Now, weren't we on our way back to the bedroom?"

"For what? There's no bed back there."

He said, "Oh, you of no imagination. I have a hundred ways around that."

"A hundred, isn't that a bit ambitious?"

"Get used to it. I am a master, remember?"

"Yeah, you are," she said, and then she laughed. She was

getting married, going to make babies…going to make a
home—in Italy.

With the man of her dreams.

Because finally, finally she was allowed to have dreams.

* * * * *

MILLS & BOON MODERN IS
HAVING A MAKEOVER!

The same great stories you love,
a stylish new look!

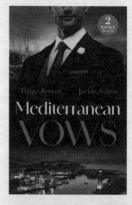

Look out for our brand new look
COMING JUNE 2024

MILLS & BOON

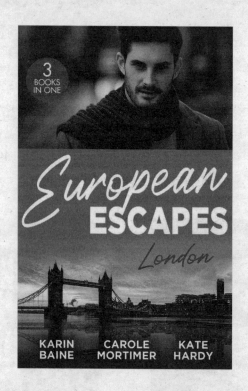

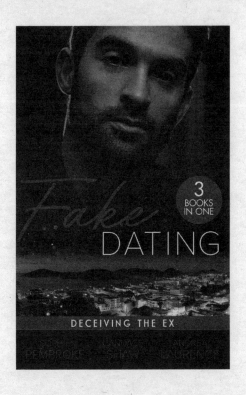

LET'S TALK
Romance

For exclusive extracts, competitions and special offers, find us online:

- **MillsandBoon**
- **@MillsandBoon**
- **@MillsandBoonUK**
- **@MillsandBoonUK**

Get in touch on 01413 063 232